Once

A little bit of
Australia to take
home with you.

Mary Ed

Once on a Road

Mary-Ellen Mullane

VINTAGE BOOKS

Australia

A Vintage book
Published by Random House Australia Pty Ltd
Level 3, 100 Pacific Highway, North Sydney NSW 2060
www.randomhouse.com.au

First published by Vintage in 2010

Addresses for companies within the Random House Group can be found
at www.randomhouse.com.au/offices

National Library of Australia
Cataloguing-in-Publication Entry

Mullane, Mary-Ellen
Once on a road.
ISBN 978 1 74166 907 7 (pbk).
A823.4

Typeset in 11/14pt Birka by Midland Typesetters, Victoria
Printed and bound by Griffin Press, South Australia

Random House Australia uses papers that are natural, renewable and
recyclable products and made from wood grown in sustainable forests.
The logging and manufacturing processes are expected to conform to the
environmental regulations of the country of origin.

10 9 8 7 6 5 4 3 2 1

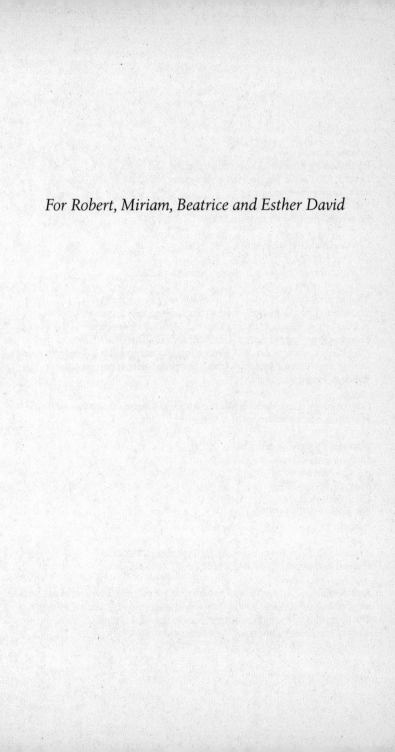

For Robert, Miriam, Beatrice and Esther David

'Nothing but death shall part us.'

The Book of Ruth, 1: 17, Old Testament

Part I

Eight years

It was the loose ends, the little details, the missing pieces that troubled Naomi, and of all the fragments and leftovers, Zoe bothered her the most. She wanted to believe that Zoe was a good person. No, she *had* to believe it. Zoe had suffered more than her fair share of bad luck – that sounded like a place to start. At least that's what Naomi, after much consideration, eight years to be exact, had finally decided. This is how she would make sense of it all – the accident, the deaths of her sons, Ben and Jesse, the responsibility of caring for her grandchildren – the whole catastrophe. And once she decided that, the other things in her life – the old anger and bitterness – would begin to disappear.

You see, Naomi was basically an optimist, a tired optimist but an optimist nevertheless. And she had begun to feel that her dead sons took up too much space. She was in the process of moving from nearly disappearing under their weight to gently stepping around them. This surprised her. At almost sixty years of age she was not expecting any real changes in herself. After all, steadily being Naomi Adams, midwife, wife, mother and grandmother, had been what kept her sane.

Naomi lived with her husband, Noel, and their two grandchildren in an old wooden cottage covered in jasmine and wisteria. It was a very forgiving wooden cottage, in which a hundred years of Sydney's children had been raised. Built first to house dockside workers, it and the surrounding cottages were now home to postwar migrants as well as refugees from the sprawling suburbs of Sydney and the isolated dusty farms beyond. Painted creamy white with Federation-green trim, the cottage was not particularly remarkable from the street. The street, in turn, was not broad or grand. But the little wooden cottages and the haphazard hill upon which they clung combined to create a certain charm to which Naomi was content to return in the evenings from the hospital.

Yes, Naomi thought, looking up at the pattern of roses in the kitchen's pressed tin ceiling, which needed a good clean, Zoe was right, *in theory*, to run away like that. It was not the sleeping dead taking their eternal rest that had scared her off. It was the living, those remaining: Noel, Naomi and of course Zoe's two sons, Chris and Max. The walking dead, as Naomi had thought of herself back then.

It was difficult to change the way she thought about Zoe, with her piercings and black clothes. She had to remember that there was a time when she had felt differently – before the car accident – and perhaps now there could be a time again. Zoe had not left her and Noel with the small boys after the accident on purpose. She had serious injuries. How could Zoe possibly have looked after two babies on her own? Be reasonable, Naomi. Noel ended most conversations about Zoe and the boys this way – stop blaming Zoe. Be kinder! Think what she went through!

Naomi was ready to admit that he had a point.

She *could* change the way she felt about Zoe. She *would* breathe life into the idea things could be different between them. She *had* to be more flexible about this. It was time.

Beyond the high-rise, out on the fringe of the city, Zoe's head rested against a greasy train window. Her hair was a tangle of knots, which she tugged at while she thought about how she'd come to leave her children with her in-laws and how she could have let eight years pass without taking them back.

She'd left them for reasons that had made sense to her then, and seemed to make sense to Naomi too. But Zoe hadn't left them, so much as *lost* them. Not in a misplaced sort of way. She'd lost the idea of them. The idea of herself as a mother.

It is possible to forget about your children. Oh yes, it is possible. All that stuff about 'once a mother, always a mother' or 'a mother's intuition' – well, it is rubbish. Zoe had read in a magazine about a woman on a sinking ship who, in her panic to save herself, had plain forgotten she had a baby. And after the accident, with a bit of help from an assortment of drugs and booze and other things, Zoe too had forgotten about her children. She'd had to forget lots of other stuff as well, or do stuff that hurt more. She'd succeeded for quite a while, close to eight years to be exact. But, for once, that wasn't the real issue now. The real issue was whether it was possible to be a mother again when she'd been so crap at it the first time. Meg, her patient case worker, seemed to think it was, and Zoe wanted to believe her.

She had been in awe of Naomi. She could still remember (which in itself was no mean feat) feeling shy and nervous around her. Ben and Jesse and Noel, they were all such push-overs, but Naomi was a rock. And now? She was probably still a rock – once rock, always a rock. And once a junkie? Zoe didn't persist with that thought. Not today.

She squinted through the grime at the paddocks beyond. She used to know every station between Kingswood and

Central, every burnt-out car, practically every clump of onion weed. She'd been staring out of these train windows all her life. But today it was different. Meg thought she had a real shot with the Department of Housing. There was more than a chance she could finally leave her supported accommodation.

She looked carefully at her pale reflection in the train window. Her long, lank hair, her blank face. Zoe hadn't known much eight years ago, but she knew she wasn't caring properly for her two small children. If you'd asked her, before the accident, whether she loved little Chris and baby Max, she couldn't have really said. She could have spoken know-ledgeably about every shade of blue, or anything else to do with colour and form, but love, well, that was something else. Zoe thought she'd loved them. Now things were different. Of course she loved them. She was their mother, for Christ's sake. Love didn't have to be more complicated than that. But when they'd been babies, she'd had to hold back part of herself in reserve, or she felt as though she'd disappear altogether.

When she'd left the children with Naomi, she'd told herself she was still a child herself, far too young to look after them properly. But Naomi? She was made to be a mother, any idiot could see that a mile off. She knew everything there was to know about it. It was practically her profession. Zoe remem-bered fumbling with Chris's feeds, way past when she should have been fumbling with breastfeeding. He was losing weight, not even back to his birth weight at six weeks of age. Naomi got rid of all the breastfeeding books and grimly put a bottle in his mouth. It must have been a big deal, because they never spoke about it again. Chris was bottle-fed by Ben from then on. Max, well he didn't even get a look-in. Zoe knew her failure at breastfeeding was a major blow to Naomi.

Had it been fair to leave the boys with Naomi, the best-possible-mother-in-the-world? Or should she have tried harder to look after them, even when she was in such a mess herself? Had it been the most maternal thing she could have done at the time?

She stood and stretched – her weak ankle aching – before moving back down the aisle of the carriage in an aimless, slow walk. Who could she get a cigarette off? Anyone worth talking to?

The train lurched and stopped suddenly. Zoe fell sideways, landing awkwardly on an elderly couple. She struggled back up.

'Shit. I'm sorry,' she said to the back of the couple's heads, sliding her feet back into her thongs and picking up her backpack. 'Not thinking straight today.'

But Zoe had a sneaking suspicion that perhaps she was finally beginning to think straight. Meg was right. If she could get back her kids, she'd have the first real chance in a long while to start over. They were the key. Why had it taken her so long to realise it? Of course they belonged with her.

At that same moment in the inner city, Naomi gripped the handle on her back door and pulled hard, further gouging at the arc in the floorboards. The door needed re-hanging – another job waiting for Noel's attention. Its narrow glass panes caught the last of the day's light and threw it back in a million tiny pieces. The garden was more than overgrown; the wisteria was beginning to strangle itself. Funny, she hadn't noticed it until now. Noel rarely set foot out here. It held no interest for him. For a boy from a farm, an inner-city garden contained little curiosity, and besides, it gave him dreadful hay fever.

Whatever Noel didn't care for, he didn't notice. The jobs around the house would have to pile up for a very long time before he would see them, *really* see them. Naomi envied him this. She, on the other hand, noticed everything, and filled up on details rather than the more substantial main course of ideas and possibilities. The passionfruit needed a brutal pruning. The grape was trailing off the trellis in long tendrils. She knew she had to take action before the winter began, she couldn't leave it up to Noel. And yes, she would try with Zoe. She would give them both a chance to make things right. She must be ready when and if Zoe turned up again.

Vital signs

It was an indisputable fact that Naomi knew a lot about babies. She had parcelled and packaged them for close to forty years. Her kitchen noticeboard was covered in their small mementos: thank-you cards, photos, footprints, handprints. She felt grateful and elated when she looked at them – the future: babies with thick black shocks of hair and eyes as big as Mariposa plums, others with wrinkly red washerwoman hands, or Cupid faces with runny violet eyes; mothers with steady and true gazes, tentative fathers with big thick fingers. She knew about how babies slept and the mechanics of breastfeeding. She understood meconium aspiration and webbed feet. She knew all about love at first sight and fontanelles the consistency of soft-boiled eggs. She wouldn't trade midwifery for the world.

Even so, it was only recently that she had begun to have the deep, healing sleep of her youth again. She thought about that kind of motionless rest when your breath is imperceptible, like a baby's. Her nights had been so broken for so long that she had begun to wonder whether deep sleep really existed. Working shifts for many years hadn't helped. But it was more than that. She had become uneasy in the dark. It was not so much the dark, as the dark thoughts. And so, at her kitchen sink not all that long ago, she had made her decision to change the things she could. She would think differently. She would sleep deeply again. It was possible.

When she felt uneasy, Naomi thought about babies. After all those years and all those deliveries, she could honestly say that each birth still held some magic for her. On her very first shift she delivered a breach, but healthy, baby boy. A good omen for her career, a midwife said to her at the time. Midwifery was full of predictions. As a midwife she was trained to locate and read signs. She measured signs of change in skin temperature and heartbeats. But the change that she sensed now in herself was altogether different – something profound – and she was quietly optimistic about it.

'As the baby is held for the first time, questions arise. Some are immediate – the sex, condition and appearance – others more remote – life expectancy, vocation, genes, IQ, the ultimate balance of happiness and tragedy. Hope even,' one student read softly from Naomi's class notes, before coming to a complete stop.

Naomi nodded encouragingly. 'That's right. A midwife is operating on two levels at a birth. It isn't just practical support that you are offering. Things like hope inevitably spring to mind and are useful. Don't dismiss those thoughts and feelings because they are not scientific measures of some vital sign.'

They moved on to a case presentation: one of Naomi's Sudanese families.

'My concern here is about the size of the baby. What should I do?' Naomi threw the question to the students. They sat huddled around her desk looking at the casenotes. The small, windowless room was very quiet for a moment as they read, lips pursed, eyes darting like pairs of mice across the pages of notes. Outside, the clinic's waiting room was full. They could hear the distant wails of a toddler demanding a sleep or a feed. Naomi thought about how she'd loved those lost, pared-back years when Ben and Jesse were babies and she had literally given herself completely to their needs; her life had been reduced to sleep and food and warmth.

'Blood pressure is good. Other signs? What would we look for?' Naomi prompted.

The students began to fidget with their pens.

'Previous unsuccessful pregnancy,' Naomi said, consulting the casenotes. 'Is that relevant?' She waited, her head of thick hair, which she kept cut short, poised ready to listen and, hopefully, nod.

'Yes,' all the students agreed.

Naomi nodded. 'And again we come back to the crux of being a midwife. Unique in the field of medicine, our obligation is to care for two patients, not one: the mother and the child. Each has an individual right to life.'

The students wrote in their notes silently for a moment. The most fidgety lowered his pen to ask thoughtfully, 'If a situation developed at the delivery where only one of the lives could be saved, which one would you save?'

All the students looked earnestly at Naomi. There was always one student every semester who asked *that* question, of all questions, and Naomi always thought, why?

'Well, you'll probably never have to face that one, unless you are a volunteer with MSF in war-torn Somalia or somewhere. It doesn't happen too often round here.'

Naomi looked forward to the new students each semester. She loved their intensity and the chance to speak about beginnings rather than ends. She had a wide mouth – made for talking, her mother had said. But she didn't want to talk about dark, improbable choices that day. She was determined to stay positive, even about a student who asked such a predictable question.

It had taken eight ruined years to reach this point, when she felt that perhaps her grief, like the drought, might be lifting. That she might be able to rebuild her life with Noel and the boys. That things were possible again. She was emerging into the daylight. Images and sounds were clear and precise as ruled paper. Her life seemed to be bubbling and buckling, rising to meet her like the asphalt on a hot January day.

'Which one would you save?' the student persisted. The kind of student who asked this question on the first day usually did.

Naomi paused. Birth and death – there they were, insistent, up front, day one.

'Did you know that there is no word in the English language to describe a mother whose child has died?'

The students looked at her blankly. That wasn't the answer they were expecting.

'It's not the right order of things, is it?' she said. 'I mean for a child to die before a parent. How very sad. But a mother is a custodian. A mother is everything, and nothing.'

Naomi paused to let the students speak if they wanted, but none did.

It was not until she had nursed her own dying mother that Naomi had truly understood the right order of things between mother and child. A mother went ahead, to beat the snakes out of the bushes, to show the child how it is to *be* and then to *be gone*. Her mother had died of old age, no longer able to speak, eat or drink, curled up in a bed on the verandah of a country hospital, still holding Naomi's hand. It was the right order of things. But when Naomi lost her own adult sons, she simply wished that she too was dead.

She stood up to bring the class to an end. 'It is a more complicated question than it seems.' She squinted at the students. 'It's not my decision to make; it's not yours either. There would be many other people involved in a decision like that. The husband or partner. The obstetrician.'

This was a big question, the balancing of which they would probably wrestle with for the rest of their careers. She had.

Circles

Noel realised he'd had a narrow escape from yet another early-morning, whispered, pyjama-clad argument with Naomi.

He and Naomi knew each other deeply. And this was important to Noel. This was all that was needed, surely? He knew that Naomi had loved him once, fiercely, enough to take his breath away. He knew that she loved fresh figs and goat's cheese and raw pistachios. He knew that she loved to sleep without dreams. As a lithe young woman (he hadn't forgotten a moment), she lay on her back, spread-eagled in the middle of the cast-iron double bed that Noel tried to share with her. Noel hugged the side and wondered how such a small woman could take up so much room. In all the other aspects of their life together Naomi was unusually compact and efficient, apart from when she climbed into the bed they shared. Noel learnt to sleep on his side, back turned to her closed eyelids and pointed chin, her unpredictable elbows and knees. Noel gave in.

But then, the unimaginable happened. His sons – *his* Ben and *his* Jesse; *his* flesh and *his* blood – died. He and Naomi were left with each other, back where they had started. Only then he realised that he didn't know Naomi anymore and possibly, just possibly, he didn't even like her. And he realised this long before she did. That was the hardest thing – knowing it when she didn't; and her increasing lack of curiosity to inhabit his world with him.

In Grenfell all those years ago, Naomi was fearless – tearing it up, terrific, wild, daring. She had freckles dusted across her forehead and the bridge of her fine, upturned nose. She had a shock of thick black hair, full of cowlicks and kinks and curls. Naomi was cute and sassy and confident, all things that brainy, bookish Noel lacked. They had been in the same classes at Henry Lawson High, but quiet, awkward Noel didn't stand a chance. He couldn't keep up with her and the rest of them out on the Weddin Mountain Road in their old utes, racing, drinking and more racing. So he waited out his time until he could leave. And out of the handful of girls that made it to the big smoke all the way from historic Grenfell, Naomi was the one who ended up rolling on the lawn in his clumsy embrace in the quadrangle of Sydney University.

Noel turned his face to Naomi, her freckles now sunspots and lesions but her nut-brown eyes still intense and sharp as broken glass. There was not an ounce of fat on Naomi. She did not stand still long enough for it to accumulate anywhere. Her thick strong hands with short, practical square nails could catch a slippery newborn just as deftly as whip up a pavlova as light as cloud. Her tongue could tear strips off him, she could be as caustic as stinging nettle, and yet. And yet . . .

'What is it?' he asked, barely concealing his indifference to her domestic detailing of their lives. After the boys' deaths it was as if she took to the detail of things. Always looking down; needing glasses, literally, for the first time in her life.

'Noel, when are you going to fix the back door? I nearly broke the glass in it the other day, trying to open it. It needs re-hanging.'

15

Noel. Naomi said his name with that certain inflection in her voice. *I thought we agreed that you would do so and so; I asked you this before, yesterday, last week, last month, last year and you said yes. Then why haven't you done it yet? Where are you? Are you reading while I'm working? Are you hiding from me? Are you ignoring me?*

She had a right to expect that he would amount to more than he had. He knew that. Short-changing her, as he had in almost every respect – except in matters to do with his boys, whom he had loved more than life itself, and Ben's two small sons, Chris and Maxy, who were his night and day, his reason for being. In his semi-retired, or under-employed, late fifties, he was happiest immersed in the small boys' sporting commitments. Since the deaths of Ben and Jesse he walked around Naomi in small, concentric circles, where once he had circumnavigated the earth.

After he and Naomi graduated from university – he a fully-fledged electrical engineer and she with a BA – Naomi wanted to return to Grenfell. He flew off round the world, and eventually all the way back to her. He had to work out the mathematics of his love for her before he could inhabit it. He knew he loved Naomi when he had flown in excess of 100,000 kilometres, circumferencing the earth, more than once (an equatorial circumferential measurement); when he had written more than 10,000 words to her from houseboats in Kashmir, beside the stone money of Yap, inside the zocalo of San Cristobal de las Casas; and when he asked her to come to him, to be with him, and she did. Finally he held her in frosty Beijing, in the circle of his arms, and they had been circling each other ever since. A circle is simple, he had been taught. A closed curve. An interior and an exterior. A special ellipse in which the two foci are coincident. But he no longer believed this. Nothing that involved two was simple.

'Soon,' he replied.

And just when he thought that they would never stop talking about the back door sticking, Max's swimming lessons, the hockey team's uniforms, the right high school for Chris, the neighbour's cat – that he would die with a hockey score stuck in his head – Naomi had spoken about Ben, that morning, for the first time, out of the blue, in what felt like a hundred years.

And he nodded and smiled at whatever it was she was saying, some observation, some passing remark. He didn't care about the words. Instead he was watching her lips move and her eyes sparkle, the way a proud parent's do. The way she was speaking about Ben invited Noel in rather than pushed him out. Just an offhand comment, as though they were normal parents in a normal life.

She had decided something. He wasn't quite sure what, or whether it was a good idea, but something had changed in her. And he wished he had been paying more attention. Nonetheless, Noel, now almost sixty years of age, slowly made room for a little hope to grow between them where all had been despair.

Blood is thicker than water

Chris rinsed his paintbrushes slowly, watching the water gush down the plughole. He wasn't the hurrying kind. He chewed slowly (so slowly that Gran said he practically digested his food in his mouth); he rode his bike home from school slowly (Max always beat him); he read slowly, making sure that every word was right before moving on to the next. He did not like mistakes. The smear of magenta (his favourite colour) across his yellow (his most un-favourite colour) school shirt was a mistake. He hoped Gran wouldn't be too angry about it. She didn't like mistakes either. They had discussed it. They discussed heaps of things like that, and usually they agreed. Funny though, they never discussed you-know-who (and he didn't mean Voldemort, because they had discussed him). Grandpa discussed *her* though. He said that Chris used to like *her* very much and that he should study hard at school because she would be asking him all about it when she came round. It might be any time now.

'Hurry up, Chris,' a boy said behind him. 'Yer wasting too much water!'

Chris turned off the tap really hard. His fingers were strong. Stronger than most other ten-year-old boys', Gran said. All that piano and clarinet practice had tightened the sinews and joints that held him together under his skin, or so she said.

Chris glanced up through the old school windows onto the street. There she was, the woman in bare feet, standing across the road. The pedestrian sign said 'Walk' but she just stood there.

'Would Year 4 please hurry up!' The teacher's voice carried out into the corridor behind Chris.

His classroom was on the western side of the building, away from the road. He had a feeling the woman was there often, but he had no way of knowing. This was the third or fourth time Chris had seen her. The last time was not long ago, when he retrieved a runaway soccer ball from outside the school fence. It was the same woman. She was on that side of the road then too, Chris was sure of it. That time the woman had been sitting on the bus-stop seat.

'Sorry,' Chris said to Cameron, who was next in line and getting a bit stroppy. Chris wanted to turn away from the window, to ignore the woman, but instead he walked along to the next window. His paintbrushes were still dripping magenta and the paint now ran down his hands and forearms in small rivulets. What a mess.

He craned for another look, but the woman was gone. He decided that she wasn't really his mother, but he liked to imagine that she might be; that she loved him secretly, from afar. She watched him like a private detective of the heart and she knew all there was to know about him: his shoe size, the birthmark on the back of his leg, his awkward fall from the monkey bars last year and his broken collarbone. She couldn't speak to him though, or the spell would be broken. A bit like the story of Ariel in *The Little Mermaid*. Her voice would be beautiful, she would have perfect pitch and, like him, an ear for music. He saw 'her' in the strangest places: at the football oval, in the supermarket, on the bus. She was more like a guardian angel than a mother. He wasn't sure whether he was angry or sad about her. Chris got those two things mixed up.

There was a lot of stuff Chris wanted to know more about, and it was not the solar system or polygons. He wanted to know more about who he was. Christopher Adams, aged ten. He asked questions, but they were the wrong questions because of what he didn't know. *Why did my mother leave me with you, Gran?* That was one. He'd asked Gran many times, but she didn't seem to know exactly. He decided that she made up her answers, because she said something different every time. Thinking about his mum made him a bit sad. He talked to Grandpa about it and Grandpa said it was all right to feel a bit sad, and if he liked they could feel a bit sad together. Gran, on the other hand, was always saying, 'Cheer up, sonny Jim, it can't be all that bad.'

Chris played hockey in the Under-11s and he liked playing the piano and that was about it. He didn't mind his school, but when he was old enough he wanted to go to the Conservatorium of Music. Then he could concentrate on the piano and he wouldn't have to worry much about all those other subjects. His teacher said to Gran at the student-led conference that there was an 'air of quiet desperation' about him. Chris had heard her say it. He didn't know exactly what she meant, but it was serious because she said it in a low voice and Gran just nodded.

Chris was waiting to grow up and change things. He kept busy. He liked to swim and Gran put him in squads at the Leichhardt pool. He wasn't what you would call a fast swimmer. Not like Max. Max was a champion and Chris got sick of being compared to him. 'Do you know how bad it is to see your little brother win all the ribbons every time?' Chris explained to Gran. She didn't agree. She said that she had a little sister, Sarah, and when they were young Sarah was always better than her at everything. He just had to deal with it. Gran was always telling him to *deal* with things. It was practically her favourite saying. 'Christopher, just deal with it!' Chris's favourite saying was, 'Whatever,' especially because he knew Gran really hated it.

He didn't tell Gran that he had started seeing his mother everywhere. He thought it would upset her. Lately Gran had been a bit funny. Too cheerful. He didn't tell Max either. They were close, just about as close as brothers almost two years apart could be. Not friends. Definitely. Not like the twins in Chris's class, who wore the same clothes on weekends. The only time Chris and Max wore the same clothes was when Max was wearing Chris's hand-me-downs. Definitely not close enough to discuss Mum.

Up until now Chris had thought Gran was pretty cool, for a Gran. She loved music, or she did a good job pretending she did, Chris thought, because he had never seen her play the piano. Chris, on the other hand, couldn't *not* play it. If he walked past a piano he had to sit down and play something. Sometimes he stood up and played as well. He loved the sound the piano made, the sound of a piano key. His favourite note was G. It was perfect. That probably sounded really stupid – to like one note more than another. Chris knew you had to use all the notes to make a tune, but he liked G a lot. He used it all the time. He improvised. That's what his piano teacher, Kerry, called it. Chris could spend hours improvising. He tried writing music down but mostly he found it too hard. Probably as tedious as writing a book, he thought. Word after word on a blank page until you had a hundred of them. He remembered the way a piece sounded and played it like that. Someone else could write it down one day.

The gleaners

Naomi and Noel had an old book that Max liked. He'd found it on the top of the bookshelf last Christmas, covered in dust. It was small and packed hard with words, like an adult's book. He'd had to clean the cardboard cover with a damp face cloth before he could even see any of it. Through the grime an Egyptian head appeared first, then some reeds. An old book about old stories – even better. Ever since, he'd kept it beside his bed and asked his grandmother to read it to him from time to time. She used to read it to Ben when he was Max's age. That was one reason why Max asked her to read it to him. Max asked her where she got it but she couldn't remember. She thought that Aunty Gwen or Aunty Evelyn had given it to Ben when he was a boy. Anyway, Max thought, it was really old. It smelt old and it didn't have many pictures. The pages were the colour of a ripe banana. The other reason he liked it was that it contained a story about a woman called Naomi. He liked the idea of Gran reading a story about someone named 'Naomi', because that was her name. To Max she was just Gran, but to the rest of the world, apart from Chris and Grandpa and a few other relatives, she was Naomi Adams.

There was a whole stack of stories in the book, but the one

he liked best was called 'The Book of Ruth', although some-times Max got mixed up and called it 'The Book of Naomi'.

'Not that one, *Max*, surely?' His grandmother usually said his name with a bit of exasperation, but then she read it anyway.

Max liked the story because it was short, no one died espe-cially badly and it had a happy ending. He was all for happy endings. In the story, they were hungry for a lot of the time, and Gran shook her head when she got to the part about 'gleaning'. She said that they must have been very hungry and desperate in those ancient times. She said this with her reading glasses halfway down her nose and Max believed her. She looked so serious with her glasses like that.

'These days we don't need to glean, by hand, as such,' his grandmother explained, and she knew a thing or two about gleaning because she grew up on a farm in a place called Grenfell. When she said 'Grenfell' they all knew it meant a farm surrounded by other farms, bushranger's gold hidden in the Weddin Mountains, sheep with pink-eye and Grandpa's famous hay fever.

Anyway, in the story, everything could be used and nothing needed to be wasted. That's why there was plenty of food these days – thanks to good modern farming practices. Max hoped she was right that there would be plenty of food for absolutely ever. She was usually right about most important things, and that was truly excellent because Max liked food. Always had, always would, according to Gran. You could even say that Max loved food. Max loved it all – the cooking, the chopping, the mixing. The setting the table – not so much. The cleaning up – well, even less. The smell of it in the oven was pretty good though. Max liked thinking about food, but not when he was too hungry. Whenever he had a nightmare, or he felt a bit sad, he thought about food. Gran, in Max's opinion, was a great cook. *That* was the single best-ever thing about her. That, and her being a nurse. Max's friend Harry hated food. How was that possible, Max wondered. Harry only ate when he was hungry, and that was all there was to it. Harry's mum was an okay cook too. Max told Harry's mother that he liked her muffins, even if they were, as Gran said, 'out of a packet'. They talked about food in HSIE. Healthy food, that kind of thing. That took the fun out of it a bit. Not that Max was fat or anything, because he exercised, and he made his grand-mother too. He played hockey and swam like a fish. Squads. He loved that word. It sounded so fast.

'I'm quite a good swimmer, for my age,' Max said.

His grandmother swam too. She teased him, 'You swim just like me.'

That was a scary thought. Did Max swim like a girl? You couldn't be too careful. It was easy to make people laugh by a mistake.

Max admitted that he and Gran had a lot in common, but he wished that she didn't make him do music. That was defi-nitely for girls. The possible exception was Chris, who would die without his piano.

'I hate piano. Trumpet's not much better,' Max said, often.

The only good thing about piano was that he could smell Gran's cooking while he practised, because she was always cooking something. Or sometimes she ate her breakfast by the piano while he practised. The smell of cooked porridge always reminded Max of the C major scale. At Harry's house Max got to eat meat pies and hot chips from the shop. Gran, on the other hand, made her own. She told Max, 'That's because I grew up on a farm and we had to make everything. That's the way it was.' That was practically his grandmother's favou-rite, number-one saying, 'That's the way it was, Max.' Or 'is', depending on what she was talking about.

Gran said she preferred the city because she liked the food and the people were more interesting. This didn't make much sense to Max – how could people be more interesting in one place or another? They were just people. Weren't all people pretty much the same? And, besides, didn't she miss her farm? Max thought he would, which brought him back to the gleaning. He thought about that word. It described him. Gran and Grandpa had 'gleaned' him and Chris. It described how they came to be living in Annandale.

'Why did Mummy leave me?' he had asked Gran and Grandpa more than once.

Gran's lips went all white. 'It wasn't anyone's fault,' she said. Grandpa didn't say much on that subject either, and that was strange because usually you couldn't shut him up.

He thought that perhaps he was such a small, quiet baby that his mother didn't notice she'd left him behind. Leaving Chris behind was another altogether different matter in Max's eight-year-old head. When he closed his eyes and tried to think about being left behind, he saw a round baby Moses stuck in the reeds on the River Nile, like on the cover of the old book.

Gran must know more about why his mother had left them. Her silence on the subject made Max feel a bit uneasy.

All the tea in India

It was eight years since that winter afternoon when Naomi and Noel stood motionless in the hallway trying to absorb the content of a Constable Thompson's telephone call. Their two sons, Ben, aged twenty-two, and Jesse, aged nineteen, had just been killed in a car accident on the Bells Line of Road. Zoe, Ben's wife, Naomi's daughter-in-law, had been transferred to Katoomba Hospital by ambulance where she was in a stable but critical condition.

Where another mother and father might have collapsed in grief, Naomi and Noel stayed calm and quiet, ever so quiet. And before they began to attend to the devastating details of Ben and Jesse's deaths, they numbly held each of Ben's children – Chris, the dimpled, busy toddler, and Max, a wide-eyed six-month-old – between them as if for the very last time too.

Throughout the following long years, Naomi gave many pieces of advice to her birthing mothers, including this: *when the pain is unbearable, don't dissolve into it. Stay strong. Remember who you are.*

That winter afternoon Naomi did not accompany Noel, dear shuffling Noel, to the hospital morgue to identify their beautiful sons' dead, burnt bodies. Instead she went to Zoe, leaving Max and Chris in the flustered hands of Noel's two older sisters.

Naomi and Noel had spent barely a Saturday together since. Instead, Noel had taken his grandsons to hockey, or athletics, or swimming, and Naomi had headed off to the fruit and vegetable market.

Naomi took the light rail to the market at 8 am every Saturday. She poked and prodded bunches of bok choy and dried shiitake mushrooms. She haggled over the price of Middle Eastern apricots and chilli-fried peanuts. She was a regular and many of the stall owners gave her an extra bunch of fresh mint or a ripe nashi pear. Back at home she washed the vegetables and laid out the food ready for the lunch.

Noel was next season's very experienced, rather than old, hockey coach, and that morning he had taken Chris's Under-11 team – the Jets – in a successful pre-season practice session. The males in the household were pleased with themselves as they sat down with Naomi to a lunch of bread rolls and ham and salad.

That summery lunchtime Naomi felt exasperated by the heat and humidity, as if humidity was a cantankerous house guest that had overstayed its welcome. Bring on autumn, if only to see the back of humidity! She was also cross because she had squashed a bag of expensive ripe figs. Still, it was an ordinary Saturday in the full swing of summer and hockey tryouts and young boys.

Noel had just sat down and started eating when he clutched his chest. 'Pain,' he gasped, looking deep into Naomi's eyes and falling forward onto the side of the dining-room table with a sickening crack of skull on wood. Naomi dropped what she was doing and skidded around the table, stumbling over his discarded thongs. Although Noel was not much taller than her, he was thickset and about twice her body weight. He had fallen doubled over, tangled in the legs of a kitchen chair. She struggled to lay him flat on the floor. Max was at the back door, standing motionless about three feet away, a hockey stick still in his hand. Chris was in front of him, tying his shoelace. Naomi pulled Noel over and started thumping his chest.

'Chris, call the ambulance!' she said. 'Quickly.'

But Chris shrank down further over his shoe as if he had not heard. Naomi turned to look at him. A tennis ball was rolling down the slope towards the back fence. Instead, Max swept past her and grabbed the telephone receiver, dialling the emergency number.

She tried not to sound too shrill. 'Tell them it's off Booth Street.'

Max knew his grandfather's address – he had, after all, lived here all his life – but Naomi thought he might be thrown by the question. At eight years of age things easily unravelled, and at fifty-eight too. She was finding it hard to get her own breathing under control. 'Nearest cross-street is Booth Street,' she repeated, trying to keep her voice even.

As she thumped on Noel's chest, Naomi did not look back towards Chris. She could not help him. Her focus was Noel, and a heartbeat that refused to come.

'Noel,' she whispered, 'Don't.'

She continued to pound on his chest, but she could see that, despite her best efforts, the life was seeping out of Noel. His flesh was turning grey.

Max spoke into the phone carefully and clearly, not a sign of panic in his voice. 'My grandfather is sick. My grandmother asked me to call the ambulance.'

She heard him clear his voice and give his address.

The cottage's tin roof expanded in the heat – *tick, tick, tick, tack* – like an erratic heartbeat.

'Noel,' she called, gently feeling again for a pulse in his neck. He was cool to her touch. She brushed the hair back from his forehead, both to check the temperature of his skin and to feel his solid mass beside her, as she had felt for the thirty-five years of their marriage.

She started mouth-to-mouth. When her lips touched his she realised that he was not coming back to life, but she continued, torn between staying in the present, because she knew that shortly she would not even have this with Noel, and a desperate need to bring him back from wherever it was he had gone.

A flock of cockatoos swooped across the backyard screeching – a terrible, unhinged sound. There was a faint lull in between trucks braking, motorbikes accelerating, kids shouting. The ambulance arrived, its siren making one last protest before fading out in the street outside. Noel's death seemed to Naomi to be stopping everything.

'He had so many things to do!' Naomi said, turning away from Noel's grey, bloodless face, surprise in her voice. She ran her hands through her damp hair and wiped the sweat off her forehead with the back of her hand. The two ambulance officers moved chairs out of the way and made room. Naomi found herself thinking, room for death to take Noel away.

'We'll get him straight to hospital,' the younger of the two ambulance officers said.

'What's the point?' she said slowly. 'He's dead.'

The officers continued to prepare to take Noel with them.

'We need to ascertain that for ourselves,' said the older one.

Naomi moved aside, disliking their strange hands on Noel. She wanted to protect him from this final indignity.

'I'm sorry you have to go through this, Noel,' she said to his lifeless body.

The men worked their way slowly through their laminated pages of protocol. They were tight-lipped and intense. The older one timed everything by his large wristwatch. The other listened to Noel's chest at intervals through his stethoscope and reported, 'Negative, negative, negative.'

Naomi and Noel's local doctor, Greg Bird, finally arrived and the ambulance officers relaxed a little.

'Time of death, fourteen hundred hours,' Dr Bird said.

Naomi almost remarked, 'Punctual,' but she knew this would sound crazy, so she just nodded and began to feel exhausted.

The theory, the medical world, none of it really mediated this thing called death. Noel was dead. She now turned to face him squarely. It was a fact. Noel no longer flinched or teased or smiled.

Chris was crying silently. Max stood, hidden behind his brother, sobbing.

The ambulance officers had moved Noel to a stretcher and were speaking to Dr Bird in low voices. Naomi heard fragments of their conversation: 'No history of coronary heart disease . . . She's a midwife out at . . .'

She moved back to Noel's side once they had completed their paperwork. Chris was now hunched up in a ball in the corner, Max beside him. Suddenly she wanted to yell at Noel, 'How inconsiderate of you!' She lay her head on his chest and wished she could beat his arms and shoulders with her fists, and sob, really sob. *Can't you see that Chris and Max have been through enough already? How could you let them down like this?* But these were accusations she would never make in front of her grandchildren. *How could you leave me!* Naomi wanted to scream. *You're a coward! How dare you give up! How dare you be so selfish!* But just as swiftly she was angry with herself. How could she have wasted so much of their precious time together being cross and miserable and disappointed?

The younger ambulance officer was packing away the defibrillator and sharps container when Naomi sat up and asked him, 'Could you help me lay him on our bed?'

She knew that they needed to get going; they needed their stretcher back. She felt dizzy when she stood.

'Just let the funeral director come here and pick up his body later,' she said, pre-empting Dr Bird's question as it hovered on his lips. It was as if she was speaking another language. The ambulance officers stared at her, unused to people taking control of such a situation, being capable of thinking about what to do next.

But Naomi knew what had to be done. She had washed and lovingly wrapped many dead babies for distraught mothers over the course of her career. She had made handprints and footprints and marvelled at the smallest nail on the smallest toe of a dead baby as she prepared a mother to say her final goodbye. She knew what had to happen next. She did not want Noel's body to go anywhere near a hospital when the choice was finally offered. On a hot, humid Saturday afternoon, there would be no one in the funeral home's office so this would be an after-hours call – double the cost. But Noel would have preferred to stay here with them a little longer than to be put in some cold fridge in the bowels of a hospital. Especially a hospital, of all places, where a death is such a failure.

After the officers had moved Noel, she rearranged the pillows under his head.

'Bring in a couple of chairs, Chris,' she said.

He did as he was told quietly and put them next to the bed, but no one sat down.

'Is he really dead?' Max said.

'Yes,' Naomi said. 'There's no bringing him back.'

❧

Lying in bed with Max that morning, Noel had been telling him about walking the Helambu Trail in the Himalayas. It was one of those increasingly rare moments when Max cuddled down in between Noel and Naomi. At ten, Chris was too independent, but Max was still open to and curious about their world.

'You walk up and down these huge mountains,' Noel had begun in his quiet voice with a faraway look in his eyes, 'and they are only the foothills! At night you come to a small village. You ask which villager takes in guests. You go to that house and pay them some money to sleep on their floor, perhaps with them in the same room. They cook on an open fire and you eat things like rice and dhal and roti.'

'What's roti?' interrupted Max.

'A kind of flatbread that you roll and dip in the dhal,' Noel answered. 'You drink tea together and – guess what – there's no chimney, so the room is quickly full of smoke.'

Naomi thought now about how Noel loved mornings best and she clung to the remnants of that morning. What an ordinary Saturday it had been. A Saturday morning in which Max and Noel talked about tea.

'In India, when the train pulls into a station, a man sells you a cup of tea.'

Noel had paused and asked Max, 'But what do you think he put the tea in, Maxy?'

'What do you mean, Pa?'

'Well, there are no paper cups – too expensive. How do you think they sell you the tea?'

Max shrugged.

'They pour it into small clay cups. Cups that can be crushed under your foot. Crushed under your foot . . .' Noel paused to think about this for a moment, 'when you're finished, because that's all clay is, cooked earth. That way, the clay returns to the earth from where it came.'

~

Naomi picked up Noel's thick, lifeless hand. She stayed as still as he was. Then she turned it over so she could see the palm. She traced the calluses and his lifeline with her forefinger. Normally this would have been enough to send him into fits of giggles, Noel was so ticklish.

She laid her cheek on his palm. Outside, the phone was ringing, voices Naomi didn't recognise were audible. The front door was open and a gust of wind moved down the hallway and around her, lifting the bedroom curtains, raising the dust from the floorboards. Unfamiliar feet stepped across the threshold into the gloom. A full kettle rolled on a forgotten boil, *boiling*, *boiling*, *boiling*. Naomi remained quiet beside Noel and let the life of the house go on around her, without her for now. What if they could all just go back one step, to the way things had been before lunch? Close the front door. Turn off the kettle. Rearrange the chairs. Sit down at the table. Unwrap figs that weren't squashed. Begin lunch again. Tell each other the hockey score. Tell each one that she loved them. Tell Noel that she loved him.

She raised her cheek from his open palm and called out to the boys, 'Come, say goodbye to your grandfather.' When they entered the room she took Max's hand and looked at Chris.

'Chris?' Max said cautiously to his older brother as he edged closer to Noel's lifeless body.

When Ben and Jesse died Noel had been the practical one.

'Come, Chris,' Naomi said to him, looking him steadily in the eye.

He shook his head, *no*.

She had felt her sons' deaths like a physical blow. Caring for Ben's two little boys was the only thing that kept her sane, ensured that life went on.

'That's okay,' she said, thinking about her refusal to go with Noel to the morgue. And about Zoe, who, although she had been in the car, could give no coherent account at the inquest of what had happened. Because she was Chris and Max's mother, Naomi had stopped short of demanding answers from her.

'I understand,' she said gently to Chris.

How many times did the car roll? Why had they crashed? Why was Zoe driving? She had stopped short for the sake of the grandchildren. And for Noel. He knew it would not bring back his sons.

Now, though, she would have been completely different with Zoe.

'What will you do?' Dr Bird asked.

Naomi shrugged.

'Take care of the boys,' she said tentatively. 'That's what Noel would have done.' And with that she stood up. 'He was a better person,' she said aloud. 'He was a better parent . . . grandparent,' she corrected herself, 'to the boys than me.'

'Naomi,' Greg said, 'what nonsense.'

In the bedroom Max had fallen asleep on the floor, while Chris remained watchful by the doorway. Naomi could feel herself slipping down the slippery slope. *Why couldn't it have been me to have a heart attack, not Noel?*

Max woke suddenly and began to sob, 'Grandpa!'

'While we have each other, we can get through anything,' she said to the boys slowly. 'Noel used to say that to me when things were really bad.'

Chris stood at her elbow, silent, dry-eyed, stunned. Naomi knew that Gran, the Gran she projected to them, did not admit that things could get really bad.

'Take strength from the fact that your grandfather was wise, and that he loved you so very much. Always remember that.'

'Gran, you're not going to leave us too?' Max cried.

'No, of course not.' She hugged him, as if her body heat could warm his little-boy heart.

Mouldy suit

At almost sixty, death was something you fought daily with a regimen of yoga and exercise and diet. Even so, Noel's death was bewildering. It wasn't violent and messy like her sons' deaths. It was a textbook heart attack. Just like that, Noel, her husband of so many years, was dead. Mid-mouthful, one sunny Saturday over a lunch of bread rolls and ham and salad.

That night, after she had allowed Noel's body to be taken to the funeral home, she lay curled up on his side of their double bed, alone. She could feel the indent of his body. Noel, from the neighbouring farm via the whole wide world, the only man she had ever loved and the only man who could have loved her all the way back. She had not come to know this the easy way.

She lay still and fell in deep, heart-thrumming love with him all over again. But just as soon as she did, she remembered the fights, and the resentment. The arguments over money, their grandsons' endless music practice, and of course Zoe. She remembered the way Noel poured milk on his cereal, and how he ignored her while he ate. Most mornings while she stood at the kitchen sink in her nightie and slippers, a naked Noel quietly walked around her. They sometimes, but not always, acknowledged each other softly, with a tilt of the head. 'The grandchildren' had been her shield against any intimacy for the best part of the past decade. But she didn't need much of a shield. Noel had given up long ago. He simply and literally walked around her. Sometimes he had exploded like a thunderous firecracker. *Are you alive?*

Naomi rolled over heavily. 'I'm alive,' she said flatly.

There was old age and *old* age. To Chris and Max, Noel and Naomi were ancient, but Naomi knew that in the back of Noel's mind he was planning a retirement in which they would travel endlessly together. 'I really want to do the Gobi!' or 'Let's go to Tahiti!' He often said such a thing after reading the travel section in the newspaper, or when he was frustrated and bored with the routine of their life. Naomi preferred to chafe under the pressure of mounting bills. Noel seemed to grow more impractical with time. 'Let's just get up and go!' But since Ben and Jesse's deaths, Naomi had not been able to contemplate going anywhere. Chris and Max's guardianship had been enough of an excuse. She knew she was completely stuck, but she kept her panic and dread to herself and simply became more and more reserved in the face of Noel's plans.

'I'm alive,' she said into Noel's pillow, crying bitterly.

At almost sixty she remained the same Arts undergraduate who had kissed Noel at university that fateful lunchtime on the lawn. She had surprised herself because he was literally the boy from the farm next door – there had been so many jokes about that at their wedding in Grenfell. She dutifully endured his older sisters Gwen and Evelyn's advice, she let Noel tease her little sister, Sarah, and he had finally curbed his desire to travel far and wide, as if these were tests he had to pass to be able to love her properly. They had come all this way to the city to study and find their futures, and had instead found each other. Last time she had looked she was a no-nonsense girl from a small country town. Flirting was not something learnt on a farm. There was nothing romantic about life on a farm, or so she thought. So once she had flirted with him, she was not sure what to do next. Luckily Noel didn't seem to know either.

Naomi thought hard about him, trying to recall traces of the Grenfell boy with the sparkling brown eyes and long wavy hair who slowly, methodically, laughingly overcame every obstacle that she placed in his way. Noel left university and climbed Kilimanjaro. Noel sailed down the Amazon. Noel crossed the Sudan. And always Naomi refused to accompany him, too busy with her women's collective to travel anywhere. Nevertheless, Noel persisted. His letters from these far-flung places gradually coaxed their relationship into life. 'You are my Kilimanjaro,' he wrote. 'The Nile is the most romantic river in the world. Where are you?' Naomi bought a map of the world. 'I miss you more than all the gold in the Taj Mahal. Climb the Great Wall of China with me. Please.' Noel enclosed a single star-anise in that letter and Naomi bought a backpack and a one-way ticket to Beijing. Looking back, she now knew their marriage and life together had survived where others had failed largely due to Noel's patience and his small acts of kindness.

Then there was her decision to train as a midwife. She didn't have the stomach for a career in rape crisis counselling or a women's refuge. Midwifery was a positive alternative. It was logical. She applied logic where ideals had failed.

Noel was dead. She wanted to be with him more than anything else. She was furious for being the one still alive. This was how she remembered feeling, finally, at the death of Ben and Jesse. Furious.

'Was he just too old?' Max asked.

'A bad ticker,' Naomi said slowly. Or was it not a bad ticker at all, but a broken heart?

There was a box in the corner of the attic. It was full of Ben and Jesse's papers and photos, things like their birth certificates and the inquest report. Occasionally Max had asked to see inside the box and Noel had taken it down from the attic and told the story of Ben and Jesse and their short lives. Max asked less and less to see inside the box; Chris, never. Of all the things in that box, the photo of their caskets was the hardest. Naomi wondered why she had a photo of their caskets. Who took it? Who gave it to her?

On Sunday morning Naomi woke to find herself still in her clothes from the day before, but in a different life. Widow. She turned over the word to examine it closely as she sat up slowly on Noel's side of the bed. Widow. It belonged to someone else. It came with floral ensembles and matching shoes and handbags. She watched the muslin curtains sigh in and out. Dust particles swirled in the sunlight above her dressing table's abandoned pots of hand cream and hairbrushes. Her positive thoughts of a few weeks ago, where were they now?

So much of her was still missing, had been missing ever since her sons died. There were questions to be answered, secrets to be unravelled and grandchildren to be cared for. And without Noel, it would all be much harder. She beat the pillows with her fists. It had only been recently that she had been able to listen to him again, to stop blaming him, to hope.

Breathing hard, she lay back down, perfectly still, and let his death roll over her.

Widow. Naomi was now officially a widow. She had just turned some kind of damn corner! She ran her fingers absent-mindedly through her hair, which stood on end as if the shock of Noel's death had burst out through the top of her head. Max appeared in the doorway. She held out her arms and he cuddled into her, head burrowed under her collarbone.

Noel's heart had been broken a long time, Naomi thought. The knowledge that it was now too late to mend it was physically painful. Why had she not made more of an effort to reach him, to get in touch with Zoe? Acted sooner. It would have helped them. She was sure.

Suddenly there was a funeral to arrange and Noel's sisters, Evelyn and Gwen, poured the fury of their grief into it. Nothing was left to chance. All contingencies were covered. No detail was too trivial. Naomi stood in her grubby sweat pants and t-shirt, looking out of the kitchen window into the overgrown backyard, without seeing any of it.

The boys kept up a haphazard vigil: Chris silent and still, Max fidgeting and noisy. Relatives arrived from Grenfell; women from the neighbourhood popped in with food; old friends cleaned up the kitchen and let themselves out.

Family was everything to Noel. Not just Naomi and his sons, but *all* their family: sisters, cousins, aunts, uncles, sisters-in-law, second cousins twice removed. Anyone with the surname Adams was all right with him. Noel had loved the connections between people. When he met new people he teased out those they might know in common: 'Would they be the O'Keefes from Victoria? Did they have a daughter, Fiona?'

Evelyn and Gwen lived together in Sydney, nearby, and had made clucky phone calls and emergency lamingtons and meat loaf for Noel most of his married life. Meat loaf, of all things. No one ate meat loaf anymore. Well, Noel's family did. With Worcestershire sauce. Evelyn and Gwen arrived clutching a meat loaf every now and then, worried that Noel wasn't getting enough protein or iron or TLC. Naomi was altogether too vegetarian for them.

He had an eccentric, shambling sense of style. If Naomi had asked him to wear a suit, it might have killed him as surely as the heart attack. He was so very sensitive, Evelyn and Gwen always said.

'The funeral people want Noel's suit and shoes,' Gwen said.

'Why?' Naomi asked.

Gwen and Evelyn were making cups of tea and toast with honey. *Good for shock, dear.* Chris stood beside Naomi, brushing her cowlicks flat against her head with his hand. Max scraped his chair back across the floorboards abruptly and they all looked at him.

Gwen frowned.

'To bury him in, dear,' Evelyn said, thin-lipped.

It took Naomi some minutes to grasp what it was that she must do next.

'Noel's one good suit is in the wardrobe,' Naomi said, finally rising up out of her chair. 'I'll get it.'

In the sunlight they could all see that the suit was covered in Sydney's special brand of mould. A powdery bakers' flour mould, blooming across the shoulders and along both lapels. Almost dust, really. Mould, one of the few things that she disliked about this place. Sydney, the greatest city on earth, Noel liked to say. He would *have* to say that. He had tethered Naomi here. His good shoes were covered in mould too.

'It will have to be dry-cleaned,' Evelyn said, indicating the suit. 'The shoes I can fix up with a bit of polish.'

Naomi would rather lay him to rest in his beloved thongs, shorts and t-shirt. He hadn't worn those very good shoes since Ben and Jesse's funeral anyway. She didn't like the idea of linking the two events through something as mundane as shoes. Could she take on Gwen and Evelyn this morning over dry-cleaning a suit and polishing shoes? What would Noel do? What would he want her to do?

Noel needed sun and heat, and humidity too. A boy from a working sheep and wheat farm, he was drawn to the physical world and the dictates of soil and water. He was tuned to the high frequency of sound and thought. He'd wanted to be cremated – he had told her this early on. Just one of the many things they had talked about, back in the days when their life together was still before them and possible to rejoice in. They discussed where they would live and travel, and how they would work and be in the world. They had never talked about what would happen if Noel died first though.

Don't be foolish, Naomi thought. People can't die of broken hearts. For God's sake, it's medically impossible. She was not just a well-meaning mother of two (deceased), grandmother of two (alive), she was also the nurse in the family, after all. People die because their hearts stop ticking, or their bodies get too old. People don't die from grief. If they did, Naomi thought, she should be dead. Long ago.

She was in shock. That was all. Shock. *Still* in shock. They never spoke about it; not the shock of their sons' deaths, but the actual thing itself. The mangled bodies. Noel had wanted to talk about it. He had started to talk about it many times over the past eight years, but each time Naomi shook her head. She blocked her ears. She got up and left the room. And he did not follow her. The deaths had taken the fight out of him. And this terrible thing came to lie between them in bed, sit at the breakfast table with them, walk to the shop with them;

driving a road through the old-growth forest of their lives.

Naomi had turned fifty a week before their sons' fatal accident. She had received her highly esteemed Midwife Practitioner certificate, finished menopause, and was looking forward to the second half of her life. One week later she stood in a corner of her kitchen, refusing to identify the bodies of her two dead sons. Fresh from a car accident. Cold from the mortuary's fridge. White sheets covering their side-by-side corpses. Were their lovely faces burnt beyond recognition or was every freckle still there to be counted? She would never know. Noel alone knew, because she had abandoned him to it.

So now Naomi reminded herself that she had to share him with his two older sisters, who had loved him all his life.

'Thank you, Gwen,' she said slowly, handing her the dusty suit and shoes. 'Will there be a drycleaners open this morning?'

'If there is, I'll find it, dear,' Gwen said. 'Everything will be perfect for our Noel.'

In a partnership of so many years, abandoning Noel to identify the bodies of their sons and her difficult relationship with Zoe had come to define too much about Naomi, to have too much prominence in her marriage. She had closed her grief over her sons like a book and placed it on the top shelf where no one could find it. Sometimes she would take it down and turn it over, even begin to open it to see inside. But there was, thankfully, always an interruption. The constant care of Chris and Max saw to that. And now, the one other person who had wanted to read that book with her was dead.

Well, Noel had been almost the only person. There was always Zoe. And wasn't it time to give Zoe another chance? Hadn't that been the plan?

Big wide empty

Evelyn and Gwen loved a funeral the way most people like a good cup of Bushell's tea. Naomi almost smiled at the thought. She, on the other hand, couldn't stand them – the smell, the colour, the pace. The sadness.

The bathroom at the back of the house was Naomi's private place. She could cry, laugh, rant and rave in that bathroom and not worry that she would be overheard by an anxious Max or bemused Chris. It was just big enough for her and her pale reflection. Today, her lips were dark, the skin under her eyes creased like a used paper bag and her eyes themselves were the colour of two blood oranges.

Naomi thought about some of the funerals she had attended. Naomi's father had died when she was a teenager. He was a quiet, hard-working man, respected in the community. His was a well-attended funeral. Once he had died, though, it wasn't long before Naomi left for Sydney, leaving her sister and mother behind. She felt guilty about that now.

Her elderly mother's funeral in Grenfell was sad but inevitable. It was a slow service in a small country town where everyone seemed to have all the time in the world. Except for Naomi, who had to get back to the hospital in Sydney, telling herself that it was good to be busy. Nor had Sarah wasted time in resuming her life once their mother was buried. She began by opening her own hairdressing salon. That was the thing about death, it could be the end of something or the beginning. You had to choose.

The more recent funeral of her sons was a blur – try as she might, Naomi couldn't remember it in any real detail. It acted as a punctuation mark in her life. A big fat full stop.

Her thoughts were interrupted by the phone ringing. It was Gwen.

'Flannel flowers?' Gwen said, 'You want flannel flowers?'

'Yes. Any flowers without a scent. I don't want to smell roses and think of Noel's funeral. How it smells is important to me.' Naomi knew this probably sounded strange to Gwen. It sounded strange to her own ears, even fussy. Worrying about the smell of flowers. *At a time like this?* But that was what funerals were like. Full of insane passion for things lost and irrelevant detail. Gwen and Evelyn were used to her doing things a bit differently every now and then. Naomi knew this was one of those times. 'I'd like to have incense in the chapel,' she said.

'Incense?' Gwen said. 'Doesn't that smell?'

'Yes, exactly,' Naomi said.

'Well, where do I get incense?' Gwen said, flustered.

'Never mind. I have it already. Some Nepalese stuff that Noel brought back years ago.'

The crematorium was built on the top of a small rise at the northern end of the city.

Naomi sat quietly at the front of the chapel with Chris and Max, Evelyn and Gwen, and Sarah. She wore black. Behind them, the funeral chapel filled up quickly.

'Some of you here today won't know that Noel lost his two grown-up sons, Ben and Jesse, eight years ago,' the chaplain from Naomi's hospital began. 'Not that he didn't talk about them.'

Naomi inwardly groaned. The chaplain had insisted on *doing* the service and Noel's sisters thought it a good idea. She let the chaplain's words wash over her and thought instead about grass, more specifically lawn; Naomi thought about the way it smelt just after rain, the way it shone in the early morning. She thought about lying down on a vast green lawn and closing her eyes. She was so very tired.

When the chaplain looked towards her, she stood up and turned slowly to face the crowded chapel. A high stained-glass window spilled ruby-red diamonds of light across the parquet floor at her feet. She unfolded a crumpled piece of paper and, turning to Noel's coffin, almost lost her nerve. A nurse doesn't lose her nerve, Naomi thought. She began to tremble, but took a deep breath and plunged flatly into the few words she had scribbled down. 'I want to thank you all for coming today. It means a lot to me and the rest of Noel's family.' Naomi paused, feeling her words taking shape in her mouth like butterflies. There were people here whom she didn't recognise, the funeral was bigger than either Noel or her and it was beyond her control.

'Noel was a good man. Family came first. It was a simple thing for him.' This was true and it was also as far as her notes went. She looked at Chris and Max sitting in the front row. They were both looking blankly at Noel's casket.

'Like a lot of people from farms, from the bush, Noel had that "big wide empty". That's the only way I can describe it. And he carried it everywhere with him. He was a curious person – by that I mean he was curious about the world. He was also *curious* to me, full of contradictions; he travelled a lot but was happiest at home in the hammock on the back verandah. He was a positive person, even when there was no hope. He kept going, until he came to a sudden stop. His death was quiet and quick. I was there with Chris and Max, his grandchildren. It was remarkably sudden.'

Naomi stared up at the ruby-red window, her head tilted to one side. 'How utterly maddening he could be too. How much of our marriage was taken up with fights and bills and "What's for dinner? Oh no, not that again!" ' She half smiled. 'My first reaction to his death was, "How dare you leave me!" We had been through the deaths of our sons, as many of you already know, and after that he said that we had faced the worst thing that could ever happen.' Naomi sighed. 'We had faced it. But now, here today, facing this alone is just as bad.

'The day we were married the celebrant said to us, "Life looks better from inside a double bed," and it was true for us. Not always, but mostly.'

Naomi looked down at the crumpled bit of paper in her hands and began to fold it. 'A life of constant interruptions, of U-turns, of small detail; that was his life, and it was mostly a happy life. He brought out the best in people, which I now realise was his gift.' Naomi took one last look around the crowded chapel. 'The sun is shining outside, but not in here,' Naomi touched her chest, her voice dropped, and she sat back down in her chair, her hands hanging limply by her side.

The children's ensemble, conducted by Chris and Max's piano teacher, Kerry, took this as its cue to begin 'Amazing Grace'. It was the one solemn song in its repertoire. Max started a short, tremulous solo on trumpet, the instrument he played in the school band. Noel would have been very touched, Naomi thought. Thinking this way about him, with a fondness, with gentleness, with patience made it worse. Naomi thought instead about how Max wasn't a keen musician at the best of times. Had Gwen chosen the right music? What song summed up Noel? Like loads of other ageing baby boomers, would it have been 'A Whiter Shade of Pale'? Naomi tried to find the melody for a moment. Music had, after all, meant a lot to Noel. No, more specifically, sound. The sound of things. His rambling collection of sounds would have to be sorted one day: the clack of a bamboo forest in Borneo, the delighted squeals of children playing hide and seek, the hum of bees. All living things, each small and inconsequential to anyone other than Noel. To him, they held magic. Noel the hoarder, Noel the collector. She should have mentioned that too.

After his casket disappeared behind the drab grey curtain, Naomi found herself outside once again in the sun. Despite the number of people wanting to say something special in her ear, to hold her hand, to hug her, Naomi made her way purposefully through the crowd to Chris and Max. She took a deep breath and ploughed on, as she had throughout the morning. 'Have you said hello to your mother?' she said to Chris, indicating the beautiful tall woman standing next to him. She had sensed Zoe's presence long before realising who the woman in cornflower blue was.

'I know who she is,' Chris said quietly, looking straight ahead, avoiding both his mother's and Naomi's eyes.

Max stood a little way away, scowling.

The two women looked at one another. Naomi was shorter than Zoe, as dark as Zoe was blonde, brown eyes where Zoe's were blue.

They did not kiss or hold out a hand to each other. Naomi was the first to speak. Think positive thoughts. Think positive thoughts. Think positively . . .

'Thanks for coming. Noel would have appreciated it.'

As she spoke, she half-turned to the empty hearse and the white flannel flowers that had covered Noel's casket and stood there awkwardly. This is what Naomi dreaded most now that Noel was dead. Facing situations like this – Zoe, alone. It was one thing to be positive in the bathroom mirror at home, it was another to be facing Zoe in the bright daylight of Noel's funeral.

'I've really missed him,' said Zoe, tears beginning to pour down her cheeks. 'He was such a good man.'

Naomi nodded, numbly. She was not prepared for any of this.

'Noel kept in touch with me. Sent me money, photos of the boys.'

Naomi was not surprised. She had argued with him so often over Zoe.

'Why don't you come back to the house?' Chris asked in his formal ten-year-old's voice, the one he kept for debating and answering substitute teachers at school. He gave Naomi a quick sideways glance. She stiffened inwardly. Zoe, in her cornflower-blue suit, simply said, 'Yes, I'd like that.'

The wake

'There, there,' Kerry said, trying to comfort Naomi. 'It was a beautiful service. You said such beautiful words.'

'Why doesn't Zoe leave us alone?' Naomi said. It had been a long morning and now, in the safety of Kerry's car, Naomi deflated inside her black suit. Kerry's vehicle moved slowly away from the crowd. The boys were following behind in the funeral limousine with Noel's sisters. Kerry looked back at the solitary figure of Zoe in the rear-vision mirror. 'I thought you said she'd abandoned the boys?'

Naomi shrugged.

Kerry's fingers played a quick, nervous arpeggio on the steering wheel.

'What if she wants to take them?' Naomi said.

'Is that possible?'

'After the car accident, Zoe sort of disappeared. She never even said, "Look after them." She just didn't come and get them. She's like that, erratic.'

'It's pretty unforgivable!' Kerry said. 'I'm sorry, but where kids are concerned . . .'

The mangled shell of the car. Chris a toddler and Max just a baby at the funeral. Trying to take the place of their father. The formal inquest. The negligent driving charge against Zoe. Naomi flicked through the past as fast as possible.

She looked down at her worn wedding ring. The engraved chain of hearts was long gone and the ring now bit into her swollen finger. She should have had it cut off years ago. 'It's the humidity in Sydney,' she usually said. 'Makes my fingers swell. It's fine the minute we cross the Blue Mountains.' There in Kerry's car, Naomi felt her finger throbbing.

'At least we got an occasional phone call,' Naomi said. 'Other grandparents have to fish their grandchildren out of the welfare system, or the police get involved. At least we never had to go through the courts.'

'She never wanted them?' Kerry was incredulous.

'Not that I know of,' Naomi said. 'She had a bit of post-natal depression after Max.'

Naomi had been over and over this story. With friends, relatives, neighbours, teachers, even a shorter version with Kerry when she first enrolled Chris and Max in her piano lessons. People liked to hear the story. She could tell it every day if she wanted to. But Naomi didn't want to. It was bad for the boys and Noel. Noel told a different version of it. Not all that different, but more sympathetic to Zoe. His was a more thoughtful version. One in which he took the time to run his fingers through his beard while he spoke, especially through the thick curly hair under his chin. When Ben and Jesse were killed, Noel's hair turned grey overnight. Actually, Noel turned grey all over. Sudden death will do that to you. Naomi had heard about it as a nurse, but she'd never actually seen it until then.

'Zoe was full of contradictions; impulsive but lacking con-fidence; watchful without being observant,' Naomi said. 'You

51

hope that your kids pick the right person, you know? She was different from the start, but you hope. Not that I am the type to want a lawyer or a doctor in the family. I wasn't that kind of mother to them, my boys. But Ben, he was so young. What did he know about relationships?'

There was always some excuse to tell the story. People were a morbid, miserable lot. She told it these days on a strictly need-to-know basis. This was one of those times. Kerry needed to hear it and Naomi needed to tell it, to get it straight in her mind again. Without Noel, she was beginning to doubt her version of events.

'She said she couldn't face being with the children, or some such. To Noel. Never to me. NEVER TO ME. She knew better. I said to her, "Why don't you leave the boys with us, while you sort yourself out?"' I was happy to have them, you know. They were a comfort to me, something of Ben and Jesse's to hang on to. At first she called all the time, then about once a month, then whenever she moved, then from time to time, randomly – missing birthdays, Christmas, holidays. I soon lost track of her, but Noel didn't.'

Naomi thought about his secretiveness. Secrets in a marriage were never a dead end, they always led somewhere. And they had a way of not staying secret for long enough. Zoe was a good example. Secrets lifted the edge of double-bed sheets and ate away at the precious, delicious centre. For a long time Naomi's marriage had been straightforward and clean-cut. No labyrinths, no hidden snakes and ladders. She was too much of a country girl to have it otherwise. Noel was hers, all hers – he belonged to her, his first loyalty was to her. Whenever there was a dispute with Ben and Jesse, Noel and Naomi were united; there was no getting between them. But all that changed after the accident.

'Despite everything, she has a right to a relationship with

the boys,' Naomi said. She would be positive about this. After all, wasn't this what she had wanted? To find Zoe?

Kerry looked in the rear-vision mirror and turned the wheel carefully. Her Mercedes slipped smoothly away from the cemetery and down towards the coast. 'I wonder about that,' Kerry said. They were now skirting the city. The high-rise buildings stood packed together like a bunch of teenagers at a bus stop and the rest of Sydney crept away over the scrubby sandstone towards the Pacific Ocean.

'I need the love of those boys in my life too,' Naomi said, and she began to cry softly.

'You mustn't give up,' Kerry said in her piano-teacher voice, a voice that was used to demolishing students' objections to practice.

'Give up? I don't know the meaning of the word. Noel had to die to get away from me!' Naomi said, blowing her nose and sighing. It was the first time she had thought about it that way, and then she thought about all the sad jokes she could make to put people at ease at the wake. Because that would be the purpose of the wake; to tell stories and ease the pain. Perhaps to put people right on a few things too. Naomi would have to work hard to have a sense of humour. It was a bit hit and miss – sometimes her humour was too dark, too bleak and altogether too bitter.

'The boys have a right to a relationship with both of you,' Kerry said quietly after a pause.

'She abandoned them!' Naomi shouted.

The traffic was more congested closer to the city and Kerry had to manoeuvre them carefully around roadworks at Rozelle.

'I'm sure she doesn't see it that way, and if she does, she won't feel good about it,' Kerry said, breaking the silence that had fallen between them.

'Good about it? I bet she won't even admit it. How can I let her back into their lives?'

'Isn't it a bit early to worry about this?' Kerry said, turning the corner into Naomi's street.

'I don't think I have a choice.'

Kerry pulled into Naomi's driveway and Naomi sat up straight, smiling fleeting hellos to people milling about on the front porch, mainly the smokers.

'She destroyed my family,' Naomi said quietly. *Her family.* Naomi knew that it was impossible for one person to destroy a family and that she was being 'over the top' about it, as Max would say, using words such as 'destroy' and 'abandon'. 'Uncool,' Chris would say. And Noel? What he would say right now didn't bear thinking about.

Kerry sat silently.

'I thought I knew her, but you never truly know someone. I mean, what they are capable of,' Naomi added.

She let her words wash over them. She had seen women mad with pain, joy, happiness, grief. She had seen it all and she had felt those emotions as well. She sat staring straight ahead.

Finally Kerry said, 'I'm sure you don't need any more advice, and you've probably been thinking about what you'd do in this situation for years, preparing for this moment. I apologise if this seems . . .'

'What?' Naomi said, cutting her off. She had no plan. She did not know what to do next. She had almost convinced herself that the boys did not have another, *real* mother. Zoe was not real, at least not the Zoe that Naomi thought about. Seeing Zoe in the flesh, though, had been different than she expected. She was not prepared for her solid lines, the clear blue of her light eyes, the thickness of her fair hair and the indisputable presence of all these things in Chris and Max.

'I think you should take the initiative.'

Naomi took a deep breath. 'I'm so angry with Noel. If he hadn't died, this would never have happened.'

'Oh yes, it would. Better to bring it out in the open. Bring it to a head now. It may not be as bad as you think.'

Despite her attempt at optimism, Naomi suspected that Kerry was wrong. The limousine pulled up behind them and quickly she got out of Kerry's car to usher the boys inside the house, as if that would keep them safe from Zoe.

Inside there was a lot to do. Gwen and Evelyn produced aprons from their handbags and went to work. Gwen made punch. Evelyn cut up fruitcake. Naomi drank tea, but around her the alcohol flowed. Sarah stood washing up at the sink in her jeans and riding boots. 'The smell of the scones makes me homesick,' Naomi said, politely refusing one proffered by her elderly neighbour, Signora Toto. This strange place, Sydney, where elderly Italians made heavenly scones that rose gloriously. In the back room a friend of Noel's had the slide-show underway. Naomi moved through her own house like a stranger, as if seeing it for the first time: the chipped and yellowed paint, the cheap, clapped-out furniture, the dust on the lampshade. She should have known this was going to happen one day and cleaned up a bit. She would be able to clean up now, she promised herself, as if there were comfort in the prospect.

The boys played fitfully outside. Dressed in their best clothes, they moved stiffly. Chris was teasing Max, holding the soccer ball just out of his reach. Max pushed Chris and Chris elbowed him back. 'Ya sook!' he spat the words at Max, a new meanness in him. Naomi turned her back. The bluntness of children on such a day was almost unbearable.

The slideshow in the back room had people gasping and gawping. There were slides of Noel as a boy, graduating from electrical engineering, at work, at their wedding, with their two sons as toddlers. Naomi smiled and cried at the same time.

'Wonderful life together,' a woman said, indicating them posing for a shot on the Great Wall, another in Red Square.

'It wasn't easy,' someone interjected.

Naomi paused before speaking, and then admitted, 'No, it was never easy, but that wasn't the point.'

'Noel was often out of work,' another said.

Naomi stood up straight. She felt very alone.

'Here's to Noel, my lover,' Naomi said, sensing Gwen in her twin-set and pearls wince at the word 'lover'. Nevertheless, she continued, 'My constant and true friend.'

Glasses and china rattled and tinkled in people's hands.

'It took Noel a while to find his life's work, but eventually he did. He loved the challenge of setting up his own sound studio. Things went well in the early days. But then, about ten years ago, Noel's studio went . . . Well, basically broke, with the advent of digital technology,' Naomi said. 'As many of you already know, we nearly lost our house, everything.' Naomi stopped.

There was an awkward silence.

'Then we did lose everything. We lost our sons.' Naomi said. 'About that time, though, Chris and Max came to live with us, and we somehow started again.'

A few of the neighbours clapped.

'Noel was out of work for a while, which was great for Chris and Max . . .' Naomi nodded at them. 'And then he got his job at the radio station, and after that he set up his own business as a television repairer, which he loved. He loved to fix broken things. He saw value in things that other people discarded. All he ever wanted to do was to make things right. And that was how we got on with our lives.'

The people listening began to relax and move, thinking that Naomi had finished, but she had not.

'I took Noel for granted, thought he'd always be there,' Naomi said, pausing before continuing. 'I first met him about fifty years ago. Some of you here today had the privilege of knowing him for a long time too. His sisters, who basically raised him . . .' Naomi looked at them and smiled. 'Thank you.' Naomi scanned the crowd. 'Our school friends too.' A few grey heads in the crowd nodded. 'You take someone for granted. You waste time being petty, being selfish, being short with them.'

Mary's husband said, 'Hear, hear,' as if Naomi was proposing a wedding toast.

'I've been thinking a lot over the past few days, trying to find a way through everything . . .' she trailed off. 'This could be a time for new beginnings,' she said abruptly, looking at Zoe.

An hour later, the hospital chaplain bailed up Naomi against the back door. 'See this as a gift, a way to learn,' he said.

Naomi nodded politely. She had been about to thank him for coming, but his patronising tone and words made her want to kick him in the shins.

'Never waste a moment. You must treasure every moment because one day it will be gone,' he continued.

What he had to say was perfectly reasonable; nevertheless it made Naomi seethe with sudden anger. She did not want his advice. She wanted to scream at him, *Have you any idea what you are talking about?*

His pager beeped. 'Excuse me,' he said, leaving her open-mouthed. Naomi looked around. She was alone, except for Zoe. Over the past eight years Zoe had grown from a skinny girl into a tall willow of a woman. Her blue eyes seemed sharper, lighter than Naomi remembered. Her face was still the beautiful oval that it had been eight years ago, but now there were shadows under her eyes.

Naomi managed a smile and began to choose her words. She had a broad mouth made for talking, straight teeth for straight words, but before she could start, Zoe interrupted her.

'I want the boys,' she said as she flattened her back against the wall. She had eaten nothing, drunk nothing, preferring to stand quietly in the hallway, alone for most of the wake.

'I've never stopped you seeing them,' Naomi said, looking over her shoulder at Max in the garden. The afternoon light caught all the gold highlights in his dark hair. His straight-as-a-die hair. His beautiful, thick, blunt hair.

'I know, but now I'm ready to take them, thank you.'

Naomi's good upbringing formed questions on her lips, rather than accusations. It would seem like bad manners to fight at Noel's wake. They were family, after all. *Zoe* was family. So she asked Zoe the simplest of questions. 'But how will you care for them?'

'I'll manage.'

Another dead end.

Zoe, the destroyer. Some things never change. *I'll have the children now*, as if she were asking for a drink. Just like that. When would she take them? Where would she take them? Had Zoe actually thought about any of this? Probably not. Did Naomi have a right to know? A DAMN right, she decided.

'I understand, Zoe, I really do,' Naomi said. She had, after all, been trying to be more understanding. 'But before you do anything drastic, remember that they're settled here.' Naomi stopped herself from adding 'with me' for fear of making things worse.

Chris hovered nearby, keeping an eye on them both. Max chose to ignore Zoe, his back turned to play a wild game of tennis on a stick with his friend, Harry.

'They love their school and friends,' Naomi continued. 'They're happy.'

Zoe remained silent.

'You can visit whenever you like,' Naomi said, trying not to sound desperate.

There was a longer silence and Naomi thought she could hear a small baby crying somewhere just behind the talk and music.

'Thank you for all you have done, but it's time. It's the way it should be. I want the boys,' Zoe spoke firmly and clearly.

Naomi knew that it had taken guts for Zoe to confront her, an older woman, her mother-in-law. They hadn't spoken much even when they lived in the same house together; they hadn't needed to. Zoe had been respectful, trusting, loyal. Never a burden. Although she found her inscrutable, Naomi liked having her around, at first. She confided to Noel at the time that she liked Zoe, but she wished that Zoe and Ben had met later. Nonetheless, she was determined to let them find their own way forward. They needed to live a bit. They were too young to settle down. Noel, unhelpfully, had reminded her about her own youth, about when they fell in love. Things were different then, she said. Ben was different. He was not patient and forgiving Noel.

Zoe had always been one of those watchful people that Naomi had to pry things out of. Not today though.

'What is this about?' Naomi said.

Zoe shrugged.

You'll have to do better than that, Naomi thought.

'Are you trying to prove yourself as a mother, or something?' Naomi pressed her, a little more rudely than she meant to.

Zoe appeared to have already lost interest in Naomi. She looked away, her eyes flicking in a hollow, disengaged way over the women chatting in the kitchen.

She should try to give Zoe a second chance. Wasn't it good that she was showing some interest in the children? Didn't she deserve to be taken seriously? Hadn't Naomi just begun thinking that anything was possible? Noel would have wanted it. But to lose the boys . . .

Zoe turned back to Naomi, and looked at her blankly. 'What?'

'You can't have them,' Naomi said quietly.

Blisters

Zoe walked slowly down Naomi's old wooden front steps, her shoes clattering unevenly, and turned left. She had dressed carefully for Noel's funeral. No nose stud. Only one set of earrings in each ear. Eyebrow piercing removed. The cornflower-blue suit instead of her normal black, although on this occasion that would have fitted right in. It didn't particularly matter to her that the suit was second hand from the Mt Druitt St Vincent de Paul. Meg had taken her shopping and chosen it. Blue for the sky, blue for her eyes. Careful. She had been careful for Noel's sake to pay her respects. And she was careful because she wanted to show Naomi that she had changed. That she was ready.

'What I meant to say was, if it wasn't for *you* and Noel,' she said quietly to herself. 'Well, you know. Thanks for everything. I really wish Noel was still here. I've changed, for real this time. I know this is not about me, at a time like this and all, but I wanted you to know, Naomi, because I think Noel *did* see that. Shit,' Zoe said, wiping her nose with the back of her hand, trying hard not to start crying again.

It had come out wrong.

'Noel was such a good father!' she said into the silence that was his death. 'Practically the best.'

And he had been, in Zoe's opinion. He had also been her connection to Ben and Jesse. She didn't see much of them in Naomi, but they had been there in Noel, in spades, if you asked her. But no one did anymore, except for Meg.

'Thanks for everything, Noel, and I mean everything. All the hugs and the emergency money – I know you couldn't spare it – and the funny cards. I love The Far Side now too. But, anyway, the worst thing about you being dead is that I can't tell you how great the boys are. I know you know and everything. But they are big now and I got to see that, because I lost most of the photos you sent, so I can stop wondering about what they look like and how tall they are, all the time, you know, and I got to ask Naomi for them back. My boys. Wow. I surprise myself sometimes. It wasn't that hard and I didn't really mean to, it just popped out.'

Zoe stopped abruptly and turned around, absent-mindedly pressing the side seams of her skirt against her legs with her long fingers.

'Max is the spitting image of Ben,' she said, looking back at the house. How had that little ball of screaming blue murder already turned into his father? 'And Chris, his face has got so long, like Jesse's.' Zoe sighed. 'When I saw them, I had to stop myself from shaking. Max, then Chris. I wanted to hug them, but I didn't. I thought I might scare them. I remember those old relatives from England turning up when I was a kid and how they wanted to touch me. It was revolting. Children need their space, just as much as adults. Meg was right about that.'

Two boys who looked about Max's age drove past on their bikes. 'C'mon!' one said to the other.

'Max,' Zoe said softly, and started to cry. 'He was acting so tough, just like me. Just like me. You knew that, Noel, didn't you? It's all just front, as my old da used to say.'

Zoe stopped and took out her Ventolin. She inhaled two puffs before beginning to walk again. 'Actually, I'm pretty hopeless. Sorry, guys. Naomi is probably right, you are better off without me. But Meg said I should at least, you know, try with you. That you'd appreciate it, or something like that. So what d'ya say?'

Zoe started to walk more quickly, a nerve above her eye beginning to tick. In the good old days she would have got wasted to deal with this. But she was not doing that anymore. She was responsible, right? She had learnt the meaning of that word with Meg. Naomi had tried to show her what it meant too, but back then she couldn't even begin to grasp it.

Zoe had a limited emotional vocabulary, Meg said. She had explained to many counsellors, including Meg, that she was the offspring of two well-meaning but essentially limited ten-pound Poms, a couple of Geordies called Sandra and Dennis. Her pale, short mother was determined to 'fit in', and if that meant keeping her Geordie mouth shut and getting used to flies up her nose and in the corner of her eyes, then so be it. Zoe remembered how Sandra bought a pair of thongs and paisley hot pants at the newly opened Penrith Plaza to 'fit in'. Kingswood grew up around them. But Zoe did not belong to the fibro-clad suburbs in the west of Sydney, though she had been adrift on the tide of their vast plains for most of her life. The only time she had fitted in anywhere was with Naomi's family.

Zoe tried to remember what she had worn to Ben and Jesse's funeral, but she could not. She was never one for clothes – colours, yes, but clothes, well, she wasn't interested. Her mother had said so, all those years ago, and it was still true. Tall and thin, she could have been a model if things had been different, if *she* had been different.

I am very different to Naomi, she told herself. Naomi, with her nut-brown eyes and her short hair and thick hands. Naomi, who throughout her life had been mistaken for a boy. Naomi with her wide mouth and pointy chin. Zoe had tried to sketch Naomi, but somehow her back was always turned. It had almost been too much, standing there in the house at the wake. She could still feel Ben's presence there. In the scribble on the doorframe: 'Ben, 180 cms'. Ben. Meeting him had changed everything. She thought of him as big and beautiful and incandescent and brilliant. Jesse was different. Darker and moody and hard to read. Falling in love had felt so right. Then why did this house feel like a crime scene?

Zoe had not meant to say she wanted the boys in quite that way. Just singing it out like that. She was so overcome at seeing them, especially Max, and feeling that she had already lost so much time with them. She felt like a mum. Where did that come from? She said out loud, 'I want the boys.' She shook her head as if to see whether the thought could be dislodged.

It was time to make things right with Chris and Max, and taking responsibility seemed the place to start. She'd managed to stop drinking and swearing. She was calmer. Not so angry, not in as much pain. She'd done the meditation course that Meg prescribed. Yoga next. Employment? Well, not just yet. But soon. Anything was possible, well, almost anything. Nothing would bring back Noel.

She walked, briskly at first, north along Johnston Street. Max is angry with me, she thought. His small eight-year-old eyes had been hot and red. Zoe reached the harbour's edge at Blackwattle Bay and stopped abruptly. Under the trees on this cloudless day small schoolchildren in gold school shirts were running about. They moved in groups of two and three. One ran up the grassy mound and the others surged behind. They flowed back and forth, like phosphorescence on the edge of a wave. The teachers called them together and set them off in small packs to run across the park. They were weaving through the giant fig trees, around the oval and back across to the water's edge, their shirts dotted throughout the park.

'Enough time has passed,' she said aloud to the seagulls circling overhead. The sky was a true, clear azure, and she found it inexplicably reassuring. She continued to watch the schoolchildren. A group of boys ran past her. The leaders jogged neatly, the pack in the middle moved more loosely and those at the back walked, stubbornly.

She often watched children like this, from a distance. She liked this park on the western edge of the harbour, with its ship-salvage yard and cranes swinging. She liked to look at the harbour from here, through the debris and chaos of a working foreshore. She looked at the world this way, *aslant*. Her sculptor teacher had said so. She found industrial landscapes beautiful. She loved scrap metal. She had made an elegant sculpture in the salvage yard here once, long ago.

The other things Zoe liked about being here were the small hills that ran down to the harbour and the glimpse of a church spire through the rooftops, or a lone Norfolk Island pine. She had tried to paint this, paint its layers. It was all so very different from the flat, sparse western suburbs.

Zoe turned and headed back up Johnston Street until she reached Parramatta Road about twenty minutes later. The sound of the traffic was deafening, almost loud enough to silence the voices in her head. 'You can't go back. You can never make it right. Don't complicate your life with the children. Not now. Not yet. Just one step at a time. Naomi will never forgive you.' Despite the garish car yards and the hot afternoon sun on her face, she ploughed on. Westward.

By nightfall she reached 'home' – a back bedroom in the Mt Druitt supported-accommodation service. Funny, Mt Druitt always felt like a depression in the land, not a mountain. Tonight, though, she felt different, more optimistic. She had taken a step, she had found a way forward.

Zoe opened her backpack and took out Noel's funeral booklet before sinking into an armchair, a camel-coloured piece with slender teak legs that she had picked up off the street. Her feet were a bloody mess of blisters. She hobbled to the window and opened it. On the cool evening air she could hear television shows and people arguing and babies crying. Zoe could hear everything there was to hear, she could understand everything there was to understand. Her life had suddenly smoothed out, made sense. She closed the window.

Fragile

When most of the people had left, Chris pushed past his grandmother and three aunts drinking wine or something out of teacups. It definitely wasn't tea. He didn't say excuse me and Gran didn't insist. That's how he knew they weren't drinking tea. He shut his bedroom door carefully behind him and pulled the shoebox out from under his bed.

He opened the lid and took out the paper inside. 'A sculptor of powerful and brilliant talent,' the headline said. Zoe's massive metal sculptures were described as 'organic', whatever that meant. He wasn't so interested in her art – although he liked art – he was more interested in her, his mother, just looking at her. It was hard at the funeral, there were so many people, so many interruptions. He had thought she might be there, and she was. Grandpa would have liked that. He was always saying that he wanted them all to be a family again, but only when Naomi was ready. He said lots of nice things about Zoe, like what a great artist she was, what a great person before the accident, and how after the accident things were different. At first she couldn't walk properly, then she was sick. When she was better, she was going to come round. He was always saying that she would 'come round'. For about five years Chris had thought she probably lived in the next street from the way Noel spoke, so he took to riding his bike slowly around the neighbourhood. But when he pressed Noel about it, he said he wasn't sure where she lived these days. Noel sent her things care of her relatives at a place called Kingswood. Grandpa was good at keeping in touch. So was Chris.

In the newspaper article Zoe's face was nice, a half-smile on her thin lips. She looked directly at him. Her light hair was pulled back off her face, but loose around her shoulders. Dressed in black, she had folded her arms for the picture. There was a watch on her arm, which Chris thought strange. Gran always said that Zoe was late for everything. How many times did Grandpa dress him, ready for the promised visit from Mum, and then she didn't arrive? Six times? Maybe more. Chris remembered Grandpa on the phone with her not that long ago. Grandpa knew where to find her, at least that's what Chris thought, hoped. 'Where are you? Did you forget? You promised them, remember? Can I come and get you? How much money do you need?' Sometimes Grandpa asked Aunty Gwen to help her too. 'Can you take this to her, if you're going past?'

The caption on the newspaper photo said, 'Zalum and son, Chris, aged 2.' They'd been doing captions at school. Chris wrote one the other day for Cameron's cartoon about school. He had the school sliding down the hill towards the park. Chris wrote, 'Oops, there goes the neighbourhood.'

In his mother's photo Chris stood beside Zoe holding onto her leg. He looked up at her, not at the camera. They had the same eyebrows, the same light hair and light blue eyes. She was tall, he knew that now. It was hard to tell from photos. He liked the fact she was tall – all the tall kids at school got to be in the back row of the school photo. They stood up straight and had the most distance to fall if they stepped backwards. And he was one of them.

'Zoe Zalum's works are born in fire, literally. Her welding technique is dazzling, showing great control and attention to detail,' the paper said. 'She has a brilliant career ahead of her as a sculptor. Watch this space!'

But Chris was more interested in this bit: 'I want to dedicate this exhibition to Naomi Adams. She believed in me.'

Chris wondered what exactly his grandmother had believed in. He understood the idea of believing in things that you couldn't see, like Santa Claus or God. But what did it mean to believe in a living, breathing person? And did Gran believe in Zoe now? What made a person stop or start believing in someone? Why had his mother singled out Naomi, and not his grandfather or his uncle Jesse, and especially why not his father?

When the newspaper asked Zoe about her own mother and father, she said, 'I divorced my family long ago.' The newspaper said she wouldn't say anything else about it. How cool is that? Someone asks you a question and you don't have to answer it.

Chris had been wondering about how she divorced her family; it worried him. She might have divorced him too, without telling him. But after today at the funeral, he knew better. It was unreal to stand next to her at last. She smelt nice. Not in an eau de Cologne way like Aunty Gwen and Aunty Evelyn, but more like the outdoors. Fresh. Was that possible? See, that was the kind of question he would normally ask Grandpa, and now what? Who could he ask? He didn't want to think about Noel being dead right now. He didn't want to cry anymore. His eyes hurt.

Max didn't think much of Zoe. Chris knew because he didn't say anything to her at all, and usually you couldn't shut him up. What a pity. She seemed really nice. Perfect even.

Once, Mum and Gran had been close. Chris liked that, because it meant that once she probably liked him too. But now it was all but impossible to talk to Gran about her. She didn't think Zoe was a good mum. Not that Gran said anything exactly, but Chris could tell. It was something to do with the car accident: it had changed everything. Hello, of course. Earlier that day, outside the funeral chapel, when he was standing with his mother and Max, he imagined for a moment what it would have been like if his dad was standing there with them too. He would have felt strong, for sure. At times like that he really missed having a father. Grandpa had been the best, but it wasn't the same as having 'Benny', as Grandpa called him, around in person. Chris hated the way all that stuff made him feel. His throat hurt. He was all for the future.

'Fragile but forceful, Zalum's exhibition is full of works that are not what they seem at first,' the review said. Chris agreed. The article included pictures of several of her works. They were massive, random, cool, whatever. Chris didn't have the right words to describe sculpture.

He knew it wouldn't be long before he could walk around Sydney and see her work. She must be famous by now. There would be pieces of her sculpture in public places, like the Domain. Last term they went to the Opera House on a school excursion and he saw a sign pointing to the Domain. Chris was sure she was close by.

He folded the newspaper carefully and replaced it in his box next to his picture of Dad. He felt so heavy whenever he thought about Dad, because then he thought about all the other dead people in his family. Cameron went on and on about his father being so old. He must be over forty or some-thing. Well, Grandpa was really old. So what? It's better than being dead, Chris had said to Cameron. Gran didn't mind talking about the *old* dead people – she could tell him who his great-great-grandfather married, that sort of thing. It was all written down somewhere in a church in Grenfell. Chris could find the names of all his cousins and second cousins and their dates of birth if he wanted to. But he knew there was another, new story, which Gran wouldn't tell him about; one that he would like to tell one day when he collected all the pieces, because he was the beginning of it.

Attachment

How far would you go to protect your grandchildren from their mother? Live with her, or kick her out? Naomi knew this sounded a bit extreme to any normal grandparent, if there was any such thing. Most mothers-in-law didn't ever contemplate such ideas. Court action? Would you take the law into your own hands and kidnap your grandchildren? Move interstate or overseas? Can anyone say you have no right to do these things if those children are at risk?

There was a time when Naomi had asked Zoe to move in with her and Noel and the boys. They tried a few times, but in the end, Zoe burnt too many bridges – coming and going, stealing what she needed, leaving a trail of broken hearts, especially two small ones, and maybe Noel's too. They didn't speak about it after Naomi had changed the locks and thrown out Zoe's belongings onto the footpath. Naomi had been the one to show Zoe the door, not Noel. She realised that she was too shattered after the accident to be able to help Zoe too. Would things be any different now?

After Zoe left the funeral, Naomi was scared to even talk about what she'd said, because in doing so she would make it real. But Sarah had watched them and overheard some of it.

There was no pretending that it hadn't happened. That night Sarah, Gwen and Evelyn, as well as Patricia, an old friend and midwifery colleague, sat at the kitchen table and went over it from every angle.

'No right!'

'No way!'

'Someone put her up to it,' Sarah said.

'She looked a lot better, I thought. More together,' Naomi said.

'She ignored me,' Evelyn said.

'Who does she bloody well think she is?' Patricia said.

'The boys' mother, that's who,' Naomi said, ending the discussion and gathering up the used cups.

Naomi had read stories in the newspaper about fathers kidnapping their children. She thought they were just crazy types. What about those fathers who bombed the Family Court? She used to think she would never allow that to happen to her family. But it had. Not in a way that she expected. But now she had to answer that question – how far would you go?

'It's all my fault,' Gwen finally blurted out. She had been sitting quietly until that point. 'I'm so sorry. I rang her and told her that Noel had died.'

'Gwen! How could you!' Evelyn said.

'I don't know,' Gwen said, twisting a table napkin between her fingers. 'Noel asked me to, you know, help her.'

'Never mind. It's not Gwen's fault,' Naomi said.

Naomi knew that Noel's funeral had been a catalyst, an opportunity to change the way things were between Zoe and herself. After all, wasn't that what she had wanted? Change? Resolution? A way forward? Instead, she found herself resolving to do her best to keep things as they were.

She picked up the empty teacups and stood up. She was still dressed in her black suit. She walked barefoot around the table to the sink and placed the cups there. The rest of the women stood up stiffly too, finally ready to leave.

Outside, the stars were shining. Noel and Jesse used to look at the stars through a telescope. It was somewhere in the attic. She should get it out for Chris and Max, they were about the right age now. Naomi found herself suddenly crying. She rested her head against the smooth wooden beam in the centre of the verandah. Countless attachments had been formed there: hammocks, basketball hoops, pot-plant holders, all holding out hope of something to come – sleep, leisure and beauty. Why did she say no to Zoe in that way? Naomi had answered her intuitively, but what if her intuition was wrong? Sarah followed her sister out onto the verandah.

'Hard to see them clearly here in the city,' she said, pointing up at the stars. 'You all live on top of each other, yet everything seems further away.'

Candle wax

Max had a secret, his first real secret. He wanted to tell Gran but he hesitated; he thought she might laugh.

Max's secret was that he believed in God. He wanted to go to church. He wanted to become something. Catholic would do, just like his friend Harry.

Harry made his first holy communion and Max had been invited to attend. The first time he pushed through the old wooden doors of the Catholic church on Johnston Street and watched Harry bless himself with holy water, he was hooked. The towering statues, the feeble light, the dull traffic sounds through the thick, solid walls – Max wanted it all.

Gran, though, was strictly not religious. She might laugh at him. Probably, definitely, most likely.

Even the chubby old nun who played the organ was comforting to Max. She reminded him of the old woman who lived in the shoe. But more importantly, she was always there. She did not have another job, another child. The church was her life. And it was a solid thing made of bricks. That he liked.

At school Max started to go to Catholic scripture instead of non-scripture in the library. He did not tell Gran. More often than not the scripture teacher failed to turn up, but just belonging to the class felt good. Max felt he was doing something grand.

When they did go to the church they were quick to light candles (ten cents each) and 'offer up' prayers, which to Max were more like wishes on his birthday candles – 'Make Mum safe' or 'I want a new BMX bike.'

'Harry had to wear a tie,' Max told Gran after Harry's holy communion. 'They had fairy bread afterwards and everything. It was mad!'

Gran just shook her head and smiled. Grandpa would have taken a keener interest. In fact, Grandpa's funeral could have been improved on a lot. It wouldn't be hard, since it was practically the worst day of his life. No, the day Grandpa died was worse. But if you believed in God then Grandpa might come back, like Jesus. Make a return visit. At any time, apparently.

Aunty Gwen and Aunty Evelyn weren't Catholics. They were something else that began with a P or an E. They were *something* and that was all that mattered, as opposed to not being something. And, who knows, their something might just be as good as Catholic. He would ask them to take him along next time so he could compare church with church.

Right now Max was happy to go along to the Catholic church with Harry whenever he went, which was not too often – Harry did not think much of the whole thing. That was the problem with the world, the wrong people had the right things.

There were loads of Catholics at school. Why? Max asked the scripture teacher, who said too easily, 'There are more Catholics than any other religion in the world.' Max didn't think that could be right, but he had no way of proving it.

Harry was so lucky. He had a mum and a dad, for starters. He had brothers and sisters. He knew what high school he was going to. He knew what hockey team he would play for. He had a religion that was there for him whenever he needed it, and Max knew all about times of need, like when Grandpa died. Chris had his music. Gran had her job at the hospital. But Max? What did he have, other than hockey and swimming? Max needed something more, and this Catholic stuff might just be it.

The other thing he liked about religion was that it had lots of answers. Answers to the difficult things in life. The big questions. Answers to the questions that Gran thought were funny or 'too hard to answer simply'. Well, the church people liked to answer those questions. They could also tell Max what he should do, and that was handy. There was right and wrong, there was heaven and hell. The hardest question for Max was, 'Why doesn't my mummy love me?' Max thought he could ask the nun at the church and get a straight-as-an-arrow answer. Definitive. Ever since he had decided to ask her, Harry had not been to mass, but Max knew where the church was and he would go there himself sometime, when the time was right.

Max was sure Grandpa was with God, but did that mean that his mother would go to hell? If she didn't love him, would God punish her for being a bad mother? Or was God punishing Max? Why? What did he do to deserve this?

Max couldn't remember his mother before he'd seen her at the funeral. She was just a feeling. An awkward feeling, in fact; a complicated and difficult feeling. He'd seen pictures of her – there was one on his bedside table. She was smiling and hugging his father. It was cold and they were wearing scarves, mad scarves that she'd knitted. All kinds of colours, and way too long. Gran had other photos of Zoe with Dad, but Max had stopped looking at them, so she had kind of faded with time.

'Zoe,' Max said to himself, forming the word with his lips. She'd always been 'Mummy' to him, but from now on he decided he was going to call her Zoe, or just plain Mum. Naomi had always been 'Gran' and occasionally, very occasionally, 'Naomi', when he was being cheeky. Gwen and Evelyn were always 'Aunty Gwen and Aunty Evelyn' and Noel had always been 'Grandpa'. But he was so good at being a grandpa that he could even have been a friend if you didn't notice how old he was. Grandpa liked hockey the same amount as Max, maybe even a bit more, because Max really liked swimming as well. And Grandpa liked Gran's lasagne the same amount as Max did. Had liked, he corrected himself.

Max wondered if Mummy, Zoe, he corrected himself, was a Catholic. Perhaps she too loved religion. That was the problem with having a missing parent. You didn't know things that you should and there were always too many questions. His father was a complete dead end. But Mum was different. Max wondered what kind of information she might have.

Max had been feeling uneasy since Grandpa's funeral though. What if Mum did take him to live with her, as Chris reckoned? Where did she live, anyway? Could he still go to his school? Would he have to get a new school uniform? What would the undefeated Under-9s do without him? Gran said that Mum would not be taking him anywhere, and that he should see her taking an interest in him as a good thing. She said it was just about Mum wanting to stay in touch with him and Chris, to be part of their lives. But Max was not so sure it would be that simple.

Cracks

Naomi returned to work not long after Noel's funeral and went through the motions of dealing with her clinical load. She had developed what she described to Patricia, her friend and co-worker, as 'arthritis of the heart'. There were some motions that were just too painful to go through. Feeling positive about Zoe. Feeling sorry for Zoe. Even contemplating letting go of the boys. She felt relieved to be at work, she told Patricia over a quick coffee. There were babies waiting to be born, after all!

It was not just Noel's death, or the financial stress, it was Zoe. If she allowed herself to think about Zoe, she started to breathe quickly and her heart started a rolling boil. Naomi was waiting, anxiously, for Zoe's next move. Waiting was the worst part. Especially for her as a nurse, used to dealing with crisis. But so far nothing. Just the void left by her conversation with Zoe. *So far*.

Noel's death had made a vast and relentless difference to everything. Even the smallest of things – cup rings on the table, cold toast, lost keys – now made her snap, as if her nerve endings were damaged. His funeral was such a blur. Had it really happened? Naomi could almost believe that it had not, that Noel was on some extended adventure in Africa, if it were not for the subtle change in Chris's behaviour and a new fear within her. There is nothing to be frightened of, Naomi said to herself. She could handle it. But she put a deadlock on the front door and looked over her shoulder in the hospital car park. She was reading cookbooks at night, alone in her bed, finding comfort in recipes, for God's sake.

'Do you have any family here with you?' she usually asked her new patients at the clinic. These days so few people lived their life in any one place, so few people were from this place. These families, *my families*, as she referred to them, had to pass by her to begin their new lives as mothers and fathers. She tried to be a welcoming gatekeeper, with her reading glasses perched on the end of her nose, her hair neat, short, practical. Usually she wore a wide African-print skirt and sensible sandals. But she was finding it difficult since the funeral to be her usual relaxed and accepting self.

Being a part-time midwife meant that her clinic was often full of the leftovers, the cases no one else wanted. For her, the more complicated the better; it made her feel needed. Today, at the question, 'Do you have any family here with you?' the woman sitting in front of her looked not to Naomi but across to her husband, who was translating for her. The bangles on her arm tinkled as she adjusted her crimson headscarf and frowned at him.

The African man was tall and he unfolded his long limbs as he spoke, shifting in the low, hospital-issue vinyl chair. He stood up against the bare white wall of her office.

'No, unfortunately for my wife,' he answered.

Naomi was used to speaking this way to pregnant women attending her clinic – through their husbands, their children, even the cleaner on the odd occasion, and other question- able interpreters. She preferred to use an official interpreter. Husbands and male relatives had way too much power as interpreters. She spent a good part of each day waiting for the interpreter to arrive; this time it was the Dinka interpreter. He had not turned up yet.

'It is difficult not having any family around you,' Naomi said, smiling at the woman and checking her name in the hospital notes before attempting it. 'Yom? Is that how you say your name?'

The woman nodded at the sound of her name.

The man had a faint puckered tattoo of scar tissue above each of his eyebrows.

'And you are Marial?' she said to the man. 'May I call you Marial?'

Marial nodded.

Yom ran her hand across her belly and touched her lips with her fingertips, performing a silent, fleeting prayer for her unborn baby.

'When you are about to have your child, it is diffi-cult anywhere,' he added, proud of his attempt at a joke in English.

'Your English is very good,' Naomi said. 'Much better than my Dinka.'

Marial nodded.

'How long have you been here?' Naomi asked Yom. 'In this place?'

Again Marial answered. 'Just a few weeks.'

Naomi wrote 'newly arrived' in her notes.

The phone along the corridor was ringing constantly. The ward clerk was probably at Min's morning tea. Naomi noticed the time: 11 am. She would have to hurry if she was to make it. Min, one of the young midwives, was leaving to volunteer with MSF in Africa. Already the table in the tearoom was groaning under the weight of teacakes and baklava and hummus and dried fruit.

Naomi put down her pen and picked up Yom's hand, turning it slowly over in her palm, looking at Yom's nails for signs of poor circulation and her fingers for swelling. The first thing she could tell was that, although still young, Yom had known hard manual labour; that she, like Naomi, was probably from a farm.

'How old are you, Yom?'

'Nineteen,' her husband answered. He appeared to be much older. Perhaps thirty?

Yom continued to hold her hand.

She was speaking a mixture of Arabic and Dinka, a few words of which Naomi could decipher, like 'nhialic' (God) or 'jok' (powers).

'She lost a baby in Kenya, in the refugee camp,' Marial said.

There could be many reasons for this, and without a medical history she may never know why. Naomi squeezed Yom's hand.

'It is important to keep this baby as safe as possible,' she said, turning to Marial. 'It is important to eliminate any congenital factors.' Sensing that he did not understand the word 'congenital', Naomi added, 'Or blood problems that might affect this pregnancy as well.'

'Many women die in childbirth in our country,' Marial said anxiously.

'Yes, I know,' Naomi said, looking into Yom's large black eyes.

The three of them sat in silence for a moment.

'Where do you come from?' Marial asked Naomi.

She turned at the question. It was not an unusual question, but today it struck Naomi as important. Often these ante-natal visits with newly arrived refugees were an exchange; she extracted the necessary medical history and in return had to tell her story.

'I came to this place from the country,' Naomi said, moving away the notes with her elbow, 'about six hours away.'

'On foot?' he asked politely.

'No, by car or bus, about a week's walk,' Naomi pointed northwest, as if she could get up from her chair and start out on the journey now.

The waiting room was full of people today, this being the busiest clinic of the week, but Naomi put all that to one side. She abandoned the idea of attending Min's morning tea.

'Why did you leave?' Marial asked.

Naomi smiled. 'I left a long time ago, with my husband, for work. I have lived in the city for many years now.'

'Do you ever cry for your country?' he asked, and then translated his question for Yom.

Naomi smiled at his words.

'Do I get homesick?' Naomi turned the question over in her mind. 'Where I come from is beautiful country, sandstone country. The houses are built out of sandstone the colour of honey.'

Yom began speaking, and Marial again translated. 'We are from Bargasal in the Sudan. It was a beautiful place too. Date palms and plenty of corn to feed our goats and cows. The children had full bellies, birds sang sweet songs. Our houses . . .' – Yom touched Naomi's hand before Marial continued to translate for her – 'were made of earth, the colour of blood.'

It was often difficult to get women like Yom to speak to her on an antenatal visit. Naomi was touched by her determination at nineteen years old, in a foreign country, to speak, to be heard, even if it was through her husband.

'And when the earth on those houses dried out it was full of small cracks,' Marial translated.

'How did you meet?' Naomi asked, suddenly wanting to hear their love story.

'In Kakuma, a refugee camp in Kenya,' Marial said without translating for Yom. 'Our home is destroyed in the war.'

'Now you have to make a new home,' she said.

'We miss our village and family. That place, we will always miss. It is gone now,' Marial said and then translated Yom's words. 'A better life for our child.'

Yom touched her stomach.

'Let's have a look, shall we?' Naomi indicated to Yom the examination table draped in a white sheet. Yom lay down and pulled up her cotton toab. Naomi's hands moved around the sides of Yom's belly and across the top. She produced a tape measure and held it against the very top of Yom's womb, extending it down to her navel.

After a moment's swift and silent calculation, she said, 'You are measuring about twenty weeks.'

'And what of your children?' Yom asked through her husband.

Naomi set aside the tape measure.

'I had two sons; they died. It was a car accident about eight years ago that took them from me.'

Naomi waited for Marial to catch up on the translation. Yom took hold of Naomi's hand, her eyes filling swiftly with tears.

'So, what can you do?' Naomi said, and after a pause she shrugged to show Marial that it was a rhetorical question. Yom clicked her tongue.

Naomi studied the opaque X-ray box on the wall above Yom's head, weighing up how to be now that she was back at work. She had not really considered this situation. She had looked forward to getting back to the hospital, throwing herself into the work, distracting herself, being around new life, measuring fundi, taking blood pressure, speaking to mothers.

'My husband died,' Naomi said quietly, 'suddenly, not long

ago.' It wasn't that she couldn't explain the pain she felt to people like Marial and Yom. It wasn't about loss of income or protection. It wasn't about being alone. It was about missing Noel, and the indecision. Decisions now surrounded her, swamped her. Decisions, big decisions – like how to deal with Zoe, the boys' lives, her future – had to be made and yet here she was struggling to decide what to tell patients in her clinic about her personal life.

'Poor one,' Marial said simply.

Yom clicked her tongue after he translated Naomi's words.

'It is better to be at work than at home without him,' Naomi continued, although she thought that this was probably a foreign concept to a couple like Yom and Marial.

They sat in silence for a moment. Naomi sighed. 'We will bury his ashes on a hill under an ironbark tree, to the north of here.'

Before Yom could ask any more difficult questions about her husband, Naomi said, 'I am lucky. I have two grandsons. They live with me. They fill me with laughter. I try to be a better parent to them,' she trailed off. Than what? The last time? Their mother?

When Yom and Marial left her office she returned to the notes. 'Midwife practitioner N.A. to attend birth. Pager number 4784.' She picked up the next file from the large stack in the clinic's in-tray. She could see that the rest of the midwives were in the tearoom and speeches were underway. Could she join them and smile? Not today, not yet. Just then an ambulance pulled into the emergency bay outside, siren wailing, and Naomi found herself having to call the next patient's name extra loud to make herself heard.

Walking

Zoe had spent the best part of the past few years walking. It seemed the only thing she could do. She could lose herself in a rhythm, a stride. She started to walk, limp actually, after the accident. No, THE ACCIDENT is how she thought of it. For three-and-a-half noisy months in rehab it had been her dream to get up and walk out. But she was pinned to the bed like a butterfly specimen, feeling as though everything that had been broken had been re-set a little crookedly.

The funeral was delayed and delayed until she was well enough to attend it. And as soon as the inquest finished, she stopped fighting the overwhelming desire to simply walk away from it all. Max was being bottle-fed, but she could not stand to have him near her and, anyway, he started to scream the minute Naomi handed him to her. One day she handed him back, without even a kiss on his downy forehead, and walked. Not completely, not at first. Naomi dragged her back. 'Your children need you!' Eventually this turned into, 'Why don't you leave them alone!'

Noel took quieter care with her. 'Sort yourself out. Your children are safe here with us,' he said, handing her a medium-sized backpack. 'You may need this.'

Lately, when she saw a pregnant woman in the street, she began to remember some of the other pieces of that time in her own life. Moving out of home. Moving in with Ben. Living at Naomi and Noel's. Moving out of Naomi and Noel's house and into their own flat. The robbery. Moving back in with Naomi and Noel. And, finally, returning there after the accident, after hospital, with a toddler and a baby that never stopped crying, and feeling so very alone. That memory, the last one, was a knot the size of her ripe-pear belly that Ben had so loved.

So Zoe walked, at first in circles and then, over time, in straighter lines. The pain was incredible. A filigreed work of intensity that began in her ankle and shot up through her knee and into her groin and spine. Her shoulders ached. Her neck drooped with the effort of standing, let alone walking. More pain the better, she thought. She didn't remember much about the birth of Max, but Chris's birth had been terrifying. With Ben there, and Naomi, and no end in sight. She had wanted to kill herself to make it stop. But Naomi did not flinch or look away, or become exhausted. Was that what you called an act of bravery?

Before Noel's death, Zoe had begun walking along the cross-street near Naomi and Noel's house. But she could not bring herself to get any closer. She walked with the backpack on her chest – like a baby pouch, Meg had observed. 'It is *not* a baby pouch!' Zoe said. But it was, of sorts. Because inside it was her collection. To the undiscerning eye, it may have appeared that she collected useless things – open seed pods and plastic bottle tops – but on closer inspection and if Zoe was feeling expansive, she might explain how the torn bird's nest or broken arrow was purposeful, discrete, a story part, a jigsaw piece. She had just one rule. She could only add broken things to her collection.

Since Noel's funeral she had taken to walking around the school more often. At the funeral Chris told her all about his teacher, somebody or other, and Max's teacher, Mr E. She had no trouble remembering this one thing about Max. Eight years on and a Mr E. had him learning times tables. All that screaming fury had turned into a solid mass of muscle and slippery eight-year-old sinew that knew eight times eight. This school thing was big for him, huh? She walked there to see it for herself. *Her* boys. The kids. *My* kids. She practised saying *my kids* like a mother, like she heard other mothers say, altogether too lightly in her opinion. Some days she sat on the bus seat opposite the school for up to two hours. She also liked to walk around the block. It was a big, solid block with a patchworked footpath covered in rotting frangipani and the occasional dead palm fronds that would have made a great centrepiece for a sculpture in her other life, the one she'd trashed. She listened to the voices clamouring through recess, the rustle of leaves during class time. She teased out the threads of the boys' voices from the girls'. She watched the children in subdued twos take the roll to the office, or notes to other classrooms. Sometimes her heart skipped a little beat when she saw a woman lead a small boy by his hand to school after the bell had rung. It could have been her if things had been different.

Zoe thought that if she walked hard enough and far enough, she might be able to live again. Meg was pushing her application for housing through. She just needed the boys with her and everything could begin.

Edith Cowan's nose

The money was gone. Naomi did not even know how much. One hundred dollars? One hundred and fifty dollars? If it was not in her pocket then where had she put it? She felt her stomach lurch at the realisation that she had no idea.

The yellow notes. She remembered how that morning her fingers had quickly folded the outside note along the bridge of Edith Cowan's nose. She considered herself a modern woman, but to avoid fees on excessive withdrawals per month (and to avoid discussion about it), Noel withdrew money for both of them.

Naomi straightened up. More than one fifty-dollar note. Perhaps it was only one hundred. Not the one hundred and fifty dollars that Noel had usually given her when he was alive, before she had to do this by herself.

'Thinking that it was one hundred instead of one hundred and fifty doesn't make me feel any better,' she said out loud.

Naomi felt every pocket twice. Then twice more, this time fumbling with her thumb and forefinger. She flushed hot with the knowledge that she had lost so much money. The three notes folded quickly and forgotten in her nurse's uniform pocket, forgotten there because of the morning's chores, hair brushing and last-minute homework.

She checked her purse. Surely she had transferred the money safely there? She had been interrupted by the search for a missing sock and Chris's frustration with his second instrument, a clarinet, with the wrong-sized reed: 'One and a half! I told you already, the teacher said I need one and a half.'

The car spaces at the petrol station on Parramatta Road were so small that Naomi could barely open the car door without hitting the vehicle parked next to hers. She checked on the floor of the car with equal amounts of rising indignation and resignation. Her fingers ran over the exterior of her pockets again before she got back into the car. At least she hadn't filled up the car before checking her wallet, or lost it. She could economise on the grocery shopping for the next month to make it up. Mince. Better still, no meat. They would become vegetarians. She hadn't lost her handbag. She hadn't been robbed at knifepoint. More to the point, she hadn't lost a child. This is where her thoughts inevitably stalled. The worst possibility of all. Naomi could almost think that thought without flinching. But she still felt the old familiar prick of pain somewhere inside her ribs. She *was* a mother who had lost her sons. No, she hadn't misplaced them, they were gone. Eight years later this was still a fact.

Frustration brimming, Naomi cried for the first time since Noel's funeral, shouting, 'Why me?' as she slid in behind the steering wheel, bitterness welling up, the sheer hard work of being, day in, day out.

She wondered about working in a bread shop instead of a birthing unit. The wonderful smell of bread. The fine particles of flour that cover everything – eyebrows, counters, the cash register. Would she care enough about customers to check their purchases? She cared enough about people's babies to check them and parcel them up after birth. That was logical. But a packet of bread? That took a special person.

The shift had been good. She had delivered the daughter of a Kenyan couple at 12.31 pm. Children themselves. The mother was a mere twenty-one years old, the father about the same. In her opinion the optimal age for giving birth was twenty-five. After more years than that as a midwife, she had come to that conclusion. At twenty-five a woman is still in good physical condition – not peak, but good enough. A woman at twenty-five has physical stamina. But, most importantly, she has some direction in her life. Her life has shape by then. She has completed her education, she has a career, or an idea of a career. At least that was what Naomi thought.

The Kenyan couple both spoke English. The labour was long. The father had attended the birth – a small, intense man who had remained silent when she handed him his beautiful baby girl, a single tear spilling down his ebony cheek.

They named the child Elizabeth. Three-and-a-half kilos, thirty-eight centimetres in length, a straightforward vaginal delivery. The student midwife and medical resident had both notched up another delivery attendance. There was the inevitable small tussle over who would take charge of the birth. One of the younger, more inexperienced midwives on the morning shift had wanted to stay back to deliver the baby.

'You know an old midwife told me once that midwives eat their young,' Naomi said to the younger woman, smiling. 'Only one person can "catch the baby".'

The younger midwife had hesitantly given in and left her to it. Midwives were a strange bunch. Tough as nails and yet compelled to spend their lives seeking the tender moment of birth. It was rare to find another midwife you could work with; especially a young one. They knew everything, of course, and they entered the profession expecting everything. Naomi knew; she had. Yes, midwifery could be a lonely occupation. But after wrapping the baby and stitching up the small tear in the mother's perineum, there was a moment when she felt it was possible to put everything right in the world. She felt like this after every successful birth.

The waiting room had been full – Arabic clinic today. In the sea of veils and prams and worry beads sat a woman dressed in black, not in and of itself anything to note. There were others, many in fact, covered from tip to toe in black. But this woman was hooded. Not even a slit for her eyes or mesh to breathe through. She turned her head and Naomi realised she could hear her husband's soft footsteps, able to pick them out of the cacophony of waiting-room sound.

Naomi stood still, an unusual thing for a midwife to do, her notes limp and momentarily forgotten in her hand as she watched the hooded woman, who now stood, a little unsteadily. Even the woman's hands were gloved. She was unable to walk without the man at her side because she could not see where she was going. Naomi shook her head. Nothing surprised her about women and what they did to please men, to be with men. In any given waiting room she had women wearing virtually nothing, as well as invisible women. And nothing surprised her about what men, in turn, did to these women.

Naomi turned and walked across the hall to the filing cabinet, the metal clip on the notes cutting into the flesh of her fingers. With one hand on the metal drawer, she turned back for a last look. The hooded woman stood, head tilted slightly, impervious to the waiting-room television above her head, on which an American talk-show host quizzed overweight contestants about their sexual infidelities. The woman was waiting for her husband to make her next clinic appointment.

Naomi continued her drive home along Parramatta Road, one eye on the fuel gauge, pulling up with a few minutes to spare before the children's afternoon school bell. The bell rang out each day across the small valley below their house. From the narrow terrace houses mothers would be making their way up the hill, as she had for two generations. Rubbish day as well, she noticed – the footpath was littered with large green plastic bins. She must remember to put out the rubbish, and her evening flamenco class at seven. Naomi felt like she was drowning in detail.

She stopped the car, momentarily forgetting that she had driven home to collect the boys' instruments. She glanced up at the front of her small house. She found it hardest here at home without Noel. For long stretches at work she was able to put his death to the back of her mind. But here she felt his absence like an open wound. With Noel's death, there was no retirement in sight for Naomi without selling.

Inside the house there were the cupboards that needed cleaning. Her desk overflowed with papers. The bedroom floor was covered in piles of washing, and elaborate cobwebs hung from the ceiling. Could dinner wait until she had attended to those things? No, they would have to wait until her day off.

She had forgotten about the money by the time she swung her legs out of the car, but there in front of her in the gutter lay a flat fifty-dollar note. Then another, and another, under the front wheel of the car. Naomi bent and picked them up, scraping her knuckles on the unforgiving bitumen in her rush, her fear that the wind might come and blow them away almost overwhelming her. One of the things about surviving the death of her children was that when something was taken from you, you sure as hell didn't let it get taken again. Were the notes hers? Did they belong to Signora Toto next door? Naomi dismissed the thought. Of course they were hers, waiting there patiently all day. She put them straight into her purse.

∞

At school the boys thrust their schoolbags out to her. 'Here take this, Gran,' they said. She took the bags, relieved at their routine rudeness.

'Can I have a slushie?' they both asked, Max with his hand already in her shoulder bag, fossicking for loose change.

'No,' Naomi said. The queue was long and full of slow, squeaky kindergarten children.

The sun was warm on her tired back and her nurse's uniform was loose against her thigh. Her hair was noticeably thinning and she could feel the sun on the pink flesh of her scalp. She felt old. Nevertheless, now that she had found her money she must try to be triumphant rather than crumpled.

'Musicianship, Max. Hurry up,' Naomi said quickly, trying inelegantly to sidestep his protest or at least to contain it to the privacy of the car.

'I hate Kerry,' began Max.

Harry's mother, Mary, saw her across the playground and waved. Naomi waved back an *all well with you?* gesture. As she turned the corner, both boys' schoolbags on one shoulder, her own bag on the other, she saw two short men hurry towards her. They were wearing bright yellow fluoro jackets, a dead giveaway. One carried a notepad and pen and they looked directly at her. Of all the people in the street, they looked at her. They knew, Naomi knew. The men jumped into their car a tad too quickly and drove off.

'Ticket!' Naomi said out loud, resisting the urge to run. She knew what she would see tucked under the windscreen wiper. 'Oh, *no*.'

There under the wiper was a buff-coloured envelope. Why do they bother with the envelope, she found herself wondering. When above all else accounts must balance, surely they should put the onus on the public to pay their fines without supplying the envelope. Naomi thought about writing to someone about it.

One of the men had written in spidery uppercase, 'One hundred and fifty-five dollars'. One hundred and fifty-five dollars for a bad angle park just inside the No Stopping zone. The one hundred and fifty-five dollars included ten per cent GST, Naomi supposed. She turned to Chris and Max and burst into laughter.

'What's so funny, Gran?' Max asked.

'I'll tell you about it some time, Max,' she said, tears springing into her eyes as she broke into new peals of laughter. 'You wouldn't read about it.'

Jigsaw

Gran was always saying that Chris was like his uncle Jesse. Mostly in a good way. Since Noel's death Chris thought about the not-so-good bits of everything. He couldn't help it. It was as if his life was completely different without Noel in it. His life before was mostly happy, and his life after was completely – well, often – not. It was like playing a cold dark fugue over and over again.

Now, when Naomi said with that faraway look in her eyes how like Jesse Chris was becoming, he didn't think about how gentle and kind Jesse had been. Instead Chris remembered how especially stubborn Noel had once said Jesse was, and how he liked to do things perfectly, right off. And then there was the matter of Ben's famous temper. He had not inherited his father's generosity and spontaneity, he had inherited his temper. Great. When he got obsessed about something, he had to do it right straightaway, like painting a picture or learning a new piece on the piano. Chris got frustrated at the beginning. He hated things in bits. He liked things to be done, finished, whether it was a piece of music or a family. Chris hated the bits that were missing from his family. Like the way Gran didn't mention his mother much. She looked so serious when he asked about Zoe that he just didn't anymore.

Zoe Zalum seemed like a made-up name. Her mother must have chosen Zoe to go with Zalum for a reason. She would have always been at the end of the roll. Chris was usually at the beginning, or at least near. Between them they had it covered.

If anyone asked him now, Chris would say, no offence, but things with Gran were getting weird. She pretended that they were this happy family, but they weren't. 'Grandpa's dead!' Chris almost yelled at her on the weekend. Lately he even said he hated her under his breath, hated her for still being alive. Max heard him and he was shocked. So was Chris, truth be told, but he couldn't help it. It just fell out of his mouth and then he couldn't take it back. He was mad with Gran for being so wrinkled as well. And, worst of all, for pretending. Things would be different if she had died and Grandpa was alive. Better, probably. Chris thought that his mum would have come over by now to take them to live with her. Grandpa would have let her. No fuss.

The new hockey coach, Harry's older brother, was hopeless. Noel and Chris had respect for one another and that was really important. Chris wished now that he had asked Noel more questions, especially since the respect thing between them had been big and all. Questions about his dad, especially. Dad's favourite hockey player? Subject at school? Music? Song? Car?

Since Grandpa died, Gran acted like Chris was going to be next. Don't run! You might slip over. Wash your hands. Put your shoes on. Don't walk with the bread knife. Loads of things like that, annoying things. She used to be fun and now she wasn't. She was behaving really weirdly, acting like she was his mother. No, like she was *better* than his mother. She didn't say that exactly, but almost. But she couldn't confuse him like she confused Max. Chris knew who she was and she wasn't his mother.

It wasn't that he didn't like her all the time, to be fair. They had been close before. He liked the way she got music. They could talk about it. She could talk about anything, almost. Except his mum, his dad and his uncle Jesse.

Chris liked how Naomi was a midwife and a good cook. He liked how she took them swimming early in the morning before school in the summer and in the holidays.

He had heard her crying in her room lately. At first it worried him, but now he just wanted to ignore it. To make the bad feeling go away, he thought about how he wanted an iPod. A computer too. A Nintendo Game Boy. Action Man Robot Atak. And his mum. No offence, but he just thought about what he wanted.

Rocks and paper

'Mrs Strowl yelled at me and Harry today because we didn't have our folders for music and drama,' Max's thin voice exploded from the back seat of the car. Thin, even for an eight-year-old. Kerry thought he might make a good soprano, but Naomi couldn't picture him in a white smock singing in a mouldy old church.

Naomi tried to remember whether she had forgotten to get the folder. Was there a note about it? Had Max even mentioned it? She couldn't remember a single thing about a music and drama folder, but she knew better than to question Max about it. They would just go around in circles.

'I'll stop and get you one at the newsagency in the morning before school,' Naomi said.

'We'll be running late,' Max said.

'Not if we know that we have to go to the newsagency,' Naomi replied.

'It won't have any.'

'I'm sure they will have something that could do the job.'

'They won't have a blue one.'

'Possibly.'

They had driven on in silence, rounding a corner with yet another inner-city café where once a smallgoods shop had been. The traffic was moving very slowly that afternoon. Naomi's red Laser was hot and suddenly too low to the ground. She sat up straight.

'Does the colour really matter?' Naomi said, feeling annoyed with the teacher.

She looked Max in the eye in the rear-vision mirror. He shrugged.

At Kerry's house Naomi entered first, followed by Chris and finally, reluctantly, Max. Kerry's grand piano was propped open and a small girl of about eight or nine was working her way through a complex piece of Mozart.

Naomi stood silently with the boys and waited for the girl to finish the section. She leant her tired back against the floral wallpaper and let the melodic piece wash over her. The music filled the room and floated out onto the street through the open windows. Another dry afternoon. The lilies in Kerry's hall vase looked thirsty, the edge of each petal paper thin and colourless.

Naomi handed Max his piano theory book. Chris already had his out and open on a page headed: 'Rhythmic Invention'.

'Place an upright line before the accented words or syllables in the following couplet,' she read over his shoulder:

Yet the grass is green today
Though the winter's here to stay.

Chris turned away from her so that she could no longer see his work.

Children were stretching out, legs and elbows in all directions, on Kerry's blue and cream Turkish rug as they began to struggle with key signatures. Max shuffled over to join them. They barely acknowledged him and he sighed.

Naomi sat down heavily on the chaise longue and listened to the Mozart for a moment longer, tapping her foot ever so gently.

The girl stumbled over a small section and Kerry asked her to play it again.

'Ta te ta te, ta *ta-te-ta*.' Kerry clapped her hands to the rhythm behind the girl's head.

Max looked across the room to Naomi and she nodded almost imperceptibly. Here was the evidence, Max's look said. See, Kerry is mean. His eyes narrowed.

Naomi sighed. How to convey the idea of practice and discipline to a small boy like Max? Max was so like Ben and therefore like her. Physically, he resembled his father. Shorter than Chris, thinner legs, darker straight hair, olive skin, no freckles on his nose as Chris had. Hazel eyes. Chris's were ice blue, like Zoe's. Both Ben and Jesse had Naomi's brown eyes. Max, frailer at birth, had more of a struggle to get going than Chris in those early years. Now he was growing stronger, becoming a natural athlete. His shoulders were quite square. He would be tall enough to make the basketball team one day, if he wanted. 'If he wanted' was the critical factor with Max. Like Ben before him, he was physically capable, but emotionally? Naomi was not so sure.

More and more she believed that Ben had been like her and Jesse had been like Noel. Perhaps their premature deaths enabled her to think like this, and if they had lived they would have contradicted her, the way children do. They would have changed, not just been reduced to full stops in the Adams family line.

If they had lived . . . This is often where she stopped herself. There was no point. They were dead. To an extent, ever since, she had been pretending to be alive herself. Her focus remained tightly on the day-to-day minutiae of life –

work, school, dinner on the table, piano practice. She had wordlessly picked up the pieces of their broken lives – Chris's, Max's, Noel's, her own – and kept going.

Zoe? She had loved her quickly, tried to welcome her into their family. Love would fix her. That was the practical thing to do. Ben had found an unusual young woman. Her beautiful, talented daughter-in-law. Then, just as quickly, Naomi had hated Zoe. Zoe, the survivor. Zoe, the woman who had walked away from her children. It was hard to hate an absence though, and these days Naomi tried not to hate anyone.

She could barely remember her sons' faces, just fragments – snatches of conversations, little more than words and disembodied voices. One such memory of Ben was a spectacular fight with him when he was about Chris's age. She was standing behind a closed door with Ben banging his bare fists on the other side and she clearly recalled the realisation that he was now stronger than her, that she would lose the battle, and, in that moment, that he hated her. She also realised that Noel would never have found himself in a situation like that one.

Max mouthed, 'Can I go home yet?'

'No,' Naomi mouthed back.

Chris, meanwhile, sat quietly working on a theory paper. His hair was darkening to almost the colour of Max's. Like Jesse before him, he was special. All children are special, of course, but Chris was special to her. She had been at his difficult birth, and when he had finally been settled and wrapped up, she carried him around the bed back to Zoe, Naomi said, 'He's a rock!'

After so many years as a midwife, she knew. There were two kinds of babies: rocks and paper. To Naomi, Chris still looked the same as he had on day one. Chris, the anchor for Max, and for her. The calm one, as Jesse had been before him.

Naomi expected that Max would overtake Chris in many ways, but he would never be his rock.

'Do your work,' Naomi mouthed at Max.

Max rolled his eyes and sighed.

Chris, on the other hand, was completely absorbed. His eyes were intense, his face still. When Kerry clapped her hands and called for attention, Chris did not hear her at first.

'Christopher,' Kerry said in a quiet voice, and he looked up. Naomi marvelled at the control that Kerry could exert over such an eclectic group of young children.

'Could you play your piece for us, please?' Kerry asked.

Naomi looked at Max as Chris took his place at the grand piano, as if to say, 'This is what it is all about, Max. Pay attention.'

Max shrugged.

'Minuet in C Major by Franz Joseph Haydn,' Chris said quietly.

The mood in the class lifted as Chris began to play, and at the same time the afternoon's southerly change blew through the open front door.

'I'll go and buy your blue folder,' Naomi mouthed to Max.

Max nodded and turned to listen to his brother play with elegant, measured, precise control.

Gavin

The local community garden was an unlikely place to find someone like Zoe. Most days she wandered there, eyes down, thinking about the ground and all that lay under and in it.

Zoe did not need to please people. Zoe did not finish people's sentences for them. Zoe did not nod while she listened. Zoe did not blink enough, her mother once told her. Her teeth were too sharp and her smile was too fleeting. When she looked in the mirror she did not always recognise the unblinking woman who stared back.

Zoe did not look in a mirror these days anyway.

She liked the community garden though. She could lose herself in its plants – behind the cornstalks, underneath the passionfruit vines, above the strawberries. She planted, watered and snapped off the old growth between her sculptor's fingers. Her tomato plants grew on stakes at crazy angles, but they were happy and fat and disease-free. She experienced a sense of achievement here in this garden that she had not known for eight years.

There he was again. The big lanky man with eyes too close together, his woollen beanie pulled down over his ears. He took long steps around the garden beds, walking with his head thrust forward. He wore board shorts and workman's boots without socks. Sometimes he wore a shirt, but not often. He always wore a nail bag tied round his waist and sometimes he carried bits of wood, making edges for the garden beds. The carpenter, Zoe called him.

It was possible to think here, to sit with a pool of sunshine on her back and to dream again. So far the community garden had been mainly her work, and now this other person, about her own age, was there too. They were often the only two in it. The local council had begun the garden for the elderly residents, but they were too scared to use it. Rough neighbourhood and all that.

After the man in the beanie had paced up and down the garden beds he usually stood completely still, or sat down abruptly and crossed his legs, raising his hands palm upwards to the sun. Listening to voices, Zoe reckoned. She knew how to recognise the signs. She had, after all, learnt to calm the voices in her own head by walking.

Zoe had watched him carefully for days and then weeks. She was practised at being invisible. It was the lightness of her hair, the fairness of her skin, her thinness, her age. It hadn't always been this way. There was a time when someone as solid and capable as Ben noticed her; when the press courted her and galleries liked her work. When she shone.

Zoe watched the man from the safety of inconsequence. He seemed wound up a little crookedly, like a spring in an old bed mattress. The width of his shoulders formed a straight yoke for his body. He only seemed to relax when he could lose himself in the work of the garden. Zoe sensed that she and he had something in common.

Today he was very agitated. Was it the cooler weather? Zoe handed him the stone she had been holding in her hand, a worn piece of quartz.

'Smooth as silk,' he said, turning it over with his square fingers. He grinned up at her, sitting back on his haunches. He smelt of earth and salt.

Zoe smiled.

'Gavin,' he said.

'Zoe,' she replied.

Kernel of joy

'You might be the ones to hear the baby's first cry,' Naomi explained to the students as they stood outside Birthing Room 3. The three female and one male midwifery students were huddled to one side of the birthing-room door, halfway down the wide hospital corridor. They waited for the cry but it did not come.

'Any questions before we move on?' Naomi said eventually.

One of the students, a young woman from Lebanon who was wearing a hijab, looked at Naomi.

'What happens if there's a complication?'

'Good question.'

Naomi drew herself up, trying to breathe life into her answer.

'Not all births go to plan. No matter how good the ante-natal care, sometimes the birth is very difficult, despite our best efforts. A first birth, for example, can take longer, require more intervention. But there is no way of knowing really, and in any case the theatres are above us on the next level.' Before the student could ask more, Naomi added, 'And we will tour them tomorrow.'

Just then they heard the smallest of throaty cries. All the students smiled, Naomi too – she was relieved. 'That's the best sound in the world,' she said, lightly touching the shoulder of the Lebanese student.

They stood listening, caught up in the moment.

'It's very difficult to give birth without the language,' the Lebanese student said, quickly. 'My mother gave birth to five children in Australia, five children in Lebanon. She can't speak a word of English. As soon as I was old enough, I had to interpret for her.' She stopped abruptly and then added, as if it was an afterthought, 'I watched her give birth to three.'

Naomi nodded.

'Any of you others ever attended a birth?'

They all shook their heads.

'Good training for midwifery,' she said, turning to the Lebanese student. 'You have to be prepared for anything.'

'I'm never having a baby, but!' the student added, with a nervous laugh.

'Becoming a mother is a profound experience,' Naomi said gently.

Naomi turned and looked up the long, busy hallway. Midwives emerged from rooms. A husband arrived with a striped bag. Pagers beeped. Despite the cool blue walls and linoleum this birthing centre was not a calm, neutral place. Behind each of these doors babies were forcing their way into the world, sometimes ripping through flesh to get there.

Naomi thought momentarily about the sheer number of births she had attended. She had lost count. She remembered very little of many of them now. She shuffled them in her memory like a pack of cards. Sudanese ones; Tibetan ones; Bengali ones. Lying under all these births like granite boulders were her own sons' home births. Then Chris's birth. Zoe had been terrified. Naomi should have known then that something was not right. And at Max's birth, Zoe had seemed distant, remote somehow. Max had been ten days overdue, eventually induced. Naomi attended both and held up Max to Zoe, who at first didn't – or couldn't, as she had come to think of it – take the infant in her arms. Ben had taken him and held him. Another boy, a known quantity. A son would fare better with Zoe than a daughter, and two sons would be better than one; they would always have each other.

Seeing an opening, one of the students, a short girl who had not spoken before, asked Naomi, 'Why did you become a midwife?'

'I wanted to work with women. Make a difference. That sort of thing,' Naomi answered lightly.

'Have you?'

'What do you mean?'

'Have you made a difference?'

Naomi paused.

'That's a tricky one. You know that one in ten pregnant women suffers violence, or at least that's what the stats say.'

The student waited.

'And I think if I can help make that woman's birth experience a positive one, maybe there's a chance things could get turned around for her.'

It was rare that a student challenged Naomi, but when they did, she was strangely grateful. It reminded her that she was opening their minds to new possibilities. Naomi knew that hungry look the short girl had – she wanted more of this kind of teacher–student exchange. It was real.

'I've seen women turn up here clutching tiny scraps of paper with hand-drawn maps of how to get to the hospital,' Naomi told the students. 'Occasionally I see families in which baby girls are unwelcome. Some women come in with boot marks in their bellies and bruises around their necks. We try to develop a close and caring relationship with all our mothers. Sometimes it's the only kindness they've seen in a long while.'

'How come . . .?' the same student began.

'We'll have to leave it there,' Naomi said abruptly. She couldn't stop herself thinking about Zoe. Had she been able to develop a close and caring relationship with her, all those years back?

'But . . .' interrupted the Lebanese student.

'The afternoon handover is beginning and I have to go to my grandkids' music concert. Can't be late.'

'What do you get out of being a midwife?' It was the same small student, she was at least half a head shorter than the rest of them. Naomi bent towards her and paused, trying to find the right note to begin her answer with.

'Most people greet a baby with enormous joy, but a few can't.'

'Yes?' The student's face was an open question.

Naomi dropped that line of thought and decided to keep it simple: 'Joy. There is the possibility of a moment in every birth of pure joy.'

The other students looked slightly uneasy at her answer, but the small student nodded.

'Not many people get to experience that every day at work,' Naomi concluded quietly.

Yes, there was the ever-present battle to stop a woman's perineum from tearing; there was the monitoring, the paperwork, the stripping and remaking of beds, students and their questions, the other midwives; but on the whole it was all about that small moment, a kernel of joy.

'Joy,' the student repeated.

'Write that down,' Naomi said over her shoulder.

'Joy,' they all said out loud.

'Delivering babies is a privilege. Don't ever forget that. If you find one day that you have forgotten it, it's time to leave the profession. Midwifery stands outside the nursing

110

profession as a profession in its own right.' Naomi was now at the door. 'If you have any more questions, we can deal with them tomorrow.'

Blue tattoo

They lay together bathed in the afternoon sunlight pouring in through Zoe's bedroom window. The bed was unmade and the sheets smelt of lemon. Her naked body was translucent in the wintry light except for her scars: the amethyst slash across her abdomen and the violet seam winding its way round her ankle. Gavin's bands of tattoos on his arms and legs were smudged blue with time.

He ran his finger along the edge of the scar that marked where she'd had her spleen removed after the accident.

'Does it hurt much anymore?'

Zoe had been thinking about her children, her *sons*, when Gavin spoke. How big Chris and Max had grown, how strong and handsome.

She turned to face him and sighed. 'Yes, sometimes.' But what she was really talking about was Ben and Jesse. Ben. She had loved him, perhaps. Now she wasn't so sure. Her love for him was tinged with regret and guilt. She closed her eyes. She didn't want to think about Ben today. Jesse was different though. Yes, she had loved him, just for a moment it seemed now, before he died. Tall and quiet and happy to let her be. Jesse was there. Always in the background of her life with Ben, and if she had to describe Jesse, she would use just one word. She would say he was 'true'.

Gavin asked her, 'What is it you're looking for, Zoe?'

Perhaps he thought that it would have something to do with him. It was a bit early to tell. Maybe there could be something between them, but Zoe was cautious. She was happy to sleep with him; however, she was in no rush to get into a relationship. That was a whole other matter. She preferred to keep it casual, to keep everything casual, except her kids. Her children had to come first. At nearly thirty years of age, if she didn't find a way to make them come first now, they never would. She didn't want to have that conversation with Gavin just yet.

A high, thin cloud passed across the sun and they both shivered. Zoe shrank back against Gavin's sinewy forearm.

'Forgiveness,' she replied.

We will rock you

The double classroom filled quickly with parents, as well as brothers and sisters, and the air grew hot and sticky. Year 1 students' work hung low in rows from the ceiling. Brightly crayoned clown-face after clown-face bobbed back and forth as parents brushed past them to take their seats.

Suzy, the conductor, a cheerful young woman with long black hair and lip piercings, turned and addressed the parents. 'We've been working hard all day on these pieces at our special workshop. Thanks for coming along to hear us.'

Behind Suzy the children puffed out their chests and sat quietly, all except for the boy on the drums, who was a fusspot, according to Max. The cymbals crashed as the boy bent to pick up his drumstick. He raised his eyebrows. The rest of the band ignored him but Suzy gave an exasperated shrug.

Suzy was a very different music teacher to Kerry. It was almost as if the two spoke different languages. The boys reckoned that Suzy was the kind of teacher that parents liked. She *said* all the right things, but when the parents weren't there she was mean. Naomi translated this as Suzy holding them accountable. Kerry, their piano teacher, on the other hand, was always mean. But because Naomi sat in on the boys' piano lessons with Kerry, she knew that *mean* in Kerry's case meant exacting.

Suzy, in her grubby hipsters, was evidently less tense, the more philosophical of the two teachers, but no less passionate.

Naomi waved to Max and Chris as they played a short warm-up in the scale of C. Max's eyes sparkled as he followed Suzy's every move, his trumpet high and proud. Chris played his clarinet, head down, eyes on the music.

Naomi felt her cheeks flush red and she suddenly found herself fighting back tears. The band was wobbling through the first movement of Beethoven's Ninth. Each child could play in unison, keep time and be content to be a small part of something larger. She felt the weight of that journey on her shoulders in a way that she had not stopped to consider before. This was not the first children's concert she had attended, but it moved her in a way that no other had. She was getting soft in her old age – in a life rubbed raw without Noel.

Many of the small children could barely be seen behind their music stands and instruments. It seemed as if the smallest boy played the tuba, or perhaps it was just that the tuba dwarfed him.

Naomi stood beside a quietly spoken woman in jeans and a polar-fleece jacket. 'Great, isn't it?' the woman whispered to her. Just then, the band began its laborious rendition of 'We Will Rock You'.

As she spoke, a man, Naomi presumed it was the woman's husband, came up behind her and placed both his hands on the woman's shoulders, turning her in the direction of their child. The woman did not react, as if this was perfectly acceptable and routine. There was a frustration in the flick of his wrists that hinted at something sharper. Her jacket momentarily rose around her shoulders and fell back in an undignified way. Naomi followed the man's intense eyes to a small child, playing flute in the wind section. In some cultures the head and shoulders are sacred, Naomi found herself thinking, but here they could be used in a piece of husband and wife shorthand.

Naomi straightened her own shoulders. Noel had never laid a hand on her. Theirs had been a more cerebral combat, but over the years, as a midwife, she had come to understand that violence was a part of daily life for some families. And even when she had been spared violence in her home life, her sons had nevertheless met a violent, senseless end.

Naomi remembered how little she cared for herself or Noel when Ben and Jesse had died. She pushed away food with a shrug, preferring to sleep with little Chris folded in her arms or to wheel Max in the pram. Deep down she knew that she had never really regained the ability to care for herself, and now it was too late for Noel. Noel, if he were still alive, would have arrived late this afternoon. Too late to catch Naomi's brimming eyes or the two pieces Chris and Max performed. He would be dressed in his ad hoc way and now, too late again, Naomi was glad that he had been so eccentric.

Mostly, Noel had dressed in what Naomi referred to as 'found items' – a mishmash of hand-me-downs always finished off with a pair of thongs. He was quite a handsome man, but it was hard to get past the clothes. The way she saw it, some people were just not meant to wear clothes. If clothes were food, then Noel had no tastebuds. She found herself smiling at the thought. Without him she could be more anonymous, just focus on the music, and for that Naomi was momentarily grateful.

Poor Noel, his allergies had been bad that past summer. He refused to use his nasal spray, and in a crowd like this his sneezing and nose-blowing would have carved out a small arc of space around them. It would have been just Naomi and him, as if they were what mattered, all that existed for that moment. This was how it had been all those years ago too, travelling through China and Russia.

∞

When the concert was finished, Chris and Max filed out of the brightly lit schoolroom smiling, each chewing on a sweet. 'Well done,' Naomi said to both of them as they emerged into the early evening gloom.

'Being at school after dark is creepy,' Chris said, hunching his thin shoulders. He hugged his clarinet and Max handed Naomi his trumpet.

The three of them stood together for a moment in the cool evening air. The rest of the children and their families were clustered in small groups, chatting and basking in the concert afterglow.

'There's a bit of snow in the air,' Naomi remarked, looking up at the sky.

'Need to take the lambs in,' Max chimed in. She smiled at him. This was something she often said, usually when it was time to come in after a big day of playing, or when she tucked him into bed at night.

The woman who had stood beside Naomi during the concert was also outside, holding her child's flute.

'Any dings, any bits missing?' Her husband appeared at her elbow, an accusing tone to his question. The child turned, and now that she was close Naomi noticed that she had a black eye as well as two butterfly clips holding a small stitch together on her cheekbone.

'No,' the child replied in a small voice.

The man smiled quickly at Naomi and, turning to his wife

and child, said loudly, possibly for Naomi's benefit, 'Come on! State of Origin is on at eight!'

'What happened to Pixie's eye?' Naomi asked Chris as she boiled pasta for their dinner later.

'Her little sister ran into her,' he said, 'and her tooth cut her cheek.'

'Poor thing.'

Chris ran his finger round the edge of a dinner plate, weighing up his words. 'You know, Pixie's flute got broken at the first rehearsal. Her parents had to buy her a new one. Her dad was very angry.'

How it feels to be a mother

'I can't help you get your children back unless you trust me, Miss Zalum,' the solicitor said. 'May I call you Zoe?'

Zoe nodded.

'Call me Sophie,' the solicitor said.

'Sophie,' Zoe repeated and took a quick hit of her Ventolin. Her asthma had been bad today. It was always worse if she had to meet new people, especially smart young lawyers like Sophie.

Sophie bristled with intelligence and efficiency. It took all Zoe's concentration just to keep up with Sophie's line of questioning. 'I see your sons are ten and eight?' she said.

Zoe clutched her backpack to her chest and shifted in her chair before she nodded. 'Yes.'

'What happened?'

'I left them,' Zoe began.

'Left them?' Sophie said.

'I was too young. I wasn't ready,' she said.

'You were a student?' Sophie said, fishing.

'Yes. Sculpture. People said I had a lot of potential; I had some possible commissions.'

'But then you got pregnant,' Sophie said.

'Yes, I got pregnant. Having the children changed everything. I couldn't work. I was depressed and then I had a car accident and ended up in hospital for weeks.'

'It's all in the file,' Sophie said, cutting across her.

Zoe looked at Sophie and weighed up how much to tell. It could not possibly be all in the file. All of it? All the mess?

'No, I don't think it is all in the file. I was a drug addict,' Zoe paused to clarify it, not that it mattered to anyone except her, 'addicted to painkillers. Then I became a full-blown nutcase. Depressed. Psychotic. Schizoid. You name it, I developed it. I was in and out of so many hospitals and therapeutic communities that it'd make your head spin, Sophie. I even lived on the streets for a while. You're telling me that's all in the file?'

'Are you taking drugs now?' Sophie said quietly and firmly.

Zoe shook her head.

'You're sure?' Sophie demanded more loudly. 'Because that will go very badly for you.'

'No!'

'You'll have to submit to a urine test,' Sophie continued.

'Easy,' she said lightly.

'Do you have a diagnosed mental illness?' Sophie asked, pen poised over the file notes.

Again Zoe shook her head.

'Are you getting treatment for your depression?'

'Yes,' she said. 'It's called a community garden.'

Eight years ago Zoe might have been more expansive, tried to help Sophie more, told her about Meg and Gavin and how she had stayed in touch with Noel and Gwen and so on, but she had learnt that it was better to say nothing. Zoe knew that the more she said, the more she would confuse someone like Sophie. She knew that she sounded unconvincing cast as the aspiring mother. She sounded like any other junkie mother; she *looked* like any other junkie mother.

'I left the kids with my mother-in-law,' Zoe said. 'I knew that they'd be safe with her and that it would take some time for me to straighten myself out.' The half-truth was calculating. She had a calculating nature that at times surprised her. Ben was a calculated risk. Being here was another. Even so, Zoe thought of herself as more risk-taking than calculating. But there was more to it than that. Zoe was a survivor.

Sophie looked at her. 'I have two children myself. I know how it feels.'

Zoe felt perplexed. Someone like Sophie could not possibly know how it felt to be in freefall, to hit the bottom and to pull yourself back up and away from the edge, to know no reason, to not recognise yourself.

'I know how it feels to be a *mother*,' Sophie clarified.

The O and the K

Chris was up Harry's tree lying along the branch imagining that he was a leopard in Africa. Chris thought that was where leopards came from. There or India, maybe. He watched the footpath below. He could even see the ants walking up and down where Harry and Max had spilt their Poppers. He watched everything carefully these days. Chris nudged the Tarzan rope with his finger on the top knot. What began at the top with a gentle prod quickly had the rope swinging in large, looping circles at the bottom. Watching and waiting.

OK. He liked the way his mother said the word OK. Chris practised saying it to Gran the way Zoe said it. He didn't tell her that was what he was doing though. He didn't want to share it with her. The O was longer and louder than the K. Chris thought about that and he knew it would be OK. But where was Zoe? He was getting sick of waiting for her to show up. She said, 'I want the boys.' Chris liked the way she said that too. He had heard her right there at the funeral so he knew it was true. He knew from the way Naomi had been ever since that it was true. He told Max and Max looked doubtful, like Chris was making it up. But Chris didn't lie about important things, things to do with their mother, and what she said and how she sounded.

So, any day now, Chris told Max; but that was a while ago. Chris was a person with patience. His teacher said so. Patience. He looked it up on Wikipedia to check its exact meaning. 'Patience is the ability to endure waiting, delay, or provocation without becoming annoyed or upset, or to persevere calmly when faced with difficulties.' It was the first word he looked up after Naomi got him and Max the new computer. It wasn't easy to be patient though. He was beginning to hate everything. He taught himself new pieces on the piano but he played them too fast or too slowly. Kerry was never happy with his work. Lately he had decided to try to write down his compositions. The short ones. His bedroom floor was covered in scraps of handwritten manuscripts. He played hockey. He drew pictures. Every time he started to feel worried about things he thought about that O and that K.

The circus

The waiting room was beginning to fill up. Phones were ringing, people were speaking loudly, babies and children cried. These sounds were comforting, reassuring to Naomi, still struggling with her grief over Noel's death. The world around her continued and she took strength from that. Turning over the first file, she told the students, 'The first woman I'm going to see this morning is a Caucasian, twenty-two, first pregnancy, history of intravenous drug use.' Naomi paused and looked at the students. 'What will I be on the lookout for?'

'Drug use?' the Lebanese student said.

'Yes, of course that's very important. Why?'

'Associated risks, HIV? Hep?' she offered tentatively.

'And nutrition, diet,' Naomi added.

The Lebanese student raised her hand. 'Infections?'

'Anything else?' Naomi waited, but the students looked blank.

'What you'll notice here is a constant tension between what is best for the woman and what is best for her baby.'

An orderly appeared at the door. 'Samples for Path?' Naomi shook her head.

'In addition to a general physical examination, including height, weight and blood pressure, several lab procedures are included: tests of urine and haemoglobin and serology.'

'Sexually transmitted diseases?' the Lebanese student asked.

'Yes, we'll take bloods. Anyone squeamish at the sight of blood?'

'Just Rodriguez,' they said in unison.

'Might be hard to find a vein on a junkie,' the Lebanese student remarked casually.

Naomi sat forward in her chair and looked intently at each of them: 'Try not to prejudge the woman. There's a fine line between clinical diagnosis and judgement. We need to keep an open mind, view the woman as a whole person.'

Naomi knew that if she taught these students anything useful at all, it would have to be acceptance. After all, hadn't that been the very thing that preserved her sanity?

'The blood will also be tested for its Rh property, whether it is . . . ?' Naomi looked expectantly at the students.

'Rh positive or Rh negative,' the other student offered.

'Why?'

'Can't remember,' the student admitted.

'Shall we find . . .' Naomi hesitated as she looked for the name of the woman on the notes, 'Chelsea in the waiting room?'

The waiting room was full. The Iranian clinic was open and all the women in there were entirely veiled in black, except one. A thin, fair-haired young woman sat staring off into the distance. She was wearing a tank top and low-cut jeans, a tattoo covering one shoulder. There was something familiar in the way she sat low in the chair, her thin shoulders hunched slightly forward. Zoe?

This was Naomi's nightmare. That Zoe would randomly

turn up at the clinic. That she would be pregnant with another child, and another child, and another. For all Naomi knew, Zoe had indeed gone on to have more children. Noel had always maintained that they would know when, and if, Zoe had more children but Naomi was not so sure.

'Zoe?' Naomi said, approaching the young blonde-haired woman tentatively. The woman looked through her. That empty, glazed stare. The junkie stare.

'Zoe? Don't you mean Chelsea?' the Lebanese student interrupted.

'I mean . . .' Naomi stumbled over the name. 'Chelsea?' Naomi looked down at the notes in her hand again for reassurance.

Chelsea stood. She slipped her feet into her thongs and, clutching her shoulder bag, padded across the carpet to Naomi. The Iranian men eyed her with a mixture of suspicion and desire, worry beads flying through their thick fingers. The women held their children close.

'Chelsea, I have some student nurses visiting,' Naomi said, forcing a smile. 'Do you mind if they sit in today?'

'Sure, they can sit in on the circus,' she said with a dismissive flick of her fair head.

Truly

Max really and truly loved Gran. He loved her hands. They weren't beautiful hands or anything, they were old and wrinkled. But they were strong hands. They could plunge into really hot, soapy water in the kitchen sink and find a missing fork. They could tie broken shoelaces and snap the stem of a flower in two, but more importantly they could put a Band-Aid on a cut finger quick-smart. Max could rely on those hands.

Gran had the medicine box open on the kitchen table and disinfectant and Band-Aids out. She swabbed Max's bloody knee efficiently and gently at the same time. Max tried not to cry. It stung like mad.

'It'll stop stinging in a mo,' Naomi said. 'How about a hot chocolate in the meantime?'

Max nodded.

This would never have happened if Grandpa had still been their coach, Max thought as he looked at his injured knee. Harry's older brother didn't know a thing about hockey. He was less than useless.

Max loved Gran deeply, but not completely. He watched her pour the milk into his favourite cup. There was the hole left by Grandpa, and since the funeral a small part of Max's

127

heart was now roped off for Zoe. Mum. He had started to think about that word. It seemed a strange, too-short word that would take some getting used to. But if she ever did decide to be his mother again, he would be ready. He would *try*.

Part II

Popped

Zoe was sitting halfway down the train carriage, looking through her reflection at the houses and cars beyond the train tracks. She did not see houses and cars though. She saw instead her mother's life in Kingswood. A thirsty expanse of struggling lawn, a small wooden fence that wouldn't keep out a cat and a fair-haired, child-sized Zoe, eyes semi-closed against the sun. Her mother was still there in Park Avenue, Kingswood, but these days she had retreated behind the venetian blinds and frosted glass panes. Zoe tried not to think of her mother, but sometimes it just happened. In fact, the harder she tried not to think of her, the more thoughts about Sandra popped into her head. And her father? Dennis had popped out of her life last year, before she could really make things right. Perhaps his death had started all this 'making things right' stuff. Dennis had gone out to buy a packet of cigarettes and never returned, his life burst out of him under the speeding wheels of a semi-trailer as he crossed the Great Western Highway.

It wasn't that Zoe was having second thoughts or anything. She was simply having thoughts. Right now she was thinking about Naomi. Bad thoughts too. Couldn't she see that the children belonged to Zoe?

She put the thoughts about her mother-in-law to one side – Naomi was so broken that it was impossible to break her any further. She would think about the boys instead. She would be ready for them in a way that her mother had never been ready for her. Nothing about them would surprise her. She had a place to live and enough money to survive. She had Gavin to help. She could do this.

The letter

When Naomi saw the contents of the letterbox, she knew. These days there was little apart from bad news in the mail – bills, belated sympathy cards, junk mail, more bills. There it was, an envelope bearing the name of a firm of family-law solicitors: Underwood. Naomi hesitated – perhaps she would simply not open it. She could leave it there. Or, better still, write 'return to sender' across it. She shuffled through the rest of the mail, an invitation to get broadband, a local precinct meeting notice, a Thai takeaway menu, a roof repairer's card, and back again to Underwood Solicitors.

Chris and Max's mother wanted them. That was better than their mother not wanting them, surely?

Naomi knew how slowly the wheels of bureaucracy could turn. She would buy more time, drag it out, delay after delay. Perhaps the boys could complete primary school in peace, somehow.

Naomi's day at the hospital was still ringing in her ears. It had been pretty routine, which meant hectic as hell. She had examined Yom again. Marial presented her with a bunch of fresh coriander from among their parcels of shopping. She was touched, but had no time to dwell on their meeting, conscious of the long list of women waiting to be seen. No time, that is, until now.

The baby was small for gestation. 'I will order an ultrasound,' she had explained to Yom and then switched on the Doppler. Yom's face split into a big toothy smile when she heard her baby's heartbeat.

'Marial!' Yom had called out to him, delighted.

Naomi had continued to move efficiently through the examination, as the pungent smell of the coriander filled her office. Better than latex gloves and antiseptic swabs any day.

'Her baby is speaking to her today,' Marial explained from the other side of the curtain.

'Then ask the baby to speak in English please, Marial,' Naomi had said, coming around the curtain. 'The interpreter is late and we can't wait for him.'

Marial smiled. He had teeth as crooked as tombstones. He adjusted his shirt collar and resumed the role of interpreter. Yom asked about Naomi's grandchildren. Naomi frowned now as she recalled saying to Marial, 'You remember everything, don't you?'

He had smiled, 'You are belonging to us.' Marial searched for the right word in his limited English vocabulary. 'We want to help you.'

From the other side of the earth, from inside a war zone, from a treeless refugee camp and still they wanted to care for her. When they looked into her eyes, they could see her, really see her.

'Thank you,' she said, humbled, and before she realised what she was doing, she blurted out, 'Now my daughter-in-law wants to take them from me!'

Marial's eyes narrowed. 'Surely you will live together?'

Naomi shook her head. No, not possible. She had tried that before with disastrous consequences. Zoe had stolen, cheated and lied. Naomi didn't like the person that Zoe forced her to become.

'But you can help each person,' he said.

'Other,' Naomi corrected him absent-mindedly. 'If that was possible, we would have done it by now,' she said wearily. Since Noel's death Max was often under Naomi's feet, at a loose end. Chris was increasingly withdrawn – it was hard to know what he thought or felt. She observed him sitting down at the piano, swaying towards the keys as if about to start, but then veering off. She refused to add Zoe into the mix.

Closing the front door firmly behind her, Naomi walked briskly through the house to her bedroom, picking up the broom on the way.

'I have a huntsman the size of a dinner plate that needs dealing with!' Naomi said. She had taken to speaking to herself loudly and firmly since Noel's death, as if to take herself in hand. Not that Noel had ever talked to her that way. The voice she used came from before Noel's time; it came from the farm in Grenfell. Her father spoke that way to his dogs.

There, on the ceiling fan in her bedroom, the huntsman sunbathed in the light from the north-facing window. She was tempted to leave it alone, except that lately it had invaded her dreams and made her uneasy in the middle of the night.

She picked up the broom and poked at the fan. The spider leapt sideways and so did she, mirroring its movements. Now it dangled by a long thread over her head. Huntsmans had bad timing, running across the car windscreen when you were changing lanes, or falling in your lap at someone's dinner party. Huntsmans were stupid and big and hairy, the Great Danes of spiders.

'Of all the places to be, this one decides to dangle over my head,' Naomi said. 'Enough!'

They faced each other squarely.

'You're just looking for trouble,' Naomi said, crazily swinging the broom a little wide. As she did so, she could feel the firmness of the letter in her pocket – stiff, unyielding. It must have taken Zoe quite a bit of effort to generate that letter.

She knocked the fan and it wobbled, showering dust all over her bed. The huntsman shimmied up the stem of the fan towards the ceiling.

The letter involved a visit to a solicitor, getting the solicitor to agree to act for Zoe and to write the letter. Paying some money – or proving she was eligible for Legal Aid.

Naomi swung the broom furiously, her arms and neck arched painfully towards the ceiling.

The letter meant that Zoe was definitely serious.

The spider sat there out of range, so still it could have been a shadow.

The letter was an escalation.

Naomi's wild swings arced above her head. Her broom collided with one of the blades of the fan, *clack*, wood on metal.

Perhaps, just perhaps, the letter was a sign that Zoe had changed. Naomi mulled this over as she whacked the fan again, this time harder, firmer.

The spider lurched forward, confused, two of its legs raised as if to question her.

Naomi turned over the idea of change in her mind. Did she really believe that people could change? She had been open to the possibility just before Noel's death. There was a small part of her that was pleased Zoe might have changed, but she could not afford to dwell on this for too long, or she would lose her nerve.

She swung hard. Again and again. Thrashing and slicing through the air like a Samurai warrior. She caught the edge of the fan, *thwack*. This time the force of the blow tore it from the ceiling. It hung there for a split second, gaping, grinning at her. Naomi gasped. Then the whole thing crashed down, bringing a large piece of ceiling plaster with it.

'What have I done?'

The fan and its mounting plate bounced twice on her bed before skidding sideways, shedding years of dust then rolling to a full stop.

Naomi threw down her broom and above her the huntsman disappeared into the attic through the hole left in the ceiling.

'I trusted you with my firstborn. Didn't I deliver both your sons? Despite my better judgement, I welcomed you into my family!' Naomi was shouting now.

The dust swirled around her, each small individual particle suspended in the thick afternoon sunshine.

When her heart had stopped pounding, she said quietly, 'And now?'

Chris and Max might not feel the same way as she did, she wasn't sure. Children were so unpredictable. What did they know? Naomi sat on the edge of her bed, tears now running down her cheeks.

'Gran?' Max called, the front door slamming shut a moment later.

There were light footsteps on the wooden floorboards outside her bedroom.

Naomi looked at the bedroom clock. 3.30 pm.

'Gran?' he called again, this time a small note of uncertainty in his voice.

137

'I'm in here,' Naomi replied thickly, hoping to reassure him. She wiped her small pointy face with the back of her hands quickly. One, two.

'Gran?' Max's head appeared around the doorframe.

Representation

Less than a fortnight later Naomi found herself sitting in another lawyer's office, one near the hospital, one recommended by a (now divorced) staff surgeon.

'I like to help people,' Colin Eastman said, sitting forward in his chair. His office door was a frosted glass panel bearing fine gold letters: Colin Eastman, Family Law Specialist. From where Naomi sat she read it backwards: tsilaicepS waL ylimaF, namtsaE niloC. It made her think of Hungarian folk songs and Mevlevi dervishes.

Naomi wanted to believe him, to trust him. She even managed a small, encouraging smile, but it didn't travel as far as her eyes. She didn't want his help, she wanted justice. She wanted respect and protection.

'You help people, Mrs, er, Adams, in your profession,' he continued, looking out of the window, not at Naomi.

Naomi pushed the letter from Underwood Solicitors across the desk to him. It was pristine, the envelope still unopened.

'What do you make of this?' she asked.

He looked at her carefully and then opened the letter, slowly, gently, as if its contents were sleeping.

On her side of the desk, Naomi clasped her hands across

her shoulder bag, a pen between her fingers. She glanced down at her skirt. She had dressed quickly for work, without attention to whether the skirt matched the top, just that it was clean.

Colin turned over the letter in his hand. 'It's a standard claim.'

'Claim?' Naomi wanted to press him for more but she was having trouble engaging her mental gears.

He ran his hand over his chin; a pair of gold cufflinks caught Naomi's eye. 'Your daughter-in-law, isn't it?'

In his voice there was a trace of private boys' school, somewhere behind his flattened Australian vowels. Naomi was used to picking through people's English. The 'isn't it' was a dead weight, not a real question, nor punctuation either.

'If you go to court, you won't get what you want. No one will. You'll have to come to an arrangement, a compromise. The court will work out a deal and the deal will be flawed. It is never all one way or the other.'

Naomi cleared her throat. She had picked out the key words – 'You won't get what you want' – from Colin's advice.

'But I can't agree to let her have the children. She's a virtual stranger to them.' Naomi was speaking in bullet points, her chest tight. She ran on, 'My husband has died. They're settled where they are – school, friends, sport, music.'

'How much are you prepared to spend?' The solicitor cut across her. He did not want to hear the details of her case. They would get to that, but by then he would be being paid to listen to her. 'I know that sounds rude,' he continued, 'but this could take all your savings. You need to be prepared for that. You need to think about that now. The other stuff comes later.'

'That seems like a strange place to start,' Naomi said, frowning.

'You will not get justice. You will get a settlement. The minute you hand a decision over children or property to a third party, you lose control of the process.' The solicitor leant forward; he was sure about this and he was sure that Naomi did not understand it, but that she would eventually digest the information in the solitude of her own kitchen or alone in a busy city coffee shop. More importantly, how much would this grandmother be willing to spend?

'No doubt to you the most important question is whether justice will prevail,' Colin said a little patronisingly.

'Spare me the lecture about justice,' Naomi snapped. 'I realise I have a fight on my hands.'

Soft spot

There was a time when Zoe had admired Naomi, looked up to her, been awed by her. Naomi was fearless. She talked about things like sex and politics. She was not afraid to contradict a police officer. She read books. She did not suffer fools. She swam in the ocean. She argued with Noel about French philosophy. She went to the film festival. She took photographs. She wore outrageous earrings.

Zoe could not imagine her own mother ever being like that. They didn't discuss anything important. It wasn't their way. If her mother talked, Zoe didn't listen.

Even though Naomi was strong and bold, she could be warm and soft with Zoe. More importantly, Naomi was the first older woman that Zoe took seriously. Naomi actually listened to what she had to say. It was terrifying at the start. When Naomi listened she concentrated, she looked Zoe in the eye. She asked questions. It was as if what Zoe had to say was really important. Zoe's mouth would dry up, she would be lost for words. She would run out of breath.

Zoe heard Naomi tell people about her daughter-in-law's kind nature, her talent as an artist and her bright future.

When the children were born, Naomi was there – a solid rock, Zoe's anchor, even when things began to spiral out of control after Max's birth. Naomi made space in her life for Zoe in a way that her own mother could not.

Zoe tried not to remember Naomi this way. It made everything that much harder.

Band concert

Whenever Naomi was asked to describe what it was like to be a grandparent carer, she said it was 'like running a marathon'. She had thought long and hard about this. It wasn't the sprint against time that was motherhood. No, it was more about pacing yourself. If she was asked to give advice to another woman or man finding themselves in a similar situation, she would say, 'Get fit or you'll be no use to anyone.' There was other advice she could add, such as, 'Don't expect too much,' and 'Stay calm and practical and organised,' but lecturing wasn't her style.

'Do you have your clarinet books?' Naomi sang out from the kitchen.

'Where are my shoes, Gran?' Max asked.

'You left them by the heater.'

Max ran past her, in the wrong direction, in his socks and school pants, pants that needed letting down *again*, Naomi noticed.

'The heater, Max,' Naomi reminded him. 'You'll need a shirt too,' Naomi called out. 'Chris, do you have your books?' she continued without looking up from the sink. 'We'll be late,' she said, to no one in particular, sloshing the dirty breakfast dishes around in the hot, soapy water.

Chris hovered beside her, books, clarinet in hand. She turned and almost fell over him. 'Great. Out to the car,' she said, giving him a cursory once-over. Hair done. Clean school shirt. Musical instrument and music. She wiped her hands on a tea towel.

'Where are my shoes again, Gran?' Max said.

'By the heater.'

Naomi gathered her car keys. 'The band-concert note?' She picked up her shoulder bag. 'Has anyone seen it?'

She opened what she referred to as 'the school drawer', a kitchen drawer bulging with things to do with the boys' lives – school, music and sport. Max's spelling sheet lay on the top, then his superstar award for 'Excellent improvisation work in Drama', a Year 2 class list, a school newsletter, Max's awards folder on which he had written: 'Get ready to see my awards – all of them! THANK YOU!'

She lifted up the folder and the other papers on top of it, and kept riffling. An assessment notice for child-care benefit, a prospectus for the Conservatorium of Music, a newspaper supplement on Gallipoli, the school-camp notices (which she had painstakingly paid off in small instalments), Chris's clarinet teacher's invoice, Ben's English dictionary, which Chris, in Year 4, could now use, but didn't. She straightened up.

'Is this what you're looking for?' Max said, waving a blue notice headed 'Instructions for Parents and Carers Taking Children to the Annual School Band Festival' under her nose.

'Where was that?'

'In my trumpet case,' Max said.

Naomi grabbed a couple of bananas as a stop-gap afternoon tea and collected Max's instrument and his music. At the front door he stopped still. 'Better bring a jumper?'

'Yes, quickly now!' Naomi said over her shoulder as she opened the car door for Chris.

Signora Toto appeared at her front door as Max ran out with a jumper under his arm.

'Ciao, Signora Adams,' she started.

Naomi's heart sank. No time.

'Ciao, Signora Toto,' she said quickly. 'We're off to a band concert.'

'Eh?'

'Band concert, *musica*, for the children, *si?*' Naomi tried as she dumped Max's musical instrument and the makeshift afternoon tea onto the back seat next to Chris.

'It's a nice Sydney day,' Signora Toto began.

'Yes, lovely,' Naomi quickly agreed. 'Max!'

'Signora Adams, where you go?' Signora Toto asked.

'Band concert.' This time Naomi did not bother trying to translate it. She raised her eyebrows. 'We're a bit late.'

Never having done this before, Naomi was worried that they might miss the meeting place. As she drove, she took out the instructions and studied them at the traffic lights. She steered them towards the university, the traffic around them full of families and young people headed to parks and beaches. They drove through the Lebanese quarter and its falafel restaurants and on down Cleveland Street to where it opened out under elephantine Moreton Bay fig trees. It was easy to be swept up in the sunshine and the warm afternoon.

At the university Max quickly dropped his trumpet into Naomi's arms and ran off to play with a couple of the other boys from the band. Chris hovered closer to her, methodically eating the bananas.

There were school bands from all over Sydney. Naomi watched them milling around – some neatly dressed, instruments polished, bright faces. Then there were the other bands like the one Chris and Max belonged to – drab school uniforms, boys wearing earrings, spiky hair. Naomi smiled. She had never done anything like this with her own sons and she was quietly excited to be given a second chance to be here.

'Eight dollars admission,' the man on the door said.

She scraped together the money from the loose change in her bag.

'I have it exactly,' she said, pleased. She had made good use of the loose change at the bottom of her bag for many years, it gave her a quiet sense of satisfaction.

According to the program, twelve bands were to play before the boys' band. Naomi took out her knitting.

The first band was a jazzy knockout. Shiny buckles on their berets, a smiling, happy performance. The next one was even better – loud, brassy. Naomi dutifully clapped for each, wondering how the boys' band would hold up. The parents around her kept creeping forward as seats were vacated by other parents leaving after their child had finished.

Suddenly the boys' band was announced. Another parent, who knew Naomi slightly, whispered as she pushed forward, 'A lot of the bands don't turn up.'

Naomi put down her knitting and, catching Chris's eye, waved to him. He smiled back, his eyes shiny, excited.

'I felt so alive,' Chris almost shouted at Naomi in the car on the way home, waving his hands about. 'Gran, I felt so alive!'

She nodded. 'I know, I could see it on your face.'

Old men

Zoe had this fantasy. Gavin would build her a studio in the country. She would make new sculptures and exhibit her work in Paris and Rome, and fall in love with him, like she had not with Ben but had with Jesse – quietly and deeply.

In her dream she married this new Gavin, only he looked like Jesse and sounded like Jesse and acted like Jesse. Not a white wedding or anything, just a simple party at home – their home. This time she married the right one. They planted their own garden and collected wild honey and made a chicken pen. They had an olive grove and thick jasmine twisted around the solid verandah posts, potted mint and parsley and bright red chillies. The boys came to live with her and they grew tall and strong. Gavin taught them to skate-board and snowboard. They loved him like a father. He built them things. He lived to be an old man; the boys grew old as well. Before that, they did well at school and became famous for something, everything. She had friends. Lots of them. She made delicious creations in her country-style kitchen. Things that used the eggs from her chickens, such as pavlovas and rich, creamy quiches. She had another baby that she could push in the stroller to the shops to meet other mothers. This time it would be a girl. They would all love this baby and Zoe would call her Naomi because she wanted her to grow into a strong and wise woman.

Mediation

Naomi understood that at the end of the court process she might no longer recognise herself. It was the same way with birth: women were transformed by the experience. They were often unrecognisable two years later when they appeared at the door to her clinic with baby number two, or three, or four. At least they had a baby or babies to show for it, but as she sat opposite the court-appointed counsellor, she realised for the first time, that there was a real chance she would lose the boys.

'I know I have a fight on my hands,' Naomi began.

'That's *not* how we like to see it,' the counsellor said.

'I wouldn't be here if we could come to an agreement,' Naomi said sharply. Renewed anger – deep personal anger – gripped her. It was palpable today. 'There is no way I'm going to let Zoe have the boys,' she added, surprising even herself.

The counsellor, a young man dressed in a smart two-piece suit and tie, raised his eyebrows. She felt another shot of anger at this, which she struggled to control. He remained silent.

'Tell me how you like to see it, then?' she asked.

She had arrived early for her mediation and had walked slowly through the court building, catching snatches of conversations – 'The affidavits say the opposite' and 'Will we reach a decision today?' and 'I've left the documents at home, again!' – and then she stopped listening and started looking. The court was a modern building, the last one having been destroyed by a bomb about ten years earlier. There was no reference in this modern place of business to its past troubles, at least not in the public areas.

Painted the same ripe apricot throughout, nondescript art on the walls, the courthouse could have been any government office block. There was a playroom for children with a cubby house. Naomi looked at the security screening and the people streaming in through the front door. They were old and young and weary and scared, people in all their inglorious shapes and sizes. It was the same in the hospital waiting room. Naomi loved the transformative moment when people in the waiting room dropped their cloak of anonymity and became someone with a story, a medical history, a family, a home, dreams, desires.

In the building there was a camera mounted on every wall and alarm switches in the women's bathrooms, which held reminders about domestic violence. At the front door, hadn't she passed through a bulletproof glass door and a metal detector? There was tension in the air, despite the faint Percy Grainger compilation being piped throughout the waiting areas. A newborn baby began screaming. Today that sound had the same effect as fingernails across a blackboard. She got up and walked quickly away down the corridor.

The counsellor's office was painted the same ripe apricot and furnished with low lounge chairs around a redwood coffee table, not dissimilar to those found in a hotel foyer or doctor's waiting room.

Outside his office she had waited quietly for her number to be called. The woman sitting next to her, a veteran of two divorces, three biological children and three step-children, told her, 'Grandparents have a perfect right to apply for a residency or a contact order under the *Family Law Act*.'

Naomi had nodded.

'But often they're not aware of their rights,' the woman had added.

'What about your children's grandparents?' Naomi asked.

The woman shook her head. 'Some are better than others. I have six sets of grandparents to coordinate, and several of them are not on speaking terms with me,' she had laughed.

'The court wants to find a settlement,' the counsellor was saying.

'Settlement? I don't want a settlement. I thought this was the justice system?' Naomi said, her voice rising.

The man looked at her impassively.

'Not a good way to begin,' she said to him. 'I'm sorry, I . . .' Her voice trailed off. Excuses? What excuses could she list to a court-ordered counsellor? Hadn't he heard it all before?

'It's my job to stop people like you . . . Naomi,' he said, after checking her name on the notes in his hand, 'and your daughter-in-law, Zoe, from going to court.'

Naomi nodded. 'I completely understand. I don't really know what I'm doing here. I can't believe this is happening.' Naomi thought of the two boys. Right now they were at an athletics carnival.

'It's very distressing, but see it as an opportunity,' he said implausibly.

'I think we're probably what you would call "intractable",' Naomi said with a small laugh to hide her sudden shame.

'I'm afraid I don't believe in that term, intractable,' he said. 'And please own this. None of this "we". I want you to talk about *you*, give me more of *you*.'

Naomi smiled tightly. 'I understand.'

'Good. Tell me about yourself,' he said, pen poised over paper.

'I'm a midwife, nearing retirement now. Was married to the same man, Noel, for more of my life than not. We were never rich but we had enough to get by. A couple of kids. Although I never took our life for granted, I didn't question it either, you know?'

The counsellor nodded.

'Then suddenly it all changed. My sons hardly had a chance to grow up before they were both killed in the same car accident. You read about things like that in the paper and think how hard they must be for the family. Well, I used to, then it happened to me. But you have no idea. I've seen it at work too – people losing babies, stillbirths. None of it prepares you. I used to think that things happen for a reason, but now I don't. I'm bitter about what happened to my family. That's the good part about raising my grandkids, they just get on with their lives. And my job, at the hospital, you know, is a bright spot too.'

'So you like your work?'

Naomi said nothing.

The counsellor sat still. He reminded Naomi of Max's stuffed toy gorilla, Troy. It was something about the angle of his head in relation to his shoulders. He had no neck. Probably an asset in his line of work.

'I find this a bit of an ordeal. Since my sons died, I don't have much patience, sometimes,' Naomi said after a pause.

The counsellor sat forward in his chair. 'Good, we're getting somewhere now.' He wrote something down on his notepad.

Getting somewhere, Naomi thought to herself; nowhere I want to go. 'My eldest son, Ben, married a woman – a girl, really – Zoe,' she said.

She could not afford to make mistakes with this man, but things were popping out of her mouth all over the place. She knew he was probably writing down things like 'resistant' and 'difficult', that she had to show him she could get herself under control, but somehow she just couldn't. This man was forming an opinion of her, scrutinising her 'affect', her demeanour, her dress. Her stupid open sandals. How she told her story was as important as what she said, and she tried not to flinch at the thought. 'Zoe was with Ben and my other son, Jesse, in the car crash. She survived. They both died.'

Naomi paused. She felt short of breath.

'Zoe and Ben had two sons, Chris and Max, both of whom have lived with me practically all their lives, on and off, even before the accident.'

'Tell me about your daughter-in-law,' the young man said, interrupting her.

'I don't really know what to say. To be honest, I don't know her now. I haven't spoken to her properly in maybe five years.'

The counsellor waited for her to continue and she obliged, after a pause.

'The Zoe I knew was a good person. Perhaps a little too young to be a mother, but well enough intentioned, you know?'

Naomi relaxed a little, remembering the way Ben had proudly introduced Zoe to her and Noel. Naomi had tried to keep an open mind. Later, she had pretended she was delighted that they were having a baby. She had also pretended that Zoe was the daughter-in-law she had always wanted.

Naomi laughed. 'I had high hopes. I thought she was capable of greatness. She was talented and beautiful, such a free spirit. I was proud of my sons, and therefore proud to be Zoe's mother-in-law.'

This was such an oversimplification, but it sounded plausible to Naomi. 'It was just that she became a mother too young,' she added.

'Children too young,' the counsellor repeated, looking intently at Naomi. He was not at all interested in Zoe, Naomi realised with a start. He was asking about Zoe to form an opinion about Naomi herself.

'Things between her and Ben were rocky after the birth of Max. She wasn't coping, she had a bit of postnatal depression.' Naomi's lips were suddenly dry; she took a sip of water. 'She became difficult to reach.'

'What happened after the car accident?'

'After the inquest, Zoe completely lost the plot and eventually disappeared. I don't know how to explain it. We each dealt with our grief differently. My husband kept in touch with her, helped her, gave her money. He died suddenly about three months ago. Zoe turned up at his funeral and demanded the boys. That's it.'

'Did you tell the children that you were coming here today?'

Naomi swallowed hard. She knew this question went to the heart of the matter. What kind of relationship she had with the boys.

'No,' she answered honestly.

She had toyed with the idea of telling them everything, and at first she had intended to, attempted to, but the only thing she had to hold onto was the idea that this would all go away.

The counsellor wrote in his notes.

'These boys are children. They deserve a childhood,' she said. 'Please write that down as well.'

Pick up

Naomi mulled over the session with the counsellor, turning it this way and that in her mind, as she drove home through the early afternoon traffic. It was not the things that he had said, but rather what he had forced her to say. She saw herself through his eyes. Unconvincing, old, dogmatic.

At school the buses had already arrived back from the sports oval. Children wearing their different-coloured t-shirts representing the four sports houses – Menzies, Monash, Barton and Chifley – milled around.

'The kids look tired,' said a young mother at Naomi's elbow.

'It was a hot day for athletics,' Naomi remarked.

'Will this drought ever end?' The woman sighed.

'No time soon,' Naomi said. 'The ground must have been very hard.' She looked down at the dirt around her sandals.

'Most of the turf on the oval has disappeared,' the woman continued. 'Soccer.'

'Which house won?' Naomi asked the woman, preparing for the inevitable heartfelt discussion with Max.

'Barton,' the woman replied.

'Oh no,' Naomi laughed. 'Don't tell me Chifley came last again!'

'I'm not sure.'

'Probably,' Naomi groaned, 'they usually do.'

The boys belonged to Chifley and had left this morning in their green t-shirts with both their chests puffed out.

The woman collected her hot child and turned to go. 'Which kids are you—' she said, hesitating, and adding the final 'rs' clumsily.

'My grandchildren, Chris and Max Adams.'

While they had been talking, the playground had gradually thinned out. Suddenly there were hardly any children left. Naomi looked around. Harry was playing on the equipment.

'Have you seen Max?' she asked him.

'He went home from the oval,' Harry said.

'Who with?'

'The lady at the sports oval.' Harry picked up his bag and ran off towards Mary. 'His aunty?' he shouted over his shoulder at Naomi.

'No,' Naomi whispered, as she began lurching across the playground towards the principal's office, 'his mother.'

The school principal was a tall, thin man with a slight stoop. The late afternoon sun cast long, lonely shadows across his desk. Naomi sat opposite him on the edge of a low vinyl chair. He was casually dressed in a shirt and slacks. Every time he moved he revealed a small 'v' of sunburn at his open collar. 'A long, hot day,' he said to himself as he cradled the phone on his shoulder.

'You must alert the police if the children turn up,' he said over the top of the phone.

Naomi nodded.

'Your daughter-in-law knows where you live, right?'

'Yes,' Naomi said through bloodless lips. 'Perhaps I should go home and wait there?' she asked him.

But he wasn't listening.

'You must inform the school about these family matters,' he said crossly to Naomi, and then spoke into the handpiece, 'Missing persons. Yes, I'll hold.' He looked down at Naomi, 'I thought their mother was dead?'

'She was.'

Naomi was vomiting in the bathroom when she heard the front doorbell. She ran to the door and opened it. On the doorstep stood Gwen and Evelyn clutching a Pyrex dish full of meat loaf.

'Don't tell me you forgot we were coming to dinner?' Gwen said, smiling and glancing across at Evelyn. They exchanged a brief I-told-you-so look.

'The boys are missing,' Naomi said.

The two sisters' smiles froze.

At 7 pm two police officers appeared at the front door.

'We have interviewed the boy from number one-three-seven,' said one of the officers, consulting his notebook.

'Harry,' Naomi said.

'You say the alleged abductor is,' he consulted his notes again, 'the boys' mother?'

'I think so. They wouldn't just go off with anyone.'

Noel's two sisters hovered behind Naomi in the hallway. Harry and Mary walked up the front steps and stood behind the police officers. Naomi felt nauseous again.

At eight there was another knock at the door. Naomi, Harry, Mary and Noel's sisters were splayed out around the kitchen table like a pack of playing cards. All snapped to attention but stayed put, except Naomi.

When she opened the door, Zoe and the boys were standing on the front doorstep, Max shivering slightly in the cold. The feeble front-porch light cast them in a thin, yellow glow.

'The boys never stop to knock,' Naomi heard Gwen say quietly in the kitchen.

Naomi looked from Max to Chris to Zoe. She wasn't sure whether she should be grateful or angry.

'Where have you been?' she asked, looking at Chris.

Max barged in past Naomi and grunted.

Chris looked at the ground.

'Zoe, I was so worried about the boys,' Naomi said.

'No need to worry,' Zoe said brightly. 'We would have phoned, but I didn't have any money.'

The two women looked at one another.

'How will you get home?' Naomi asked.

Zoe shrugged.

'Let me give you twenty dollars,' Naomi said, turning from the door. 'Come in,' she said over her shoulder. She turned and nearly tripped over Noel's sisters.

'No. Got to get going. It's late,' Zoe said, her quicksilver smile and bright eyes flashing in the dark of the doorway. 'It was great to see the boys,' she said brightly. Chris hung back behind her.

Naomi chose her words carefully in front of him. 'Next time, just tell me first, okay?' Her mouth was dry, her heart pounding in her ears. As she handed Zoe the money, her hand shook slightly.

'Gee, thanks!' Zoe said.

'How did you manage to get home from the oval?' Naomi asked Max later as he lay stiffly in bed.

Noel's sisters had pursed their lips and departed, washing up before they left, the family dinner in tatters. Harry and his mother slid out the door, giving Naomi a wide berth.

'We walked,' he said and rolled over, away from Naomi.

'I'm unhappy this happened to you,' Naomi said.

'I had to go because of Chris. I saw them across the oval; he just went off with her. I missed my race! I had to run to catch up with them!'

'I'm sorry,' Naomi said.

'I didn't know how to get home from there,' Max said, starting to cry, 'and Chris wouldn't help. I told Zoe to ring you up. "Gran will come and get us," I said, but she didn't have any money.'

'It took all that time to walk home?' Naomi asked.

'Yes,' he sobbed, 'I was so scared.'

'There's nothing to be scared of, Max. Zoe is your mother and she means well. You did the right thing to go after Chris. Grandpa would have been proud of you.'

'She doesn't feel like my mother. She smells different, she says strange stuff, she doesn't know about hockey or AFL or anything.'

'What strange stuff?' Naomi asked, but Max was already asleep, exhausted.

Father's Day

Naomi got up early, alone. She made a pot of organic tea and raised her cup. 'To Noel,' she said quietly. Naomi had taken to talking *about* Noel, no longer *to* him, as she had done in the first months after his death. She would not remark on the fact that it was Father's Day to the boys. She would get through it as she had all the other anniversaries – Noel's birthday, Ben's birthday, Jesse's birthday, her wedding anniversary, her birthday – with little or no fuss, and if possible without mentioning Father's Day at all.

The house was quiet and warm. The sun had regained some of its heat now that winter was finally ending. She looked out onto the garden, as she had all those months ago, and thought about how she had wanted to give Zoe another chance back then. And now? She was fighting not to.

'Let's go shopping,' she suggested over breakfast.

'Max's idea of hell,' Chris said quietly.

'Do I have to go? Can't I stay and play with Harry?' Max began.

'I thought we could get some more software for the computer,' said Naomi, interrupting him.

After Noel's death the first thing she had done was buy a new computer for the boys. It was the biggest purchase she had made in several years. She and Chris researched it carefully. She spoke to the teachers at school, she quizzed other boys' parents, she read catalogues. She poured so much energy into that purchase. She even spoke to Sarah about it, more than once. 'It's not open-heart surgery,' Sarah had complained. 'Just buy the thing. It'll be out of date in two years anyway.'

'Can I go to Harry's, please?' Max tried again.

'Father's Day sucks,' Chris announced. 'They had us make stupid Father's Day cards at school.'

Naomi almost dropped the plates she was clearing from the table. If she had not been so preoccupied she would have remembered to speak to his teacher.

'So the stupid teacher said I should make one for my grandfather.'

Naomi noticed the way Chris referred to his teacher. He had, up until now, really liked her. She wanted to ask, 'Stupid? Since when did Miss Peters become stupid?' but she waited, sensing something else coming.

'But I don't have one of those either,' he paused, 'or not that I know of.'

It was so long since Chris had even alluded to his mother's side of the family. Probably it was way back when he was a preschooler. Naomi looked at him closely. Since meeting his mother at the funeral Chris had been different in small and subtle ways. He was never outright rude, but there was a creeping resentfulness, a sullenness, a new distance. And as a result, Naomi had backed away, telling herself that she must allow him more independence because he was growing up, because he was missing Noel, because he was like Jesse, because he was like Ben – everything she could think of, except that it was because he wanted Zoe in his life. She walked around him, the way she had walked around Ben. At ten years of age he held Naomi captive at arm's length.

Zoe's family remained a bit of a mystery to Naomi. Sandra and Dennis and a cat, she thought, or maybe a dog. There was definitely a pet. They were plain people, Zoe a virtual jewel among them. Not country people, not refugees. Just ordinary immigrant battlers, deeply suspicious of Ben and Jesse. Actually they were deeply suspicious of their own daughter. Naomi had tried with them. They weren't bad people, but they had nothing in common with Noel and Naomi, who couldn't help but see them as two people flattened by the dull and relentless suburbs of Sydney. Suburbs that Noel and Naomi only passed through, quickly, on their way somewhere else. But back then, one afternoon they had found Park Avenue and eaten vanilla slice and cheesecake with Sandra and Dennis and marvelled at how their families were now united, and made unspoken vows to become friends for their children's sake. They admired the Afghan hound, or was it a Persian cat? And Dennis's tomato plants. And after that? Zoe's parents were narrow people without curiosity, in Naomi's opinion. That day in Katoomba Hospital, with Zoe hanging between life and death, they had clung to Naomi, and she to them. But after the funeral of Ben and Jesse, in her bitterness Naomi stopped trying. She had cut them loose.

'So? I just helped Harry with his dad's one,' Max chimed in.

'Father's Day sucks, that's all,' Chris concluded. She wanted to contradict him, for Max's sake, if nothing else. She wanted to say something smart and insightful. Something that would touch him, but nothing useful would come to mind.

'I miss him too,' she finally said. 'Every day I have to remind myself not to forget him, even a little bit.'

Max left for Harry's house and she left Chris at home on the new computer. She headed to the bright, shiny shopping mall. She had to be with people.

Naomi had worked her way through the bookshop, KMart, Oxfam and was about to enter the organic supermarket when her hospital pager went off.

'Yom's baby,' she thought. She had been expecting this. If the baby did not come today, it was to be induced tomorrow. It was now day ten, the final possible overdue day. Some babies were divas from the start, others by contrast were very accommodating. Naomi had a theory – as she had about most things that mattered to her: people began life as they meant to live it. When she asked mothers what they had been doing while they waited for their overdue baby to arrive, some said they were still working, others said they were finishing off the nursery, even more said still preparing it! Some babies waited for their mothers to complete these tasks, even if that meant being ten days overdue. Yet others were simply bursting with life and the telling of it from the moment of conception and couldn't possibly wait forty weeks to be born. And then there were special babies, who arrived really undercooked, as tender as lambs, who would carry that tenderness with them for the rest of their lives.

Attending the delivery herself was not something she offered to every woman in her clinic. In fact, the hospital actively discouraged it as too expensive. But Yom was different. This baby was special. Naomi had a personal investment in a good outcome. If she was honest with herself, she hoped that this birth and the joy it would bring to this small family would mark the end of her own intense grieving.

She telephoned the birthing unit. An agency midwife was on duty – all the more reason to attend the birth – and told her that Yom was six centimetres dilated. Could she please come in? In the notes it had said to notify her.

Naomi made a second call to Chris. 'I have to attend a birth.'

Chris grunted. She could hear the television in the background.

'Where's Max?'

'Harry's house.'

Naomi hesitated. Chris did not help.

'You go across to Harry's too. I'll phone Mary and tell her to expect you shortly.'

'I don't want to.'

'Why?'

'I'm watching something on TV.'

'When it finishes, go across to Harry's.' Naomi tried to make her voice sound firm but fair.

Perhaps she would be home in a matter of an hour. False alarm? Swift birth? It could also be a long while before Yom gave birth. Naomi may have time to go back and forth a couple of times to the hospital. She dismissed the small suspicion in her mind that for the first time she was making an excuse to avoid Chris.

Marial was sitting alone outside the special-care nursery when Naomi finally found him. Yom had been attended by Ellen, a midwife with an active dislike of Naomi, and was now in the recovery unit after an emergency caesarean delivery of the baby.

'The baby's heart rate was dropping,' Marial explained, his eyes large and frightened, lowering his hand dramatically in a series of big swipes.

'Interpreter? Did someone get a Dinka interpreter?' Naomi said.

Marial shook his head. Naomi squeezed his hand. 'I'm sorry I wasn't here sooner.'

She gowned up. In the special-care nursery Ellen and the registrar were still working methodically, calmly, on the baby, a boy. Under the bright lights he was a stark, bloody mass of grey muscle and bone, not moving, not responding.

'We have a very sick baby,' Ellen said quickly to Naomi. 'The heart rate is still very low.'

'Perhaps I let her go too long,' Naomi said quietly.

Ellen shook her head. 'Now, don't go blaming yourself.'

'He's a bad colour,' Naomi said.

'Flat, very flat,' Ellen said.

'Where's the attending paediatrician?' Ellen shouted across the nursery.

'On his way,' one of the surgical team sang out.

Naomi sat beside Yom in Recovery and wordlessly held her hand. She lay on the theatre gurney, her head turned, her large eyes fixed on the door as if it might open and deliver her baby to her. Tears ran slowly, silently down her cheek and onto her pillow.

Naomi kept going over and over it – was there anything she missed antenatally? Any signs that this baby was not well? Had she been too distracted by her own problems to care properly for Yom, or any of her other expectant mothers, for that matter?

Her friend Patricia, coming on for the evening shift, appeared at the door of the recovery unit. Naomi left Yom for a moment to step outside with Patricia.

'I know what you're thinking. It's not your fault. Your practice was completely sound.'

'Should I have ordered another ultrasound, Patricia? The baby was small for its gestational date. We knew that.'

'So? There was no other indicator. You couldn't possibly have known this would happen.'

Marial was still sitting alone in the corridor and when she had finished speaking to Patricia, Naomi motioned to him, 'Come with me.'

Inside the special-care nursery a quickly assembled team was getting ready to transfer the baby to the neonatal intensive care unit at Westmead Hospital.

Naomi led Marial through the crowded nursery to where his son lay, so they could have a small, quiet moment in between the beeping of the monitor, the phone, X-rays and the incessant oxygen pump.

'You can touch him. You won't hurt him.'

Marial tentatively reached out to touch the baby's small hand. The child in turn curled his fingers immediately, tightly around Marial's forefinger.

In the recovery room next door Yom was waiting patiently to be transferred with the baby. The interpreter had now arrived and Naomi left Marial with his son and took the interpreter next door to Yom. She asked gently through the interpreter, 'Do you have a name for your baby?'

Yom's eyes softened.

'Deng,' she said hesitantly, as if in giving the child a name she was allowing herself some hope.

'Deng. That's great.'

'It means rain,' Marial said simply when Naomi asked him a little later. 'Child of the . . .' He hesitated, trying to find the right word in English. 'The child of the pieces of rain.' Deng still had his finger gripped. 'Will he . . . ?'

'We can't say, it's too early,' Naomi said.

Patricia appeared and began to speak to him in a mid-wifely fashion. 'I can tell you about the equipment and what it all does.'

Naomi moved away. Ellen was preparing her handover to the transport team. Deng was finally ready to be transferred.

How long had Naomi been at the hospital? Six hours? No, seven. The time! Where did Father's Day go? She had never called Mary. Naomi thought about the boys at Harry's house. 'Got to pick up the kids,' she said aloud, tearing off her overgown and hurrying towards the hospital car park. If she left now, she could get to Mary's before their bedtime.

'Yes, I got caught up at work,' Naomi repeated tersely.

Evelyn and Gwen politely shook their heads. 'You should have told us,' they said in unison. 'Chris was very distressed by the time he called us.'

'I arranged for him to go to Mary's across the road. I don't know why he didn't.'

'He didn't ring us until at least five.' Gwen looked at her sister.

'Almost six, I'd say.' Evelyn drew herself up.

'Usually he's happy to stay with Mary. Before, you know, Noel,' Naomi said. When she was at work Noel had taken care of the boys, she wanted to say, but what was the point? She pushed on into the brightly lit hall and dumped her bag on the lounge before sweeping through the house to the boys' bedroom, leaving Evelyn and Gwen standing in the sitting room.

Chris now lay on his bed, fully dressed and deeply asleep. Naomi turned away from his door. Noel's sisters ambushed her once more.

'He wouldn't eat or drink anything,' Gwen said, shaking her head.

'Max?' Naomi asked.

'Still at Harry's house,' they both answered.

'Thank God for Mary,' Naomi said, cranky with tiredness and more exasperated with Chris than she'd like. What had possessed him to call Noel's sisters? Why hadn't he gone over to Harry's, as she'd asked? She couldn't bring herself to even thank Gwen and Evelyn. She was so annoyed with Chris.

The garden

Naomi stood at the kitchen sink cleaning dirt out of her fingernails and looking out onto the garden. Chris had taken up Noel's spot in the hammock with one of the Harry Potter books in his hand, his lips moving ever so slightly every now and then. How quickly he had stepped into Noel's shoes. How much he reminded her of Jesse, lying there as vigilant as a cat. It was something about the way he concentrated; the intensity that he brought to everything, whether it be navigating a piece of music or finding his place in the world.

Naomi had spent the afternoon pulling out most of the garden. It had taken her months to get to this point. She had pruned back the grape and dug up what was left of the vegetable patch: the parsley gone to seed; dried stalks of long-departed beans, bitter lettuce, brittle passionfruit leaves. The new water restrictions prevented any hosing. What was left of the garden would have to wait for its life-giving water.

Chris did not move to help her. He showed no curiosity about what she was doing. He was revealing to her the new, watchful but aloof Chris. Naomi remembered Jesse being like this as a teenager, his need to live parallel to her. She gave him his space.

She opened the back door to better survey her afternoon's handiwork. The door swung smoothly. She'd had a local handyman in to re-hang it and now its glass panels no longer shuddered and refracted light she felt a pang of regret. One less memory of Noel.

Chris scowled at her. Naomi held his eye briefly before he dropped his gaze back to his book.

She found herself watching over the boys with a new intensity. What if Zoe kidnapped them? The newspapers were full of stories about estranged fathers kidnapping their children. These thoughts made her jumpy and anxious when she wasn't with them. She made sure she was at school waiting for them every afternoon before the bell rang. She felt that if she let them out of her sight she might never see them again. She knew this change in her was no good for Chris. He hated it.

His grip on his book was suddenly furious and intense.

'What is it?' he said impatiently, without looking up.

'I never asked you how it was seeing your mother again?'

Chris didn't answer her, but he stopped reading.

'Must have been a bit of a shock. To see her there, I mean. Just turning up out of the blue like that,' Naomi said.

'Not really,' he said, still staring at his book, now wary.

What if Zoe took them someplace from where they couldn't get back to her? Naomi had begun dreaming about it.

'I'm sorry,' Naomi said, a mocking tone creeping into her voice. 'You must be running into her everywhere you go?'

'As a matter of fact, I do see her around. A lot.'

Naomi hadn't been expecting this answer and she didn't know whether to believe him or not.

'What do you mean?'

'She hangs around the school sometimes, you know, at recess and lunch. I can see her through the fence.' Chris turned a page in his book. 'She just misses us, I guess.'

Naomi nodded. There were so many things she could have said, things she *should* have said, but what was the point? She knew all about missing sons.

Lemonade

Zoe was thrilled. She had her own place at last, all sixty dollars per week of it. It said so on the lease that she had just signed. A Department of Housing two-bedroom townhouse in a quiet street in Mt Druitt.

She opened the mission-brown front door, ignoring the scratches around its fleshy, pockmarked keyhole, and walked straight through from front to back. When she reached the back door, she turned around and retraced her lopsided steps. Ten paces. She liked that. The hallway ran from the front to the back door, and with both doors open you could see all the way through to a small backyard, patchy grass and all. There was a pile of rubbish in the backyard, which Zoe would examine carefully later, not now. She noted the Hills hoist clothes line and tried to imagine it full of little boys' school uniforms. Beyond the back paling fence was a reserve planted with lemon-scented gums. She could smell the eucalyptus right now.

Zoe walked back inside more slowly now, in and out of each of the five rooms. The walls told stories: a faint shadow where there had been a picture, or perhaps even a painting once; a scuff mark; a protruding nail head. She opened all the windows and turned on and off each of the light switches.

Twice. She might be able to work here, put a shed in the backyard and who knows? Sculpt, even? She stood at the kitchen sink and turned the tap on and off. The cupboards were empty. Not for long, she said to herself. She took off her backpack and put it in one of the mission-brown kitchen cupboards (there was nowhere else to put it until she got some furniture).

She was happy to see that this was the last townhouse in the row. No one on the other side, just one immediate neighbour to deal with. Zoe hadn't always disliked people, it was just that for so long now they had usually seemed to dislike her.

At the top of the narrow stairs, she walked into the first bedroom and stood at the window looking down into the backyard. She could get a basketball ring put up for the boys.

At nearly thirty years of age she felt like a parent, even if it was just a part-time parent. Sophie had said the house was contingent on the boys' weekend residency with her. At first, at least, it would have to be weekends only. But if that worked out well, anything was possible. She practised aloud: 'Go outside and play with your basketball, boys!'

'What're you saying?' It was Gavin at the front door.

Zoe ran down the stairs smack into his arms. She gave him a hug. He kissed her and laughed. 'Happy now?' he said.

She nodded and smiled. They stood together looking at the grubby hallway and the narrow stairs. She squeezed Gavin and dared to imagine a future in this brown brick-and-wood-plank townhouse, a *bright* future here with her boys.

'I hope there's enough room for them,' she said.

Gavin shrugged.

∽

Zoe spent that summer cleaning. She scrubbed the townhouse from top to bottom. It felt good to smell the sweet ammonia from the bathroom. She tacked up sheets as curtains. She cleaned the fridge with vanilla and warm water and thought about what food she would eventually put in it.

Gavin found her a spare single mattress and she decided to put the boys in her bed, she would take the spare mattress on the floor. She got sheets and pillowcases from St Vincent de Paul, and a secondhand indoor plant with long, dark green tendrils.

She bought potato chips and lemonade at the local supermarket with her sickness benefit, soon to be her supporting parent's benefit, she hoped. She watched ten-year-old boys on their skateboards in the park and tried to breathe in the essence of them.

She worked in the community garden and picked basil and lettuce.

She bought an alarm clock and waited for the court to set a date.

One night, two days

Max was exhausted already, and a whole sad weekend lay ahead. How many hours had it taken to get to Zoe's? A car trip with Gran to Blacktown. She didn't say much, except that they were to look after one another, and Zoe too. Then a graffiti-covered train ride with Zoe. A bus ride and a walk around a graffiti-covered block from the bus stop.

It looked like Zoe had made a big effort. Gran had told him to make a big effort too. Chris was making an extra-big effort. If everyone made a big effort, it should all be easy. The only problem was that Max didn't want it to be easy. He wanted his old life back.

Chris practically bounded through Zoe's front door. 'That bus driver was totally out of line. Did you see how he almost hit the Stop sign?'

Zoe smiled and nodded. Max walked behind silently, dragging his backpack along the ground. Long silences didn't faze Zoe. In fact, she didn't even notice how quiet he had been on the bus. She said something like, 'Made me feel giddy.' How can almost hitting a Stop sign make you feel 'giddy'? Max thought.

There was only one word to describe Zoe's place. Brown. Brown carpet. Brown cupboards. Brown grass.

Max's heart was beating a bit too fast and his tummy was full of small white moths. If he opened his mouth, they'd fall out everywhere.

'This is so cool, Mum,' Chris said.

Zoe beamed at Chris with pride and gratitude, and perhaps even, yuk, love. It made Max feel weird. He wanted to say something smart like, 'We're not supposed to speak to strangers,' just to take that smile off her face. Today the tryouts for the Glebe hockey club were taking place. Naomi said he couldn't try out if he was going to be away every second Saturday. He would be letting down the team.

'Sit down,' Zoe said, motioning to the one and only chair. It was brown and covered in darker brown stains.

'Stop being so random, Chris,' Max said under his breath, but loud enough for Zoe to hear. 'We're not staying long!'

That was exactly Max's problem though. They were staying for one night, two days – altogether far too long in Max's book. He dumped his bag on the floor. The carpet was greasy and smelt faintly of dog and cigarettes. It was the colour of a dog too, a brown one.

Chris and Zoe ignored Max.

'Something to drink?' she asked brightly.

'No, thanks,' Max said.

'Like what, Mum?' Chris said.

There was that word again. How often was Chris going to say 'Mum'? Every sentence? It was so obvious.

'Lemonade? I used to like that when I was your age,' Zoe offered.

'Okay then, Mum,' Chris said happily.

'Since when do you drink fizzy stuff, Chris?' Max accused Chris loudly.

'Since now,' Chris said testily.

Max turned on his heel and walked up the stairs. He could hear Zoe's voice behind him saying, 'Take a look around, make yourself at home, your room is at the top of the stairs.'

At the top of the stairs he entered the room. There was one double bed with brown sheets and a brown blanket. He'd be sharing with Chris then. He walked straight over to the window and stared out. There was practically no backyard, but behind the back fence there was a bit more space and a few trees, and he could see a couple of green leaves on them. He could kick a soccer ball there, he supposed. He sighed.

Uppity

The light streamed through a bank of high windows. Naomi sat in the office chair and thought about that light. She could just glimpse the true blue of the sky. She thought about truth, and then she thought, again, about chance. How was it that she was sitting here, at this point in time? She struggled to digest what was being said, to give it her full attention.

'The only signs antenatally were that she was overdue and the baby seemed small for gestation,' Naomi repeated quietly, almost to herself.

The consultant looked through the casenotes in his hand again.

Naomi was seated in front of the Internal Incidents Investigation Panel – the hospital's lawyer, the critical incidents investigator, the risk manager, the head of nursing services and a medical consultant. They were all a good twenty years younger than her. These days, hospitals had more managers than things to manage. They, no doubt, had university degrees, probably even Masters, in hospital administration. She shook her head and tried to concentrate better. All these people looked like they were just out of high school.

'You ordered a second scan?' the risk manager asked.

'Three actually.' Naomi indicated the casenotes. 'You'll find the last one was done just a day before the birth.' She twisted her wristwatch and checked the time.

'History of a stillbirth?' the head of nursing asked, looking up from the notes in front of her. She was wearing a business suit. Naomi found herself thinking that she couldn't deliver a baby in a suit like that.

'Yes,' Naomi conceded.

'Despite the history of a stillbirth, you let her go beyond her due date?'

'The history is unreliable. It may not have been a stillbirth, we don't really know.'

It was always the same with an unknown and newly arrived refugee. Naomi could have given the panel a short history lesson about postcolonial Africa, but decided against it.

Deng was making progress and was almost ready to go home from Westmead. Naomi knew; she had kept in constant contact with the nursery, monitoring Deng's progress herself. His brain scans had become increasingly promising. Naomi was quietly optimistic about his long-term future; she had told Marial and Yom this. They agreed and told her that they felt the same.

The consultant shifted in his chair. Naomi knew that he didn't like her. He had made it known around the hospital that he didn't have much time for midwife practitioners. They had too much power. They trod on medical toes. They were uppity.

'It says in the report that you admitted to another midwife to leaving the pregnancy too long without intervening.'

'Patricia?'

'I can't say.'

No, not Patricia. Patricia would never have reported a

conversation like that to an investigation team. Then who? Who else was on? Naomi thought hard. Of course, it would have been Ellen.

'Am I being accused of some negligence here?' Naomi asked the doctor.

'We are undertaking a thorough investigation of all aspects of the case.'

'And the fact that the paediatrician didn't turn up, I expect will be taken into consideration?'

'We are investigating the standard of antenatal care you provided. Please confine your comments to that.'

Naomi frowned.

'I did nothing wrong,' she said flatly.

The panel watched her impassively from behind their desk. How long had she worked here? Twenty years? She was close to the longest-serving midwife. And what about her status as a senior midwife? She remembered her first day at the hospital. She had successfully delivered a breach baby boy on her first shift. A good omen, which she tried to keep in mind as she looked at these people opposite her.

She had even been one of the staff consulted on the hospital's new design. Then there was the time when she had been considered management material and approached by the head of the hospital to climb the corporate ladder. She had thought long and hard about it. Noel was supportive. But eventually she decided that what she loved best about her job was the women and babies, and that if her work was to be meaningful, she had to remain with them.

It was hard not to take this personally. Did these people want her out?

'You have just a year or two to go before retirement?' the head of nursing asked.

Naomi sat forward in her chair and nodded. She smiled at the panel, despite the fact that something inside her felt wrong. Something had broken and Naomi doubted she could fix it. For the first time in her career as a midwife she doubted herself.

Courtside

Zoe lingered in the magazine section. Did being a mother mean reading magazines like these? She picked up *New Idea* and looked at the garish cover. Or did it mean washing up other people's dirty plates? She suspected it meant you had to do things quickly and simply. She had always suspected it meant you disappeared into your children's lives. Being a mother was about to become a reality, her solicitor said. Almost 100 per cent. The court favoured cases like hers; it liked to 'rehabilitate' mothers. Zoe was sure she had meant to use the word women, not mothers. She didn't think it was possible to rehabilitate mothers. You either were one or you weren't, surely? But she certainly wasn't going to ask that question now.

'I lost you in the crowd,' Sophie said, coming up beside her and looking at the *New Idea* in her hand.

'Sorry,' Zoe said.

'We're due back in court in ten minutes. Are you sure you don't want a sandwich or something?'

Zoe shook her head and quickly put the magazine back on the rack.

She did not like or trust the courtroom. It was too official – the colour and the shape of the large jarrah timber bench, the Australian coat of arms not far enough above. She hated sitting there, knees together, quietly waiting for the judge. It felt like being in church. She hated the judge's eyes, direct and unflinching. The court asked too much of her. They wanted to know where she lived, how much money she paid in rent each week. How bad her asthma was. It was more complicated than she thought. It was extremely personal and too practical.

As they left the newsagent, Zoe could see Naomi's back disappearing through the revolving doors at the front of the courthouse. Naomi walked slowly, with her eyes to the ground as if she had lost something. As if she had already lost, Zoe thought.

'Naomi knows,' Zoe said aloud.

'What?' her solicitor said.

But Zoe just shook her head. 'Nothing.'

It was there in the angle of Naomi's elbow, in the tilt of her head and in her step. It was being a mother, no doubt. It made you care in a way that could only end in defeat and tears. Zoe thought nervously, not for the first time, that perhaps this was all wrong. What if Naomi had been right – the boys were settled and happy with her. But surely they needed their mother? They had crossed the point of no return. She slowed down, not wanting to catch up to Naomi in the queue at the security screen.

She did not mean to make Naomi unhappy. That was not the intention here. She knew that she should feel grateful to Naomi for taking care of the boys. That was what her solicitor had said. But it was hard to feel grateful; she didn't really understand that feeling. She'd never known being a mother without Naomi. When the boys were born, Naomi was there. When Ben died, Naomi was there. Max was more like Naomi's son than hers. But she wanted them back now – properly, not just every second weekend. She thought about her house and remembered that it was now or never. She was ready.

Interim hearing

Justice Wilson was a small compact man. Clean-shaven, dark hair, nice suit. He was not remarkable-looking, except for his sharp raven eyes. Good for picking over carcasses, thought Naomi. The judge's associate, an older woman, sat down abruptly and began typing.

'Tell me why this matter is before me.'

No introduction, Justice Wilson just looked straight at Colin Eastman. Naomi and Zoe had appeared before him previously. Naomi knew the drill; his lack of introduction had annoyed her then too. After all, she was a beginnings specialist. Introductions were her stock in trade and she thought it was important to get them right. What kind of a birth had Justice Wilson's been? Did he crown in a taxi, or slide onto the floor of the hospital lift? An abrupt nature from birth? Naomi knew all about nature and nurture. Babies had minds of their own. Or was his abruptness an occupational hazard? Those raven eyes did not give much away. They took everything.

Colin cleared his throat nervously. His gold bracelet glinted below his cuff. Colin had been reliable, dependable, compassionless. Yes, Naomi was quite satisfied with her choice of solicitor.

'This matter was before you on the fourth of August, Your Honour. There has been a breach of the orders. I'm instructed that, since the matter was before you, the scheduled contact has not taken place according to the orders.'

The court fell silent while the judge read the affidavits. Naomi could hear the thrum of the airconditioning. She wriggled her toes free of her sandals and onto the thick, plush carpet. She stared hard at the Australian coat of arms behind the judge's bent head. And now they must wait. Naomi found it difficult enough to concentrate on a bus, easily distracted by the other passengers as she was. How the devil did you read and absorb something as important as an affidavit while a room of people stared at you? Naomi thought about Deng – his tiny, wrinkled fingers, his big eyes. Yom was having more success with the breastfeeding. She hung onto that small but important success.

'There was also an incident where unscheduled contact took place,' Colin continued.

'I plan to speak directly to the parties on this matter,' the judge began. His fingers fluttered to his wig and then down to the notes before him.

So this is the law of the land in action, she found herself thinking. The best this country has to offer. Her head shook ever so slightly. It amounted to not much more than a shudder.

Naomi stood and Zoe's solicitor turned to Zoe and asked her to stand.

The judge paused and looked at Naomi purposefully and then at Zoe. They could never be mistaken for a mother and daughter; one tall, one short; one dark, the other light. It went far deeper though, Naomi thought, seeing herself and Zoe through the judge's eyes. She thought that she was essentially a functioning human being, trying to get on as best she could, not asking too many questions, not expecting too much, while Zoe, on the other hand, filled holes ravenously, reaching for anything and everything; the stars and the moon if necessary.

'It would appear that you cannot come to an agreement without the intervention of the court. The court-ordered mediation has not served any real purpose.'

The judge paused to let his words sink in.

Naomi stood stiffly. She looked at Zoe and noticed her formality. The impression she gave Naomi was that of a schoolchild before the principal. Zoe did not look at Naomi. Refused to? Naomi looked away.

'The family report is not yet complete?' He wrinkled his forehead in annoyance but was careful not to direct his question to any of the parties before him, instead focusing on the corner of the file in front of him.

'Yes, that is correct, Your Honour,' Zoe's counsel replied.

The judge again consulted the file. 'Miss Zalum is doing well with her counselling and job search. She has secure housing through the Department of Housing where she has lived for the past half year. She has demonstrated a real desire to have her children back and create a family.'

Naomi bit her lip. She did not like the direction this was heading. Colin Eastman looked straight ahead, unflinching.

'While the court has taken this into account, it is not the deciding factor. It is the court's opinion that Miss Zalum has made a real effort to be reunited with her children and that is to be recognised.'

'Yes, Your Honour,' Zoe's counsel replied.

Colin remained silent.

'I am going to set a new direction. It appears that the contact arrangements could do with some improving. Is that your opinion, Mrs Adams?'

'What arrangements? Zoe breaches any and all arrangements you put in place,' Naomi snapped.

The judge ignored her. Beside her Colin stiffened.

'Having heard all the applications, I remind you that it is the court's opinion that the children need a relationship with both of you, their mother and their grandmother, and that these relationships can be positive.'

'Yes, Your Honour,' Zoe's counsel replied again.

'We are not interested in dwelling on the past here. We are making a whole new set of orders to create a new beginning, and the court expects you to do the same.'

'If I may, Your Honour,' Colin Eastman began, but the judge rolled on over the top of him.

'It is the court's opinion that the children will have a better chance of the relationship they need if they reside with their mother rather than their grandmother. There is a very real danger in this matter that these children, who have already lost a parent, may lose another. With adequate supports in place the court feels that their mother will be a positive element in their lives and vice versa.'

'I couldn't agree more, Your Honour,' Zoe's counsel began, but the judge was stopping for no one.

'I hereby order that from this day the court grants a *trial* residency of the two children to Zoe Zalum.'

Naomi gasped.

'The family report is to be completed,' the judge continued.

'Yes, Your Honour,' said Zoe's counsel, stepping into the breach.

'Unsupervised contact visits should take place every second weekend with their paternal grandmother, Mrs Adams.'

Naomi gripped the bar table.

'Contravention of these orders is a serious matter, punishable by jail. Pursuant to the *Family Law Act 1975*.'

Naomi was now shaking with rage.

'You are making a terrible mistake.' Naomi eyed the judge fiercely.

'Please calm yourself, Mrs Adams, or you will be in contravention of the court,' the judge said.

Colin Eastman put his hand firmly on her arm. 'No,' he cautioned.

Outside the court, the judge's associate was already consulting the parties to the next matter. The waiting room was full of elderly men and young women and sulky teenagers and small children eating chips. Barristers leant against the walls, clutching files and speaking into mobile phones.

Naomi walked purposefully over to Zoe. 'It's all about you, isn't it? Did you ever think that they were happy with me, settled, doing well at school? Are you happy now? You got what you wanted.'

'Naomi, I didn't want . . .' Zoe trailed off, her sunny smile now gone as she backed away.

'Call it off then!' Naomi snapped.

'I can't,' said Zoe, shrugging apologetically.

Naomi turned, both furious and distraught. The waiting room was silent, everyone had stopped to watch what Naomi would do next.

'Don't let this happen to your family,' Naomi said to the room loudly.

A couple of tall, serious young women with no-nonsense hair and wearing beige business suits emerged from nowhere. They each packed a small handgun on a slender hip. Deadly, life-size Barbie dolls, Naomi thought. Federal police officers. Before they could reach her, Naomi turned on her heel and fled the building.

Dudesville

It was proving easier to slip into this new school than Chris had expected, and until recess everything was going pretty smoothly. He had a nice new teacher. He had found it easy enough to get up in front of the class and introduce himself. This school would be nothing compared to dealing with Noel's death, or piano exams. These were only kids, after all. This was just another classroom. The one tricky part was when the teacher asked him about playing the piano.

'Christopher, you apparently play the piano rather well?' she prompted.

'No, not me,' he lied.

The teacher let it go, thank goodness. Who told her?

'He don't play football? Can you believe that?' The boys milled around the entrance to the boys' toilets, blocking Chris's way out. The shortest kid kept watch and another kid, a fat one with a rat's tail, leant against the toilet door, staying in the background. He didn't say much but the others kept looking at him. He watched Chris closely.

An annoying little kid in trackies said, 'You don't 'ave any money in yer pockets! You don't play football! What are ya? Gay?'

Chris looked at them. They were fat and little and ugly. He watched the boy with the rat's tail as he dragged slowly on his cigarette. Chris knew he was acting like he wasn't interested, like he was above all this, like he wasn't here, but he was. There was this kid back at Annandale who was always picking fights. Naomi said there was always one. This kid was in Year 3 when Chris was in Year 2, and he made Chris his special project. For some reason Chris just got on his nerves, that's what Naomi said. Well, he hoped this wasn't going to turn out the same way. He didn't need that kind of extra attention.

Then Chris thought about the sunny playground beyond. There were trees there, menacing, big, spindly things. He looked again at the doorway. There was a teacher on playground duty somewhere, but that wouldn't save him. How many boys were in front of him? Most of his class? He couldn't rely on the teachers day after day, every time he had to go to the toilet. No, there was nothing for it. He would have to get it over and done with now. It had been a mistake to come into the toilet block first up, but it was too late to think about that. The boy leaning against the door slowly smoking that cigarette was probably the leader.

Then the boy with the cigarette abruptly lost interest in Chris, which was some sort of signal to the others to do the same. The rest of them started to push past him. Suddenly, he was of no interest to them.

'I play hockey,' Chris said, as if a firecracker had just gone off in his head. He smiled. 'You know, with a big stick?' He motioned hitting a ball with the stick to the boys. They turned to watch him. He took a long swing and at the last moment

191

whacked the kid nearest him in the stomach. Hard, like he knew what he was doing. He even surprised himself. The kid went down and the other stepped back, shocked.

'Hey, dude,' he heard the fat one say.

Chris had obviously crossed a line.

'I'm ready for a game of hockey any time,' he said to them as he pushed roughly past them. That was the last time he would do anything in fear. He was now officially fearless. He had waited so long for this: to be here with Mum (definitely) and Max (maybe), to make his family work out, to be able to say, 'Mum', just like all the other kids. He was going to be somebody here, it would be great. Life with Mum would be great. They were a family now. He would make sure of it, even if he had to cook for Max. This new life would be so much better than the old one. Max was the only problem so far. He sat, miserable as a wet cat, on a bench in the sunny playground all by himself. No recess snack, no lunch. Chris would get that right tomorrow. They just had to get through today.

Random

Mr Epsom, or Mr E., as Max referred to him, had been his all-time favourite teacher. Maybe it was because he was old, like Grandpa, but Mr E. never lost his temper with Max. He let a girl bring in her cat for news one day. Mr E. told lots of stories about when he was a boy, even one about his cat and when it got an abscess after thirteen years and Mr E. had to have him put down. He was a bit strict. Hands in the air, no yelling out. Mr E. banned the word 'random' from their classroom. Gran didn't like it much either.

But here in the demountable classroom it was different. Everything was different. Max had a young teacher, Miss Lin. She was kind but her voice was a bit soft. The kids didn't always do what she asked and he felt sorry for her. He didn't feel too sorry for Zoe though, at least not the way Chris did. Chris said that she was *really* nice, that she was *really* trying. Max didn't see it. Chris said he had to give her a chance, a fair go and all that. But where was she half the time? And Gavin – what a pain. Always in those baggy shorts and no shirt, fiddling with his baseball cap, turning it backwards or something. Not very sun-smart. Even Chris couldn't bring himself to say he liked him. What a loser, what a no-hoper. He would have been a dobber at school, for sure. Mr E. would have no time for Gavin. Max was sure Gavin was nothing like Ben had been or ever would be, or Jesse, and that the way to explain his existence in their lives was that Zoe had no taste. Chris and he had been polite but had enforced a strict non-engagement policy where Gavin was concerned. They hadn't come all this way to deal with the likes of him.

Enough about Gavin. He was so random.

On a more interesting note, Max had noticed something about Zoe the other day. Something that Chris probably didn't know. He saw that she had a tattoo, a real tattoo (Gran made him promise no real tattoos, ever. What would Gran say?) on her back, low down. It was the letter C and the letter M, sort of inside each other. It made Max feel a bit gooey. Must have hurt too. A lot.

To Max's surprise, Chris was suddenly the older brother he had always wanted. He stuck up for Max in the playground at recess when some little annoying kid took his hat. He waited for him after school, mainly to protect him from the big kids at the shops. He set the alarm to get up and made their lunches and got Zoe out of bed. If they had to have a note signed, he forged Zoe's signature, really authentic. He even let Max wiggle his loose tooth.

At their old school, Chris was just some kid who nobody noticed, and he certainly didn't look out for Max. Here, he played basketball at lunchtime with the big boys and had opinions about everything. Well, more than he did at Gran's. He said he liked the new school because the uniform was cooler and there was better stuff to eat at the canteen, like chips and doughnuts and chocolate milk. He was going to get a job soon, maybe delivering the newspaper. Chris was good at tidying up the townhouse too. He said it was good that they didn't have a TV – there wasn't anything worth watching on it anyway. He was saving up to go to Timezone. The new Chris had plans. Lots of them.

There were trees here, and birds and grass. Chris said he liked that, but all this fresh air and sunshine didn't hide the burnt-out cars and dumped rubbish and graffiti. And how was he going to get the electricity turned back on?

It was all a bit random for Max. The changes in Chris also made him nervous.

Last day

There was a time when Naomi could tell you the most popular boys' and girls' names. In 2000, the year of the Sydney Olympics, they had been Joshua and Jessica. Naomi could also tell you that Joshua and Jessica had peaked in popularity by 2002, although she thought both deserved to retain their number-one status a little longer. These names were now shelved, to be rediscovered by a later generation. More recently, the exotic and slightly sibilant Isabella had topped the list.

Naomi kept a list of her all-time favourite names. These names rarely appeared in the top ten. Names appealed to her for a range of different reasons. Some because of their sense of history and stamina: Silas or Agatha. Others for their onomatopoeic qualities: Pipi. Ben and Jesse had been names that Noel loved, and Naomi grew to love them too. Ben was a name that shot off the end of her tongue while Jesse escaped between her teeth.

What's in a name? Everything and nothing. It was Naomi's quiet opinion that there were names that suited babies and names that were ridiculous on them. Reginald was perfect on a red-haired baby. Alexandra worked well on certain petite, dark-haired girls. Dorothy could do, at a stretch, on a fair-haired, blue-eyed baby. Then there were names that suited a particular baby, and no other, as if the baby had been born to fit the name and not vice versa: Glen or Hank. Hannah was another personal favourite, one she had set aside for that elusive daughter she was never to have. She would have liked more children, especially a daughter. But Ben and Jesse had filled her quota.

In the end it didn't take much to resign. It was a quick decision. Naomi wrapped the baby, a three-kilo boy – was it Mohammed? Mustafa? Michael? – handed him to his mother and decided she couldn't do it anymore. She returned her ID badge to the human resources department, filled out a couple of forms and she was out, long-service-pay-approval pending. It was as simple as that. Her career as a midwife was over.

She hadn't really thought about the end. Perhaps that was her problem, she didn't think about endings enough. It was more than an occupational hazard, she realised that now. But here she was, at the end. How did you end a career, Naomi wondered. When did you make the decision? Ever since the investigation into Deng's birth she had been thinking about it. It was terrifying to stop being a midwife, but it was also terrifying not to. Every birth was no longer special. Her windowless office was now an oppressive box of ice-cold air. Babies would go on being born, but without her. It wasn't a defeat, she'd simply had enough.

She had attended many farewells over the years. Specialists, nurses, orderlies – each person's retirement was so very different, some joyful, others sad. Naomi was determined that hers would be neither. The change would be good, it would be another beginning.

After Noel's death, it had been almost impossible to describe the pain. There were many times when she simply pretended that he was still alive rather than deal with his death. She still felt guilty for not telling the butcher; she'd simply stopped going to his shop. She could speak about Noel's death now, a year later, so that was progress of some sort. How she was coping with the loss of Chris and Max was another matter. She couldn't bear to talk about it and yet she had to. She had to tell all kinds of people – teachers, friends, colleagues – but her words were hollow, often lost in the soft flesh at the base of her throat. Eaten, half-swallowed to stop her wailing.

Naomi's last day at the hospital included a farewell morning tea, and true to form there was too much food. Plates of honey-soaked baklava, rosewater Turkish delight, hummus, tabouleh, koftit ferakh, dates and a chocolate cake. The gifts included a large suitcase, a framed photograph of the birth centre's staff, a card and a bunch of flowers. No mention was made of the reasons for her resignation. Ellen was nowhere to be seen.

'Ellen's management material,' Patricia had said glumly after Naomi's debrief on the investigation into Deng's birth.

'She'll probably get promoted to head of department if she keeps it up.' Naomi laughed grimly.

Patricia now said simply, 'You'll be missed.'

Naomi juggled all the gifts and cards and a box of bits and pieces from her office, mostly photos of babies and thank-you cards, down into the staff car park. She lingered there, taking in the rows of vehicles. The parking attendant, Rodney, who'd worked at the hospital as long as she had, walked slowly towards her. Rodney did not do anything fast, he was a very calm influence in the car park. He had seen it grow from a dirt paddock to a multistorey concrete monolith.

'Sorry to hear you are leaving us,' Rodney said politely.

Naomi burst into tears.

Rodney shifted his weight from one foot to the other.

'Time to go,' she sobbed.

Skate park

Chris was in. He was one of the brothers. Now he could hang out at the skate park with the rest of them. It was something to do, a place to go. He liked coming up with excuses, he liked the possibilities that kids like Dane presented. It was brilliant.

'I'm good for it,' he said to Dane.

He wished he'd listened to the Juvenile Justice talk a bit better. What was the penalty for underage smoking? Driving? Stealing a car? Then again, so what? That was the old Chris, worrying about stuff like that. The new Chris was totally brave and fearless.

Dane handed him the packet of cigarettes.

'Tomorrow at school,' Chris said, putting the packet into his pocket. It was hot in the park. Not much in the way of shade, still no rain. Everything was burnt. Paint peeled. Dead grass. Graffiti.

Dane nodded. Chris could be trusted. He could deliver the packet without getting caught, whenever, wherever. He'd show Dane how it was done.

'Toilets. Recess,' Dane said.

'Easy,' Chris said.

'You don't even like smoking,' Max said when he was looking through Chris's clothes for any spare change later that day.

'Don't be a loser, Max,' Chris said, shoving the cigarette packet back into his pocket. 'It's to be cool.'

Max looked upset. 'Gran won't like this one little bit,' he said, pointing to the cigarettes. 'Besides, those guys – Dane and those dudes – are not cool, they're mean. They pick on little kids, even *girls*, you know. That's really low.'

'Gran doesn't need to know,' Chris said, standing between the bedroom door and Max, blocking his way. 'No word to Naomi, okay?'

Chris liked Dane's mean streak, admired it, even, except he didn't call it mean. He said Dane was tough.

Max looked at him and shrugged. 'Whatever.'

Cheap haircuts

Naomi sat on one of Kerry's uncomfortable rickety chairs and waited for the concert to begin. Chris had barely touched the piano for the past few months. It would be a big job to get him ready for the Conservatorium's auditions. Now that he *resided* (as the court described it) with Zoe, he had proclaimed he wanted to put his lessons with Kerry on hold, until he was more settled. He'd told Naomi he had bigger things than piano practice to worry about now, though he wouldn't say what they were.

Deep winter, thought Naomi.

'Welcome to our concert,' Kerry greeted the assembled mothers and fathers.

The small children sat on the floor in the front and the older ones leant against the wall. In this room, with its Persian rugs and French windows and chintz curtains, it was possible for Naomi to forget her unhappiness for a little while. Here, in the warm pools of buttery light, she looked closely at Chris, a dishevelled eleven-year-old in a black t-shirt and grimy jeans, and Max beside him, now nine years old. Both boys needed their hair cut, thought Naomi. Perhaps Just Cuts would be open and she could scrape together enough money to take them there as well as for dinner at Broadway shopping centre.

Chris and Max looked so different to the other children, all of whom were polished and ready to play. Keen parents and grandparents sat around her with video cameras at the ready.

'Could all performers please take a piece of paper and write on it your name and the name of the piece you're performing,' Kerry continued.

Naomi had watched Kerry do this at other concerts. The paper was so that she could give each child notes on their performance.

'We have a wonderful program of music for you this afternoon. The children have been working hard on their pieces. The exams will be held later this year.'

Kerry was wearing a chartreuse blouse, matching lipstick and a full-length black skirt and black pumps. The grand piano was open and commanded the centre of the room.

There were quite a few performers, and Naomi let the music wash over her. The pieces were more complex from Grade 3 upwards. She particularly enjoyed the Chopin.

'Our final performer this afternoon is Chris, who is going to play Beethoven's Sonata Opus 27, Number 2,' Kerry said.

There was a small ripple of interest from the audience. Naomi sat up straight.

'Also known to some of you as the Moonlight Sonata,' Kerry added.

Chris sat down heavily at the piano and looked expectantly at Kerry.

'Oh, you'll need me to turn the pages, won't you?' she said, bobbing up to stand beside him, smiling sweetly.

Chris grunted. He bent forward and hunched over the keyboard. He paused and then began the opening sequence with perfect control and pace. Naomi could see the intensity of his concentration in the swan-like bend of his neck and the thrust of his shoulders. He moved through the first movement flawlessly. At that point Naomi realised that she was almost holding her breath. She relaxed and smiled. But then Chris faltered. He couldn't get through the next section. He made a couple of abortive attempts and then abruptly gave up. It wasn't like the Chris she knew to give up like that. He stood and half bowed, before moving off to slouch against the wall once more. The audience clapped weakly, uncertain as to what had happened. Kerry moved to the centre of the room, her face slightly flushed.

'Sometimes we have to work on smoothing out our performance,' she said quietly, looking straight at Naomi before adding a more general, 'Thank you, girls and boys, for your wonderful work this afternoon.'

Naomi nodded. Chris's playing, what was left of it, was still mesmerising.

The following evening, before returning the boys with haircuts to Zoe at Blacktown Station, Naomi found Chris's sheet screwed up in a ball on the floor of the car. On it Kerry had written, 'You always have such a powerful story to tell when you perform. The first movement was riveting. The second should be of equal strength.'

Naomi stared out through her dusty car window. Teenagers in flannelette shirts and trackpants moved aimlessly around the station. The cold night air had seeped into her bones as she watched Zoe and the boys walk off. Zoe's public housing estate was not a safe place to walk around after dark, a repository of stabbings and drug dealers and vulnerable single mums. Naomi had tried to quiz the boys about Zoe's place. Did it have a TV? Did Zoe have a fridge? Did they each have a bed to sleep in? They didn't answer most of her questions, but she drew her own conclusions from what they didn't say. They didn't tell her about having fun, but they did ask to take their hockey sticks and the cricket bat.

Absolutely

When Zoe was a little girl, which felt like a lifetime ago, she used to sit with her father on the banks of the Nepean River while he painted. She gathered perfectly shaped sticks and feathers and small, smooth river stones and piled them into a cairn-like structure. She could spend an entire Saturday afternoon selecting just the right stones. Every time she and Dennis returned, the cairn had been changed. Sometimes it had been added to – a chip packet shoved on the top like a small flag, or a hairclip or Barbie doll's head – and sometimes it had been diminished. Once, the stones had been used to prop up a trailer, the sticks burnt in the barbecues. Dennis asked her if she was upset. Zoe wasn't – it wasn't meant to be a permanent thing. But the cairn, in its many manifestations Zoe's first artwork, became a local fixture, and when vandals knocked it down the *Penrith Press* reported it. She eventually progressed to more sophisticated sculpture, but there was often a reference to that early riverside cairn in her work.

So, here they were. An empty Saturday afternoon sprawled ahead. Now that Zoe had downgraded Gavin somewhat, she would have to get used to thinking up all by herself what to do with the boys. Max was Mr Fidget and he had the worst timing in the world. He always had an emergency when she was in the bathroom or on the phone. Chris, on the other hand, never needed anything. He wouldn't let her help, at all. Chris was Mr Laidback. Eleven going on twenty.

'Do you want to go to the park?' Zoe said, standing up to stretch.

'Yes,' said Max, rushing to the front door, his hand already on the door handle, yanking it up and down.

She noticed Chris hesitate; he had been playing the table like a piano.

'That's right, you play, don't you?'

'Used to, a bit.'

'Gran's gonna get him a keyboard to practise on at your place. He's really good at the piano,' Max chimed in.

'Great. I can play chopsticks. Can you play that one?' Zoe asked.

Chris scowled at Max.

'What?' Max said.

At the park they sat on the grass under a milky autumn sky. Max kicked an empty drink can in and out of the broken fenceposts. Chris hung off the monkey bars. And Zoe thought about the cairn by the river at Penrith.

The following Monday morning Zoe was a little late for her session with Meg. She admitted that it was mostly hard work beginning motherhood with an eleven-year-old and a nine-year-old.

She asked Meg, 'Don't get me wrong, I love it, but perhaps if I had seen them more, had them from babies, it wouldn't be so hard now?'

Meg did not offer an opinion. 'What is hard about it?' she asked.

'Hard? Everything. School uniforms, school books, school newsletter. Not having a computer is a big problem. Or a TV. Chris reckons he doesn't want one, but Max likes to play games and watch *The Simpsons*. It's a bit quiet in the evenings. They reckon they don't get any homework. Sport? They need kit, socks, shoes, mouthguards. This talking-to-teachers-and-other-parents stuff is really hard, especially when I don't know anything. Or the kids seem to know more than me. Then there's feeding them and not being able to leave them alone. Doing the shopping. Trying to fit it all in between nine and three.'

Zoe stopped, smoothed her hair back and tied it into a business-like ponytail before continuing. 'Sometimes I can't help it, I just have to get up and start walking. I call into an NA meeting or a church service sometimes. I have spent so long walking to sort myself out or to fight the urge to do something stupid, it's a hard habit to break. I am basically a shy person. It's hard being a parent when you are shy.'

'But, I am curious, do you feel closer to your sons now that they are living with you?'

'Yes, I do. Of course. How did I ever live without them? It feels right, most of the time.'

'Do you find being responsible for them a problem?' Meg asked.

Zoe wasn't too sure what Meg meant, so she didn't answer the question. Responsibility was still something she was coming to terms with.

'When they are with Naomi, I just sleep. I'm exhausted.' The strain of being a mother – her mother always spoke about that. But it was THE STRAIN, the way Sandra spoke about it.

'Yes, but that is what you are *doing*, how are you *feeling*?'

'Great.'

Meg waited for Zoe to elaborate, but she didn't.

'What does the future hold, Zoe?'

'I don't know.'

'More children with your boyfriend?'

'No.'

'Not feeling more maternal yearnings?'

'No. But I do love my kids more, better than before.'

'Good.'

'Absolutely, one hundred per cent. I think that getting the house was a big part of it, to start with. But having them with me has also changed me. I think for the better, but you'd have to ask someone else about that.'

Since living with Chris and Max, Zoe had been able to move on in many ways. She and Meg spoke less and less about THE ACCIDENT.

'I know you, Zoe, and I can see a big change in you. Congratulations. Now you just have to keep it up.'

'Absolutely.' Zoe sounded a little less enthusiastic than she had meant to.

More mediation

'What is there left to mediate?' Naomi said.

Six months ago she might have bothered with etiquette, waited to be addressed, let the counsellor feel that he or she was in control, but not anymore. At the security screen this morning another grandmother had told Naomi as they waited in line to be searched, 'We've been to court six times. The court gives the mother access but she doesn't exercise it. Then twelve months later she turns up demanding to see her daughter. The child doesn't want to go.'

Naomi found herself thinking wistfully of the years when Zoe had buggered off. She watched the effect her words *what is there left to mediate?* had on this new counsellor.

'Zoe left them. She had no interest in them. I don't want them to reside with her. End of story.'

The counsellor coughed. 'Why don't you get some legal representation?' she asked.

'Because I've run out of money. I'm now reduced to self-representation,' Naomi answered. She tried to sound practical rather than defeated. 'I only use my lawyer when I absolutely have to.'

Naomi felt her reduced circumstances in every bone of her body. She had taken pride in her appearance, had her hair coloured and bought decent clothes, but not anymore. Now she wasn't working she was running through her savings at an alarming rate. She had her long-service-leave payment, but she had spent too much of it on barristers and solicitors, just as Colin had warned. For all his shortcomings, she appreciated his directness about money. She would have to sell the house at this rate.

'Get some advice then?' she added.

At least this counsellor was about her age and seemed more practical, shockproof. She was different to the last one, and the one before that. More relaxed, more experienced, but equally treacherous.

'I don't need advice. I've had advice,' Naomi snapped.

The counsellor wrote down something on a piece of paper.

'I lost any dignity I had long ago,' she continued. 'Isn't that part of the process? See who folds first?' She'd be pretty used to people spilling their guts, Naomi thought.

'It must be very difficult for you,' the counsellor said, without looking up.

'Has Zoe turned up for her sessions?' Naomi asked. It was hard for her to contain her anger.

'I'm not at liberty to discuss that with you.'

'I bet she hasn't. And you know what, I bet that will somehow be my fault too.'

Earlier in the waiting room she had held forth to another woman, 'Many grandparents have spoken to me about the stability and security they provide for their grandchildren.'

The woman had nodded and Naomi had taken this as encouragement to continue: 'These kids are in unsafe situations.'

The woman, who had initially been nodding and agreeable, had shrunk back in her seat and begun glancing around for an exit.

'Then these parents drop in and out of their children's lives, causing havoc. You know, broken promises, erratic contact. Then they use the legal system to punish us grandparents!'

Behind the closed doors of the room the counsellor attempted to get the session back on track. 'The family assessment is to be ready in time for the final hearing.'

Naomi nodded.

'Basically, the court was happy with the boys living with you, apart from the incident where they were left unattended while you delivered a baby . . .' Here the counsellor's voice trailed off as she read further through the notes.

Deng's delivery.

'I did not leave the boys alone. Chris, I don't know why . . .' She stopped short of accusing Chris and tried not to show how angry she felt.

'It was not the only factor,' the counsellor said, before moving on. 'The last six months with Zoe have proceeded smoothly from the court's point of view.'

Naomi listened carefully. The counsellor was going out on a limb here. She probably wasn't supposed to give her this much information. The counsellor frowned, but kept her eyes firmly on the notes in her hand. Mediation training, Naomi thought: avoid eye contact with berserk grandmothers, it only encourages them.

'What do you mean, *smoothly*? That's a matter of interpretation, surely,' Naomi interrupted. 'The boys are rarely ready for me to collect them on my contact visits. They have nits, they've lost weight, their shoes are falling apart and they are usually still wearing their school uniform when I pick them up on Saturday morning.'

The visits over the past six months had been miserable and usually began at McDonald's, Naomi watching, silent, while they ate ravenously. They remained tight-lipped about their circumstances. Questions such as, 'How's the week been?' drew a shrug.

'What did the boys say about their mother?' asked Naomi, trying to peer at the report.

'They would like to live with her.'

Naomi paused. This was not something she had planned for. She had presumed they would want to return to her and their friends. It was simple, surely.

'They feel responsible for her,' the counsellor continued. 'They worry about her when they're not there to take care of her. They think that she's better with them around. She eats better, sleeps and so on. Her life has meaning with them in it.'

Naomi closed her eyes. How old are these children? Where did their childhood go? Why are they held responsible for their mother?

'Your daughter-in-law is proposing to continue the twelve-day/two-day split with you. She has them during the week and you would have them every second weekend, as it is now.'

'No,' Naomi said, stubborn lines around her mouth setting.

'Any point in trying to negotiate with your daughter-in-law?'

'We've had every intervention under the sun – counselling, mediation, court orders, the lot. All the court has done is twist and distort the truth at every turn.'

'Grandparents find the family court system and its rulings particularly difficult,' the counsellor said, adding, 'Just *try* to make this work.'

Miserable Max

They were late. Despite everything Chris did for him, Max was still miserable and Chris was losing patience. 'Where did you leave your shoes last night?' Chris asked as he pulled up their unmade bed.

'I dunno,' Max replied unhelpfully.

'Max, you're almost ten years of age!' Chris said, sounding just like Gran, which was more than scary. Strangely, he and Dane both had to look after little brothers. Gran would skin him alive if he didn't look out for Max, and Max would tell, for sure. Dane didn't have anyone telling him what to do. He just did it. And he had more than one brother.

Max shrugged.

It was hard not to notice how thin he was becoming. His hair was greasy and needed a cut again. His school shirt was too short in the sleeve, and his trackies were torn. Not a cool little brother at all.

'You can't go to school with one shoe,' Chris said, feeling a lump in the end of the bed, inside Max's sleeping-bag.

'We don't have any more bread,' Max said, resigned to his role as the bearer of bad news.

Chris reached into Max's sleeping-bag and fished out the missing shoe. He threw it on the floor at Max's feet. 'I'll get some bread. If you don't hurry up now you'll miss breakfast at school.'

'It's yuk, that breakfast,' Max said.

'Stop whining, Max.' Chris was short with him today. He was hungry too. He was sick of being Max's mother. At first it had been kind of fun, but now it totally wasn't. 'You didn't even look for your shoe, Max. Come on, we're late!'

'I'm sick of trying to cheer you up, you know,' Chris said moments later, after they had climbed through the back fence and were on their way. 'This is our life now. Just accept it, why don't you?'

Max didn't say anything. That was a first. Usually he moaned on about missing Gran or Grandpa, but today he was silent. Chris glanced sideways at him. He waited for an outburst, but Max kept his head down. Chris felt uneasy.

The night sky

The stars were too bright and it was too cold to stay still for long. Chris tried all the parked cars he passed. Bingo, an unlocked door. He opened the driver's door quietly; just a click and a dim interior light popped on.

It was a nice car. Not fancy or anything, but it smelt nice, like one of Naomi's vanilla rice puddings and hand cream, or something. No McDonald's rubbish on the floor. He eased into the driver's seat and closed the door. The light clicked off and he sat there, resting his head on the smooth steering wheel. He hunched further down in the seat. A piece of Mozart that he played last year suddenly filled his head. He hummed a few bars of the melody.

The seats were worn so it was easy to get his fingers down the back of the driver's seat, where there was a bit of change. But for now he didn't want to take any money, he just wanted to sit there.

He felt Gran's presence here – the indentation of a worn-out back against the seat and the way it was pushed as far forward as possible. The person who owned this car was probably a grandma too. They might even have a piano in their house. He only got to practise at Naomi's once a fortnight, which he knew wouldn't be enough to pass the Conservatorium audition. There was no way he could practise at Mum's even if he wanted to – the keyboard Gran had bought him had disappeared. He couldn't tell Naomi – she would blame Zoe. The only place that had a piano was the St Vincent de Paul shop on High Street. It was there in the front window for everyone to see. Five hundred dollars, they wanted for it. He had asked them about it one day, when the shop was almost empty, careful that no one like Dane would overhear him. It was a Nicholson with a steel frame. The ivory keys had long ago been replaced with plastic and it needed a tune, but it was still a beauty. He could see that a mile off. The piano had been in the window as long as he had lived in this place, and he took comfort from that.

Mothers

Chris was bouncing up and down on Zoe's bed like a drongo, like he owned it. Zoe laughed. Chris was acting like he was a little kid or something, instead of the cool dude that he pretended to be at school and at the skate park. This was definitely not cool Chris. This was cuddly Chris and it made Max want to vomit. Max hung back, sitting a little distance away near the door. He wondered whether Zoe would notice if he wasn't here, whether she and Chris even noticed him in the room sometimes.

'So, if both my grandfathers are dead, and I know all about Naomi, what about my other grandmother?' Chris asked, just like that, so boldly. Max noticed the slight change in Chris's eyes and how he called Gran 'Naomi' in front of Zoe.

Zoe ignored him and pulled on her sweater. 'Get off my bed,' she said, and then remembered to laugh.

'Not before you tell me about my grandmother, *your* mum,' Chris said, looking her steadily in the eye.

Max looked at the floor and shook his head slightly from side to side.

'Get off my bed,' Zoe said with more determination. 'There's nothing to tell. You wouldn't like her.'

'What's her name?'

Zoe looked annoyed. And she didn't say anything at first, but then she said, 'Sandra,' without looking at Chris.

'Sandra,' Chris said, rolling the name around his mouth like a peach pit.

'Can we visit her?'

'No, definitely not,' Zoe said as if that was the end of that, but Max knew better. Mothers were never the end of something.

'Why not?'

'Because . . .'

Chris kept bouncing up and down. Max thought for sure that he was wrecking Zoe's bed. Chris was pretty big – well, he was tall, bigger than Dane and them. Max wanted to tackle Chris and make him stop being an idiot. Couldn't he see that Zoe didn't want to talk about it? Why was he being so stupid?

'Because why?' Chris said.

'None of your business,' Zoe was getting cranky with him.

'Who says?' Chris wasn't being cute anymore. He was bouncing harder and harder. He sounded just like Dane and the others now. Gran would say they were a bad influence and she'd be right, as per usual.

'I do,' Zoe said. She slammed the wardrobe door and Max thought that the door might fall off any minute because it bounced back open and nearly hit her in the face. Zoe didn't have many muscles but she could still slam a door good and hard. Gran hated it when people slammed doors, any kind of doors – car doors, front doors, back doors. Grandpa was always saying she should live in a tent and Gran agreed with him – less housework living in a tent.

Those were the days.

'Shut up, Chris,' Max said.

Ever

Zoe knew it was just a matter of time before Chris asked her again about his father. He wanted her to tell him *everything*. He had said so. When she said, 'There's not that much to tell,' he looked angry and Max rolled his eyes. It was clear she would have to do better. But how much do you tell an eleven-year-old boy? What was the point of going back over it all, and what could she tell him that Naomi had kept back? Ben was perfect and I was his mistake? Should she make up stuff? But then she'd never be able to keep the lies straight.

It was hard to remember much about her own father now he was dead. He had been Sandra's project. That's what Zoe had liked most about Ben, that he was never going to become a project. If anything, Zoe was his project. He was Mr Capable and Confident.

For a tall man, twice the size of his wife, Dennis wasn't allowed to take up too much space in their home. He'd been killed by the semi-trailer only two years earlier, but already his opinions, his face, his voice were fast fading. When Zoe tried to think about him, she could only see Sandra. It didn't help that she had almost no photos of him – she had lost all that stuff long ago, at some rehab unit, a friend's flat, on a train seat.

How would she describe Dennis to Chris? Because that was where she would have to start any discussion about Ben, for some reason which she didn't fully understand. Dennis was clean and tall, his fair hair parted neatly on the side. He was a carpenter, a simple man from the north of England. Always red in the face. He wore short sleeves and shorts, even on winter days when the frost burnt the front lawn and Zoe's shaved legs were blue in her short, short school uniform.

'It's hot 'ere,' he said, a lot.

'Why did you come here then?' Zoe shouted at him when she was old enough, when she was wearing her mother–daughter matching hotpants, learning how to be just like Sandra. 'Go back to England. Nobody likes you. Nobody wants you here.'

He never raised his voice to her or her mother. He dutifully handed Zoe her pocket money from his wallet and when she stole from him, he acted as though it had never happened. He spoke to her in his most polite voice, as though she was better than him. And she was. Zoe was his princess, he was always telling her that. Sandra was always telling her too. Zoe knew now that she had been more like a tyrant.

Sandra liked improving on things. She improved their house. She improved Dennis. She had him playing tennis. Doubles, with other smiling husbands and their pert wives. They ate smoked oysters and drank moselle afterwards. Zoe could remember cringing at Dennis's puffy fingers on the stem of his plastic wine glass.

So between tyrant Zoe and self-improvement guru Sandra, what chance did her father have? Zoe sometimes wondered if his death had really been an accident. God knows, she had been tempted to do the same at times.

After Dennis died, the first thing Zoe realised was that he didn't need improving. He'd been just fine as he was. He could do things with those puffy fingers. He made Sandra a red-brick palace to live in. He grew beautiful tomatoes. He was a better painter than a tennis player and that was more than okay with Zoe. He liked watercolours the best. His paintings were fussy, small landscapes of the Nepean River or the Blue Mountains. They were okay. Self-taught is how she would describe him to Chris.

When Chris and Max first moved in, fathers – Ben, in particular – was one of the things that Chris most wanted to talk about. *What was my dad like? What do you mean you don't know? You can't remember that? Naomi can. She says that Ben was a know-it-all. She says that Ben was really smart and artistic. He was good at everything. Football. Swimming. Singing. Cooking. SKATEBOARDING. SNOWBOARDING!*

'Don't yell, okay?' Zoe eventually had to say. She knew what it felt like to be Dennis for the first time in her life.

Sandra

'Sandra says she wants to see you,' Zoe said. She smiled grimly.

Max knew immediately who Zoe was talking about, but Chris pretended not to know.

'Who?' he asked.

Zoe smiled.

'Her mother, who do you think?' Max said. 'You know, the one you were asking about on the bed.'

Chris looked puzzled but Max knew he was faking it; just playing with Zoe, teasing her.

'My *mum* wants to see you,' Zoe said. 'She hasn't seen you since you were babies.'

Max was not sure about this news. How come, after all this time, this person, his other grandmother, would suddenly want to see him? Being with Zoe had made him very wary of adults who suddenly wanted to see him. He did not trust Zoe's judgement. This missing grandmother, who was she? Where did she live? How come they hadn't seen her before now? Max didn't like Zoe's kind of surprises.

They caught a train and then walked. Max didn't mind the walking as much as he had when they first came to live with Zoe. He had grown used to it over the past year or so. Zoe seemed to know where everything was. She always turned down the right street.

Max was also getting used to the time it took to get to places. With his head against the glass window of a train or a bus, he spent hours anticipating stuff, imagining what might happen next. He thought about him and Harry riding their bikes on the weekends at Gran's. Or his favourite thing – now that he played soccer at school – winning the World Cup in a nerve-racking match. There was being rich, having so much money that he could have a lunch order every day. Eating Gran's baked dinner. And then there was Noel and thinking of all the great things they would do together if he was still alive – and this wasn't a sad thought anymore. Like fixing a television set or playing hockey on Saturdays and winning the competition. Or watching the footy together on a Saturday night. Noel telling him stories; sometimes they were annoying, but mostly they were interesting. It was just nice to be with someone telling stories in a patient, quiet voice, the one Noel used to put on before Max went to sleep.

Sandra's garden was bare: a single flat piece of lawn then perfectly straight concrete. Her front fence was practical. Hard to describe to Gran, Max thought. The red-brick house was neat. That's what he would say, neat.

Max did not have a good feeling about this place.

Inside everything was wrapped in plastic. There was a plastic carpet protector. On the table there was a plate of party cakes, all wrapped in plastic. Fairy bread too. There was a plastic cover on the lounge, but, strangest of all, Sandra herself had a plastic shower cap on her head and plastic washing-up gloves on her hands.

Max tried not to stare. Sandra was nothing like Zoe. She was short, pug-nosed and dark-eyed. She seemed a lot older than Zoe, and even Naomi. She shuffled through the house behind them, wringing her hands in her pink washing-up gloves.

Chris was being so charming. 'Nice to meet you, Grandma. We've been looking forward to this. Your house is very nice.' Why? Max wondered.

Sandra greeted Zoe politely. Sandra was very formal with all of them.

Zoe immediately began removing her shoes and indicated to Max and Chris that they should do the same.

'Don't touch the walls,' Zoe said.

Chris, who was leaning on the wall, immediately straightened up.

When they had taken off their shoes Zoe said, 'You need to wash your hands too,' and she pushed them down the hall towards the bathroom. Sandra watched them from the safety of the kitchen doorway.

'It's all right, Mum,' Zoe said in a slightly exasperated voice.

Zoe was quiet on the way home in the train. Max and Chris watched her in the reflection of the window. She looked mean, Max thought. She caught Chris's eye.

'You wanted to see her? Now you've seen her. See what a nut she is?'

Circumstances

Naomi took her cup of tea out to the front verandah, as she used to in the days when her own boys, and then the little boys, lived with her. In those days it was to get away from the noise, the clutter, the eternal washing-up, to find some peace.

These days it was to be nearer people and to escape the nagging, niggling thoughts that accumulate in the minds of the lonely. It was also to avoid looking through her kitchen window at her garden. When had it got so overgrown? The peppercorn needed more than a few branches lopped off. It must be shedding terribly onto Signora Toto's newly replaced tin roof. Her drains would soon be blocked again. The olive tree was twice the size it should be in its spot against the retaining wall, and the vegetables under the water tank had gone to seed again.

Signora Toto was washing her front steps and she called out to Naomi. 'Ciao. How are you, Naomi?'

'Not too bad.'

'You too quiet over there, eh? How's the boys?'

'Okay.'

'Still with their mum? That's a good thing, no?'

'Yes, that is a good thing. At least it should be.'

'And Christopher? Is he going to Il Conservatorium di Musica?'

'Yes, I hope so.'

'There was music, always music, in your house, Signora.'

Naomi nodded. Especially in summer on those long twilight Saturday evenings, after an afternoon of sunburnt cricket, when Chris would play his nocturnes for her and Noel. They would sit out the front, their heads almost touching, bent over a photo or the newspaper or a piece of music. Max usually rode his bike up and down the street with Harry until it was well and truly dark. Garden moths and mosquitoes would swirl in on the end of the dusk through any open windows. Chris liked to say they had come to hear him play. Sometimes there would be dinner guests to entertain. Family mostly, but occasionally new friends, who marvelled at how good Chris was. And he would play hard, louder, longer, and Naomi would hope for greatness in him.

She sipped her tea. On mornings like this, there was always Ben or Noel's voice in the back of her mind. For more than thirty years she had been justifying herself to Ben, her first-born, a consummate nagger while he was alive. Strangely, his nagging hadn't stopped when he died. In fact, it got worse. He held Naomi captive, just as more recently Chris had.

When Naomi was having trouble with Ben, as she was this very morning, she sat on the front verandah and tried to ignore him. She thought instead about the timbre of Noel's early morning voice. It was as soothing to her as rocking a sleeping baby.

This was not the first fight she'd had with the posthumous Ben, and since Chris and Max had moved in with Zoe Ben had really stepped up his tirades. He filled the corners and the cracks of the old wooden cottage. Sometimes she had to go outside into the unkempt garden because she couldn't breathe for the presence of Ben in the house. Naomi found herself arguing with him while she waited in queues at the supermarket, at Blacktown Station to pick up the boys, at the swimming pool doing laps. Not just in her bed, as it had been that morning – one of his favourite haunts.

'Speak to your lovely wife, not to me,' she said out loud.

'Eh?' Signora Toto poked her head over the front fence.

'Nothing. Just talking to myself.'

Mind-reader

It was trying to rain, but it couldn't. The air was dull and still. The bus was late and when it did come there was just one seat left. It was ten already – Zoe's Access to Work and Training course at Blacktown TAFE had started without her. She bit her lip and crossed her legs, first one way, then the other. Oh well. Someone on the driver's radio was talking about love. Everything was always about love. How when you are first 'in love' it is like a mental illness. You can tell when someone loves you by what they do, not what they say. Which was interesting. She nearly missed her stop thinking about that one.

Gavin was there at the entrance. Sometimes Gavin'd be places, ahead of her, doing things, like that first day when she met him in the veggie garden. Like he was a mind-reader. She'd be minding her own business and he'd appear out of nowhere. It could be when she was at Centrelink or TAFE or Westfield, as if he knew ahead of time, ahead of her, even, where she was going. She kind of liked it, knowing that he was near and all. 'Be near me,' she had said to him once, at the beginning.

'Checking up on me?' she said, smiling with her whole face, including her eyes, like the lady on the radio had said:

'Tell him you love him with your eyes.' Did he understand her language of love?

He looked right through her and took her phone.

'What're you doing?'

'Seeing if you're texting anyone you shouldn't.'

Zoe watched him fumble with her little pink phone, the one he'd bought her at the post office for her birthday. She took a step back and looked at him. She wanted to gather his dreadies back into a thick coil at the nape of his neck, but she hesitated to touch him. He looked messy, like he'd slept in his clothes again. His breath was sour. She weighed up the idea of skipping TAFE – she was late already. Maybe they could go over to Westfield and get a coffee together. Go window-shopping. That sort of thing. She loved window-shopping.

'You can't be living on your own with the boys. It isn't safe.' He'd said it over and over and now he was saying it again.

She took another step backwards, away from him, away from TAFE. She wished it would rain, soft swirling warm rain. 'What brought this on?'

He was that kind of person. He repeated things until he believed them and she even believed them. He knew right from wrong. More than most, he said. He told Chris and Max how he didn't have much of a childhood and they should be grateful for having such a great mum. Sweet. He knew important stuff like how to survive. He was street smart. Really clever. Could have been the prime minister if he'd got an education. He was always saying that to the boys.

'I want to move in to keep an eye on you,' he said, handing back her phone.

Was that his way of saying that he loved her?

Should she let him move in? It wasn't the first time he'd asked. She wasn't particularly attached to her clinker-brick townhouse with its Hardiplank walls and north-facing front windows. But she liked to be there and shut the front door. It was all hers and the boys'. They could be a family together there and it had taken a while, but they were really getting somewhere now.

'Those boys need a man to keep them in line. You can't do it.'

Gavin. What a funny bloke. With his plans for expansion and world domination every two seconds. Busy ordering her around in the community garden one minute, hanging at the skate park another. Doing favours. Helping his mates. Hassling Centrelink. His spelling was terrible but his maths was good. He knew the minute they short-changed him. He was practically on a first-name basis with the counter staff.

Zoe shrugged. He certainly wasn't going to build her a studio in the country. He was altogether too hectic sometimes. She kept avoiding the question. She made excuses. She blamed the Department of Housing. She even blamed Meg. But she was running out of excuses. And Gavin didn't seem interested in anyone or anything else but her.

Gavin squinted at her.

'I'm late,' she said, stepping lightly around him and into the building. She was sick of the sun on her face. 'I thought it might rain. I was hoping that it would.'

Gavin reckoned he knew everything there was to know about raising kids. But he'd never been one himself. He'd had to grow up fast, that's all he'd say about it. Gavin was really good with the boys, firm but good. So what was the problem? Why did she hesitate? Should she speak to Meg about it? Zoe knew what she'd say. A big fat no.

Gavin was wrong about the boys. They were *her* boys. And he was wrong about her too.

The holy card

There was not much to Zoe's townhouse. The double bed where Max and Chris slept, and the single mattress for Zoe on the floor of the other bedroom. A fridge, a microwave, a coffee table. No telly, no phone. Broken gas stove, broken heater. That was it, fully. Almost. Except for the small holy card that Zoe had slipped into a corner of the window frame.

Max took the card down and read it aloud.

'Make Time
Make Time to THINK . . .
It is the essence of power.
Make Time to PLAY . . .
It is the secret of eternal youth.
Make Time to READ . . .
It is the wellspring of wisdom.
Make Time to PRAY . . .
It is the greatest power on earth.'

Mr E. at his old school would have had a field day with all those capitals in the middle of sentences. Anyway, if prayer was so powerful then why was Max still living here with Zoe? He had prayed, even lit a candle, to be able to go back to his life with Naomi. Zippo. God was not listening. Except about food. It was lucky the Salvation Army served that breakfast at school. They called it the Breakfast Club. Funny how they had a breakfast club for the poor kids who didn't have any food at home, but they were all fat anyway. How was that possible? How random. His P.B. was six slices of toast and Vegemite. When it started getting cold in the mornings he'd tried hot tea for the first time. It needed plenty of sugar and milk to make it drinkable, but at least it made him warm. After school there was an afternoon tea at the church. The biscuits weren't too bad at all – shop ones, not homemade. But you had to get there early.

The church didn't have statues like Harry's church, but it felt safer than Zoe's place. He turned Zoe's card over in his hand. She had this small card and nothing else. She must believe in God too then. Was it the same God as his? That would be nice. It would be something they shared – the first thing, as far as he could tell. He smiled.

The Salvation Army ran this town, Max decided. They ran the youth centre, the employment centre and the street-art club. It seemed to him like the street-art club was just another way of saying 'graffiti', but they called them murals and graphic design. There were lots of clubs in this town. A homework club in the school library every day after school. A design-and-make club. A reading club.

Max put the holy card back and turned his attention to finding something to eat for dinner. Only five more nights till he could go to Naomi's for an overnight visit. He wondered if she would make him lasagne. She made the best lasagne. The meat sauce was just runny enough, the melted cheese on top was perfect, the white sauce was silky. His mouth watered. How could he make sure Naomi cooked it for him? He didn't have any money to telephone her. He wouldn't have to, he decided; Naomi would just know.

Freakin'

Dane was pure evil. It said so on his pencil case. Chris liked that. It felt like Dane could turn out to be the first real friend he'd had here. But he didn't want to push it. He acted like Chris the cool dude around Dane, he didn't say too much. He definitely didn't crack any jokes, especially none of Max's. They just hung out and shared drags on cigarettes.

By 'friend' Dane meant someone who would take a bullet for you. That's how Dane talked about things. They talked like this behind the lunch shed at school and at the skate park after dark.

The Year 6 girls steered clear of Dane. He had been known to throw a ball, hard, at their faces if he didn't like the way they spoke to him. The teachers looked the other way – well, mostly. Every now and then a new one started – the teachers were always leaving, or sick or something – and Dane would have to educate him or her about the ground rules. The primary playground boys' toilets at recess were definitely off limits to anyone except Dane's gang. Dane was the top of the canteen queue and last into class. He didn't pick up papers, even when everyone else had to.

Dane stole stuff all the time. But never from 'the brothers'.

There were school rules and there were everything-else rules. Dane had been caught stealing from the office lady's handbag. The principal said he had to return what he took and apologise at a school assembly. Dane said no way, so it looked like he was going to be suspended again. He didn't seem too worried about it. He didn't worry about things like that; they weren't important to him. He was too busy for school anyway, there were so many other things to do. Sometimes he was that tired he fell asleep in class. Chris knew because he watched him.

Chris was tired too. Staying up late, staying out late, going out late, that was all new. Gran would not like it. Especially the tagging. Graffiti, Chris loved that word. It reminded him of an arpeggio – three equal yet distinct tonal parts. *Gra-ffi-ti*. *Ta. Ta. Ta.* What Gran didn't know, though, didn't hurt her.

Fully mad

Naomi's kitchen had a special place in Max's heart, even more so these days. It was a place with the promise of good things to come. It was easy to talk here, the chairs were comfortable and the right height for the table. It was a great place for a catch-up snack as well as a feast. The table could be extended, which was very important. So important that it used to be Grandpa's job, in the old days. And on really special days like Christmas they would take the table outside and put Gran's white linen tablecloth on it and have candles and all the works. Gravy in a gravy boat, that sort of thing. Not too much fuss, but enough to make it special. It was usually Max's job to light the candles, and tonight he would ask Gran if they could have some at dinner, for old times' sake.

Naomi was happiest in her kitchen, Max thought. She was relaxed and busy at the same time. Just how she liked to be, he reckoned. She wasn't the sort of person who liked to sit down much. Neither was he, come to think of it.

'It was fully mad,' Max said to Naomi as he paced back and forwards.

She smiled. He liked it when he made her smile like that. It was how a *mother* was supposed to smile. Not like Zoe and her random jokes he didn't understand. Anyway, he was here now and he was enjoying telling Naomi all about Chris's friend.

The lasagne bubbled away in the oven and he could smell the onion and fresh garlic. He was so hungry that the only way he could stop himself from opening the oven door and grabbing the burning-hot lasagne was to pace.

'Dane was saying how his brother had done a crime to go back to jail so he could die there.'

He had developed a bit of eczema since he moved to Zoe's, especially on his ribs. Naomi was always giving him ointment for it. He gave his ribs a good scratch now and thought about dying in jail. Then he thought about how annoying it would be to have eczema in jail.

Naomi had stopped smiling. 'Are you sure?'

'His brother has AIDS or cancer or something, and he said it would be the best place to die,' Max nodded.

'This was at school or on television?'

How many times did he have to tell Naomi that Zoe didn't have a television?

'At the skate park,' he said calmly. Honestly, keep up, Gran!

'Did he say what the crime was?'

'Not really, just something bad enough to give him enough time to fully die,' Max said, eyeing the lasagne.

Naomi shook her head but didn't say anything. Max thought she had changed. She seemed older and thinner and more tired. No twinkle.

'Dane's mum knows Zoe. They went to school together.'

That reminded him of Zoe's scary mum, Sandra, and how Zoe had taken them to see her. It turned out she lived just a few suburbs away, but she never visited Zoe. That seemed weird. *She* was weird. And she'd never acted like she wanted to meet him, or Chris, for even one minute. And after the visit

Zoe was totally different – all angry and sharp and fierce. After she'd got dressed up to go there and everything. He was kind of disappointed that Zoe's mum wasn't like Naomi. He thought about telling Naomi about her, but before he could she cut across him with a question.

'Is this Dane a nice kid?' she said, taking the lasagne from the oven and placing it on a breadboard in the middle of the table, to join a green salad and a fresh, sliced baguette. Max had set the table.

'Yeah, Dane's all right. He's Chris's friend, not mine,' Max said. Dane was scary, but Gran didn't need to know that because it would worry her and because Chris had it all under control, he hoped.

'Well, I guess that's all that matters. And doing your best,' Gran said. She sounded a bit lame really.

Picking up the egg flip, Max handed it solemnly to Naomi. 'He'd really like your lasagne.'

On Monday Max was still thinking about Naomi's lasagne. He was thinking about it so that he wouldn't think about his argument that morning with Chris.

'Here, Miss,' he said as he sat on the carpet in 4C while the roll was taken.

What a pain it was to have to try. When he lived with Naomi he didn't *try* to do anything. He just did things, like eat lasagne. What an extra pain it was to be trying and for no one to notice. 'I am trying,' he had told Chris in a fierce whisper so that Zoe wouldn't hear them arguing.

Just then the teacher turned to Max.

'I've noticed how hard you are trying, Max. I'd like you to present your news first today.'

Max took a deep breath and nodded dutifully. He smiled grimly at the teacher and marched out to her desk. He could see Dane's little brother, Nathan, in the front row, flicking a rubber band.

Max surveyed the rest of the class. The little space where he had been sitting might be his place here for now, but he vowed it would not be forever.

'My grandfather told me once about how in India they drink tea out of cups and then you smash them.'

'Awesome,' someone said.

'You get to break things?' another person said.

Max frowned. 'That wasn't the entire point of the story,' he said, but then he couldn't remember. 'The point of the story was . . .' The class was listening now but Max hesitated.

The teacher tried to help him. 'What did you want to say, Max?'

'How the cups are just made of dirt,' Max began.

The class erupted into laughter.

'Drinking dirty tea,' one kid sang out.

It was hard to tell Noel's stories. He was forgetting them.

Family report

Max sat uncomfortably in the armchair next to Chris and was suddenly aware of the state of his and Chris's trackies and runners. Both needed a good clean. He noticed how Chris put on a bright smile. Max looked at him carefully. This was the new Chris again, all outgoing and mature. All interested in what the counsellor had to say. Acting like a grown-up, even though he was only twelve. Just because he's got pubic hair, he thinks he's fully adult, Max thought.

'Like I said before, Mum needs us.' Chris had now said this three times, in fact.

Seeing the counsellor for the court-ordered family report was gruelling. The counsellor asked some tricky questions, but Chris was way ahead of him in Max's opinion. Chris had told Max that he would handle it. Another thing Chris would handle for him. Max wanted to trust Chris to do the right thing. Who had bailed him out of a bashing at the shops? Who found him lunch to take to school? Who forged Zoe's signature on the school notes? Max was dying to add, 'Naomi needs us too!' but he was a bit scared of what Chris might do if Max crossed him. A lot seemed to ride on this session today with the counsellor. What if they just told the counsellor the truth? Max had argued this point in bed last night. That's what they were meant to do, tell the truth.

'They'll take us away from Mum, and then she'll die,' Chris had said. 'And then we'll have no one.'

'But I'm hungry all the time, Chris, and you are too!' Max felt like hitting his brother on the head. Was he stupid or something? Zoe was a grown-up and could take care of herself.

The counsellor turned to Max. 'What do you say?' he asked and, consulting his notes, added, 'Max.'

Max could feel Chris stiffen beside him and wait for his answer. Why was it like this? Why did they have to choose? It was so unfair. He was suddenly very angry with Chris; he was the problem here, forcing Max to choose between him and Gran.

'It's complicated,' Max said at last, staring at the carpet, the colour of a big pink tongue.

'How so?'

'I just want everyone to be happy, you know?' Max said slowly.

'Yes, I do know,' the counsellor said. 'You'd be really surprised to know the number of children who come in here and just want to make their parents happy.'

Max was slightly offended at being called a child. These days he didn't feel much like a child. He had far more responsibility and far more free time, but he didn't like it.

'Well, we only have one parent left,' Chris said, suddenly sounding a bit tired, 'and we don't want to lose her again.'

The counsellor nodded and wrote something down on his clipboard.

'Max?' the counsellor asked again, looking at him.

The way Max saw it, he only had a few possibilities. He could go to Gran's by himself, but then he would have to worry all the time about Chris at Zoe's. They could both go to Gran's, but Chris would take off, or worry about Zoe all the time. They could both stay at Zoe's and be miserable. He would worry about Gran a bit of the time, and miss her all of the time. But Gran was basically okay, whereas Zoe was totally random. Who did he feel the most responsibility for? Gran? Zoe? Chris?

'What Chris said,' Max replied quickly, biting the inside of his lip.

Chris had better have made the right decision here, Max thought to himself.

Contact

A week later, a little sallow and withdrawn, Chris walked in through Naomi's open front door silently and sat down at the piano. He played a miniature fugue in the key of D minor.

'How was the party?' Naomi asked when he had finished.

'Good,' he answered without turning, his eyes downcast.

Max burst through the front door. 'Gran, can I go to Harry's for dinner?'

Naomi turned to face him with a basket of washing in her hands.

Max continued, 'We're going to watch the footy and eat meat pies with tomato sauce!'

He was clearly delighted to be spending time with Harry. During this contact visit Naomi had barely seen him or Chris; both were off with their old friends doing 'stuff' as they called it.

Naomi laughed. 'Sounds like fun!'

'You can come too, if you want.' He wasn't sure about the right thing to do here. Should he leave her at home, should he invite her to join in the fun?

'No, I've got the washing to sort,' she said, 'but thanks for thinking of me.' The boys had arrived with two plastic garbage bags full of a fortnight's worth of dirty clothes. She had been washing all day. On the stove behind her a big pot of chicken noodle soup was thickening and reducing. She was just about to add the last touch to the dish: coarsely chopped parsley. A loaf of rye bread sat on the kitchen table with a kitchen knife next to it for hungry boys to help themselves. Usually she struggled to make enough food to keep pace with them: homemade hummus and bread for snacks, an omelette, vanilla milkshakes, spaghetti and meatballs. It was never enough.

'It's Saturday night,' Chris burst out. 'Why don't you ever do anything?'

Naomi frowned at him but Chris had already stormed off to his bedroom.

An hour later Naomi knocked on his door with his washing.

'Chris, can I come in?'

Chris grunted.

His room reeked. Musty. Sour. Unwashed. He looked pale. His breath, his hair and his skin smelt different now that he was living with Zoe. Probably all the fast-food he was eating, Naomi thought, feeling a little more defeated. She knew deep down that it was more than that. He was changing, growing away from her. She wanted to bundle him up and throw him in the bath, but she knew that time had long gone.

'How's school?'

Chris turned his face away and sighed.

'I'm tired,' he announced to the wall.

'You must be,' Naomi agreed.

She put down his washing and stood in the doorway patiently.

'I'm doing the best that I can,' he said flatly.

Naomi nodded and waited. Chris turned over.

'It's not that I miss you and Noel,' Chris paused.

Naomi noticed that he had referred to Noel by name, and not the familiar 'Grandpa'.

'It's not that Zoe needs help, and Max,' he continued. 'It's that I don't know what I'm doing in this family.'

Naomi remembered Ben and Jesse going through the same thing. Adolescence, of course. Chris was a boy on the cusp of adolescence. She was torn between telling him that he was special and destined for great things, and the scientific facts.

'If your father and mother had not been who they were, you would not be you,' she said carefully.

Chris listened, rigid, his eyes focused on the top of the chest of drawers.

'At the moment of conception any one of four hundred million male cells – spermatozoa – had an equal chance of becoming your particular biological father; only one did.'

She remembered having this talk with Ben, but she was sure he had been older. She had been very open with her children about sex, as both a midwife and modern mother. Fat lot of good it did. Nonetheless, she must do the same for Chris.

'And no two of those four hundred million spermatozoa were exactly alike,' she continued. 'Each had a slightly different chromosomal make-up. The chromosomes containing helixes of deoxyribonucleic acid, DNA, are those parts of the body cells that carry the blueprint of offspring.'

Chris remained silent and watchful. She knew he was listening carefully, but she wondered what he was thinking about.

'When the two sets of blueprints – one from the father and one from the mother – are combined, a unique product results. In your case, by one chance in four hundred million, that unique product was you. If any of those other spermatozoa had fertilised the ovum from which you were created, you certainly would have been a strikingly different person, perhaps even a girl.'

Chris looked at her. She had his attention now.

Naomi smiled at him expectantly, but he remained grim.

'Sometimes I wish I could go backwards, to when Grandpa was alive,' he said in a small voice.

Naomi's smile slid a little.

'But with Zoe too,' he continued.

There was a pause, and Naomi turned to start folding the washing.

'Why don't you like Zoe?' Chris asked, point-blank.

He was not like every other kid, she reminded herself. He was Zoe's son.

'It's not that I don't like her, it's more complicated than that,' Naomi said, turning back to him.

'I don't understand,' Chris said angrily. 'Either you like her or you don't.'

'Let me tell you about when I first met her,' Naomi began. She moved from the doorframe towards the dressing table, where she carried on folding Chris's clothing and sorting it into piles: socks, undies, shorts, t-shirts, pants.

'Zoe was studying photography. That's where Ben met her. They were in the same class. He told me she was the most talented student in the class. He took me to her exhibition; it was very promising, apparently.' Naomi watched Chris in the dressing-table mirror.

'What was it like?'

'The only way I can describe it is ghostly – full of fog, or mist, I suppose, and veils and clouds. Very other-worldly.'

'Black and white or colour?'

'I can't remember now,' Naomi admitted. 'Ask Zoe?' she suggested.

Chris shrugged:

'She dropped photography and started sculpture. She exhibited once or twice, but she was too erratic and unreliable for the galleries.'

'What kind of sculpture?'

'Big metal structures inspired by nature and her endless *walks*; tubas, lantana, succulents; soft, refined forms with intricate structures within the structures, like Zoe herself.'

Naomi watched Chris absorb this new information about his mother. 'I told Ben to invite her out.'

Chris looked surprised.

'Oh yes, you see things were very different back then,' Naomi said, smiling knowingly. 'But I think it took him a long time to work up the courage to do so, and that's saying something because Ben was quite confident and outgoing, especially with girls.'

'Girls?'

'Yes, girls. He always had a girlfriend. He knew how to talk to girls. He was handsome,' Naomi smiled.

Chris thought about this for a while.

'Were you very proud of him?' he asked.

'Yes, very, like I am of you. You remind me of him sometimes.

'Anyway, one day I came home from work and Zoe was sitting at the kitchen table with Ben, drinking tea,' Naomi continued. 'She had long, thick straight hair and a really beautiful face. Same eyes and small upturned nose as you, actually.'

Chris ran his hand over his face slowly.

'I could tell that Ben was in love with her straightaway. A mother knows things like that. Especially a mother of a son.'

Chris sat up. 'How was he in love?'

Naomi thought hard, and after a long pause said, 'At first, he was very solicitous.'

'What's that mean?'

'Extra nice to her,' Naomi explained. 'He was lovesick.' Naomi stopped and looked at Chris carefully to make sure he was following her. 'It will happen to you one day too. He was so in love with finally being in love that he couldn't think straight. That's what I think, anyway.'

'In love?' Chris pondered the idea of his parents being in love. He had often wondered about this. How had they been together? Had they loved one another?

'Probably, after a while, Ben was too overwhelming for Zoe. I'm not sure, though,' she said.

'Why?'

'I think he was too forceful. He was very outgoing. He couldn't wait to get married. He just wanted to be with her, which was lovely. He meant well, but I don't think that he was a good listener. Anyway, Zoe practically moved in here with us that day, until they got their own place. But that's not what you asked me, is it? Why don't I like Zoe?'

Chris shifted on his bed again and remained silent.

'She was very quiet. She was watchful; a listener, you know? That wasn't so strange to me, having grown up on a farm. A lot of country people are quiet and hard-working. It's why she was such a good artist. She was an observer and a collector.' Naomi thought for a moment and then added, 'It's not that exactly. It's that she was so careful. She wasn't carefree in the way Ben was. You know? She was always on her best behaviour. A bit secretive or something. I couldn't get to really know her. I thought that she was a deep person.' Naomi shook her head crossly. 'Then I realised that she was a bit afraid of me . . .' She broke off and fell silent for a moment before continuing more quietly, 'Ben did everything for her.

Practically waited on her. Jesse and Noel cooked and cleaned for her. They all loved her. I asked her about her family and she said, "My family and I are divorced," refusing to say why. I knew what it was like to leave a family behind, because I had left Grenfell to start my life with Noel here, where we thought we could make a better life. But I didn't really understand a child divorcing a family. I pretended that I understood, but I didn't.'

'She was an artist.'

'Yes, she was an artist, but that's no reason,' Naomi met Chris's wide-open twelve-year-old eyes.

'It's delivering so many babies; you begin to see patterns in people and families.' Naomi faltered again. It was difficult to speak openly to him, from her heart, about her feelings for Zoe. She and Noel had argued so often and so long about this. Frustrated, hushed, bleak, hateful arguments which always left her feeling as though she had lost.

'Go on, Gran,' Chris urged her.

'I began to worry. I just wanted them to be happy. Then when things began to get tense at home – it can be hard with an extra person – Ben announced that they had got married and were moving out.'

'Didn't you go to the wedding?'

'No, I wasn't invited.'

'Why?' Chris asked. His face wore that all-too-familiar bewildered expression. She had seen it so many times when it came to Zoe – from Noel and from Ben, though never Jesse – that she had banned it. Her own face had set into a kind of disbelief and finally cynicism, when it came to Zoe.

'I think, to them, their marriage was private. Parents were irrelevant, that sort of thing. Kids can be insensitive – until they have their own, that is. Jesse went; he was their witness.'

'So you were pleased when they moved out?'

Naomi placed the piles of clean clothes into Chris's empty overnight bag. The room was so quiet that the clock on the kitchen wall could be heard, two rooms away. No screaming jets coming in overhead to cause her to pause mid sentence, to have more time to gather her thoughts. No cat scratching at the door to be let in. No Max running down the hallway, yelling out, interrupting. Just the two of them. Naomi stopped fiddling with Chris's washing and turned to face him. This is how she had felt with Ben at times.

'In a way it was worse, because at least when they were here at home I could keep an eye on them.'

Chris looked perplexed.

'They were so young, Chris. Then suddenly Zoe was pregnant. Ben was working two jobs to support them. I was really worried that the baby was coming before they knew who they really were. Zoe was not ready. And then they had you!'

'They didn't want me?'

'No, of course they wanted you! We all did. You know Noel was so proud of you, kept making excuses to take you to the shops so he could show you off. Jesse read endlessly to you. I looked after you too. Zoe tried her best to be a good mother, but she didn't know how. Soon Max came along and things started to get more difficult financially. Ben was getting work as a photographer, but it was hard. He needed expensive equipment to be a photographer. One day, Zoe left the front door open and they were robbed. He lost his cameras. Everything. No insurance.'

Naomi placed the last of Chris's clean clothes in his bag and pressed down on them to close the fraying zipper.

'Noel and I suggested that they move back home with us, so they did. Zoe was unwell after the birth. It can take a lot out of a woman.'

Naomi chose her words carefully. She omitted to tell him that Zoe had had severe postnatal depression; that she had wandered down to the harbour's edge in her night-dress, ready to throw herself in, and if not for the kindness of strangers that would have been the end. He would see it as Max's fault. She remembered that time as a hushed time: Zoe curled up in a ball; Max sleeping; Ben agitated, confused, frustrated. She remembered little about it in any real detail now, except snippets like brushing Zoe's long hair and Dr Bird's visits.

'Zoe tried to get back on her feet. Perhaps she even needed to have a bit more time in hospital, but she didn't want to. She was such a free spirit, to be cramped up in a hospital ward would have been a terrible thing for her. I thought we could take better care of her at home, and at the same time we took over more and more of the care of you boys.'

When she had recovered, the only thing Zoe would do, as Naomi remembered it, was go for walks, long walks. Walks around the city, walks around the park and down to the harbour. Sometimes barefoot, even in winter.

'Then what happened?' Chris was chewing his bottom lip. Naomi knew that now she had started, he expected her to finish. But how?

She picked up the t-shirt that Chris had thrown on the rocking chair and sat down absent-mindedly with it still in her hand. She rocked the rocker gently with one foot. Noel had bought her this chair after the birth of Ben. She had rocked two generations of boys with earache, nightmares and fevers here. She had read them stories in this chair as well. *The Adventures of Tarzan*, *Swiss Family Robinson*, *The Lost World*, *Treasure Island*. She listened to the chair roll against the floorboards for a moment and felt a certain comfort from the familiar sound.

'We were secretly just trying to get our hands on you,' Naomi said, closing her eyes and smiling at the memory of Chris as a baby. 'We just couldn't get enough cuddles and kisses!'

Chris looked disgusted.

'You were such a beautiful baby boy – so open, happy,' Naomi said smiling now, 'such a joy to have in the house. Always singing little songs.'

'What about Zoe?' Chris persisted, his voice louder.

'She got better. She wanted to be a good mother. I believe that.'

Naomi looked at the bookcase. 'You should take some of these with you. They're a bit dusty but they're worth reading, or even re-reading.' She scanned the shelf. 'Ha! Do you remember the story of Ruth, but we called it "The Book of Naomi"?' she said, plucking it off the shelf. 'I must have read you that story a hundred times when you were a boy.'

Naomi appealed shamelessly to Chris's vanity. Of course he was still a boy – a bored, confused boy – but in that one sentence Naomi gave him the same consideration she would an adolescent, and they both knew there was a distinct difference between the two.

He did not reply but turned his face towards her.

'Or maybe it was Jesse. He loved that story; so did Max. I thought you did as well, but these days I get a bit mixed up sometimes. Anyway, it is a small story, in and amongst a number of other old stories gathered in the Bible.'

Chris rolled his eyes.

The Bible was such a loaded subject, not that Naomi ever let that get in the way of anything.

'I used to read that story because even though it is called "The Book of Ruth", it is also about a woman called Naomi. I read it when I was a child. Someone gave it to me and as I had an unusual name, I read it to find out where my name came from. You know the way you do as a kid? Anyway, in the story Ruth helps Naomi, even when she doesn't have to. They go on a journey together.'

'What's the point, Gran? Get to the point.'

'That is the point, entirely. I think you could find some inspiration from it, or stories like it. Look, here is your father's copy of *Aesop's Fables*. Now that you are growing up, these old stories will make more sense.'

Naomi put the two books on Chris's bag. 'Take them with you. I don't want them back. I know the stories.'

'We were talking about Zoe, and then you went off on this random tangent?'

'Zoe. Well, Zoe. I think —' Naomi fumbled with a series of beginnings. 'Zoe was just starting to get on top of it all, then the accident happened, and Ben's death. She was in a great deal of pain with her leg. She was very sick . . .' Naomi started, drifting off.

Chris rolled over and off the bed. 'Let me help you with that, Gran,' he said quietly, taking the washing basket and what remained of its neatly folded washing out into the light of the hallway.

Smokin'

The thing that struck Max was the noise, the constant roar. At first he wanted to block his ears, but that would be uncool. It was like a whole pile of giant mosquitoes and angry bees and a wild herd of African animals all mixed up together. The next thing was the smell – oil, burnt rubber, hot chips. Zoe had been serious about Eastern Creek Karts, and now they were here! It was totally mad and brilliant, and just wait till he told Harry about this.

'You have to be eleven or older,' the girl behind the counter said, a piece of chewing gum between her back teeth.

Gavin frowned. 'In Queensland it's eight years and over!'

'What about him?' Zoe said. They all turned to look at Max. He had that sinking feeling. He looked big enough, didn't he?

'How old?' the girl said, her gum now wrapped around her front teeth.

He suddenly seemed to be the only person who knew his age. 'Ten,' Max said.

'He can go in a double. With an adult.'

Max looked at Zoe. He prepared himself to be disappointed. They would get this far, and then something would happen that she hadn't thought about and they would have to go home.

'Gavin?' Zoe turned to him.

'Sure, I'll take him,' Gavin said.

'Why can't you instead, Mum?' Chris said, moving between Gavin and Zoe.

'Not me. I don't drive,' Zoe said, shivering and turning away.

The woman behind the counter said, 'That'll be forty-six dollars for one ten-minute single and one ten-minute double.'

That sounds like a lot of money, thought Max. A lot of money for Zoe from her pension, but Zoe handed it over without saying anything. Like she did this every day. She had the six dollars in small change and the forty dollars in twenty-dollar bills.

'There's a two-hour wait,' the girl said as she handed Zoe her tickets.

'That's no problem.'

There were no problems today. They were in. Max would get a go after all.

They sat in the grandstand, just like all the other families. A man, a woman and two kids. They fitted in, but, even better, they fitted together. They ate hot chips and drank Coke. Max was happy. Zoe was happy. It was all good. Zoe smiled at him and he smiled back.

Chris sat a little apart. He was a bit edgy or something. More like his old self when they lived at Gran's. Stupid, thought Max. What a waste.

'There's nothing to worry about except having a good time,' he said to Chris over the noise of the engines when Zoe and Gavin went to check out the adult track. Chris grunted.

Sometimes he could be a real pain.

'This is the best karting I have ever seen . . . Better than anything anywhere else in the world,' Gavin said when he returned, and Max believed him. Gavin was random, but he knew things.

Once they were in their kart, Gavin gave him some advice: 'Always brake in a straight line. And when you apply brakes, make sure your foot is off the throttle.'

Max wasn't sure what a throttle was, but he nodded anyway.

'Make sure your turns are smooth. Don't be too aggressive with the steering wheel,' Gavin said.

The steering wheel. He gripped it, and then released his fingers and gripped it again. He liked that feeling. He moved the wheel from side to side.

'Accelerate at the apex of the turn. It's important to think about corners ahead,' Gavin said.

Max said, 'Too right,' and they were off. It took all his concentration to stay on the track.

'Try to use the whole width of the track to maintain your speed,' Gavin yelled. But Max was too busy concentrating to reply.

They went round and round, at first quite slowly, then as fast as possible. He crashed a couple of times but not too badly for a beginner, as Gavin said.

'It was mad, Mum,' Max said to Zoe when they finally came off the track. His eyes were bright and sparkling. 'Can we go again sometime?'

Zoe nodded.

'Where's Chris?' Gavin asked, looking at the crowd.

It was almost evening and the crowd was thinning out. The night races were about to start. Max could feel the atmosphere building.

'He had his go yet?' Max asked, looking around.

'Where *is* Chris?' Zoe said, standing up.

Seeing Zoe acting like a concerned mum made Max feel good. She looked good, for a mum. Above the sound and diesel fumes he almost felt proud of her.

'He'll turn up,' Gavin said, pulling her back down onto the bench beside him and giving her a cuddle.

Brothers

Chris was hanging out at the skate park after Max was asleep, especially on the nights when Gavin was hanging around at home. He didn't feel so creeped out by Gavin when he was at the park. Dane liked hanging out there too. They had noticed how alike they were. Sometimes it was just the two of them; Chris liked those times the best.

Dane wasn't so proud of his older brother, Danny. He told Chris that personally he thought Danny was a loser. For getting caught mostly, but also because he'd been a bit of an arsehole to Dane when he was little.

Chris wondered what that meant exactly. With Dane it could mean anything from taking his pocket money to sexual abuse. Chris thought it was probably better not to know.

'All the bad stuff I have to do is because of him,' Dane said. This didn't really make sense to Chris because he saw Dane do plenty of bad stuff at school, which Dane's older brother couldn't even know about from prison. 'And now he's dying.'

'I know,' Chris said.

'We have to stick together, but,' Dane said. Chris wasn't sure whether Dane was referring to his brother or him, so he just nodded.

'I don't want to go to prison to see him,' Dane said and shivered. 'But I go. I don't want him to come after the others.'

Chris guessed that he was talking about the other kids in his family, his little brothers. Max had one in his class. In fact there was one in nearly every class at the school.

Chris thought about Max. He was probably at home having nightmares. He hated sharing the same bedroom, and most of all sleeping in the same bed as him. There were times when Max was so annoying that he wished he didn't have a little brother. It was like the glue that had held them together all this time had reached its use-by date.

'Don't ever make me come after you,' Dane said to Chris without looking at him.

'Like where would I be,' Chris said, the Chris that was all fearless and strong. 'Brothers. Right?'

Dane looked at him for the longest time. Dane was mean and fat, but he was something else too. You could take him home to Naomi and she'd probably think he was okay. Not that he had any manners, or anything, but what he did have was time for people – certain people. Dudes talked to him. You saw him everywhere you went round here. He knew all the places. He never went home except to sleep, even after dark in winter when it was *so* cold here. It was like Dane didn't feel the cold. He watched and he listened. He didn't say too much. He was a quiet dickhead. To Dane everyone was a dickhead. He'd probably say that Gran was a good dickhead. In Chris's opinion, people were down on him because of his brother more than anything. If you asked Chris, with Dane it was like there was something in him that had been broken and had never quite been fixed, that's all.

'Don't ever make me come after *you*, too,' Chris said.

'Brothers,' Dane said, quietly.

Nits

After Eastern Creek, Max had one of his bright ideas. Grandpa had loved his bright ideas. Gran too, but not so much, like the time he had the bright idea to put a sultana up his nose like Mr Bean and Naomi had to get it out with tweezers. But he'd had better ones, like the invention of the famous Adams family chocolate meringue. Even Chris liked that one. He'd like this one too, Max was sure.

As usual Zoe came home at dusk, through the back door – never the front – and slung down a pile of dirty vegetables from the community garden in the kitchen sink. She was singing to herself. He liked her singing voice; it was all light and airy like a vanilla sponge cake. She had a few other things under her arm that must have caught her eye on the way home, including a purple frisbee, which raised a little low-level interest in Max. Might be worth trying that out. Usually the things she brought home were broken. She said that she *preferred* broken things. Weird. They now had a broken boogie board, a broken bike, a broken cat cage, a broken couch, and that was just in the backyard. She had another collection in her room upstairs. Sometimes she sat and tore up bits of paper, which she colour-coded. She said they were for her book.

'We need some heat,' Max said, coming into the kitchen from the gloomy lounge room.

Zoe turned at his words and switched on the light. She glanced down at him briefly, a hello-there-you smile playing around the edge of her lips. But then it slid sideways.

'What the hell did you do?' she said, taking a step towards him and slapping his face.

'Ow!'

'What did you do?' Zoe yelled right in his face.

'Watch it!' Max said, backing away from her.

She was scary up close. He could see all the pores in her skin, and her nostrils were ugly, especially her nose-stud hole. It was red and vicious, like her eyes.

Zoe had that same ability as Chris, to sneak up on him. She moved like a cat, Chris too. Max was the only one in the family who never surprised anyone. Well, now he had.

'To stop the nits,' Max said, holding the side of his face and trying to wriggle away from her. 'What's it to you? What do you care?'

'I am your mother,' Zoe said, rolling the word 'mother' around her tongue, sounding just like her own mother. He was shocked and confused by her action. This fight had been coming for a long time, ever since Grandpa's funeral: tracks laid, gauge set, as swift as the Indian-Pacific and just about on time too. The two of them stood squarely facing one another, standing their ground. Max's stubbly head was a shocking mistake, Zoe knew it. Max knew it too now.

'Your beautiful hair,' Zoe said, her voice trembling as she reached out to feel his head where his thick, straight hair had been. 'There is so little beauty in our lives.' She began to cry.

Max looked uncomfortable. 'Didn't think you'd care that much.'

261

'Well, I do care,' Zoe said, tears streaming down her face. She drew Max to her and held him. He stood stiffly at first, but when it became clear she wasn't going to let go any time soon, he relaxed. She smelt of tomatoes and basil, probably from the garden.

When Chris walked in, Zoe was still holding Max and both mother and son were sobbing.

'What's wrong?' Chris said, in a panicky voice.

Max realised that he probably looked like a plucked chicken. The hair clippers (found last week by Zoe) were not the sharpest. He hadn't really meant to cut it all off, but he was sick to death of scratching. He held the clippers, felt the weight of them in his hand for a while, then plugged them in and pressed the 'on' button. They made a mad noise, like Aunt Gwen's choppers on fast-forward. He tried to mow a bit, just a little bit at the front, but it ended up being more than he planned. It was harder cutting your hair in the mirror than it looked. A *trap for young players*, as Grandpa would have said. Anyway, it looked really mad for a while, but then it stopped looking mad and started looking sad, so he had to cut the rest to match it. There was hair all over the bathroom. Zoe would probably want to put it all in a paper bag marked 'Max' and call it an artwork.

All things considered, he thought he didn't do a half bad number one, but he couldn't see the back. He was hoping Chris might check it out and tidy it up for him.

Max tried to smooth down his school shirt, pulled out of shape by Zoe. It was great not having the nits though. 'Lots of kids at school have number ones,' he said between sobs.

'What are you crying about?' Chris said, sounding increasingly suspicious.

'About everything that's wrong,' Max said between sobs, and, with that, Zoe cried even harder.

Final orders

Naomi felt a new destructive force in her life: herself. Now that she was no longer working, for the first time in her life she found she had aches and pains. Her hips hurt at night if she lay too long on her side. Her wrists ached, the joints in her fingers were stiff each morning, and she found it hard to get out of bed. Her knees were swollen and didn't bend enough to get in and out of the bath easily. She moved the TV set into her bedroom and watched it any time of the day or night. Whole days lost their shape. There were blanks in her diary, which once was full of appointments. She made mental lists of the jobs that needed to be done, but didn't do them. She waited until the day before the boys arrived each fortnight to get some semblance of order back into the house.

Friends tried to encourage her to do a course at the local community college, or join a seniors' exercise group. She nodded and smiled, but delayed picking up the phone. Patricia dragged her to Blacktown once a month to help with an African women's support group.

'If I could just get a decent sleep,' she heard herself tell Sarah on the phone. When did the word 'just' creep into her vocabulary? Naomi hung up the phone and tried not to laugh out loud at herself. Just? It was not there before. That was a word that should be banished, along with 'perhaps' and 'well'.

Raised all those years ago to be a farmer's wife, she still looked to the sky for inspiration. Naomi looked for signs of cloud, but they remained high and thin. When the drought breaks, she thought, I'll know what to do.

'All stand and remain standing.'

The judge, a bespectacled man in a wig and gown, entered the court. A good-looking man in his fifties with a full head of steel-grey hair; fit, athletic even.

Court 13 was panelled in blond wood. The high-backed chairs they sat in were a furious pink, and there were the unforgettable ripe-apricot-coloured walls. The colour made Naomi feel sick. Every element clashed like a bad symphony. Naomi wondered how anyone could make proper decisions in such a place. 'Proper', that was a word she heard in court, 'sensible' another; words that she didn't hear much in the rest of her life, or for that matter associate with Zoe.

Naomi tried to focus on the matter unfolding before her, but found herself wondering about the judge, as she had during the interim hearing. Did he have a straightforward nuclear family – a wife and two happy, healthy children? Was work in the Family Court an occupational hazard? What happened when a judge's family imploded? How would he, as a father or grandfather, dispute contact and residency, as they called it these days?

Naomi had stood in this court for three judges in six appearances in the months since Noel's death. Outside, it was already winter again. An initial hearing; interim orders;

breaches of the orders; a couple of 'no shows' by Zoe; and today the final hearing. Right now, though, this final hearing felt sudden. She supposed the importance of it caused her to feel that way. A panicky, useless wish to turn back rose in the back of her throat.

The court officer handed the judge the thick file marked in black, unforgiving square letters: ADAMS vs ZALUM. She held the file up to the judge with both hands, like some ancient sacrifice.

Naomi was no longer angry, no longer sad, or even surprised to find herself in a court of law. She had, instead, shrunk down to being just simply practical. Zoe was a part of her life, she had to accommodate her. She understood, now, how the court worked. How had they arrived at this point? Naomi wanted to reach across to her thirty-year-old widowed daughter-in-law and say, 'This is so very stupid!' But they had their new roles to play. Adversaries at six paces.

Zoe stood quietly next to her solicitor, wearing the same cornflower-blue suit that she had worn to Noel's funeral. Seeing it again made Naomi's skin crawl. Her hair was darker and calmer these days. She looked even more like Chris's mother. Under different circumstances she might have told her so.

At least she makes it to court now, Naomi thought. The young solicitor had done a lot of work with Zoe and Naomi could see that Zoe had grown into the role. She was the archetypal wronged, struggling single parent. Zoe had gone from a transparent waif to a solid young woman. Perhaps this was to be the making of her, after all. Naomi knew she should feel pleased and not resentful about that.

'Have you had an opportunity to consider the recommendations of the family report?' the judge asked Naomi's solicitor.

'Yes, Your Honour,' Colin Eastman replied.

'Can we establish that this contact regime is working for both parties?' he asked over the top of his glasses.

'We would be asking for an adjournment, Your Honour, to consider the recommendations,' Colin replied.

'But that's just what I asked. Have you had an opportunity to consider the recommendations of the family report?' the judge snapped.

'Some limited consideration, Your Honour,' Colin mumbled.

'I'm here till six-thirty; let's see if we can't sort it out today,' the judge said briskly.

The family report had arrived, handed to Colin in the corridor by the children's representative that morning.

'And what about you?' the judge said, turning to Zoe's solicitor.

'Yes, Your Honour. We have read the report and we will be seeking final orders today.'

'I will stand the matter in the list,' the judge shot back. It was clear that this was his court and no one else's. And with that he stood and swept out of the court.

Outside the courtroom, Colin directed Naomi along the apricot-pink corridor to one of the small discussion rooms. He closed the door behind him. Naomi sat down tentatively.

'The family report,' he began, and, taking a deep breath, changed tack. 'You are going to lose on the residency of the children.'

Although Naomi had sensed this was coming from the way Colin had sniffed and fidgeted his way through the report that morning, leafing back and forwards through the pages, it still hit her like a brick. It was a physical thing. She clutched her belly, her empty womb. Her head throbbed. It was a disaster.

'Why?'

'The boys still feel' – he paused and searched for the right word, shifting in his seat – 'responsible for their mum. They feel that she's better off if they live with her. She takes her asthma medication, eats better, sleeps and they can keep an eye on her.'

'That's great. The boys are awarded to her because they feel they must look after her.'

Colin shifted uncomfortably in his seat.

'They have expressed a real desire to continue to live with her.'

Naomi sat back in her chair and gripped the armrests.

'They want to live with you too. It's not that they don't want to live with you. But if they have to choose, and they have expressly stated that they do not want to choose, but if they have to choose, then they choose Zoe.'

Naomi smiled despite herself. 'I have raised them well, too well for their own good.'

The solicitor studied her carefully, bracing for an outburst. Usually at this point the relinquishing party would be lashing out.

'They are good boys,' she continued quietly, 'and I don't want to make it any harder for them. If that is their wish, then so be it.'

She slumped forward in her chair, her eyes down, her head bowed.

Colin Eastman was already scanning the rest of the document.

Naomi didn't know what to do with her hands. She turned them over. Work-worn hands. Chipped nails, dry skin. There was her old wedding ring biting into her flesh. She would get it cut off directly. What would Ben make of all this? She shuddered to think.

'Contact will continue at Blacktown Station, the changeover point being the bus bays at the car-park end of the station,' the solicitor droned on. Naomi knew she should be paying attention to this detail, but she couldn't. She was too tired, too lost.

Back in the courtroom, the judge wrapped up. 'I dismiss all outstanding applications and cross-applications and I remove all issues from the pending cases list and I order that all material produced on subpoena be returned.'

He paused and looked at each of the women closely.

'That's the formal part. I would also like to congratulate the parties for reaching this agreement. I have no doubt, particularly for you, Miss Zalum, it's been a difficult process, but it is a sensible process. It recognises with great respect to you the reality of your present position.'

Zoe nodded and said a faint, 'Your Honour.'

Naomi fidgeted with her wide African-print skirt, pleating it with her thumb and forefinger.

'You will note that the children's representative, in preparing the orders he has, makes it clear that this is not an end of matters for all times. In effect, I suspect what is being said is, the future is up to you.'

He now turned towards Naomi. She waited calmly, refused to feel defeated yet.

'Mrs Adams, so far as you are concerned,' he said steadily, 'the orders recognise your part in the children's lives, and they recognise your continued part in their lives on a final basis. Now that does not mean, lest there be any misunderstanding, that this is set in stone and for all time. Things can change, and if things do change, it may well be appropriate for the residential status of the boys to change. That's for the future.

'The future for all *four* of you – that is, both of you ladies and the two boys – in my view has been very much improved by these orders.'

Naomi wondered whether a judge could be wrong. Wasn't he meant to be wise? Perhaps *she* was wrong? She thought about the first mediation she had attended, where the counsellor had begun what she could only describe as shaping this outcome. It had always been about the outcome. Not about justice at all.

'They are sensible orders. They are workable orders and they lead the way into a future that can only benefit the children because of their ongoing relationship with both of you. I am satisfied it is an entirely appropriate arrangement. I'll have copies of these made for each of you.

'Is there anything further from your client's point of view?' the judge finished, turning to Naomi's solicitor.

'No, Your Honour,' Colin Eastman replied, straightening his cuffs.

'Anything more?' the judge turned to the other party.

'I thank Your Honour,' Zoe's solicitor said.

'Thank you, I'll adjourn,' he said, closing the folder in front of him, and with the briefest of smiles sweeping out of the courtroom before Naomi could remember to breathe.

'All adjourn,' the court officer said. 'This court stands adjourned.'

Winning

In the car on the way to the court that morning Zoe had been silent. She hadn't slept. She couldn't put a sentence together. Sophie didn't seem to notice. She spoke quickly and firmly to Zoe; she would get residency. The matter would be settled today; the final orders were to be made. Zoe was going to win.

Her lawyer's words bounced around inside Zoe's head, making her feel hollow. Win? Had Zoe ever won anything in her life? Naomi, on the other hand, was not one to lose. There was something wrong with this picture. And Zoe felt sick with anxiety about it. What if they had got it all wrong?

She had walked from the car park to the court on legs that didn't work properly. Her weak ankle ached and she had to stop suddenly to vomit in a rubbish bin and again in the gutter outside the court. Sophie stopped too – she was on the phone now to another anxious client – and patted Zoe's back.

When they entered Court 13 Naomi was already there. She was always there. Zoe took her seat at the bench, two high-backed swivel chairs away from Naomi. In this court, they had sat close together. Sometimes when all was quiet – usually while the judge read something – she could hear Naomi's watch tick.

She was feeling light-headed and dry round the mouth. Everything was too loud again. Her lawyer coughed up a polite hello. Zoe added a tremulous hiccup, as if to say, oops, I'm here too, but Naomi kept her eyes fixed straight ahead.

And then it was like it always was. From the minute the judge swept in it all happened very fast. He was an impatient man. He interrupted counsel and asked them to get to the point. You had to think quickly. Stand up. Sit down. Sophie jumped out of her seat to hand a piece of paper to the associate. Her empty chair rocked slightly, leaving a gaping hole between Zoe and Naomi. Zoe took a deep breath and turned to Naomi, but Naomi stared straight ahead, like she was made of stone. Then the judge was speaking. He was asking Zoe and Naomi to stand. She looked him straight in the eye. He was being all fatherly and wishing them well. His lips moved but Zoe couldn't keep up. He was speaking too fast. 'Slow down,' she wanted to call out, 'this is important to me.' She would order the court transcripts. She sat back down, her back perfectly straight, and her jaw clenched. She felt the colour rush to her cheeks. Then Sophie was congratulating her.

'A good result. You got what you wanted,' Sophie said in her ear. When Zoe continued to look blank, Sophie added, 'You won, *silly*.'

When Zoe was little she had been a good runner. At her first sports day in kindy she had surprised herself and won her race. All the kids were suddenly thumping her on the back. Big kids too. It was terrifying. Meg had warned her from the very beginning that winning was always more complicated than losing. Meg was always saying stuff like that. All Zoe knew was that it made her feel scared, regretful and pleased all at once.

There was a time in her life when Naomi had been a better mother to her than her own mother. There were things that Naomi knew about Zoe that no one else knew; dark, sad regrets about Sandra's mental illness or her own descent into postnatal depression. Perhaps Naomi had forgotten it all. Perhaps it meant nothing to her now. Lately, as this court date approached, Zoe had begun remembering; Naomi had brought her back a box of chocolates from a holiday in Tasmania once, made her moist banana cake when it was the only thing to stop the morning sickness, took her to the opera to see *Cosi Fan Tutte*, sent her a card on her twenty-first birthday, delivered her two sons, made her welcome and finally showed her the door when she deserved it.

That very morning she had woken in the middle of a dream – she rarely dreamt – in which Naomi was at the door. 'I've come for the boys,' she had said.

Just then Naomi turned to Zoe briefly.

'If I had known what this would be like . . . I never meant you any harm,' Zoe said quickly. She could feel the bile rising again in her throat. She felt sweat starting to pool in her armpits and run down her spine in between her shoulder blades.

Naomi stood up, her hands loose by her sides. She turned away from Zoe and back to the coat of arms, as if she could find the answers there. She looked so very small.

Since Noel's funeral Zoe had been working towards this. There were many times when she could have stopped, but she hadn't. Her need to have the boys had grown, not diminished. It had made her do things that she didn't want to do. Perhaps that was what being a real mother was all about; finding the strength to keep going, being prepared to have the fight for as long as it took. It had made her stand here in court, time after time, when it would have been so much easier to stay in bed. And now she finally had what she wanted. The boys were to 'reside' with her. She liked that word.

Naomi picked up her bag and walked silently away. The noise of the waiting room rushed in like the tide as she opened the door of Court 13 for the last time.

'I have to rush back to the office – another case, I'm sorry . . .' her lawyer said.

The registrar gave Zoe a noncommittal nod. Sophie shuffled her papers roughly and jammed them back into her thick file. Zoe stood up, gripping the table to steady herself. She managed to pull herself together enough to say, 'Thank you' to Sophie, who seemed, for a moment, relieved.

Outside the next case was ready and waiting. Zoe understood those people waiting out there; their expectations and intention. There would be other women who came here, before a judge, to convince the world that they should be given their chance to become a mother with a capital M. Never again for Zoe though. This was it. She looked down. It was time to retire the cornflower-blue suit. She was daunted, but she'd walk through that waiting room with her head held high. She would be the best mother possible.

Dancing

Naomi wriggled out of her skirt and pulled her top roughly over her head. The room was spinning a little. She stepped out of her underpants and pulled off her bra. She giggled and steadied herself by striking a flamenco pose.

The man on the bed leered at her. The music started. She began to slowly spin around the bedroom, her hands, one over the other, moving up and over her head until they hung there like two unfolding flowers.

The man took a drink from his glass, neat whisky. Naomi could smell it on his breath as she moved around the bed. She closed her eyes. The flamenco music swelled and ebbed. A male singer's voice rose up and over his stormy guitar and Naomi gave herself completely to the music.

She moved gracefully, her naked ivory-white breasts in profile against the deep red plush wallpaper. With her fingers curling and stretching she brought her hands down the length of her torso and up again. Then she took a series of small, trembling steps before turning away from the man on the bed. She ran her hands through her hair, her naked back arched towards him. He groaned but she was already working herself into a frenzy of stamping as the singer's voice rose in a crescendo of clicks and wails.

She turned and turned and turned, finally swooping down to kneel. In profile now, her head bent forward, touching her raised knee, nothing moving except her heaving chest, her hands weaving their way up again above her head. Just like the Spanish women in her flamenco dance class had said, all the best dancers were in their fifties and sixties.

Suddenly the music died. Naomi turned. 'It's four in the morning, for Christ's sake. Come to bed.' The man's words were slurred a little.

Naomi stopped and steadied herself. She blinked.

'Noel?' she asked.

'Who's Noel?' A stranger's voice, now muffled as he rolled over onto his side.

Naomi remembered the bar, meeting a lawyer of all people. Was this the man from the bar? She peered at him. She couldn't be sure.

'No, not Noel.'

The man began to snore.

She stumbled to her skirt, knocking over a small stack of CDs that she had worked her way through. They clattered to the floor. She froze. Suddenly, modestly, she held her skirt in front of her chest, but the man snored on.

She had to get away and get back to her life. Was this her life? She pondered the question for a moment. No. This was not her life and she dressed quickly.

She looked at the man again. He was certainly not Noel. She could remember leaving the court and feeling empty, going to the bar, an upmarket bar in Norton Street. She had no plan beyond that. When was the last time she had eaten? The wine and whisky soured in her stomach and she lurched out of the house onto the early morning street. It looked familiar, so she began to walk.

'Walk it off,' she told herself. 'Just start walking.'

The stabbing

The time it took to live your life just kept expanding. There were so many things to do at Gran's, but here it was like one long Christmas holiday. For a while, it had been great, but, especially now it was permanent, Chris was beginning to wonder if this was all there was. He'd felt some serious boredom lately.

It was an overcast night, full of high wind and barking dogs. Chris was aimlessly kicking a can along the road when he heard something. A man's voice. Raised in anger, surprise? Chris turned his head. It was coming from the skate park. There in the distance he saw two people standing close together.

He walked towards them, hugging the shadows carefully, keeping his eyes on them. When he was about a hundred metres away and hidden by the thick grasses, he stopped. He looked around carefully to make sure that there wasn't anyone else around. He couldn't be sure, but he thought he could make out shapes of figures on the play equipment.

One voice sounded like Dane's, but he did not recognise the other person's.

Dane said something that Chris couldn't quite make out. He sounded a bit uptight, his voice all high and squeaky.

The man turned to walk away.

The wind carried their voices eerily close. 'I'll get the money for him. I just don't have it now,' the man said over his shoulder towards Chris, like he was a sincerely nice guy.

Dane was having none of it. 'That's bullshit. He's given you so many chances. He's running out of time. He needs it now.'

Dane was silent.

Chris watched, perfectly still. His open-mouthed breath was quick and shallow and smelt like vinegar. The Dane he knew wouldn't take that kind of crap from anyone at school.

The man began to walk away and then Chris saw Dane take out his double-edged flick-knife and shout something to the man, who turned and laughed at Dane. Like it was all a joke. Perhaps it was, he was pretty convincing. Then he ran towards Dane and grabbed for the knife. *Staccato. Agitato. Prestissimo.* And Dane locked onto him. They swayed back and forth like they were slow dancing for a second or two. Dane was strong, but he was just a kid. Chris wanted to yell, 'Leave him alone,' but this wasn't the playground, this was some other different game with different rules.

Frozen, Chris stayed hidden in the native grasses along with the bush cockroaches and empty chip packets. His feet felt as heavy and as lifeless as piano legs, his mouth dry. His head was full of clashing *messa di voce* harmonic minor scales, *descending, descending, descending.*

It was all quiet for a second except for his own breathing. Dane slumped forward onto the man and they both fell down. He could hear Dane crying now, quick little moans – up and down, up and down. The man was kicking out. He rolled quickly, almost frantically, away from Dane. Dane was not moving. Chris didn't wait to see what happened next, he turned and sprinted away.

Part III

Sore eyes

hris was used to the way missing someone made him feel. For most of his life something had been *missing*. He was practically a missing professional. He had still missed Zoe for a while, even after he found her. Missing Dane and missing Grandpa, or the idea of his dad, or Gran, were in completely separate categories. He felt different about each one and he had come to realise that no two missings were the same, could ever be the same.

Dane's death was complicated and shocking and unfair. Dane had been many things – smelly, rude, mental, wild – but above all these he had been a friend to Chris. Those times in the park – late at night, when they were together, not saying much – felt special, different. Dane, with his rat's tail and chipped teeth, had been the best kind of friend, and it had been a friendship that snuck up on Chris and took him by surprise. Dane had spent time with Chris, not because Chris could do anything, or give him anything. He didn't even know that Chris could play the piano. Chris made sure of that. And now, after Dane's death and the events of that night, Chris knew that things were about to change for the worse. He was confused. Why hadn't he tried to save Dane? Why couldn't he move his feet that night? What stopped him? It was the same way when Grandpa died. *Chris, call the ambulance!* But he didn't move. He went over and over it in his head.

The man who killed Dane had not been charged. No witnesses had come forward, and Chris didn't know what to do. The cops didn't have enough evidence – apparently the guy even bragged about it. Chris was scared to the bone. If only half the stuff that Dane had said about the dealers and the gangs was true, he had to watch his back.

He was missing Dane and that made him miss Naomi too. Last weekend he had to remind her that he was in Year 6 now, and then she chimed in, 'Max is in Year 4. That's right.' Naomi forgetting something like that was mental.

Chris's high-school application form arrived. It was supposed to be filled out by a parent or a guardian, but Chris knew he'd have to fill it out, like he filled out all the other forms. Somehow he hadn't quite got round to it. Gran would be onto him in a flash if she knew. A part of him didn't want to admit just yet that he wasn't going to the Sydney Conservatorium of Music. Filling out that form was too final – it confirmed that the future lay here with Mum.

In the months since he and Max had come to live with Zoe, he had not changed his mind about a single thing. He would not have traded any of it for the whole world. Until now. The high-school application form made him stop and think about his life in a new way. The future, which had been a long way away, was suddenly here, and Chris was smart enough to realise that it contained more of the same. Mum needing help. Max needing help. Friends like Dane disappearing. Every time Chris thought of that terrible night, he wanted to get up and run as far away from here as he could.

∞

Zoe hadn't come home last night. Sometimes she left them alone at night, but she usually turned up before morning. Chris knew because he slept lightly, listening for her, but all he'd heard last night were the wind and distant sirens and trains.

Why didn't Mum act a bit more like a mother? She wasn't even trying! Chris was acting like a parent as well as a son. Chris was acting like so many people it was hard to keep it all straight in his head. There was skate-park Chris – all tough and mean and fearless and breaking into cars. There was Chris, the big brother – looking after Max. There was Chris, the son – trying to be funny and make Mum love him properly. There was Chris, the grandson – polite and stuff. Then there was Chris, the blood brother, who hadn't saved his friend. And last but not least, there was Chris, the pianist – the Chris he liked most. But the Chris he most liked was disappearing, along with his dream of the Con.

'You hungry?' Chris asked Max.

Max didn't answer.

'Are you hungry?' he asked again.

Max turned his head slightly. His eyes were puffy. 'I can't open my eyes,' he said.

'What do you mean?'

'Just what I said. They're all stuck together.'

Max's eyes had been red and sore for days, and now he looked really bad. The eczema on his legs had made him look contagious enough, but now the skin around his mouth was all blotchy and dry too. Chris tried to think what to do. What could he do that wouldn't draw too much attention to them, but get Max sorted out? What would Naomi do?

Chris tried to open one of Max's eyes.

Max yelped.

Chris washed Max's face gently and combed a bit of water through his hair. He knew well enough that appearance did matter, especially when you had to interact with the system. Chris didn't ring Naomi. Last time he had shared a problem like this she had taken Zoe to court. It just made things worse for them, not better. He waited for Zoe as long as he dared, but Max was moaning and it was too much. Eventually he left Zoe a note, before taking Max by the hand and leading him down the front path.

It was one of those typical Saturdays. There was the incessant sound of a lawnmower and the smell of cut grass in the air. Even here, among the car wrecks and broken wheelie bins, someone still mowed the lawn. Their Saturdays used to be full of sport and shopping, but now they just stretched on endlessly with no shape to them.

'My little brother is sick,' Chris said in a rush when the old woman opened her door.

She was even older than Chris expected. Well, she looked older than Gran. She was as wide as she was high. Chris was right about one thing though. She was definitely the owner of the red car. Her house smelt of soap and vanilla rice pudding.

The woman opened her door a fraction more to get a better look at him.

'We live just next door,' he said, pointing back over his shoulder.

'How sick?'

Chris toyed with playing it down, saying something like, 'He's not that sick, he just can't open his eyes.' But he was afraid that if he did, the woman would turn him away. If he sounded too dramatic, she might get angry with him when she saw Max. It was hard to know. He decided to be straight about it.

'His eyes are stuck together,' Chris said.

'Wait there,' the woman said and shut the door firmly. Her door knocker was covered in a crocheted clown made out of bright orange wool. Chris wondered what else the bright orange wool had been used to make. He tried to imagine a jumper made out of it. Not possible. Socks? Not even. A scarf? Maybe. Along the edge of her front doorsteps were several gnomes and potted plants. Naomi's house – their house – had the same potted plants.

He thought about how bad he felt trusting a total stranger. But how else could he get Max to a doctor? And that was not the only reason he was here on this doorstep. Chris thought that this woman was probably a mother, that she knew how to be a mother.

A minute later she opened her door, car keys in her hand. She began clucking like a hen over Max. 'You poor old thing,' she said softly. 'Let me see your face now. Yes, that looks very sore.'

At the hospital the old woman knew exactly what to do, like she was used to doing exactly this every Saturday morning.

'Their mother sent us down here. She said we could get some medicine for his eyes from the nurses,' the woman said in her most upbeat voice.

The nurse behind the glass partition was unmoved. 'Are these boys relatives of yours, Doris?'

Chris was not sure whether he should be worried or not that the nurse knew Doris's name.

Doris shook her head. 'No, just a neighbour.'

'What's your surname again, Doris?'

'Stubbs.'

The nurse began typing it into a computer.

Doris Stubbs? What kind of a name was that? Chris didn't know any other Dorises. He relaxed a little. Doris seemed to understand everything. She probably even knew that he sat in her car at night sometimes, just because it smelt right.

The nurse didn't ask who was looking after the children – *phew*.

'You need a parent or guardian to sign the form. You need your Medicare card.'

Accident and emergency departments were all the same.

'We have that,' Chris said, producing their card. He tried not to think about what might be happening underneath Max's eyelids. The thought of pus made him feel sick.

'Their mother will be meeting us here. She's at work,' Doris lied.

'Look, it's probably just conjunctivitis. Nothing much to worry about, but it's very contagious. Wash your hands. Make sure you wash the bedclothes and his clothes when you get home. Wait over there with Doris,' the nurse said, pointing to some chairs in the waiting room, 'while I get someone to see you.'

Chris knew that this was a point of no return. It had been a difficult decision – risk coming here without Mum or stay alone in the house with Max to wait for her. He was thinking of escape strategies and contingency plans in case Doris turned out to be a wrong idea. To his way of thinking there were right and wrong ideas. It was a wrong idea to steal for kicks. It was a right idea to steal money for food. It was a right idea to lie to Gran about how well things were going with Mum, because then she didn't worry so much. It was a wrong idea to ask Gran for help, and it was a wrong idea to ask Mum for help. It had been a right idea to hang out with Dane – that way he didn't get the shit kicked out of him – but then it was a wrong idea because now he felt like he was in a lot of trouble. It got complicated if you thought about it too much.

Doris sat Max down and eased herself into a plastic chair next to him. Chris flopped into a chair on the other side of Max. The waiting room was not too busy, it was a Saturday morning, after all. A woman with a black eye walked up and down. A few people slept on the seats.

'Long wait?' the woman with the black eye said to Doris. Doris just nodded.

Every now and then Chris glimpsed doctors and nurses through the open plastic doors. They looked back at him, their faces blank, unreadable. Chris sat quietly beside Max and tried to think comforting thoughts.

'There, there,' Doris said to Max in a quiet voice, one used by the grandmas of the world.

'Why are you helping us?' Max asked in an accusing voice.

'Honestly, Max, it's as if you don't want any help!' Chris snapped at him.

Doris nodded her head. 'Max, you be careful now. You don't want to end up in the system.'

'Why? Anything would be better than this,' Max groaned. 'I can't stand it!'

'This nice lady has brought us here,' Chris began, but Doris put her hand on his arm.

'Whatever you do, you don't want to get mixed up with the system. I lost two of my kids that way.'

Max grunted. 'I don't care. I'm hungry. I want some food right now, and no more of that vegetarian stuff of Zoe's.'

Saturdays with Zoe were the worst. Most other days they could get by, but on Saturdays at her place there was no breakfast and no hope of any. Chris had a strategy though. He told Max, just stay in bed until lunchtime. It was as simple as that, and every second Saturday they were at Gran's anyway. They could eat then. There was always a solution if you put your mind to it. Although right now his stomach was really rumbling and he had that empty, cold feeling.

'I'll see if I can get us a cup of tea and a biscuit, or something,' Chris mumbled, getting up off the seat and strolling a little too nonchalantly over to the nurse's window.

Support group

Naomi walked Yom and Deng in through the front door just in time to see her friend Patricia clap her hands to make herself heard above the waiting-room chatter and babies' squeals.

'Let's start!'

Patricia waved Naomi and Yom over to the group.

'Thanks,' she said to Naomi.

'Everyone, this is my friend Naomi. She and I used to work together at the hospital. And this is her friend, Yom. Naomi is volunteering with our group today. Naomi, this is everyone!'

'Hello,' Naomi said, smiling and waving the collection of children's books she had brought with her from Leichhardt library.

There were women from East and West Africa. Some in hijabs, others in kangas with head ties, and cotton shifts in shocking pink and aqua, ochre and olive and saffron. Little girls were dressed in frilly puffy-sleeved dresses, their bright eyes downcast, clinging to their mothers.

Naomi had picked up Yom and Deng and brought them along to the group. She was given the job of helping to look after the children while Patricia and an interpreter ran a budgeting and shopping session for the women. Marial now worked shifts with a number of Sudanese men collecting shopping trolleys at Westfield. He and the other men often left a box of over-ripe tomatoes or broken biscuits that they had found at the back of one of the supermarkets for the women's group to divide up and take home. This morning there was a pile of soft, fresh strawberries still in their punnets, as well as yellow boxes of tinned fish sitting on the trestle table.

'We are so happy in Mt Druitt. A rich and wonderful place,' he told Naomi when he called her every few weeks to update her on his family's progress. 'The doctors say that Deng is so clever now. God willing, he will be studying at university soon!'

'Well, preschool, definitely,' she said. He was reaching his milestones – smiling, rolling over, sitting up, crawling and so on.

Chris had also been calling in on the 'emergency only' mobile phone that she had given him. He didn't say much, but Naomi had trained her ear to listen to the in-between in his communication. His silence about such things as Zoe's cooking, his school projects, music, or local hockey teams said volumes. He was more forthcoming about the skate park and new friends. Phone cards had become a sort of currency between them until recently, when he had 'lost' the phone. Grilling him over it did not get Naomi far. She would have to buy him another one if she wanted to hear from him regularly, but she held off. Money was tight.

This morning she put her shopping and grandchildren and mobile phones and Marial and his band of unlikely skip-dippers on hold for an hour, and instead she sat down, her reading glasses on the end of her nose, and began the story of the Three Little Pigs. The children sat in a semicircle around her, or at her elbow, or stood over her shoulder, spellbound by the magic of listening to the written word.

Shrugs

Zoe slowly washed a bright green lettuce at the sink. She eased each leaf loose and ran it under the cold water before placing it in the drainer. Chris stood beside her. He was silent and wide-eyed. He was too close and it annoyed her. Then he started to cry. This scared her. She did not know what to do when a twelve-year-old boy cried. She kept washing the lettuce.

'The day Grandpa . . .' Chris said, before pausing to get himself under control. 'The day Grandpa died was like any other Saturday. We had played a trial game. Grandpa was our coach and we won.'

Zoe didn't have the heart to tell him that she didn't want to hear about Noel's death. She just didn't want to know the detail of it.

'Grandpa went like this,' Chris sobbed and clutched his chest. 'He looked at Gran, like, "Please, help." Then he fell forward and cracked his head on the table. Gran was washing a lettuce just like that,' Chris said, indicating the leaves in Zoe's hand.

Zoe turned to face Chris.

'Gran said, "Chris, call the ambulance!" But I couldn't. I stayed back, pretending I hadn't heard her. Max's tennis ball was rolling down the slope towards the back fence and I just watched it roll.'

'There's nothing you could have done to save him,' Zoe said.

But Chris wasn't listening to her. He was staring at the lettuce leaves. He was *telling* her something and he didn't want to be stopped.

'Max called triple O. Outside, everything was quiet. Then, after a while, I heard some car doors opening and closing. I told Gran and I let the ambos in.'

It was the same as the way Zoe went over and over things to do with THE ACCIDENT. She remembered the shrug. She had shrugged him off. If she just hadn't shrugged . . . If she could take that shrug back everything would be different.

'Later – after – Gran said that Grandpa was wise and that she loved him. She said, "Everything will be okay while we have each other." I keep thinking about that.'

Zoe wiped her hands and put her arm around Chris.

'Dr Bird came with his black bag, and put his head on one side, like he does,' Chris said. ' "What will you do?" he asked, but Gran just shrugged.'

Ah, there was the shrug, Zoe thought.

' "Take care of the boys," Gran said. She said Grandpa was a better parent to us than her. That's what she said.'

Zoe felt something shift in her understanding of Naomi. The Naomi she knew was never wrong, never unsure.

'I knew that some time had passed because the sun had moved. Max was asleep but I stayed up. Gran said, "Why couldn't it have been me to have a heart attack, not Noel?" I don't think she knew I could hear her, but I could.'

Chris pulled away from Zoe and leant over the sink. He hated the wretched lettuce and he hated himself too.

'I wish I hadn't heard her say that because, then, I thought it was true,' he said. 'And now I think she was wrong.'

Nobody

Seemed like Gavin was always at Zoe's these days, Max thought as he stood at the bedroom window looking down on them in the backyard. He didn't mind so much. After the day go-karting at Eastern Creek he had made a big effort to be nicer to Gavin because out there on the track Gavin had proved he was okay. But Max knew Gavin was getting on Chris's nerves, well and truly.

Gavin was problematic, if you asked Max. He wasn't a dad or a big brother or even a friendly uncle. He was a bloke who hung around and took up a lot of space, but then disappeared when you really needed him. You couldn't rely on Gavin. That was the major problem with him. That and the fact that when he was around, he liked to talk. He talked too much, in Max's opinion. He liked to talk about fibro and tiling and pieces of wood. He reckoned that dead bodies have less than two legs, statistically speaking. Whatever that meant! When he did come over he helped himself to things in the fridge, although he was definitely not into Zoe's raw and 'nutritious' vegetarian food.

Max decided it was probably the talking that really ticked off Chris. Chris was more the silent type these days. The silent-but-deadly type. Nobody messed with Chris at school;

Chris kept to himself completely. It was funny how he had gone from Mr Popular to Mr Nobody.

Every time Max thought about Dane being stabbed, he shuddered. The principal had addressed the whole assembly about it. It made Max sick to think about it. He had seen the spot on the way to school. All by himself. The police tape flapping in the wind. It was pretty hard not to miss it.

Max could see how Gavin and Chris could be a problem. But hadn't Gavin fixed Chris's skateboard? And Chris never said thanks or anything. Gran would be *so* disappointed if she knew, if she knew half the stuff that went on and half the stuff that Chris did. It didn't bear thinking about what she'd say if she found out what had happened to Chris's best friend.

Was Gavin Mum's boyfriend? Max wondered. What did that make him? A step-dad? Definitely not. He was one of those people who was here one day, gone the next. Sometimes Max didn't see him for ages and then he'd be everywhere – down the street, outside school, at the pool. There was a time when Max thought Gavin might move in. But Mum didn't seem the type. There was her bad cooking, for a start. And who would want to live here if they didn't have to?

Max had asked Chris the other day if he thought Gavin was Mum's boyfriend and Chris had practically choked him on the spot for even mentioning it. So maybe that meant a big fat yes. And he seemed to think that Gavin had nicked his keyboard, but Max thought that was stupid. Gavin couldn't even play chopsticks.

Dry as a bone

It was hard to believe that it was two years. Two years, where had they gone? It was as if the aperture of Naomi's life had closed down since she had packed their belongings and driven them to Blacktown Station to meet Zoe for the first visit. And still Naomi was struggling to accept the fact that she had lost them for good now. There on the kitchen bench lay a small white ticket:

WAVERLEY BONDI BEACH BAND INC.
presents
SCHOOL CONCERT
Adult Ticket

Naomi could not bring herself to throw it out and yet every time she looked at it she felt such emptiness. It seemed as though just a few months ago they were at the school, the boys in the band, playing Beethoven's Ninth and 'We Will Rock You'. That warm afternoon it was possible to pretend that things were all right. Now the boys were gone – a new school, no more band, no more swimming with Max on a Monday afternoon. And Chris's high-school options were still up in the air.

The phone had largely stopped ringing for the boys, or matters to do with the boys. No more hockey calls. No more invitations to birthday parties. But Kerry kept calling. Earlier, the phone had rung and it was her. 'Is Chris going to apply for the Conservatorium?' Kerry asked. Before Naomi could reply, she ran on, 'He's not registered.'

'He says that he's been studying,' Naomi frowned. She dismissed the niggling doubt that this might not be true, just because she hadn't seen it with her own eyes. She had no reason to doubt Chris, but whenever she asked him about the Con, he was evasive. She shook her head and put her fears down to her own state of mind.

'I have some test papers I thought he might find helpful. I could bring them around,' said Kerry.

Naomi murmured her thanks and hung up. It was only a matter of a few more days, she told herself, until the children's weekend visit, when she could try to get some answers from Chris about his plans. But two weeks is a long time in the life of a widow and unemployed midwife. She washed her hands slowly. Now that the boys were settled with Zoe, it was as if she could not regain her equilibrium. She looked around her. The house was not a home any longer. The mortgage was soon going to become impossible to manage. She rattled around in each room and, as if to prove the point, she raised her arms skywards and shook them.

'I've had enough,' Naomi said.

The phone rang. Her sister Sarah sounded cheerful.

'When are you coming for a visit?' she asked Naomi.

'I don't know. But I have been thinking lately about the old farmhouse. Did you know the rosebush there must be over a hundred?'

'Sean owns the farmhouse now,' Sarah said, a chink of curiosity opening up in her voice. 'He'd rent it to you, if you wanted it.'

Sean Adams was one of Noel's most entrepreneurial distant cousins. He had bought and sold properties in the Grenfell shire for quite a while, her own childhood Mara Downs homestead among them.

'It's just that I can't pay the mortgage here for much longer. That's really the final straw for me. Now that I'm not working, I'm just worrying about it all the time. I think I'll have to sell up soon. But then what?'

'Christ, you sound like half the farmers around here,' Sarah said. 'The drought's been that bad.'

'I can't leave the boys. But their lives are with Zoe. I can accept that now,' Naomi said.

'If you lived here, you'd see more of them in the school holidays,' Sarah said. 'You know, they'd come for the whole holiday. It's too far to be going up and down to the city.'

'You're probably right. I hate this every-second-weekend visit. It's impossible. It's not enough time to really help them beyond feeding them and washing their clothes, although Chris tells me that everything is fine at Zoe's. Max doesn't say much about it. It's just now that I'm not working I notice things more. I really miss the old me, my life. This is just a half life . . .' Naomi's voice trailed off.

'Why don't you come home then?' Sarah said.

'I have to make sure that Chris's high school is sorted out. He still says he's going to the Conservatorium. I'm worried that he hasn't enrolled properly.'

There was a slight pause at the other end.

'I'll speak to Sean about the old farmhouse,' Sarah said. 'It's been empty for a while. I'll just see. No obligation or anything. You have a think about it. You could have the boys all summer long. Might be better all round that way.'

Naomi hung up the telephone and took out the box of photographs. She cleared a space on the kitchen table. The

Great Wall of China. The Eiffel Tower. Victoria Falls. Such adventures all over the world together. She heard her own young voice whispering in Noel's ear, 'I'm homesick.'

Their wedding – he'd worn sandals, she recalled, and had that dark beard. His crooked smile; she traced his lips with her finger. The photos of the first ten years of their marriage were funny: fat, newborn babies; Evelyn and Gwen in matching caftans; the boys playing cricket, riding bikes, shooting arrows, dressed up for Halloween. There was one of Zoe at the kitchen table just about where she now sat. Zoe looked high. Naomi put that thought to one side. She shuffled through the rest of the photos quickly. Chris's first day at school. Max in his beloved hockey shirt.

Naomi reminded herself that things would change; that one day she'd stop feeling so empty. But she needed to make a decision; she needed a change. She was thinking she wanted to leave the city and to return to Grenfell. Perhaps a visit was in order, after all. She had never got used to missing Grenfell. No Noel, no sons, no grandsons. Just her.

Three days later, she rose early with renewed purpose and swam laps at the local pool in the quiet before dawn. The water was glassy and warm, steam rising in the chilly wintry air. When the sun did finally rise, the sky was shell-pink.

It had always been one of her favourite things to do with Chris and Max – at the swimming pool they could simply be together. She tried to make sure that the boys, on their weekend visits, got to swim as often as possible. After their swim they usually ate breakfast at the pool's café. So that Sunday morning the three of them found themselves eating breakfast together there. Chris stirred his hot chocolate. His toast lay untouched.

'Can I have your toast?' Max asked him.

Chris nodded vaguely and sank lower in his chair, looking away at the pool below.

Max, with a mouthful of toast, offered one of his observations. 'I don't like fuss,' he said.

Naomi nodded. 'I don't like it either.'

In the last few months Max had developed new and mysterious aches in his legs that Naomi had disappointingly diagnosed as growing pains. He burst into tears of frustration over his shoelaces; Naomi said he was getting ready to become a teenager. He coughed too loudly. He spoke too soon. He took offence where none was intended. Chris, on the other hand, had become increasingly reserved. Naomi was unable to draw him out. He made his bed when he was at her house. He wrote in a diary. He played a miniature prelude on the piano but never the accompanying fugue, over and over again, losing himself, escaping into the music.

Naomi wondered again what was going on with Chris. Something had happened, was happening, to him, but she couldn't reach him. Zoe probably knew. They were close. Yes, it was time to let go.

Passionfruit

Chris sat on the floor at Zoe's. He opened his high-school application form yet again. Under 'Intended School' he so badly wanted to write 'Conservatorium of Music'. But he didn't. It was no use pretending. Chris knew that since his keyboard had mysteriously disappeared from Zoe's place, he couldn't pass the audition. He hadn't done enough practice. If he was honest, he hadn't practised properly in over six months. He ran his fingers along the form's edge. He couldn't remember F harmonic minor. He closed his eyes tight. How many flats? Was it four or five? He scratched his head. There was no point in completing the second or third high-school preferences either. He didn't want to go to any other school. Not round here, anyway. He signed Zoe's name, folded the paper and put it back in his schoolbag. It was too hard.

Next he took out the week's homework sheet. He didn't bother with homework as a rule, but he thought it was time to start making a few changes. And besides, school was some-times interesting, usually the art class or writing and working on the computers in the library. That was mostly calm and had a purpose.

'Lesson 3: Conductors and Insulators', Chris read out loud

to the empty townhouse. 'Explain: "Electricity is always trying to go somewhere." '

Chris sat with his pencil between his fingers and thought deeply about how to answer this question. He was always trying to go somewhere. How could he explain it? Mum was the same. She was probably out walking right now. She'd come home with an armful of wood or sticks and leave them by the back door. She was going to make a sculpture soon.

'Name ten conductors and ten insulators.' Chris thought hard. They did this in class, but lately he was having trouble concentrating on the board. He tried to remember what had been said. Wood? Copper? But which was which? Chris tried to visualise the whiteboard, but it was blurred and out of focus.

'List five dangerous situations involving electricity and metal.' Chris suddenly saw Dane rolling on top of the man in the park. He tried to block it out, but he kept seeing the knife in Dane's hand. In his mind he was running to him. He saw the blade as it glinted in the moonlight. Dane's elbow was at a strange angle. He was standing behind the man. Chris grabbed the man and pushed him away, like a hero would, but then Dane turned on him. Chris tried to imagine the man's breath on his neck, the knife in his guts. Would he know how to stab someone? Then Chris was back hiding in the grasses and the shadows. Watching, breathless. Dane reckoned that he learnt to stab from his brother. That's what brothers are for, Dane had told Chris once, joking around, or maybe not?

Chris was breathing a little harder than normal. He brought his eyes back into focus on his messy homework sheet. 'Your writing is too small,' his teacher told him. 'Write bigger. Be bold. What are you afraid of?'

'There's nothing to worry about,' he told himself. 'They can't hurt you.' But he was not so sure. And what about Max and Mum? If the dealer found out what Chris had seen, he might make his point through Mum or, even worse, Max. Chris stood and looked out of the window. Nothing moved in the street. Not even an empty Cheezels packet or a blade of grass. He returned to his homework sheet and tried to concentrate on something.

His English and maths half-year assessments both lay on the floor beside him. According to the reports, he was below the national average in literacy, reading, textual devices (whatever they were), syntax and vocabulary. In fact he was in the bottom 10 per cent for both subjects. Gran would be so cross if she saw these results. She had such high expectations. It used to make him mad, but now it made him smile. She believed in him. Chris looked at his hands, turning them over in his lap. He tried to remember them racing up and down the piano keys; he tried doing the scale of B flat major this time. But the memory was too thin. The last few times he had visited Gran he hadn't even played the piano. Chris sighed.

Max walked in through the back door and pushed on past him.

Chris rolled across the carpet to Max's schoolbag and took out his results. The same – all at the bottom of the graph.

It was one thing for his results to be bad, but it was another thing for Max's. He followed Max up the stairs and stood in the bedroom doorway. He was now lying in the bed, still fully dressed in his dirty school uniform. No teeth brushed. No clean pyjamas. No clean sheets. Gran would be cross – no, *disappointed*, Chris thought.

'Max? You awake?'

Max grunted, 'Whaddya want?'

'I think we should move back to Gran's.'

'What?'

'Before it's too late.'

By that Chris was talking about more than just their marks, but he had already decided that Max didn't need to know he'd seen the stabbing.

'Move back with Gran?' Max sat up. 'But I thought you liked it here?'

What was there to like? They both looked around the room as if for inspiration: the piles of dirty clothes on the floor, the dusty window, no light shade on the bare light bulb hanging from the ceiling.

'We should take Mum with us,' Chris said.

'How's that going to work, exactly?' said Max, exasperated.

'I don't know, but I'll sort something out. If you want to, that is.'

'I hate it here,' Max said.

'Yeah, I've noticed.'

'Where is Mum, anyway? That's not right. Doris says it's not right,' Max said, but Chris cut him off.

'You haven't said anything to Doris about when Mum's not here, have you?' Chris asked quickly.

'I didn't have to say anything to her,' Max said, crossly. 'She notices stuff. She knows that Mum's not here half the time. Why do you think Doris feeds me? The whole place knows that Mum isn't here.'

Chris thought about Naomi's passionfruit vine. The passionfruit would be ripe soon and he wanted to be there to eat them all.

Dreamer

Even at primary school Zoe had been the child who everyone said was a daydreamer. They always had to call out her name twice, or ask her opinion over again. She was usually the one left out of games, or the last one to be chosen as a partner for handball. She had a great way of switching off the noise. Everyone said she was vague. Aged twenty, she'd been invited by a gallery to speak about her art and she had asked, what was the point? The gallery owner had become with her when she'd repeated the question in an interview. But she had meant it. What was the point? If you had to speak about it, it lost its magic. Art exists in that space between words and knowing. Once, when Zoe was still promising as an artist, she had been asked to speak to a class of art students and the words just wouldn't come – it had been terrifying. But when she saw Chris sketching, she had found that she suddenly had a lot to say about art. (When Chris asked her to help with his maths homework, that was another matter.)

In the backyard Zoe had started stockpiling. Well, that's what Ben used to call it. She was collecting things again. Driftwood. Broken glass. Rocks. Plastic. She was like a spider, Ben had said, describing the way she approached the preparatory work of sculpting. At the same time, upstairs in her bedroom she was drawing and painting everyone she cared about and putting the results together in a book. She had been working on it for some time and it was almost complete. It was nearly ready to show the boys.

It was thrilling to be thinking about sculpture again, but it took a lot of energy. Chris seemed to understand, but Max didn't, and she couldn't explain it to him. She couldn't explain how this and the garden were sometimes the only things that made sense to her. This is where she started all those years ago, before Ben, the car accident, the children. When it was just her. It was hard to remember that time, it was so long ago.

There was a movement in the shadows. Zoe stopped what she was doing and stood back.

'You'll lose them kids, if you're not careful,' a voice said.

Zoe nearly dropped her bundle of sticks.

It was hard to see the woman in the gloom, but her voice was very clear. Zoe tried to walk past her to the door.

'You're not much of a mum, but you are their mum. You should start acting like one.'

Zoe squinted.

'My name's Doris Stubbs and I live next to you.'

Zoe nodded. 'I know who you are,' she said. She had seen Doris getting in and out of her car. She had seen the boys going in and out of Doris's house. Max had told her about how Doris had handled the visit to the hospital. She had seen her working in the community garden.

'I don't think you do. I was like you once,' Doris said.

Zoe took a step back. It was hard to imagine being anything like Doris; Doris Stubbs at art school? A promising sculptor? A mother, even?

'I was a young woman who was looking in all the wrong places for love. These kiddies are here, trying to love you.'

Zoe watched Doris's lips. They were like prunes. They twitched in between her announcements. She was just another version of Naomi. Zoe supposed that she was destined to have a version of Naomi in her life until she learnt the lessons – whatever they were. Naomi was so much more than this, though. Naomi, with her dangly earrings and her sense of humour and sandalwood soap. How dare someone like Doris, in an ill-fitting nightie, address Zoe, uninvited, and point out her shortcomings.

They stood glaring at each other.

'You need to make things right for those boys, and do it quickly before it's too late,' Doris said. And with that, the old woman disappeared back into the dark.

The Book of Change

The following afternoon, Zoe was opening the *I Ching* at random and reading out paragraphs to Gavin. 'Darkening of the light. Righteous persistence in the face of difficulty brings reward. This hexagram symbolises light hidden within the earth.'

It was one of those beautiful, runny sunsets full of warm pinks and apricot. They were cuddled up in an old armchair that Gavin had dragged in off the footpath. It was covered in faded floral print. Not exactly garden furniture, but it now sat squarely in Zoe's backyard. Gavin started kissing her, even though she was in the middle of reading. When she looked up, Chris was standing there. Usually Gavin was happy enough to be pretty reserved with her in front of the kids, but today he kept trying to get it on. Zoe dropped the book and pushed Gavin away before scrambling to her feet.

'Where's Max, honey?' Zoe asked in her best mother's voice.

'Getting changed,' Chris said, turning away from her and Gavin. He looked a bit sick.

'I thought we might go up to the pub?' Zoe said, following Chris inside the house.

Chris shrugged. He was getting pricklier around Gavin. Chris could make things pretty clear without saying a single word.

Zoe loved going to the pub. She liked the way the music made her feel all loose and ready for action. She loved the lights over the pool tables. She liked the indoor water feature near the pokies. Zoe could lose herself in the crowd around the bar. The pub was full of couples like them, people in low-key, low-maintenance relationships. Most of the women had a couple of kids with them and the men bought the kids a lemonade or the occasional packet of chips. Zoe played the odd good-natured game of pool with one or other of the women. They were nice enough. It wasn't boring, things happened at the pub and she only went every now and then. Max hung out on the play equipment and Chris, well, Chris just did his own thing.

'It's embarrassing,' Chris said.

Zoe wasn't sure whether he was talking about going to the pub or Gavin kissing her, but she had a pretty good idea that he was talking about Gavin.

Zoe thought about how things were changing with Chris; everything was becoming more complicated. Chris wanted more and more of her. He demanded things where once he asked. He shouted where he once spoke. He was bigger and growing taller every day. Soon he would be taller than her. And she was shrinking down inside herself.

'Don't be rude,' Zoe said.

She should see his teacher at school to discuss this stuff. That's what his teacher, an intense young woman, had said. Come up to the school to discuss any further concerns. Further? Zoe didn't know how to discuss the usual ones. The last parent–teacher meeting had been a disaster. She felt *so* inadequate as Chris's parent. Half the stuff the teacher talked about she had never heard of: 'student learning outcomes', 'restorative practices', 'risk behaviours'. Chris was at the bottom of the class. The teacher seemed to think it was her fault. Was it?

'Gavin is a loser,' Chris spat the words at her.

Gavin had appeared in the doorway in one second flat. He grabbed Chris and held him by the front of his school shirt. 'Listen here, you little twerp, you'd better keep your head down and show me some respect.'

'You can shove your respect up your arse,' Chris said straight into Gavin's face. Max appeared at the doorway in the lounge room.

Gavin shoved Chris hard against the wall. It stunned him. Max yelled and moved between Gavin and Chris. Then Zoe was pushing them all out of the way. 'Chris!'

'Move!' Gavin said.

But before Gavin could get past Zoe and grab Chris again, Chris turned and sprinted down the hallway towards the front of the house, sobbing as he went. At the front door he slowed a little to give it a good kick.

Chris was so angry that he could have run straight through the front door. How *could* she have sex with Gavin? Weren't they just good friends? When Max had mentioned the 'boy-friend' word, Chris could have practically throttled him. Then, just as he was trying to think of the proper way to bring it up with Zoe . . . Chris hated the way Gavin was always there. Passed out on their couch. Dispensing advice. Talking about himself.

Chris had walked out and there they were, kissing! All over each other. It was disgusting. He wanted to kick Gavin's teeth in. How could she? How dare she even touch Gavin. Gavin with his big grin and bad tatts. Who said Gavin could come in? What about Dad? What about him? This was *his* place now. He never said Gavin could come in. Was Gavin making her cups of tea in the morning? Was Gavin stealing stuff for her? No, he was hocking Chris's stuff. He was stealing from her and him!

Chris's heart was thumping so loudly it was hard to think straight. Bits of Beethoven and The Kooks and Coldplay were exploding inside his head. He pulled his hoodie up and turned south.

At the skate park Dane's brothers and the rest of them were doing nosegrinds and backsides and 180 blindsides on some other kid's board. Dane's little brother was probably wearing the kid's shoes too. Chris watched them from the shadows; they were just a bunch of ten-year-olds. But now he was careful to give Dane's family a wide berth. They hadn't spoken much since the stabbing. Chris didn't want to get involved with the family. He wanted to remember Dane as his friend, and not as one of them. The sound of board against concrete over and over again calmed him down, and after a while he could think clear thoughts again.

After the little kids had gone home, Chris wandered around for a bit. Gran would kill him if she knew he was roaming the streets like this at night, whereas Zoe didn't seem to notice. Or was it care? But she had stepped in between him and Gavin. She had tried to protect him. Yes, she tried.

He passed the St Vincent de Paul shop on High Street. The piano was gone. He stood in front of the window for a full ten minutes, just looking. He couldn't believe it. In some ways that was worse than Zoe sleeping with Gavin. Without that piano in the window, how would he remember that, somehow, one day he was going to be a concert pianist?

Chris kicked the wire-mesh cover on the window. It rattled but didn't break, and he turned and ran off down the street. He was beginning to know this housing estate, with its avenues and cul-de-sacs and parades, but it had taken quite a while. He used to get so lost sometimes that he couldn't find his way back to Zoe's. Funny – it was still 'Zoe's place', not home. Not yet. He wanted to belong, but nothing was logical here. None of the streets were straight and narrow, like they were at Gran's.

Chris melted in and out of pools of light, feeling each car's door handle as he went. He was always surprised by the number of open cars. Inside each one he ran his fingers quickly over the surfaces, and in and out of the places where there might be coins. On his third try finally – a fifty-cent piece.

The phone box was covered in graffiti, but the phone still worked. It stank of stale cigarettes. Chris dialled.

'What's up?' Naomi's voice said quietly.

Chris held the receiver tightly and stared out into the dark, empty street. Another cul-de-sac, he thought bleakly.

Naomi waited.

Chris stared hard at the gum trees and their ghostly shapes in the dark. A dog barked in the distance and a police siren moved down the motorway. At night you could see different things. You could hear everything. You could understand things properly too.

Chris thought about how he came to be here in this phone box in the middle of the night, in the middle of a cold winter night. How he missed his ordered life with Naomi. He missed the old house and her cooking and even Harry across the road. He missed Noel so much that it made him dizzy. He remembered how alive he had felt here at first with Mum. 'This is my mum,' Chris had said at the parent–teacher interview. But

Mum was not the person, more specifically the *mother*, that he thought she would be. Gran was right. Mum was everything that Gran had said she would be. Chris couldn't stay here. He was scared and he was tired. Just plain old tired. And this was all too hard.

'It's all fucked up,' he said, trying not to burst into tears.

There was a long pause at the other end.

'What's wrong?' Naomi said.

Chris tried to hold back the tears, but they began to roll down his cheeks silently. He punched the metal wall of the phone box and began to sob. His voice was cracking. He cried for all the things that confused and frustrated the hell out of him – Mum, school, hunger, Dane, Gavin, Max – until his throat was raw.

Finally, when he felt completely empty, he stopped. 'Gran?'

'Yes,' she said.

'Are you still there?' He held the battered receiver as if it was the most precious thing in the world.

'Yes,' she said. 'Go back to Zoe's.'

But he couldn't go back there just yet, and he couldn't tell Gran why. His head felt like it was going to burst.

'Chris?'

He hung up.

No smacking allowed

Max and Zoe waited for Chris to return. Gavin took a short, cursory jog around the block to look for him, but he came back alone.

'No sign of him,' he said to Zoe quietly and then left again, leaving the front door wide open. Max hoped he'd get lost somewhere and never come back. What would Gran say about all this? Chris was out of line, but so was Gavin. That was the problem with Gavin – he was always popping in and out like that, saying dumb stuff and leaving doors open. He would drive Gran crazy. Max got up and closed the door. This was a dangerous neighbourhood, after all.

Zoe didn't seem to register that he was even there. She just sat staring ahead. Max decided he was going to give Chris the biggest Chinese rope burn possible, plus a snakebite and a good hard punch and a knuckle-crack when he got back. All at once. What an idiot! How uncool. Who cares about some bloke kissing Mum? At least Gavin did the massive washing-up every now and then. Anyway, he wasn't all bad. Gavin reckoned that he could teach Max to snowboard. Gavin was all right, mostly.

Now he was stuck with Mum, by himself! Gran sometimes made Chris go to the toilet with him because Max didn't like the dark. Just wait till he told Gran all about this! She would be so angry. She might even call Chris an 'idiot' too. Although she hated that word. She might call him a 'drongo' or 'duffer', but this was far too serious for 'duffer'.

Max hoped he wouldn't get the fidgets. That would be uncool too. He *could* sit still. He had proved it. Mr E. had even said so, on his old school report.

He didn't want to think about school. He still missed Harry and Mr E. and the juicies from the school canteen, and the slushies from after-care. Right now everything sucked big time. If he had some money he would ring Gran and beg her to come and get him, Chris was ready to leave too. He said so. But he didn't have any money. Mum didn't have any. Max decided to look for spare coins at the shops in the morning, on the way to school. He had already found twenty cents on the footpath that way.

Chris had better get back here, fast. Max didn't want to walk to school by himself in the morning – it didn't bear thinking about. Past the shops where those big boys in hoodies were waiting, taking everybody's hats and lunch money. Anyway, how would he wake up in time for school? Chris did all that stuff.

Max took a long look at Zoe. He would have to speak to her shortly. He would say, 'I'm going to bed now. Good night.' But he felt sick in his stomach at the prospect of that dark room, of life here without Chris.

Max thought about God, and more specifically Jesus. Jesus would protect him in the dark. He tried to remember the prayer that Harry knew. It went something like:

Matthew, Mark, Luke and John
Bless the bed that I lie on . . .

'What should I do?' Zoe said.

Max didn't hesitate. 'Smack him,' he said.

'Is that what a parent is supposed to do?' Zoe looked at Max directly, as if for the first time. There were those same serious eyes that Max knew from his own face. How totally *not* random, he thought.

'Naw. They made some new law. No smacking allowed,' Max said, just in case Zoe thought she could smack him too. 'Gran sends him to his room,' he offered. 'My friend Harry, well, his mum fines him. I've seen it.'

'I don't know how to discipline a child,' Zoe said.

'The way I see it, Mum, it's not complicated. You're the parent.'

Zoe smiled. 'I've got no idea what I'm doing.'

'No offence, but you suck at it big time,' Max agreed. 'Gran knows how to do it better. Ask her.'

Zoe didn't answer.

'You know, we were happy living with Gran. There wasn't anything wrong with us being there.' Max turned away. 'I did wonder about you, though, sometimes, you know,' Max said.

Zoe nodded.

Max got up out of his chair. 'Are you going to call the police?' Max asked, keeping his voice even and light.

'No.'

Max was relieved. 'Good night then, Mum,' he said quickly. There was nothing else to do. No TV. No heating. It was too cold to stay up.

'I can't lose him again. I can't go through that,' Zoe said.

Max shrugged. 'He'll turn up,' he said softly.

'Goodnight, Max,' Zoe said.

'I can sleep down here, if you like?'

'Yes, I'd like that.'

Max stomped up the stairs to get his sleeping-bag and pillow. He wanted to ask her where she got his name from. It sounded strange when she said it. He wanted to ask her why she left him, and did she love him now that they were living together? Now was not the time, but Max would ask her soon, when he wasn't so tired, and she would tell him, straight. Because Max would make her.

Tim Tams

Naomi rolled back the bedclothes and swung her feet out of bed, her soles tender on the cold floorboards. Her knees were stiff from her exercise class. She could feel her tight hamstrings. She splashed her face with cold water and threw on some warm clothes, a coat too.

'Handbag. Wallet. Phone. Car keys. Licence,' she said to herself.

She put the cat out and slipped quickly out of the door and into the Laser. What was a twelve-year-old doing in a public phone box at midnight? Then she remembered Max. She went back inside to grab an emergency packet of Tim Tams. She didn't even stop to chase the cat out again.

'Bloody cold,' she said.

Naomi reversed swiftly out of the driveway. It was 1 am. Her headlights swept across the wisteria as she turned the car in the direction of Mt Druitt. There was very little traffic other than trucks as big as apartment blocks screaming down the M4.

A blunt rectangle of light spilt from Zoe's wide-open front door. It was now nearly 2 am. Naomi knocked and a heavily-tattooed man in trackpants and a singlet (didn't he feel the cold?) came to the door a little unsteadily. In the dark, in her tiredness, Naomi had a moment's doubt that she was in the right place.

'Does Zoe Zalum still live here?'

Although she had been to Zoe's on a couple of occasions to pick up the boys, to look for the boys when they failed to show at Blacktown Station, to just look when she thought nobody was watching, she still checked. All these streets and townhouses looked the same. Yom, Marial and Deng now lived in a similar house just a few streets away. Naomi liked the idea that they were nearby.

He answered yes. So Zoe had a boyfriend. Why hadn't the boys told her? She would have to put all that to one side for the moment and deal with the way it made her feel later. Right now she was only interested in Chris.

When the man just stood there, she tried again. 'Could I speak to Zoe, please?'

The man, about thirty years old, had hooded eyes that flicked over and around her uncomfortably. He was a big guy, rangy, long-limbed, all sinew and bone and muscle and tatts.

'Who're you?'

'Her mother-in-law.'

'Bit late to be calling in, isn't it? We were just going to bed.' He had his hand firmly on the edge of the door, ready to close it, the tips of his fingers – with their ragged bitten nails – white.

Zoe appeared in the hallway behind the man.

'Where is Chris?' Naomi asked her point-blank, no time for politeness.

'He's around, why?' Gavin said, stepping in front of Zoe to block her, leaning his weight against the edge of the door.

'He's just rung me, very upset,' Naomi said, trying to maintain eye contact with Zoe, who looked exhausted. She needs a good feed of red meat, Naomi thought.

'He had a tiff with Zoe, that's all,' Gavin said.

'And you are?' Naomi said, blankly.

'Gavin,' he said, without looking at Naomi.

Naomi looked away, just for a moment, as if making up her mind about something, and then she nodded. 'Hello.'

'This is Naomi,' Zoe said, still a step behind Gavin. She did not move to invite Naomi in.

Naomi continued to direct her questions to Zoe.

'Where's Max?'

Zoe stood aside and motioned Gavin to do the same. He wobbled out of the way. Behind them, Naomi could see that Max was asleep on the dirty carpet in the lounge room. He was in a sleeping-bag and he had his pillow. She felt slightly better seeing his favourite pillow firmly under his head. He was snoring quietly. Probably a slight cold or his dust-mite allergy, Naomi couldn't help diagnosing.

'Okay,' Naomi said slowly, as if she was talking to a toddler. 'What was the fight about?'

'None of your business,' Gavin said.

'Chris sounded very upset,' Naomi said. 'Let me help.'

'We've got it all under control,' Gavin said, moving between Zoe and Naomi again.

'I don't think you have. A twelve-year-old running around the streets in the middle of the night, ringing up his grand-mother on the other side of the city, crying, is not my idea of *having it all under control*,' Naomi said, standing her ground.

'If you don't get out of here, I'll call the cops,' Gavin said lightly, his eyes half closed.

'I'm just trying to help Chris,' Naomi said. 'Zoe?'

Zoe didn't say anything.

'I'm going to go out and look for him. He can't be far away.'

'Well, you better bring him straight back here, or we'll call the cops and say you abducted him,' Gavin said, his eyes sharp now.

She would not even bother to address that one. She wanted to say something like, 'I'll call the cops too, you useless idiot, and let's see who they believe?' but she didn't. She was already trying to work out how to find Chris. It made her feel sick to walk away from Max asleep on the floor, but she reminded herself that Chris was in crisis now, not Max. And anyway, she had no real chance of getting to Max past Gavin.

'She's just trying to help,' Zoe said behind Gavin in her sing-song voice.

'That's right,' Naomi nodded. 'I am just trying to help.' And with that she took out the Tim Tams. 'These are for Max when he wakes up.'

Zoe moved forward to take the packet of biscuits, trying to shrug off Gavin's proprietorial arm as she did so. 'Just a minute, babe,' Zoe said.

Gavin tore the packet out of Zoe's grip and it went spinning across the hallway. He pinned Zoe against the wall, her head hitting the pockmarked surface hard, his forearm straight across her throat, his face now in hers.

'What do you think you're doing?' he said, spit flying from between his clenched teeth.

Zoe was clawing at his forearm, coughing, gagging, trying to catch her breath. Her legs kicked out, her silver toe rings twinkling in the waxy hall light, her face was now the colour of beetroot.

Naomi threw herself forward, gripping Gavin's tattooed elbow with her strong hands and pulling as hard as she could. 'Let her go!' He swung round to face Naomi and Zoe crumpled onto the floor.

'You stay out of this,' he said, moving his weight from one leg to the other. 'It's none of your business.'

'It *is* my business. This is my family. These are my grand-children. This is my daughter. I want them safe,' Naomi shouted. 'I'll call the police if you lay another finger on Zoe, *ever*!'

Then Zoe was there, filling the doorway, her hair and eyes wild. She was as white as a sheet, her legs and arms rigid.

'Get out!' Zoe screamed at him. 'Don't you come near my family again!' Her chest was heaving. She reached out and hauled Naomi inside before slamming the door shut on Gavin. Naomi banged against the hallway wall and steadied herself. Zoe leant against the back of the door.

'Lock it. Make sure you've locked it.'

When Zoe didn't move, Naomi said, 'Did you hear me?'

Zoe nodded and started to sob – a rasping, hoarse cry – as she fumbled with the lock.

'Where's your Ventolin?' Naomi asked.

Zoe pulled her puffer out of her pocket. Her eyes large, her mouth ragged, she closed her lips around her puffer, gulped and held her breath.

The two shaken women looked at one another.

Naomi patted herself down, as if to feel for bruises.

'If he comes back, I'm calling the cops,' Zoe said, taking another hit of Ventolin.

'Amazing how Max could sleep through all that!' Naomi said.

Not working

Three hours later when Chris turned the corner into Rawson Place, he was afraid for a moment that Zoe's place was on fire. Four o'clock in the morning and the house was blazing with light, reaching as far as the scrawny grevilleas and banksia on the nature strip. There was no sound, only the wintry wind low in the bushes, which moved the leaves, making the lights of the house wink at him through the dark.

Chris circled the block first and then squeezed through the missing paling in the back fence, this time putting it firmly back in place.

The back door was locked, so he climbed in through the kitchen window, careful not to make a sound. Zoe was not in her bed but asleep in his sleeping-bag on the floor in the lounge room next to Max. He checked upstairs to make sure that Gavin was not in the house before he returned to close the kitchen window.

He made himself and Zoe a glass of Milo and sat down beside her. She was beautiful; Chris was proud of her beauty. All those years he had wondered if she was alive, and where she lived, and whether or not she had other kids. Now he knew all that he wanted to know about her. Chris had tried to live her life with her, even tried to live her life *for* her. He knew she cared about him and Max, but not in the way that he thought a mother would. There was a shadow between them. Perhaps it was her age, or Dad's death, or her art.

'Do you believe in fate?' Chris asked Zoe, when at last she opened her eyes and fixed him with her steady blue gaze.

Zoe sat up. 'Where have you been? I was worried sick. I nearly called the cops.'

Chris continued, 'Kerry does, she believes in fate.' It was the first time Chris had talked about Kerry in a long time. Kerry with her willowy fingers. 'Strong musical bones,' was how Gran described her. Kerry, who lived and breathed music; Kerry, surrounded by her harpsichords and pianos. It was her passion, as it had been his, back in Annandale, until finding his mum and putting together the pieces of his family had taken over.

'Kerry believes that the things that happen to us are meant to be,' Chris said. He smiled and handed Zoe her Milo, knowing that she didn't really understand what he was getting at.

'You can't just go off like that,' Zoe was saying now. 'Naomi was here tonight, looking for you.'

Chris looked worried. 'Gran?'

'Yes, Gran. Naomi. She was here. She came out here straight after you rang her. She was worried about you. She drove around all over the place looking for you. Gavin upset her.' Zoe paused before adding quietly, 'It was terrible.'

Chris began looking around him like he wanted to kick something or someone. He thought about Gran coming for him in the middle of the night. She was so brave. He missed her bravery. He thought about getting Max through another winter here. He thought about the stabbing and how it wasn't over.

'Do you remember how you once said you owed everything to Gran?'

Zoe looked at Chris, blankly.

'In the newspaper? You mentioned her.'

She shook her head. 'I said that?' She stirred her Milo slowly.

'I was meant to be a concert pianist, according to Kerry,' Chris said abruptly.

'You can't just go off like that,' Zoe said again.

Chris shrugged. 'You did. You left me and Max.'

Zoe and Chris looked at one another with their matching light eyes and funny eyebrows.

'Why did you leave us, anyway?'

Zoe took a deep breath.

'I want to know!'

'I don't know exactly,' she said.

'What?'

'I didn't plan to leave you. It just happened. After the accident, when I was in hospital for so long, I just sort of drifted away. I was too young to get married and have kids. I was just too young. When I left hospital I couldn't go back to my old life. I couldn't work anymore. That part of my life was gone. I couldn't do anything right, I guess. I had to leave and sort myself out. My career was over too. I couldn't do anything after the accident; I couldn't see my way ahead.'

'What about us?' Chris asked.

'I couldn't be the mother you needed,' she said as she pulled the sleeping-bag up around her thin shoulders.

'Do you think you were meant to be a mother at all?' Chris looked at her hard, as though if he did he might be able to catch a glimpse of the mother in her.

Zoe didn't answer.

Chris changed the subject. 'You shouldn't be worried about me. I go out at night a lot, most nights in fact, stealing some money for food, or just for the hell of it, you know.'

Zoe pulled down the sleeping-bag and stood up. Her mascara was thick under her eyes.

'Dane's little brother says he'll teach me how to hotwire a car really soon,' Chris said slowly, like he was letting down a tyre.

'What sort of talk is that! I don't think Naomi'd like to hear that kind of talk from you, would she now?' Zoe said firmly, taking Max's advice and trying to sound more like a parent. 'She left those for Max.'

Chris turned and looked at the crumpled packet of biscuits still lying on the floor where Gavin had thrown them. He picked them up.

'Can I have one?' Chris said. 'I'm starving.'

'Yes. Then we'll go and call Naomi and tell her that you're back,' Zoe said.

'Okay,' Chris said, quietly running his finger around the inside of the glass to get at any sweet milky chocolate crust stuck there. He thought about Max and his increasing silence, his set thin lips. He looked at his fingers, and realised that they were his own hands, not hand-me-downs from a family in Grenfell. He thought about how much he missed his piano. He thought about Naomi in her empty house.

'I don't think this is working, do you?' Chris said.

Water under the bridge

Zoe sat at the kitchen table, where the light was good, and with exquisite patience and single-mindedness removed Gavin from her book. She carefully tied it back together before packing it back into her old backpack. It only just fitted now. When did it get so thick? Its large pages bulged with dense stiffness from layers of glue and lacquer and collage and watercolours and unusual objects. On one page Chris hovered over the family, a small acrylic Rama-like figure. Around the edge of that page she had painstakingly appliquéd paper and plastic doilies into an elaborate frame.

'I want to show you something,' she said to Meg.

Wednesday. The week's dead zone for Zoe except for her session with Meg. Here she was – on time, with something to show and issues to discuss.

Zoe untied the battered art book. Today she had taken care to dress in neat and clean clothes, simple black jeans and a white t-shirt. Her hair was smoothed back into a ponytail. She was calm and clear and purposeful.

'Noel gave me the backpack, way back, when I was still a mess. He put a sketchbook inside, and some photos of the boys. Then I lost it all somewhere. Left it on a train, I think. I remembered it when I was in rehab and I got him to send me another backpack and more photos and another book. They had this artist-in-residence program and everyone was doing big canvasses of their problems and shit. It was so bad, like most prison art. I did small postcards. Watercolours and collage. That was all I could manage. Then I collected things and stuck them in my book when they made sense.'

'It's amazing,' Meg said, turning over the pages carefully. 'Every page is like a painting.'

'I started it when I thought I might not make it; I might not see Chris and Max again.'

'Yes, I know. But now? Things are different now, right?'

Zoe paused. 'Maybe.'

'Maybe? Come on, you're doing great. This is great,' she said, indicating the book.

Zoe bit her lip. 'You like it, huh?'

'Yes, of course, Zoe.'

'I'm making it for Naomi too. I want to share it with her.'

Meg turned the pages gently and Zoe watched her and thought about how she and Meg had been through so much together. Meg knew everything.

'This is your place, isn't it?' Meg asked, tilting the book towards Zoe for her to see the page.

'Sort of. It hasn't turned out to be the magical fairy-kingdom-type place I wanted it to be. We haven't lived happily ever after, exactly.'

That was an understatement. Max was depressed. Chris was depressed. She was depressed.

'Zoe,' Meg looked perplexed. 'We have been over this so many times . . .'

'But it is home,' Zoe said, cutting across Meg. She knew where Meg was going next and she couldn't face it.

'It is indeed,' Meg said, following Zoe's lead. 'Look at the detail in your picture of it here,' Meg said, scanning the watercolour carefully. 'You've found the beauty in it. I'd know those pink grevilleas anywhere.'

Zoe nodded. 'I love them. They are the best thing about living there. I love their colour and texture and the way they bring in the birds. The colour of a blush – baby pink. Did you know that pink used to be a boy's colour? It's only been around in its proper form for less than five hundred years. It was first recorded in the seventeenth century to describe a pale red rose.'

'You know a lot about it,' Meg said, smiling.

'Colour is important.'

Meg turned a stiff page.

'Is that a *pale pink* wedding cake?'

'Yes, there is a wedding going on.'

'With . . . ?'

'Someone.'

Meg didn't press Zoe. She moved on, 'And the wedding dress?' She lightly touched the bride's train. 'It looks like liquorice allsorts, the black and pink and yellow stripes. Like ribbons. You know, each and every one of these pages is a work of art, Zoe. It's truly beautiful.'

'Like I said, I lost one of these books along the way. I collected things for the longest time, but I didn't know what for. Bits of plastic. Paper. Sticks. Leaves. It feels like forever now.'

'Are you done?'

'Yes, I think so.'

'There is a new page for Chris,' Zoe said.

Meg nodded. 'And one for Max?' Meg asked, pointing to the page of a room with Max's figure standing at the window.

'And one for Naomi. And Ben and Jesse. And me. I gave Noel his own page way before he died.'

'And Gavin? Where is he?'

Zoe shook her head. She took the book, closed its mushroom-pink cover and slowly tied it up before speaking.

'I broke up with him. Gavin, I mean,' Zoe said without looking at Meg. 'He really changed.'

Meg sat up straight, 'Or maybe you really changed? Did you think of that?'

Zoe shrugged. 'Maybe. I don't think Chris likes seeing me kiss another man.'

'Who isn't his father?'

'Probably. He thinks that he is the man of the house.' She paused, then forced herself to go on. 'He told me he doesn't think things are working.'

'What do you mean?'

'He's not happy.'

It had been pretty intense at home lately, if Zoe was honest with herself. She went on to tell Meg all about the previous night.

'Naomi is really feisty. I remember that about her from before, in the early days.' Zoe was suddenly struggling to catch her breath. She took a lightning-quick nip of her Ventolin.

Meg pushed her glasses back up her nose and waited patiently for Zoe to be able to speak.

'I need her help with the boys, but I can't ask for it. After all that I have done to her!' Zoe whispered.

'Why? What have you *done* to her?' Meg asked.

'Haven't you been listening?' Her mouth was grim.

When Meg looked puzzled, Zoe ploughed on. 'I stole her grandkids. And dragged her through the courts when she wouldn't let go. I have ruined her life. I *wreck* things. That's why.'

The breeze swam in through Meg's open window, clattering against her grubby vertical blinds and lifting the edge of a child's drawing on the noticeboard, which rose up and fell back in a slow waltz with the unseen.

Zoe's eyes were streaming. She opened the book again and turned the pages until she came to one of Naomi's. She touched the hair on the miniature figure, which was made from lacquered black wool. Naomi was dressed in a nurse's uniform and surrounded by babies wrapped in brown paper, babies who would come to rest all over the world.

'In rehab they were always talking about burning bridges and I didn't know what they meant. I had to ask someone to explain it. I didn't know about that kind of stuff. But now I do. I've burnt my bridges,' she said, looking Meg steadily in the eye, 'where Naomi is concerned.'

'But it sounds like she wants to help the kids, at least, and probably you too,' Meg said, sitting forward in her chair.

'I'm so worried about Chris,' Zoe said, veering away. Meg was always telling her that dealing with chaos by creating more chaos was not a sustainable strategy, and she knew she was doing it now. But she couldn't help it. 'He is saying stupid stuff, like how he can practically steal cars. He just runs off whenever he feels like it. Since the death of his friend he has been really low.'

'Zoe, listen to me,' Meg said, gently. 'Is the past more important than your children's future?'

'I don't know. No.' Zoe shrugged helplessly.

'Let me give you a bit of advice. You have to let go of the past, no matter how terrible it was. The kids need you to. Now. You don't have time to muck around. Naomi will understand.'

At this last comment Zoe looked up in surprise.

'Because she was a mother, once, too?' Zoe said slowly.

'Yes.'

'She'd still be one, if I hadn't killed Ben and Jesse,' Zoe said, twisting the tissues between her fingers.

'What did I just say? You have to let go of all that stuff. You've made so many gains, Zoe. You stood up for your boys. You chose your boys over Gavin. You are turning into the parent that you always wanted to be. Remember? Being responsible? Having authority over your life? All that stuff. Don't look back now. You have to keep moving forward.'

Paspalum

That afternoon after school Chris sat on a log in the skate park and thought about things. Everything was changing too fast, and not the way he wanted it to. So, if going to the Con, Chris's dream for absolutely ever, didn't look like it was going to happen, then what was going to happen to him?

The skate park was unusually empty for this time of day. The sky was empty too, except for the faint trail of a jet. The grass under his feet was brown and, he thought, let's face it, largely dirt. If it didn't rain soon it would be gone. Chris sighed. He listened to a crow and thought about how discordant it sounded, like a minor third. A composer like Miriam Hyde would be able to capture that sound, as she had with the 'Jumping Frogs' piece he played once upon a time, and her 'Magpies at Sunrise'.

The seesaws were still. Not a kiddie in sight. Police patrolling on bicycles put the mums off. In their ridiculous shorts, two of them were, at this moment, doing a slow circuit of the park, like two large blowflies on a dirty kitchen table. Chris thought of the string section of the orchestra and how the violin would be both the lazy and menacing blowfly if he were composing this scene as a piece of music.

He had played with Zoe right here in this park, pushing her on the swing, chasing her like a sheepdog until she dropped, giggling, onto the grass. Yes, there had been grass when they first moved here. And shade, there seemed to be more shade in the park back then. Back when they first arrived anything seemed possible. Chris would hide in the grass pretending he still liked hide and seek, content to wait for Mum to find him. He was happy. But then, it seemed almost overnight, he was hungry and breaking into cars and stealing and giving up on his piano and witnessing a cold-blooded murder.

Chris hated the way he'd had to choose between Mum and Gran. Why did adults make things so complicated?

Max appeared at the edge of the park, and as soon as he spotted Chris he trotted over.

'How come you're not at Doris's this arvo?'

Max had definitely grown. And he looked better – no eczema, no conjunctivitis. Must be Doris's cooking. Chris had to admit that Zoe's vegetarian diet had its limits. Even so, he was too proud to ask Doris for food, and she never offered. It was like Max was hers to spoil and she didn't want to share him.

'I've got swimming later,' Max said, sitting down next to Chris.

They watched a broken swing sway in the breeze.

'Mum says that Gran's coming over tonight after tea to discuss stuff,' Chris said, twisting his mouth to stop himself crying when he said *stuff*.

'I know. Mum told me. I hope she brings some more Tim Tams and takes us home with her.'

Max pulled a piece of paspalum out of the dry earth and stuck it between his teeth. Chris pushed himself up and off the log and they walked to Doris's. Zoe was out and he felt a bit afraid of being at home alone at first. He checked all over the house to make sure Gavin wasn't lurking in a cupboard, and then he felt better. He tidied up because Naomi was coming.

He was making a Vegemite sandwich for his dinner at about 5 pm when a rock smashed through the large front window. He dived under the table. At first he thought it might have been a gunshot, and he felt relieved to see that it was just a rock. He had been waiting for it. It was a warning. He had heard about these warnings.

It seemed like minutes later and there was a police car in the driveway. What was it with this place? You could be having your throat cut and no one would lift a finger. A little rock through the window and detectives were with you like a shot.

Chris opened the door slowly. It was one of those times, like when he went to the doctor or the principal's office, when he felt like a skinny little kid.

'Christopher Adams?' one of them asked.

The other just looked him up and down.

Chris nodded.

'Is your mother home?'

'No.'

They walked in anyway and Chris had another bad feeling.

The detectives asked about everything. All about the park that night. All about Dane and his brothers, and the dealer. How long had Chris known them? Did he know Dane had dealt drugs? Had he, Christopher Adams, ever used drugs? They made him go over and over the whole thing in the park. What he had seen, exactly. Nothing about the rock through the window, until the end. At one point he thought that maybe they weren't going to mention it. He felt almost relieved to talk about it, and to show them the broken glass on the carpet.

He didn't like the way they wrote things down. Then, suddenly, Zoe came running in, her hair flying. She banged on the table and told the detectives they had no right to speak to her son without her permission. They just smiled and said there was no harm in having a chat. Then she started yelling at them. Saying all kinds of stuff like how dare they, and they didn't have any right to speak to her son. Chris watched her. She was just like all the other mums here. The cops said that this was a crime scene and she shouldn't leave her kids alone and that they'd report her if she didn't shut up. And then they drove away.

It was as if everyone was waiting, waiting for the next thing to happen. It was like the end of the second movement of a concerto. Chris could imagine the violins beginning to rise skywards.

Swimming

When the cops left, Zoe made Chris lock the doors and stay put for Gran, and she slipped quietly out of the back door. She ran down the path, through the pink grevilleas and around the corner, sprinting barefoot, no thought of her weak ankle or the cold on the soles of her feet. She ran past the shops and their treacherous pavements full of bottle tops and broken glass. Commuters were pouring off the evening train and she pushed past them with her thin shoulders and elbows.

At the pool, children's lessons were underway. A group of young fathers splashed in the shallows with their toddlers. Zoe felt a pang at the sight. She watched Max dive into the pool and swim with a grace that she didn't know he possessed. He was a different child in the water – calm, confident and measured.

She had always felt a bond, which was about the best way she could describe it, with Chris. Max had been different – a different birth, a rushed and intense labour. They had never had time to do much.

Max touched the wall first and the PCYC swimming coach bent down to show him the stopwatch. He gave Max the thumbs-up sign. Max smiled. Zoe moved towards the coach, smiling too.

'Max is good at this,' he said to her.

'Max is a good swimmer, huh?' Zoe asked.

The coach looked at her as though she was from another planet.

'Yeah. You're his mother, right?'

'He only just started to live with me in the last year or so,' Zoe said.

'Well, he's the best we have in the competition,' the coach said. 'You should be very proud of him. He works quite hard.'

'It's great to know he's good at something,' she said. 'Because I didn't know that about him.'

The coach stepped back to look more closely at her. He had a slightly quizzical expression on his face.

'That he could be good at something like swimming, I mean,' Zoe said. 'I know that he's great at lots of things . . .' she trailed off, trying to think of an example.

'Don't despair, because with a lot of these kids, time takes care of things,' the coach reassured her, assuming that Max was the delinquent.

'Yes, it's just the beginning.'

The coach nodded encouragingly.

Zoe escorted Max home, quickly. She kept glancing over her shoulder and they stuck to the back streets. She chatted to him about anything that came into her head – school, sport, maths. And Max chatted back. Perhaps he wasn't the mystery she had thought he was. She could walk him home like any other mother. Almost. Yes, the pieces could fit together, she decided.

When they arrived home, Naomi's red Laser was already parked outside Rawson Place.

'Did you get Naomi a drink of water, Chris?' Zoe asked as she came through the front door, locking it behind her.

Chris stood up abruptly.

'Are you going to tell me what's been happening?' Naomi said, pointing at the broken window.

'Someone threw a rock through the window and the police came,' Chris said.

'Why?'

'My friend Dane got stabbed.'

'Badly?'

'He's dead.'

'Your friend? A twelve-year-old?' Naomi said, looking appalled. 'His poor mother.'

Chris nodded.

'Chris, that is terrible. Horrible.'

Naomi hugged him.

'He was in trouble. A lot of trouble,' he said, pulling away from her and glancing at Zoe and Max.

Naomi looked at Zoe and then squarely at Chris. 'You stay right away from that kind of trouble. You hear? And don't you lie to me about it. Ever.'

'No, Gran,' said Chris in a small voice. 'And I'm sorry about the phone call and getting you all worried in the middle of the night.'

'I'm sorry too,' Zoe said, 'for getting you involved.'

'What nonsense,' Naomi said. 'But a rock through the window? What next? Let's sort out the window, then I want you to come home with me for tonight. All of you.' Naomi stood up and when no one moved, she added, 'Now.'

That was the frustrating thing about Gran. She was so certain.

Grenfell

When Chris had finished the bowl of Naomi's homemade chicken noodle soup, he pushed his chair back and rose wordlessly to rinse his plate in the sink. Max was still across the road up in the tree house with Harry. Naomi could hear them shouting and squealing. In the backyard, Zoe moved aimlessly around the garden beds looking for herbs.

Naomi folded her napkin and took a good long look at Chris as he wiped his hands roughly on a clean tea towel.

'What?' she said as he turned to face her.

'The suitcases?' Chris said, pointing towards the front hall where two cases sat side by side.

Naomi stood up. It was one thing for them to leave her; it was another for her to leave them, especially now.

At twelve Chris was tall – unlike a lot of other boys, his growth spurt had started already. His eyes were still the palest of blue, but his face had become sharp, his cheekbones more prominent. His skin was soft and clear, although Naomi thought it was only a matter of time before the dreaded acne hit. Ben had bad acne, Jesse none. Funny how different they had been. Chris had his father's height and Jesse's leaner build. But, she had to admit again, as she stood across from him in the small kitchen, there was a large part of Zoe in Chris. The way he moved, the tilt of his head, the expression in his eyes. They said he was Zoe's son.

'I was thinking of going to Grenfell,' Naomi said carefully.

Chris's eyes narrowed slightly and she saw a flash of something there. Anger? Fear? Resolve? She wished she could smooth out the perceived slap in her words, but it was too late.

'For how long?' Chris said, as if he had got used to adults springing things on him. His voice was flat. He sounded as if he recognised that things were not going to go his way. Earlier he had almost seemed to want his life with Naomi back, but she had learnt not to trust her ears where Chris was concerned. He was a survivor. He had survived the past two years, he'd chosen to live with Zoe, and she had to admit that in some ways he was stronger for it.

'To visit Sarah,' Naomi replied.

'How far is Grenfell again?'

'Six hours by car,' Naomi said.

'Really,' Chris said, sitting down heavily.

'Yes, really. I haven't said anything to Max yet. I'll wait till things settle down before I go.'

Chris scratched his head. He looked uneasy.

'Will we be able to visit you there?'

'Of course. I'd only be going back to the farm for a month or so,' Naomi said.

'Just for a holiday? You'd just go for a holiday, right?'

'Yes. Why?'

'Nothing.'

Naomi had given herself a stern talk about taking a break a day or two ago. It was time to face up to the fact that the boys' lives were with Zoe. Time to recharge her batteries and think about her future.

'I said I wouldn't go anywhere without you,' Naomi said.

'What if you go there and you don't want to come back?'

'I'll come back.'

'Gran, how do you know?'

'I know.'

Chris stood up tall and shoved his hands into his pockets.

'What about our weekends with you?'

'You'd only miss one or two, three at the most.'

'I've always wanted to go there, to Grenfell,' he said, sounding quietly determined. 'Is there a piano there?'

'I'd imagine,' Naomi said, 'that the place is full of them.'

Chris frowned. 'It would be a lot closer to the Con if I lived here with you again,' he said.

'The Conservatorium is perfectly accessible from Zoe's by train. When is your audition?'

He looked defeated. 'I haven't sent in the form.'

Naomi sat down heavily. 'It's never too late,' she said. 'I could ring up.'

'No, Gran, I don't think I would fit in there anymore. I've got out of practice,' he said.

'Not fit in?' Naomi shook her head. She thought about that concert at Kerry's, where a gloomy and bedraggled Chris had sat down and played the beginning of the Moonlight Sonata with such precision and control.

'I can't go. I haven't done the work.'

'Kerry would help you catch up, I'm sure. Let's phone her to ask.' Naomi reached for the phone.

'I don't want to,' he said more firmly, without looking at her. 'Just let it go, Gran. It's not important anymore.'

Naomi could no longer read Chris's expression. He had perfected his poker-face during his time at Zoe's. It was the slackness of his lips, almost imperceptibly loose, which she probably would have taken for a sign of dullness but for the sharpness in his eyes.

'What's not important?' Max asked, bursting into the kitchen and pushing Chris out of the way so that he could get a drink from the tap.

'Are you moving to Grenfell, Gran?' Chris demanded. 'We have to know. Max needs to know.'

'No, I'm not,' she said. 'Why do you say that?'

Chris looked hard at Naomi, searching, seeing something in her face as though for the first time.

They jumped when Zoe banged the back door. She was humming as she walked barefoot across to the sink. In her hands was a surprising collection of crisp green leaves.

When Naomi thought about going back to Grenfell, she thought about the dusty main street and the way it bent about a third of the way down. Sitting in the Greek café in her childhood, she was happy to eat lollies and hot chips and lemonade ice blocks while she watched people come and go. Her mother refused to eat what she called 'town food' – she stuck to her roast lamb with mint jelly and scones – but for Naomi town food had a place and a time. She always reserved her disappointment at its ordinariness.

Naomi watched the boys carefully. 'I'm not going to Grenfell yet. The main thing now is making sure you are safe and warm and well-fed. Come on, let's set the table properly. Zoe's got some salad from the garden and I have a lovely piece of cheddar somewhere that'll go nicely.'

A family

Chris felt himself changing. It wasn't just the puberty thing, and it wasn't just outward signs. In fact, it wasn't physical at all. He sat opposite Zoe on the train, Max next to her, and smiled at his mother over the top of his schoolbag. She smiled back.

'Max and I had a talk at Gran's.' Chris nodded towards Max and Max folded his arms across his chest and planted his feet wider apart. 'We want you to consider doing something a bit radical,' he said.

She nodded.

Good, Chris thought. That's what parents are meant to do, be encouraging.

'We want you to take us to live with her in the country,' he said.

The smile on Zoe's face slid.

Chris saw the way she flinched ever so slightly at the mention of Gran. 'When school finishes,' he added.

'Grenfell?' Zoe said, as if the place was sacred or something. She looked like she might jump right off the train.

'We think she'd like to go back there. We think we could help her.'

'What does Gran think about this?' Zoe asked in a hushed voice.

'We haven't told her yet. I thought we should talk about it first. You know, as a family.'

It felt good to say the word 'family'. It felt like he had got the order of things right for once. For about three seconds! Zoe was looking as though she was about to have an asthma attack.

'You don't have a choice,' Chris said without emotion. 'We can't go back to Rawson Place. To live. Properly.'

Zoe nodded like she understood, maybe. Or maybe she was just out of breath. Chris tried again. 'You can't stay on there without us, anyway, right? That's how you qualified for the house in the first place?'

Zoe nodded again, grabbing around the pockets of her backpack for her Ventolin. She took a couple of gulps of the puffer and held her breath. She was red in the face and her eyes were now bulging slightly. Chris felt uncomfortable. When she could speak again, she said, 'It doesn't surprise me that you don't want to live with me.'

Chris shook his head. 'That's not what I said. We don't want to leave you. We want to take you with us, to be together.' Chris emphasised the 'together'.

Zoe looked from him to Max, who nodded encouragingly.

'I don't want to make the same mistake again. I don't want to lose my children the way she did,' Zoe said quietly.

'I need you to do this for Max, Mum,' Chris said.

'I can think of several reasons why it won't work, straight-away,' Zoe said.

'And I need you to do it for me too, Mum,' he said, more urgently.

Zoe began to cry.

'There were these two women,' Chris said. 'One old and

one young. The young one didn't have to, or anything, but she decided to help the older woman. So at first it seemed like she was doing the old woman this big favour, but it turned out that the older woman could help the younger woman too. They became a team. And things turned out pretty well in the end. They went through some really rough patches, but they got there in the end because they had each other.'

When Chris finished speaking, Zoe said, 'I can't stand between you and what you need, but what you're asking is almost impossible.'

Chris didn't know what to say. He had told her 'The Book of Ruth', his ultimate weapon, and she was acting as if she hadn't heard him. Didn't it make perfect sense to her too? There was silence for what seemed like hours. Just when Chris thought Zoe must be thinking about something else – about Gavin, or her art – she said slowly, 'I won't lose you again, ever.'

Chris loved hearing her say this. It took him by surprise and made him feel all warm and great. He wondered if it meant yes. He would assume it did for now. He knew that making it work with Gran would be pretty hard though. It wasn't about finding something that you had lost, as it was when Grandpa died, it was about giving something back, which Zoe had taken from Gran.

'I'll think about it,' Zoe said.

Settling

There was a light knock at the door, or perhaps it was a neighbour's hammer fixing a nail in place. Naomi ignored it. It might be Signora Toto, and she couldn't face her right now. There it was again, this time more persistent.

When she opened the door, much to her surprise Chris stood on the doorstep with Max behind him, hands in his pockets. And, even more surprisingly, Zoe stood several metres behind the boys at the bottom of the steps. Naomi thought how different it was seeing Zoe at her townhouse those few nights ago, and here today. She felt none of her old animosity towards her. The fight was gone.

'May we come in?' Chris asked.

'Of course,' Naomi said, standing aside, her heart sinking at his formality. Max hugged her briefly, more like a football tackle, as Chris and Zoe walked down the hall ahead of them. They had the same walk. They both moved from the hips. They were now also about the same height.

Chris stopped in the dark kitchen. Naomi moved past him to turn on the light. Newspapers cluttered the table. The sink was full of unwashed dishes. The garbage bin overflowed. Max's eyes were round with surprise. He folded his arms.

'We want to take you to Grenfell,' Chris said, looking around, 'to live.'

'All of us,' added Max.

Naomi frowned. This was not what she had been expecting at all. When she first saw them on the front doorstep she had thought that Zoe probably needed money, or Chris wanted her to drive them somewhere. All of them in Grenfell? Together? Naomi felt confused. Hadn't the past two years been about being apart?

'It's a long way away,' she said eventually.

'We know that,' Max said.

'It's hard to come back to the city from there,' she said. She remembered how hard it had been to leave Grenfell in the first place.

'We know,' Chris said.

She opened her mouth to tell him that he could not possibly know about such things – exile and return – but then remembered that perhaps someone like Chris could.

'We wouldn't have any money,' she added. 'I wouldn't have a job.'

'Money's not everything,' Chris said.

Naomi sat down heavily at the table, her chair scraping on the kitchen floor with a sharp, discordant sound.

'Why do you want to do this?' she asked them.

'We miss you,' Max said simply, without any hesitation, as if they had discussed this over and over again, arriving at that point long ago.

'We want to be all together,' Chris said.

Naomi said nothing. Zoe said nothing.

Did Chris set this up?

'We belong together,' Max stated.

Or perhaps it was Max's doing?

The boys looked from Naomi to Zoe expectantly, waiting

for Zoe to add her bit. Naomi was trying to work out what she felt and why.

Zoe was not at first forthcoming. She seemed to be studying her sons' faces carefully.

'Mum?' Max asked eventually.

'The children are right,' she said, her face creasing into a frown.

When Naomi first arrived in Sydney she was unsettled, according to her mother. Naomi was from a long line of what they called 'settlers' rather than farmers, so she was not surprised when her mother diagnosed her loneliness over the phone as being 'unsettled'. She missed the farm and, in particular, the horizon. In the city there was no horizon. Most of the time at Sydney University Naomi studied. She was an earnest student with an open, impressionable mind, an eye for detail and a quiet determination to complete what she had started. She lived in a student college and was reluctant to follow her shadow back there every night after lectures. Occasionally, in the early evening, she took a bus down Parramatta Road, just to be amongst it. Sometimes the road would be choked with taxis bound for Circular Quay or the downtown theatres. She began to like Sydney – the busy, audacious feel of it at night, and the pleasure that the constant movement of people gave her restless eyes. Voices rose upwards, there was laughter and snatches of song, everywhere people moved towards one another. She wished them well.

Her mother had then pronounced Naomi 'settled'.

Once Naomi had settled in Sydney, she could settle anywhere and anything. She could certainly settle a baby.

She settled babies to sleep in her arms, a cot or a car. She could still change a nappy with one hand, if she wanted to. In a short while there wasn't much about babies that Naomi could not do or undo. She read them like small books, from their skin texture and jaundiced eyes to their sweet breath. As a young midwife on night duty, she would take all the babies into the lounge and play them whatever music she could lay her hands on. Naomi learnt about music on those long nights. She played Bizet's *Carmen* and Chopin's *Nocturnes*. Not a peep would come out of those heart-shaped mouths. Babies were easy for Naomi with her mix of tender curiosity and quiet opinion. She laughed about babies as though they were a temporary predicament and, briefly, when she rubbed shoulders with their new mothers and fathers, it was with not a small amount of envy and desire. And now, here, nearly half a century later, she may be about to leave it all behind. Could she really let go that easily? Never the predictable student, wife, mother, mother-in-law, or grandmother, Naomi did not easily agree.

'I don't know,' she said to Chris, Max and Zoe.

'What?' Max said.

'You take the children, and now you want me to take them back? And you as well?' Naomi said, looking at Zoe.

'That's not what . . .' Chris started. He seemed very protective of his mother. Good, Naomi thought, that's how it should be. A boy should protect his mother. There should be no question about it. But the feeling was tinged with a little jealousy too. Would he have protected her like that?

'Do you really think this could work? Isn't there too much water under the bridge?'

'We want to take you, not you take us,' Zoe said, smiling a little uncertainly. 'For once.'

'We want to take care of you,' Chris said.

'Okay?' Zoe said.

They all looked intently at Naomi.

'I want to believe you,' Naomi said, 'but I don't know if I can. Quite.'

It's all good

Max decided, *it's all good*, as Harry would say. Gran would come round. He knew it. He had sensed it in that word 'quite'. Mum would come round. Chris would come round. They would all see how this could work.

All the way back to Mt Druitt Chris was practically wringing his hands. He was such a nervous wreck these days. Dane's stabbing and Gavin and that random rock through the window had really got to him. Ever since then he had been so worried and, quite frankly, worrying. He had perked up at Gran's though – that was good to see. Mum, Max thought, was a bit stressed too. She was reading that book out loud on the train, which was embarrassing and another good reason to move to the country. She could read to the cows and stop bothering everybody else.

It's all good – that's if everyone didn't fall apart first. Gran, Mum and Chris; they were all so stressed about everything. Max hoped that Gran could get a good night's sleep now she knew they were all coming to Grenfell too. She looked really tired. Max would take good care of her in Grenfell; as long as she cooked lasagne – say once a week – he could do everything else.

Max would miss Doris, but she had other kids that needed her, and loads of grandkids to look after. He would miss the PCYC, but that was about it – from Zoe's place, that is. He would miss Harry, but Harry could come for holidays.

Max knew Gran, really knew her. She just needed a few days to think it over.

Survival

One of the great things about going to live with Zoe, in Chris's opinion, was that she was young. She could roll around on the grass with him or chase him through the house. She liked pop music and knew that the Black Eyed Peas was a band not a vegetable.

'What's wrong?' she asked him on the train on the way home.

Zoe rarely noticed things like how you were feeling. Chris knew that she must be really trying hard. After getting through the visit to Gran's, and the talk about all going to Grenfell together, Zoe seemed to be pretty calm.

'What if she means it? What if she really won't let us go with her?' Chris blurted out. 'She looked,' and he took a moment to find the right words. 'Too old.'

Gran did look different. Like thinking about leaving had almost killed her. She looked totally wrecked. Chris noticed more lines on her face, the thinness of her hair, the stiffness of her back. Had he never properly looked at her before? He shook his head. He knew what it was like to be under pressure. Perhaps Max was right – Gran needed their help. It wasn't a matter of whether she would take them with her or not, it wasn't a thing that you made a decision about. You just did it. It was a matter of survival. Gran needed him.

His eyes filled with tears.

'It'll be all right,' Zoe said.

'You're just saying stuff.'

'You have to trust me, Chris. You have my word.'

'So?' Chris said, beginning to cry. 'Words don't mean anything.'

'You're wrong. They can change everything. You just have to decide.'

Chris wiped his eyes on his grubby sleeve. 'You have to tell Gran,' he said after a pause.

'I'll tell Naomi,' Zoe said, 'everything.'

Max knew that his mother made promises she didn't always keep; that she said stuff she didn't mean. Max thought she meant well and everything, but she didn't always do the stuff she said she'd do. That was one of the worst things about being a kid. Adults were always giving you the run-around.

Max just hoped Zoe didn't let Chris down. He had his hopes pinned on her. Max would not be happy if she mucked this up, and she knew it. She gave him that look, and he gave her that look back. She knew.

Free country

Naomi rang Sarah to ask about the rent on Mara Downs. She told her about her conversation with Zoe and the boys. 'I've made up my mind. It will never work.'

'You like saying *no*, don't you?' Sarah said. 'Mum did too, that's where you get it from.'

Naomi didn't want to have this conversation with Sarah. She just wanted to tell her how it would be and leave it at that. She wanted to confine the conversation to money and dates and distance, not open up another can of worms. She could hear in the background a manic hair dryer competing with the local radio station, both blasting away.

'You can't stop them,' Sarah went on. 'It's a free country. They'll probably move to Grenfell anyway, and you don't want them living down the road. You want them to be with you. There is plenty of space on Mara. The old shearers' quarters, the machinery sheds, the feed lots – they could all be converted into accommodation.'

'I don't want to discuss it.'

'What about bringing some of those refugees you talk about too?' Sarah said, now laughing. 'Guest workers make the cherry-picking viable at Young, you know.'

'Okay, you don't have to be such a brat, Sarah,' Naomi said. 'I am trying to be serious. This is SERIOUS!'

'Come with them,' Sarah said. 'It will all work out.'

'I just don't know,' Naomi said.

'The Book of Ruth'

Zoe began cleaning while they waited patiently for Naomi to change her mind. She swept the townhouse from top to bottom, as she had when she first moved in. She scrubbed down all the surfaces. Then she washed everything – the walls, the floors, even the beds. It was as if she wanted to remove their scent, their place in the history of the dwelling.

She kept her word to the boys and took a fast train to see Naomi, as if afraid that with more time she might lose her nerve and change her mind. There was nothing else to do except speak. She could clean everything. She could wash everything. She could plant vast gardens. She could walk to Perth. She would rather walk to Perth, any day, but she knew what she had to do. What she had to *try* to do, at least. All she had to do was to find the right words.

'It's like "The Book of Ruth",' Zoe said, sitting with Naomi at her kitchen table.

Naomi frowned. Zoe, reading the Bible? What next? What

could Zoe possibly understand about that story, of *all* stories? Loyalty? Fidelity? Courage?

'It is a beautiful story. I don't know why I never read it before. But Chris gave it to me, and it spoke to me. It was the story of you and me. Two women.'

Naomi fought the urge to correct her, so surprised was she by this new, articulate Zoe.

'They have a bond that can't be broken. They are both alone going in opposite directions for most – almost all – of the time. They are opposites, but they can be together once they find a place to make a home.'

Naomi was silent for the longest time. Zoe began to think that she had made things worse by telling the story. She took a deep breath. 'I brought you something.'

She unzipped her backpack, took out her overstuffed book and handed it to Naomi.

Naomi undid the pink ribbon and the book burst open to a watercolour of the rooflines of the townhouses and the curve of Rawson Place. The oyster-pink grevilleas too.

Zoe folded the discarded ribbon and placed it on the table.

'I have worked on this for a few years. I think it's finished, for now. I wanted you to have it.'

Naomi did not move, neither did she take her eyes off the pages.

'I wanted to say thank you for what you did for me. For us, all of us. I didn't ever mean to cause you so many problems. I'm . . .' Zoe trailed off. She couldn't finish what she wanted to say. She looked at the book again. 'It is the book of us. We are all here: Noel, Chris, Max, Ben and Jesse. Evelyn. Gwen. You. Me. Sandra. Dennis. Everyone.'

Naomi was completely silent and still.

'They are going in opposite directions. See,' Zoe pointed to the Naomi figure with its appliquéd dress and thatch of thick black hair, and then over the page to the Zoe figure with a backpack. 'They are opposites, but they can also be together.'

Naomi turned the page and there she was under the heading 'Naomi the brave!' She was a diminutive figure defending Zoe against a burly man. The words 'my daughter' escaped in a bubble from her mouth.

'This is Chris's page,' Zoe said, pointing to another sheet of paper that contained a collage and an ink drawing of a big house with a large room in the roof. She folded the roof back on its hinge and inside was a typical teenager's messy bedroom. Scraps of manuscript lay on the floor, as well as a piano and music on a stand near the window. The bed was unmade. A miniature Chris stood off to one side, looking over his shoulder into a mirror.

'No more massive sculptures?' Naomi said finally.

Zoe shook her head. 'Suppose not.'

Naomi moved her eyes over the work slowly, hungrily. Jesse was there, fixing a bike in a front yard. Ben was standing in the middle of a room taking a photograph, his camera set on a tripod. The couple to one side making love were not easily recognisable. Naomi would have to examine them later.

'The detail is impressive,' she said, opening a front gate on one page with her forefinger.

'It is all about the detail,' Zoe said.

Naomi's eyes darted over the work, trying to take it in. One page had clothes made from scraps of cloth hanging from a line. The figure of Max threw a basketball into a hoop in the foreground. She ran her finger over another page, which contained intricate beading work on an elaborate ball gown with the words *For Sandra* scrawled underneath. Noticing a dangling pair of earrings that matched some she had years ago in her own figure's ears, Naomi wasn't sure whether the book made her feel uncomfortable or grateful, such was the obsessive quality and care of Zoe's work.

'The purpose of art is to provoke,' Naomi said, 'and to remember who we are and what we are capable of. Isn't that what they say?'

Zoe hesitated. Perhaps she had gone too far, too fast. But then Naomi turned and said to her, 'I hope you are right about this idea of moving to the country.' Her face was both stubborn and hopeful.

'Yes,' said Zoe. But what she really meant was, 'See, I can be as stubborn as you.'

Life with Naomi

Zoe handed her door keys back and braced herself for life with the boys and Naomi. She decided that the best way to start was to immerse herself in cleaning again. She washed Naomi's floors, the windows and the walls. The only place she didn't clean was the attic. That was for Naomi to make decisions about. Her fingernails were split and broken, not just because of the cleaning but also because she was gnawing away at them. She still had things to say to Naomi that needed the right timing. She told herself over and over that she was waiting to find the right time, that she would know when it came.

They had been living together for several weeks, but they still circled each other. The boys acted like the spokes in the middle of their wheel. They were polite and respectful and too careful with each other. There had been tense moments, such as when Naomi saw the boys' school reports.

'How could you not have noticed' – Naomi searched for the right words – 'the *downward trend* in these results?'

Zoe nervously took the results and weighed them in her hands. 'That's just it. I knew I couldn't do it on my own.'

She tried to make herself as inconspicuous as possible and Naomi seemed preoccupied with arranging the sale of the house and the boys' education in Grenfell. She retreated into conversations with her real-estate agent and the detail of packing. But one day she finally snapped. 'You've washed the linen tablecloth on a hot cycle!'

Both boys moved silently to Zoe's side.

'I just wanted to help you,' she said.

Naomi began to cry, holding the damp and shrunken, and now misshapen, tablecloth to her chest.

'Please don't be angry with me,' Zoe said in a small voice.

'Ever,' Max added in his unbroken ten-year-old's voice, the one he reserved for the teachers at school.

That night Naomi was extra polite at dinner and Chris played the piano for Zoe for the first time.

Zoe was more energetic and helpful than Naomi expected. After dreading her moving in, and worrying about all the ways it could go wrong, she had to admit: so far, so good. The house felt full of life again and she had new energy to face the move. Perhaps the boys were right, perhaps this would be the right decision after all. Hope: the key ingredient in optimism, the greatest antidote to bitterness, but the most elusive thing of all.

Naomi had forgotten her daughter-in-law's silvery laughter and her tuneless humming. These days there was Zoe's variety of herbal and scented teas – peppermint, caramel, chamomile and dandelion – and her compulsion to collect to deal with. Naomi smiled. Ten years ago Zoe had been obsessed with coffee and speed. Now there was a new gentleness about her. Her life was no longer a series of absences. And she loved having the boys back, with their cheekiness and interruptions.

There were moments when Naomi doubted the wisdom of her idea to return home. She was packing up the attic, with its dusty memorials of lost shoes and sports ribbons. Should she take the tea chest with them? Would it make things better or worse? Ten years on and decisions around Ben and Jesse were no easier. Suddenly she lost her confidence. They would never fit into Grenfell. The boys would be bullied at their new school. Chris would not start piano again. Zoe would fall apart.

But her dreams had been so vivid. The purple Weddin Mountains and the old farmstead's rose in bloom, a bonfire at night and the ice in the birdbath at dawn. A horizon. Sometimes Noel was there, sipping tea with her on the verandah. It was so real; she could feel his body heat. And sometimes she saw her boys there too. They'd felt at home on the farm – Ben and Jesse, two small, eternally freckled boys, doubling each other on a pony.

Mara Downs was waiting. A patient and forgiving place for them to start over. It was, finally, as simple as a handshake.

Goodbye

Moving away to Grenfell meant leaving behind Sandra again.

Zoe wanted to get it right this time. The old Zoe could not have faced her mother to say goodbye. If the old Zoe did make it to her mother's, she would have been drunk or too stoned to stand up straight. She didn't do goodbyes. This time, though, it was different. She didn't feel good about it, but she could do it.

'What time will you be back?' Chris asked her as she opened the front door.

Zoe closed her eyes. 'As soon as I can,' she said, and then, turning to him, she added, 'Here, keep this safe.' She took off her backpack and handed it to him.

She caught the train from Central to Kingswood and walked from Kingswood Station, as she had so many times before. But today it felt like hard work, she could not get into a rhythm.

When she finally arrived at her mother's house, she did not stop or even hesitate on the footpath outside. She knocked loudly and confidently.

It took her mother a full fifteen minutes to open the door. Zoe waited patiently for a further few minutes while Sandra unlocked the screen door but did not proceed to open it.

'I'm moving to the country, Mum,' Zoe said clearly and slowly. 'I'll be back to see you soon. I won't be gone forever this time.'

Sandra frowned, but did not say anything. She couldn't invite Zoe into the house. Zoe knew it wasn't her in particular. Sandra just couldn't have anyone in the house today. It was that kind of a day. Standing on the front patio, where as a child of about Max's age she had sometimes been fed her dinner (vegetables and meat must not touch), she tried not to let the flood of unpleasant memories drown her. Missing a school concert because Sandra was unable to leave until her make-up and hair were perfect. Being embarrassed when her mother instructed her school friends not to touch the walls. Having all her birthday parties in a park because her mother couldn't have people in the house. So many rules. Cupboards full of dinner sets that were never used. Furniture never sat on, just for show, for all the people who never visited. She thought, then, of those warm Saturday afternoons by the river with her father painting. She thought about the social tennis matches and the times when her mother had been the smiling, singing housewife.

'Do you like pink?' Sandra asked.

'Pink?'

'Yes, pink. You used to be fussy about colour. Pink.'

'What about it?' Zoe said, suspiciously.

'I was thinking of painting the door pink,' Sandra said.

'Oh?' Zoe said.

'Hot pink or lolly pink? I think it would really stand out better, but which shade? Fuchsia? Garnet? Blush? Waterlily? There are so many to choose from.'

'You can't really see what colour it is through the screen door,' Zoe said.

'I've been thinking that it is time for a change,' Sandra said.

Usually, Zoe would have started to yell at Sandra, *I'm here to say goodbye to you, and all you can talk about is the colour of the front door.* She might have kicked the grill too, for good measure.

'Yes, change is a good thing. I like all those pinks.' She paused. 'When you feel up to it, you could come to Grenfell for a visit. A change of scenery would be good for you.'

Sandra nodded and drew her dressing gown closer across her withered breasts.

'I'm sorry that I can't help you with the front door today, Mum. The boys need me. I hope you can understand that I have to try to make things better for them.'

Sandra nodded. 'You understand now, what it is like, don't you?'

Zoe rested her head against the screen door. On the way to her mother's house, she thought that her head was going to explode, but now she felt calm. She watched a trail of small brown ants abandon all judgement and march forward to their fate inside the brickwork below the door. Sandra's house wasn't the impenetrable fortress it once had been.

She nodded. 'Yes. I know what it is like to be a mother.'

The road home

The morning had been spent packing Naomi's newly acquired second-hand ute. While Chris and Naomi worked to secure the bright green tarpaulin over the boxes and luggage in the tray, Zoe scrubbed and washed Naomi's floors one final time. Max hung upside down in Harry's acacia. Naomi did wonder how she would get him into the back seat of the ute when the time came. Gwen and Evelyn had already said their goodbyes. They would follow them to Grenfell for a holiday in a month's time.

Kerry arrived quietly in her sleek black Mercedes four-wheel drive.

'It's a piece of Chopin, given to me by my music teacher when I was your age,' she said, handing Chris a thin volume of music.

They stood awkwardly together. Chris wordlessly offered his cheek, and Kerry lightly kissed it. Naomi worked on around them, tightening ropes.

'Could rain,' Naomi said.

Several dogs began a loud, grating barking, and overhead a 747 flattened out into its final approach for landing.

'There's a piano where you're going?' Kerry said, raising her voice.

Naomi did not immediately answer.

'This past year or so, Chris's practice and playing has suffered enough,' Kerry began lecturing. 'It's time to get his piano back on track. Perhaps he can have a shot at the Con as an undergraduate – you never know.'

Naomi nodded. This past year or two Chris's *life* had been suspended, not just his piano playing, but what was the point of trying to explain this to a thin and exacting piano teacher?

'Not sure,' Chris mumbled. But Naomi noticed his eyes lit up at the mention of the Con.

Kerry rolled her eyes. 'Not sure?'

Before she could draw breath, Naomi intervened. 'There will be a piano. You know country towns, Kerry. All those old, dusty pianos in elderly ladies' houses. I don't think finding a piano or an appreciative audience will be a problem for Chris in Grenfell.'

Kerry's hand fluttered. 'Good,' she said firmly.

Once the front door had been locked and they had all paused at the wooden board with 'SOLD' pasted across it, there was no more to do except get into the ute. Chris hesitated at the front gate.

'Grandpa?'

'He's coming home too. He's always with us.'

Signora Toto appeared with a chicken in an open box. 'Take it. You need it. Makes good eggs.'

Three small boys from the neighbourhood, kitted out in Glebe hockey club jerseys, appeared at the ute's window. 'Up the Jets!' one yelled as they jogged alongside the slow-moving vehicle. As Naomi pulled the ute away, Chris shrugged and Max murmured a faint 'Up the Jets' from the back seat. Without turning her head, Naomi said quietly to Max, 'They play hockey in Grenfell too.'

He grunted, his head bent low over the kitten that Harry had given him as a farewell present.

They travelled in an empty silence for the first hour, moving slowly along Parramatta Road with the rest of the Saturday morning traffic.

'The ute takes a bit of getting used to,' Chris said later, when Naomi looked set to strip all the gears as she stopped and started in the single-lane traffic snaking its way through Mount Victoria. She liked the bigger cabin with its back seat, but it was a lot heavier to drive than her little red Laser. Chris was right, it did take a bit of getting used to.

Squalling, drought-breaking rains closed in on them at Victoria Pass. Usually wrapped in a mauve gauze of haze, today the pass was lost in swirling grey cloud.

'Winter storms,' Naomi said.

Chris sat beside her in the front passenger seat. 'Do you think it could be the end of the drought?'

'I hope so,' Naomi said.

On the back seat Zoe and Max curled around each other, softly asleep.

Just out of Blayney it began sleeting, and Naomi started to wonder about stopping for something warm to drink and eat. Dun-coloured hills rolled away as far as the eye could see.

Out of the rain a car came slowly towards them, flashing its headlights on and off, on and off, the driver waving his arm up and down. Naomi braked hard, dropping the ute's speed suddenly, changing down through the gears quickly. Rounding a slippery curve, they came to an abrupt stop behind a long snake of vehicles.

Zoe and Max in the back seat were thrown forwards with

the force of Naomi's braking and the kitten fell onto the floor beside the chicken.

'Gran?' Max said, still half asleep, 'What'd yer do that for?'

'There's something ahead,' she said, turning briefly to Chris beside her in the front of the cabin, before gripping the steering wheel to lever herself up into a better position to see ahead.

Max picked up the kitten and the ute became completely silent and still. Naomi turned off the engine and it ticked away like a bomb. They listened to the sleet hitting the roof in soft gusts. No one spoke. Another car came towards them from the opposite direction, slowly at first, then gathering speed. The ute rocked as it passed and then was still. Without the demister the windows quickly fogged up. Naomi cleared a patch on the inside of the windscreen with the back of her hand. Another car, then another, passed, each shedding more freezing rain and making the ute rock on its suspension.

'Looks like it might be moving,' Naomi said eventually, turning the engine back on. She felt uneasy about what lay around the next bend.

They inched forward. Stop. Start. Crawling in first gear onwards through open farming country. Then, around the next wide corner they came to another full stop and there, not ten metres away, a car lay on its roof with its black underbelly exposed to the sky. The white side panels were buckled and scratched like boys' knees, the roof had completely crumpled, and the front windscreen had shattered. Naomi looked away at the rolling patchwork of crops and fences and took a deep breath.

Max wiped the fog off the inside of his window with his sleeve. Chris just rolled down his window and let the sleet whip his face. Zoe sat staring straight ahead, her lips moving almost imperceptibly. Naomi glanced back at her in the rear-view mirror. Was she praying?

'Are you okay, Zoe?' she asked.

But Zoe did not answer. She closed her eyes and then opened them wide.

They were moving ahead again, a policeman cursorily waving on the ute past the crushed vehicle. As they drove slowly forward Naomi could see a grey-haired man, blood streaming down his face, walking unsteadily around the car. Through a broken window a semi-inflated white airbag sagged, covered in a bright red blood splatter. She could see another person buried in the wreckage.

'People are still trapped inside,' she gasped, her hands beginning to shake on the steering wheel.

Chris looked away and Max sat bolt upright in the back. 'A 1999 Toyota Corolla,' he said.

Once they were beyond the next bend the traffic began to pick up speed again, but it was not fast enough for Naomi. She put her foot down hard on the accelerator and pulled out recklessly into the other lane.

Her rashness set something loose in Zoe.

'Stop the car, Naomi,' she said firmly.

Naomi did as she was told, on the wrong side of the road. The ute tipped forward into the ditch. The oncoming traffic began sounding horns and skidding out of the way, as the vehicle slid down into the wet earth of the ditch. Zoe kicked open her door, the cold wind stinging her face. Her fingers and nails slid across the wet surface of the door looking for something, anything, to grab hold of, before she landed damply in the muddy ditch.

'I need to talk to you,' she yelled.

Naomi numbly got out. Her legs were shaking and stiff.

Zoe clutched at her thin check shirt flapping around her

torso. The boys, all eyes, stayed put in the ute's warm cabin, just a rain-splattered windshield between them and the two women. They knew better than to move.

'I . . .' Zoe began. Both women now stood a little off to one side, between the ute and a farm fence. Naomi put a tentative hand on Zoe's forearm.

Zoe turned to wipe away the large beads of sweat on her forehead. 'I have something I want to tell you, Naomi,' Zoe said evenly.

'It's just like . . .' Naomi began, turning her head in the direction of the accident.

'I know.'

'I thought I was over it.'

Zoe's eyes were locked on the horizon, and then she began speaking softly. 'When the car finally stopped rolling, we were all upside down.'

Naomi turned sharply to Zoe. It has taken ten years for this, she thought. She had long ago given up wondering whether they would ever have this conversation. How she had railed against Zoe for withholding this from her. Blamed her. Hated her. Naomi had focused her anger at the loss of her sons on Zoe because of the absence of Zoe's version of events.

'Ben's face was covered in blood, but he was conscious,' Zoe continued.

A truck with 'Blayney SES' emblazoned across its side approached them from the opposite direction, slowed, and, after a cursory look at them and their ute, sped on around the bend to the real accident.

'"Get out!" Ben yelled at me,' Zoe said flatly, pulling a strand of her hair from across her cheek and tucking it behind her ear. 'His voice was panicky, but he was still in control.'

Zoe took a deep breath. 'We both noticed the small puff

of smoke escape from under the steering wheel. I did what he said.'

Naomi listened carefully to Zoe. These words marked the return of the Zoe whom she once knew. The Zoe whom Ben had loved, whom she had been trying to love too.

'In that moment before I climbed out of the wreck, I remembered everything, every last stupid thing, that I had ever done, and a part of me, the biggest part, wanted to stay right where I was. I tried to kill myself so many times after Max was born, you know. I was sick. And now all I had to do was sit tight. But Ben was yelling and I was thinking, *my children. My boys*. Really, for the first time it hit me. I was a mother. And I knew that Ben was going and so was Jesse.' Zoe paused. 'I'm sorry,' she said, looking at Naomi before continuing. 'I climbed out for my children. It was like going through childbirth with them all over again. The pain was unbelievable. Pulling back into myself. I was thinking that my boys had no more father. But they still had a mother. And I never forgot that, even though I tried,' Zoe paused, lost in thought for a moment. 'Another driver had stopped and he helped me. He pulled the door open.'

Naomi nodded; she had read the man's statement after the accident.

'He helped me up through the door. From the back seat I heard a groan,' Zoe's voice dropped.

Naomi flattened her back against a wet fence post. 'My darling Jesse,' Naomi said, barely above a whisper. There was something about Jesse's gentleness as a child that made Naomi kiss him lightly on the top of his head.

'Are you all right, Jesse?' Zoe said slowly, back in the moment.

Naomi closed her eyes. Even now, there were still times when she reached out to hold Jesse's small-boy hand to cross a road. She had loved him so very calmly. Jesse, the bright boy-man with his wide mouth, ready to smile his wide, slow smile, the one they shared.

'You knew, didn't you?' Zoe said, turning to her now.

'About you and Jesse?' Naomi asked.

Zoe remained silent.

'I wasn't sure, but I thought something was happening. Something *had* happened. Jesse was different around you. I suspected he loved you, but . . .'

'I loved Ben, but I don't think I ever really loved him my way. I was too young. He was so full on. He was so dazzling. But just before the accident I fell in love with Jesse. I never meant to, it just happened.'

Naomi looked up into the thick, boiling sky, the colour of a pot scourer. They stood together in the rain, both staring into the paddock beyond.

Zoe broke the silence. 'The way Ben said "Jesse" was strange. Without turning his head. I think his neck was broken.'

Yes, his neck had been broken, according to the autopsy report. But there was something raw about hearing Zoe say so now. He was still Naomi's oldest son, her firstborn. She felt his painful last moments as intensely as she had his birth.

The traffic had completely stopped again on both sides of the accident and all they could hear was the low hum of stationary cars. Neither of the women could yet look into the other's eyes. Naomi stared at the paddock's fence and a tuft of grey wool caught on the barbed wire.

'There was no reply,' Zoe said.

The rain was now seeping down the back of Naomi's collar. A fire engine sped past them, siren blaring, covering them in freezing spray.

'Through the open door I could only see Jesse's perfect

hands, one on top of the other. He was lying against the roof of the car, folded over like a piece of paper.'

Naomi nodded. The man who had stopped, the only witness to the accident, had reported that Zoe, covered in blood, had moved slowly away from the vehicle. Probably tearing her spleen with each step, Naomi thought.

'I remember dragging my leg because I couldn't walk properly. Then I was looking around to get something to prop open the door so that I could get them out. The man who'd helped me was shouting into his phone.'

Naomi would know everything, at last. Zoe was finally giving her the last moments of her sons' lives.

'Just then, suddenly, maybe,' Zoe continued, holding nothing back, 'the engine caught fire. The sound was incredible. And the heat was unbearable. But no sound from Ben.'

Naomi closed her eyes.

'I never understood that. No sound,' Zoe said, her eyes restless.

Naomi felt calm now, as though she had all the time in the world. She waited. There was more to come, she could hear it in Zoe's voice.

'I wasn't driving,' Zoe said, now completely still.

'You weren't?' Naomi said.

'I was out of the car by the time the cops arrived. They just assumed I was driving, because the witness said so. But it wasn't that way. At least that's what I used to think. But now, I guess, I don't really know. Perhaps I was driving, after all. *Was it me?*' Zoe stood lost in thought, chewing the quick of a fingernail.

Naomi turned to Zoe.

'I have been over it so many times in my head. We weren't wearing seatbelts, and the car had rolled. I don't know anymore. I said yes. I felt like a murderer anyway. I felt like

I had murdered Ben, as good as murdered him, falling for Jesse. I had destroyed everything way before the accident. I never meant to lie, especially to Ben. We were arguing about it just before the crash. Jesse was asleep in the back, so we were having this really intense argument in whispers. Ben grabbed at the wheel. Maybe I grabbed the wheel? I don't remember now. It's so messed up in my mind. For so long I wanted to go to jail. I did a lot of stuff after that which should have landed me in jail. My last memory of anything before my life went down the tube is a terrible argument. Ben was so furious with me.'

'I blamed you.'

Zoe's knees buckled.

'Noel didn't. He felt sorry for you. But I didn't. I wanted you to be the one that had died, not them. You took something from me, something that didn't belong to you. That's how I used to think about it. I disapproved of the way Noel and Gwen kept in touch with you. I thought it contaminated us, our family.'

'I murdered your sons,' Zoe said, collapsing into the wet paspalum and mud.

Naomi thought back to that sunny afternoon, ten years ago. When the police rang, the phone woke Chris, just a toddler at the time. *'Mum, Mum, Mummy!'* First the oval of Noel's distraught face swam up and away – how grey and silent he grew overnight – next she felt her own bitterness contract in her chest. She swallowed hard and cleared her throat. That afternoon, before she could absorb the shock of Ben and Jesse's deaths, her immediate concern had been the extent of Zoe's injuries.

'You didn't murder anyone,' Naomi said quietly.

'It was all my fault. All of it. It's always been my fault,' Zoe said.

'It's no one's fault. It just happened' – Naomi paused and helped Zoe to her feet. And when Zoe had straightened her thin legs, Naomi placed a hand on each of her shoulders and looked steadily into her light blue eyes – 'a long time ago.'

After two ambulances had passed them and the crushed vehicle had been towed, the police finally reopened both lanes of the road. They helped Naomi and Zoe get the ute back on the road.

'It's time to move on,' Naomi said.

The cabin was dry and full of small boys and warm kitten smell.

Max was holding the kitten in his hockey scarf. 'I'm going to call him Jesse,' he said quietly to Zoe. The chicken began squawking from its box behind Naomi's seat.

'Just don't call the chicken Naomi, okay?' Naomi smiled.

'Or Zoe,' said Zoe from the back seat, catching Naomi's eye in the rear-vision mirror.

'How far now?' Chris asked.

'Not too far,' Naomi said.

'Grenfell,' Zoe said quietly.

'It's over those hills.' And Naomi pointed south across the dashboard. 'Where the clouds are clearing.'

Postscript

Despite all the millions of words and billions of people on this planet, not many more than a handful of distinctly different and unique narratives exist. As they pass down from generation to generation, remarkably they grow stronger by being reinterpreted and retold; they are not diminished.

It was with these thoughts in mind that I began work on *Once on a Road*, the retelling of an ancient narrative about a journey away from grief and bitterness towards friendship and loyalty. The original 'Book of Ruth' is a small, oddly shaped work. The story begins with death and ends with birth. It is a rare and emotionally charged insight into women's lives and loves in ancient times. Ruth and Naomi make a peculiar pair of heroines: one older, one younger; one Jewish, one not. In the original story Naomi, exiled by a famine to Moab and grief-stricken after the death of her husband and two adult sons, decides to return home to Judea, alone. Her daughter-in-law, Ruth, insists on accompanying her, and on the dusty and dangerous road to Bethlehem she pledges her loyalty:

'Wherever you go, I will go,
wherever you live, I will live.

Your people shall be my people,
and your God, my God.
Wherever you die, I will die
and there I will be buried.
May Yahweh do this thing to me
and more also,
if even death should come between us!'

Naomi reluctantly accepts Ruth's offer and they arrive in Bethlehem destitute. Ruth becomes a gleaner, picking up the broken barley left behind in the fields after harvest. The land owner is a distant relative of Naomi's, and the lovely Ruth catches his eye. Naomi advises Ruth on how to win her way into his heart. Ruth eventually marries Boaz and has a son, Obed, whose son, Jesse, will become the father of David, King of Israel.

The idea of a mother-in-law and a daughter-in-law co-operating, yet alone pledging loyalty to one another, is almost unique in literature. 'The Book of Ruth' was probably included in the stories of the Old Testament to establish lineage, but it is so much more than that. It is a meditation on love and duty that still holds true, three thousand years later.

I began to wonder about what went on before the women's grief-stricken journey to Bethlehem. Why did Ruth want to help Naomi? What shape did Naomi's bitterness take? What made their bond so resilient and what would happen if you tried to imagine something of that story today . . .

Acknowledgements

Thanks to Jane Messer, Andrew O'Hagan, Jean Bedford, Antonia Harbus, Nellie Flannery, Janette Howe, Michael Wall, Clare 'Joan of Arc' McHugh, Catherine Hill and Meredith Curnow.

Thank you, Jack and Cath Mullane. 'The children's glory is their parents.' (Proverbs, 17:6) Thanks also to Margot Nash, UTS 2006, where I worked on this manuscript under her supervision, and Marcelle Freiman at Macquarie University, where I completed it.

Thanks, last but not least, to Helen Doogue and the rest of the Saturday writing group.